Games
of
Pleasure

Julia Ross

BERKLEY SENSATION, NEW YORK

THE BERKLEY PUBLISHING GROUP
Published by the Penguin Group
Penguin Group (USA) Inc.
375 Hudson Street, New York, New York 10014, USA
Penguin Group (Canada), 90 Eglinton Avenue East, Suite 700, Toronto, Ontario M4P 2Y3, Canada
(a division of Pearson Penguin Canada Inc.)
Penguin Books Ltd., 80 Strand, London WC2R 0RL, England
Penguin Group Ireland, 25 St. Stephen's Green, Dublin 2, Ireland (a division of Penguin Books Ltd.)
Penguin Group (Australia), 250 Camberwell Road, Camberwell, Victoria 3124, Australia
(a division of Pearson Australia Group Pty. Ltd.)
Penguin Books India Pvt. Ltd., 11 Community Centre, Panchsheel Park, New Delhi—110 017, India
Penguin Group (NZ), 67 Apollo Drive, Mairangi Bay, Auckland 1311, New Zealand
(a division of Pearson New Zealand Ltd.)
Penguin Books (South Africa) (Pty.) Ltd., 24 Sturdee Avenue, Rosebank, Johannesburg 2196,
South Africa

Penguin Books Ltd., Registered Offices: 80 Strand, London WC2R 0RL, England

This is a work of fiction. Names, characters, places, and incidents either are the product of the author's imagination or are used fictitiously, and any resemblance to actual persons, living or dead, business establishments, events, or locales is entirely coincidental. The publisher does not have any control over and does not assume any responsibility for author or third-party websites or their content.

GAMES OF PLEASURE

A Berkley Sensation Book / published by arrangement with the author

PRINTING HISTORY
Berkley Sensation trade paperback edition / November 2005
Berkley Sensation mass-market edition / April 2007

Copyright © 2005 by Jean Ross Ewing.
Cover art by Griesbach and Martucci.
Cover handlettering by Ron Zinn.
Cover design by Monica Benalcazar.

ISBN: 978-0-425-20730-7

BERKLEY SENSATION®
Berkley Sensation Books are published by The Berkley Publishing Group,
a division of Penguin Group (USA) Inc.,
375 Hudson Street, New York, New York 10014.
BERKLEY SENSATION is a registered trademark of Penguin Group (USA) Inc.
The "B" design is a trademark belonging to Penguin Group (USA) Inc.

PRINTED IN THE UNITED STATES OF AMERICA

10 9 8 7 6 5 4 3 2 1

Praise for the novels of Julia Ross

Games of Pleasure

"Beautifully written with intelligent characters . . . and an insightful glimpse into the human heart, this book is one of Ross's finest novels. You'll be captivated from page one."
—*Romantic Times* "TOP PICK" (4½ stars)

"The kind of book one can sink into . . . replete with wit and sensuality." —*Romance Reviews Today*

"Tenderness and sexiness that is just unbeatable . . . It is easy to see why Julia Ross is a bestselling author." —*Romance Junkies*

Night of Sin

"Exhilarating and highly sensual adventure romance . . . Ross's gift for creating masterful plots and memorable characters is at its height." —*Romantic Times* "TOP PICK" (4½ stars)

"A terrific character study . . . Fans will appreciate gutsy Anne."
—*Midwest Book Review*

"One of the most lush and atmospheric books I've read in a long time." —*All About Romance*

The Wicked Lover

"An exceptional writer who creates rich, compelling characters in tales of intrigue. When [Ross] adds passion to the mix, so much the better for fans . . . [Dove] is one of the most truly heroic men in romance . . . Fascinating, appealing, and unforgettable." —*The Oakland Press*

"An exciting story that sizzles with unbridled sensual desire. Lots of amusing twists and turns, a real keeper." —*Rendezvous*

continued . . .

"The Georgian period comes to life vividly here . . . Each scene is carefully crafted . . . A romance with rich details, intriguing characters, and a fabulous conflict."   —*All About Romance*

"Exquisitely romantic, utterly captivating."
—*Romantic Times* "TOP PICK" (4½ stars)

"Twists and turns entwine with sensuality and suspense to make this lush romance a genuine page-turner."   —*Booklist*

The Seduction

"Rich, delicious . . . Books like this are treasures . . . Put it at the top of your summer reading list."   —*The Oakland Press*

"Wit, lust, and just enough mystery . . . The characters are charming, reckless, and endearing."   —*Rendezvous*

"A gripping novel starring two wonderfully tainted romantic skeptics as lead protagonists."   —*Midwest Book Review*

"A superb example of Ms. Ross's outstanding storytelling talents and exceptional writing abilities. Intense emotions and passionate, strong characters are the complement to a complex love story, replete with such dastardly villains as Shakespeare might have crafted."   —*Historical Romance Reviews*

"Magnificent . . . A wonderfully tempting tale filled with unsurpassed sensuality . . . A hot and fast-paced read . . . Completely enthralling."   —*The Road to Romance*

"Ross's lush, evocative writing is the perfect counterpoint for her spellbinding tale of a wickedly refined, elegantly attired rake who is redeemed by one woman's love. Ross, whose combination of lyricism and sensuality is on par with Jo Beverley's, skillfully builds the simmering sexual chemistry between Alden and Juliet into an exquisitely sensual romance and luscious love story."

—*Booklist*

My Dark Prince

"Brilliant! Passionate, complex, and compelling. The best book of any genre I have read in a long, long while. Don't miss this beautifully written, intensely satisfying love story. I am in awe . . . Highly recommended."

—Mary Balogh

"I thoroughly enjoyed *My Dark Prince*. If you enjoy exciting, entertaining, wonderfully written romance, read this book."

—Jo Beverley

"A fantastic cast of characters . . . Julia Ross traps the reader from page one . . . Outstanding . . . A breathtaking and mesmerizing historical romance. This is romance in its finest hour."

—*The Romance Journal*

"Lovers of tortured heroes and intense stories will take this one to their hearts . . . *My Dark Prince* has a plot filled with complications and dangers—real dangers . . . [Nicholas] is as dark and hurting as any hero of Anne Stuart's . . . A tale that will grab you and compel you to finish it in one sitting . . . I don't think I'm going to forget this one any time soon."

—*All About Romance*

"Enjoyable . . . Fast-paced . . . The lead couple is a divine pair."

—*Midwest Book Review*

CHAPTER ONE

$\mathcal{R}$AGE IS A FUTILE ENOUGH ANTIDOTE TO REJECTED LOVE, but true love is elusive, even for the most desirable man in England.

His heart raw, Ryder drove his horse along the cliff road. Indignation surged hotly in his veins.

"I am very sorry, Lord Ryderbourne," she had said. "I must inform you that I have just this morning agreed to marry Lord Asterley."

She must have known that his attentions were serious. He had received every encouragement. He was a superb catch, even for an earl's daughter. Yet she had been secretly courting Asterley all along. In the end she had announced, with trembling fingers and silly little bites to her lip, that marriage to Ryder was just too alarming to contemplate, and she had accepted an amusing, penniless baron instead.

While he had delayed—secure in her shy glances and delicate blushes—Lady Belinda Carhart had played him for a fool. Apparently, even becoming the Duchess of Blackdown one day could never make up for Ryder's personal failings.

It was humiliating. Humiliating and, perhaps, a genuine hurt. There was no reason at all why any young lady should hold him in fear, especially in the face of his magnificent prospects and his sincerely expressed admiration for her.

Yet Lady Belinda had stared at him with eyes like a rabbit's. "You're so very forceful, Lord Ryderbourne. All the girls are frightened of you."

It was, he supposed, a serious shock to his confidence.

Not to his position in the world, of course. To his faith in himself.

The sensation was both unwelcome and novel. It left him feeling oddly vulnerable, to which the best answer was righteous resentment. Any insult to the male heart fuels only anger.

Drizzle wet his face. The ground was getting slick. Just ahead, part of the road surface had fallen away, carried down with the collapsing cliffs toward the sea by a landslide the previous winter. The local people had beaten a new track across the tumbled earth and another, narrower path down through the uprooted trees to the beach, but no wagon or carriage could pass this way any longer.

He slowed his horse, then stopped to gaze out over the bay. Clouds gathered on the horizon. Jade-shadowed breakers shattered white against the broken rocks of the headland.

Something bobbed, appearing and disappearing among the swells.

Ryder shaded his eyes. A scrap of wreckage, perhaps? Whatever it was, it had vanished.

He took a deep breath. Salt air filled his lungs. Rollers surged up the Channel. Spume splattered onto cliffs. Waves dashed and sucked on the shingle far below.

He loved this land. He loved Wyldshay, his ancestral home, his joy, his burden. He loved his family. His father, the aging duke, who delegated more and more responsibility to his elder son. His mother, brilliant and demanding and a light in society. His sisters, who would soon be fielding suitors of their own. And his younger brother, Wild Lord Jack—the wicked, interesting boy with the face of an angel who had left home long ago to drift about the world—gone again now with his new bride to India, while Ryder was left to both the duties and privileges of being the heir.

He had never resented it before, but now a small disquiet seemed to be gnawing at him like a mouse at a grain sack.

Ryder shrugged and urged his horse forward just as the flotsam lifted, closer to shore than he had expected. Dipping and spinning, it tossed haphazardly toward the headland.

He pulled up abruptly. A dinghy. Foundering, without oars, without rudder, spinning straight toward the rocks.

Yet something fluttered, almost out of sight behind the prow—a scrap of fabric?

Someone lay in the slosh of water in the bottom of the boat.

The gelding sank its haunches. Hooves slid on mud as the horse hurtled downhill through the jumble of dislodged trees and shrubs. Pebbles rattled, then showered past, when they reached the shingle. Riding full-tilt toward the surf, reins dropped onto his horse's neck, Ryder shed hat, cloak, and jacket. His heart hammered as he plunged his mount into the sea.

The gelding swam strongly. Cold water broke over Ryder's chest, soaking him. The saddle turned to soap beneath his thighs. He urged his horse to swim faster, his hands filled with wet mane and reins like damp rubber.

The sinking craft had disappeared among the waves.

The gelding's breath roared like dragon fire. Ryder shouted. The ocean swallowed the sounds in an infinity of moisture.

He circled his horse, shouting like a madman, when the little boat suddenly wallowed down the face of a breaker. Cold spume broke over Ryder's face.

Half blinded, he grasped at the gunnel.

A woman. Almost naked. Ivory flesh shone blue-white beneath her corset and a scrap of soaked chemise, her thighs and arms bare to the cold rain and the sea. Beaten iron-salt hair plastered over white neck and shoulders, streamed like seaweed across a slim waist. Just clear of the bilge, her half-hidden face lay pillowed on one outstretched arm.

The next wave tore the boat from his fingers.

Ryder tugged the swimming gelding back toward the dinghy. A rope trailed from the bow, coy as an eel. Reaching from the saddle, he grabbed at it. Skin ripped from his palm as the next wave lifted the boat, and his grip on the rope tore him from his horse.

Cold ocean, loud with bubbles, closed over his head. Kicking strongly, Ryder grasped the end of the gelding's tail. Fighting water, he looped a knot between tail and rope. As he surfaced and his horse turned back toward land, a flailing stirrup iron struck him hard on the elbow.

He cursed and hauled himself into the dinghy one-handed.

She was alive. As Ryder lifted her she groaned, her head falling back to expose her white throat. A red bruise marked one cheek. Streaks of color spoiled the flesh of her arms. He knew an instant of livid fury before he forced his mind back to the problems at hand.

The boat wallowed deeper as another wave broke over it. The nerve screamed in his elbow, numbing the muscles from wrist to shoulder. Nevertheless, he propped the woman against his own body with one arm and hooked a foot under the seat to jerk off one of his boots. He began to bail as if his life depended on it—though *his* life was not at stake, of course.

He could still swim to shore with one arm. Yet he probably could not carry her with him without both of them foundering.

Her life, then. Her life depended on it.

A woman. A stranger. Her bones as lovely as glass. Her long legs entangled in beauty and threat. Her hair a cloak of mystery. Her face damaged by a man's fist. Other than the purple fingerprints branded onto her flesh, her body might have been carved from marble beneath the little stone ridges of crumpled wet fabric. A sensuous, enchanting body, ripe with female invitation.

He cursed again and kept bailing.

Freed of its burden of water, the dinghy lifted. The horse swam nobly, driven by instinct straight back to the beach. The woman coughed and opened her eyes. The deft curve of her waist burned beneath his palm as she coughed again, then thrust both hands back over her head, pushing the sea-tangled hair from her forehead.

Her breasts lifted, nipples shining dark beneath the soaked fabric.

She looked up at him from bleak chocolate eyes, her lashes spikes of distrust.

He met her accusatory gaze without flinching. Of course he was aware of the shadowed triangle between her thighs; her breasts thrust up in deliberate invitation by her corset; her naked legs and cold white feet—glimmering beneath torn silk stockings as if she had run unshod over stones. Did she think he was villain enough to pay attention to anything but rescuing her? To feel anything but this white-hot anger at her unknown assailant?

"It's all right," he said. "We're almost ashore. You're quite safe now."

She shivered and crossed her arms as if hugging herself, moving as far from him as space on the seat permitted, yet her mouth quirked with a kind of wry bravado.

"So who are you?" she asked. "Sir Galahad?"

REMARKABLE eyes glowered at her beneath strongly male brows: glass-green, storm-tossed eyes, clear yet feral, like the deep ocean. Neatly barbered hair dripped water over a face ruggedly designed to please women. His soaked shirt plastered vigorous muscling. Drenched breeches painted inflexible thighs.

A tall, powerfully built man, wet as a seal. Young and strong and lean—and splendid in his masculine certainty.

"I am Ryderbourne," he said.

Miracle choked back a small laugh, dismayed at how bitter it tasted.

Just that: *Ryderbourne.* With the assumption that anyone would then know exactly who he was. Even though his was only a courtesy title, as the elder son and heir of the Duke of Blackdown his precedence was just below that of a marquess. His given name, if she remembered correctly, was Laurence Duvall Devoran St. George, but he was known as "Ryder" to his friends.

The select handful of friends!

He was only whispered about by the amusing young gentlemen who whored and drank and gambled away both youth and fortune. A proud scion of St. George, slated to become one of the most powerful peers in England. Why be surprised if Lord Ryderbourne carved a rarefied path of his own?

Miracle had occasionally seen him from a distance in London, of course, fawned over like royalty. He did not look so different now, even soaked to the skin. Lean muscles bunched and coiled as he bailed. Though his green eyes remained wary and cool, he was as attractive as they came.

So the Fates laughed as they spun their webs and decreed nothing but more trouble! Miracle would far rather have been rescued—if she had been destined to be rescued at all—by a grizzled old fisherman with a comfortable wife.

Fortunately, since they had never moved in the same circles, Lord Ryderbourne was unlikely to recognize her.

The keel scraped on shingle. The horse stopped, fetlock deep in surf, and shook itself like a dog. The duke's son tugged on his salt-ruined boot and sprang from the boat. His feet splashed as he waded to the horse and rubbed its black neck. The gelding blew through its nostrils and shook itself again. The duke's son untied the rope from his mount's tail, then strode away over the shingle to retrieve clothes he must have abandoned there earlier.

The horse waited, watching him.

He returned to hold out a heavy cloak. He had shrugged into his jacket and donned his hat. He seemed impervious to the chill rain.

"Who did this to you, ma'am?"

Miracle ignored the cloak and stared at the ocean. Whitecaps reared ever higher beneath lowering gray clouds. In spite of that odd moment of incipient hilarity, her heart felt numb, as if she were desperate. Goose bumps rose on her arms.

"No one did anything, my lord. There was an accident."

"You've been beaten." His voice resonated: rich and deep, with a piercing intelligence. "You've been robbed of your clothes and cast adrift. By whom?"

She shook her head and shivered again, worried that she might do something hideously inappropriate, that she might laugh out loud or break into bawdy singing.

He threw the cloak in a belling sweep to land about her shoulders, then held out one hand.

"Never mind. I'll get you to shelter." His mouth was set in the imperious lines of habitual command. "Come! You will die of cold."

Miracle clutched the front of his cloak in both hands. "If I only had oars, I would row right back out there."

His eyes darkened, like the glass-clear shadow in the trough of a wave. "You planned to take your own life?"

"Oh, not deliberately." She suppressed the mounting impulse to laugh. "However it might appear, I'm not so melodramatic."

"Neither am I. What's your name?"

There was insistence in it. He would not leave her alone. He would feel obliged to be gallant. There was not much she could do about it. So in defiance of fate, Miracle met his gaze and told him her third lie.

Her first falsehood had been to cling deliberately to a few more moments of blissful oblivion when she had regained consciousness in the boat, looking up at him through slitted lashes before she had been forced to acknowledge him at all.

Her second lie had been to deny that she'd been thrashed.

The third was the name that now spilled without thought from her tongue, though it was not one she had ever used before.

"Miss Elaine Sanders, my lord."

"Then, come, Miss Sanders!"

He reached into the boat and picked her up in both arms to cradle her snugly against his chest.

As if the sea had already defeated her, Miracle surrendered. Further struggle seemed absurd.

She gazed up at his face as he carried her toward his horse. His mouth was beautiful, like a carving, yet the grim lines seared her heart. He ought to laugh, not frown like a gargoyle. Of course, he did not know whom he held so completely at his mercy. Would he drop her right away, if he knew? Or would he demand one fast, sensual exchange, then leave her with a guinea? Intoxication bubbled madly in her heart, like champagne poisoned with wormwood.

"I had it wrong," she said. "Sir Lancelot."

Lord Ryderbourne stopped. His heart beat strongly beneath her ear. "What?"

"It was Lancelot, not Galahad, who rescued the woman from the water."

He stood silently holding her, while the rain thickened. The retreating waves sucked on the shingle with the grinding sound of a troll at dinner. The boat bobbed away.

"Elaine," he said at last. "She was also an Elaine. But that water was magically boiling in a tub, not the frigid ocean. The rescue was Sir Lancelot's first miracle—"

"—and his last, because it cost him his virginity and thus his mystic strength."

"I'm not a virgin," he said with precision.

As if she really were a madwoman, her gathering hilarity spilled into open laughter. Yet Lord Ryderbourne held her securely in his embrace, until Miracle finally choked down a mysterious rush of tears. Quivering like a fish on a line, suddenly drained of all emotion, she snuggled blindly into the warm cloak.

Lord Ryderbourne strode forward again.

"I might suppose, based on the nature of this conversation, that you're not a blushing maiden yourself. Yet I believe you're in shock, Miss Sanders. It's clear that you've been battered by a human fist, in spite of your protestations to the contrary. Death, if I had not intervened, was the inevitable outcome of your abandonment in that boat. I trust you're at least glad to be alive?"

Alive! Yes, she had come face-to-face with death. Yet against all odds she was alive! Was that sufficient cause for hysteria? Or was it simply a reaction to the disaster of having been rescued by this particular man?

"Since it's the only life that I have, I must thank you, Lord Ryderbourne, for your rescue. Now, if you would kindly set me down here on this beach, I can make my own way from here."

"No." He tossed her up onto the saddle, then swung up behind her. "You're more hurt than you know. You're coming with me."

"You're abducting me?"

"You're without clothes, without money, wet through, and half frozen. You have no shoes. I'm continuing to rescue you. From yourself, if need be."

He gathered reins and the gelding pranced forward, then bounded up the muddy path and onto the cliff road at the top. Lord Ryderbourne turned the horse to canter straight into the oncoming night. A goose girl sheltering under a tree stared at them as they flew past. A handful of sheep scattered. The sea turned sullen as the rain began to pelt down in earnest.

In twenty minutes the horse clattered down the cobbled street of a village, where a handful of thatched stone houses tumbled haphazardly toward a beach. Fishing boats were drawn up on the foreshore. Nets stretched on poles planted in the shingle.

They rode into the yard of the single inn. The Merry Monarch seemed grand enough, yet neglect hung over the rain-soaked yard and empty stalls. Paint peeled. Only one person came out to greet their arrival, a groom in a shabby coat.

"A room." Lord Ryderbourne vaulted to the cobbles. "A room, a hot bath, a meal. Take particularly good care of the gelding."

The groom tugged at his forelock. "My lord!"

Ryderbourne spun a coin into the man's open palm, then turned to hold up both arms. Since there was no other immediate choice, Miracle slipped into them, put her arms about his neck, and laid her head on his shoulder. Rain poured in a stream from the brim of his hat, but he turned so that his body sheltered her from the worst of the weather.

The groom took the horse's reins.

"A bran mash," the duke's son said. "An especially thorough rubdown."

"Very good, my lord!"

Miracle stared at the gelding as the man led it away. The magnificently muscled rump. The coat groomed to a coal-jet shine, in spite of its recent bath in saltwater. An animal obviously worth a fortune.

"You would trust that minikin with your horse?" she asked.

"Absolutely," Lord Ryderbourne replied. "Until the landslide swept away the road, this place handled all the coach traffic passing along the coast. Though it's cut off to through traffic now, Jenkins still knows how to take care of a horse."

"So no one comes here now but locals?"

She knew at once that her voice had betrayed her. He glanced down at her and smiled. A lovely, almost amused smile that said he was infinitely capable of laughter, infinitely quick-witted—not cold, not arrogant, at all.

"You wish for quiet, Miss Sanders?" he asked. "You want privacy? You need a place where no one will discover you? You'll find them all here."

"And you can guarantee all of that," she said, "because you are Lord Ryderbourne, heir to the glorious St. Georges. They say you might slay dragons with one raised eyebrow—"

"Do they?"

She tilted her head against his shoulder and stared up at the sodden sky as he carried her toward the inn doorway.

"They also say that you've been known to send ladies into either decline or climax—depending on the lady—with one haughty glance."

The good humor fled his face. "So which kind of lady are you?"

Miracle wrapped her arms more tightly about his neck. "Which kind of lady would you like me to be?"

CHAPTER TWO

*R*YDER KICKED OPEN THE DOOR TO A BEDROOM AND CAR-
ried his captive inside, two maids scurrying at their
heels. The room felt chill, unused.

"See to the fire, Mary," he said to one of the maids. "Alice,
bring hot soup, or tea, or mulled wine: anything hot that you
have in the kitchen."

"Yes, my lord." Alice hurried away.

While Mary busied herself at the grate, Ryder set his burden down on the rug, then strode to the bed to fling back the
covers. The sheets felt damp.

"As soon as you've finished with the fire, fetch clean, dry
sheets," he said to the maid. "And bring up a warming pan."

Mary curtsied and scurried from the room. Flames leaped
up the chimney. Warmth began to permeate the cold spaces.

Ryder felt supernaturally alive. His mystery stood like a
sapling. Long wet hair snaked down over the sodden cloak.
She met his gaze without blinking, a small, defiant quirk at
one corner of her mouth.

Beneath the ugly bruises, beauty streamed from her dark
brow to the proud column of her throat. Allure gamboled in
the sweep of black lashes and kissed at sensuous red lips. A
perfection of creation that struck him to the heart, like a jewel
suddenly discovered among seaweed. He had rescued a
woman who was more than beautiful. Her very bones were as

dazzling as a diamond. No man would ever see her without wanting her.

The air almost sizzled as their eyes met. Yet it was not only her loveliness that made the blood run hot in his veins like spring sap; it was the splendid accident of having rescued her.

Had a similar heady recognition of random fate driven his brother Jack to travel to the ends of the earth?

His pulse rapid with new awareness, Ryder turned away as if to break an enchantment. He was used to facing problems with cool equanimity. He threw his hat into a corner, then shrugged out of his soaked jacket. As if similarly released, his captive walked up to the fire and crouched down to hold out her hands to its warmth. His cloak trailed out behind her like the train of a wedding gown.

Ryder strode to the window. *Which kind of lady would you like me to be?*

Unlike Jack, he had responsibilities far beyond this woman and this incident, even though excitement still thrummed in his veins. Hands crossed behind his back, he stared out at the rain and faced the more uncomfortable realities, before he turned back to face her.

"I would prefer you to be an honest one," he said. "My days are generally quite predictable. I'm not in the habit of saving young ladies from a watery grave. Perhaps it's the common thing to be lied to in such irregular circumstances. I wouldn't know."

Her head jerked up, her skin ghostly beneath the rose pattern of bruises, her eyes dark, like those of a deer fearing danger. "How have I lied?"

"Elaine was certainly the name of the woman whom Sir Lancelot magically rescued from the boiling tub," he said. "Yet I don't believe that it's yours. Your clothing—what remains of it—is costly, the finest quality. Your hands are smooth and unblemished, those of a lady. There are marks on your fingers where you've recently removed several rings. You're not Miss Sanders. You're married. Has your husband beaten you?"

She gazed back at the fire, leaving him nothing but the elegant curve of her spine and the steam rising gently about her bent head.

"I recognize my debt to you, my lord. I don't agree that it gives you any right to question me."

"Why else would you be so afraid? No one but a husband could have such control over you."

"My situation is no concern of yours."

"I made it my concern when I dragged you from the ocean." He stepped forward, driven by this intense new acuity. "Why hide the truth from me? I'm one of the few men in England who's in a position to help you, whatever your problem."

"My only problem, my lord, is that I'm wet and cold and tired. You must be busy with affairs of your own. You should return to them."

"I cannot abandon you. You must see that."

"I may appreciate your noble impulses without agreeing that they're necessary." With clear defiance she stood and turned to look up at him. "If Elaine doesn't please you, by all means choose some other name."

"Then you admit it's not your own?"

"Does it matter? We're only chance-met strangers, after all. If I might ask for the loan of a few shillings, enough for some clothes and the hire of a horse, you need concern yourself with me no longer. That's not beyond your means, surely? Once I'm safely away from here, I shall be happy to send you repayment."

He felt almost incredulous that she should so cavalierly dismiss him. "You're offering to *reimburse* me?"

"Of course." A wry note crept into her voice. "You won't be hard to find. Everyone in England has heard of Wyldshay Castle, the magical fortress afloat in its lake."

"Nothing magical about it," he said. "Simply a large and anachronistic pile of stone."

"Only the heir to infinite privilege could say that."

"And only a man of such privilege can promise to take care of any difficulty and mean it."

She stepped forward, clutching the cloak to her throat with both hands. "Then you will make me a small loan?"

"No," he said. "I will not."

Color drained from her face, as if she faced a sudden rush of panic. "Why not?"

The door latch rattled.

"Come!" Ryder said.

His mystery walked away, cloak trailing, to sit on a chest at the side of the room.

Mary and Alice entered, one with a pile of fresh sheets balanced on top of a warming pan, the other carrying a tray. Darting shy glances at Ryder, Alice set down the tray on a small table near the hearth, then went to help her companion make up the bed.

"Will there be anything else, my lord?" Mary asked when they were done.

"A tub and cans of hot water," he said. "Bring toiletries, as well—everything a lady might need."

"The water's heating now, my lord. Jenkins will bring up the tub." The maids bobbed their heads and left.

Ryder examined the tray. "Ah! Mulled wine! Our landlord has provided his best. The Merry Monarch kept excellent enough cellars, until the landslide plunged it into disaster."

Hugging the cloak, his mystery stared at him. "Why won't you help me?"

"I am helping you."

"I cannot be found here. I must leave!"

"Not until you've rested and eaten." He filled two glasses. "Have some wine! You'll feel better."

She looked away as if exasperated. "They all know you here, don't they?"

"I've spent my entire life riding over this part of Dorset. Wyldshay dominates the countryside hereabouts like a mailed fist hammered down onto velvet."

"And that," she said, standing to face him again, her eyes flashing, "is a splendidly apt description of my situation, also, don't you think?"

She was wet and hurt and bedraggled. She was magnificent. Ryder held out a glass, the wine warm and scented. She took it as a lady might take a posy from a child, with a gracious little nod of the head, then sat down in a chair near the fire. He leaned both hands on the rail of the opposite seat, the table with the tray at his elbow.

"What's so apt?" he asked.

"The delights of being at the mercy of the heir to a dukedom," she said. "The mailed fist keeps me pinned in this room. The velvet pretends an elaborate courtesy, as if no overwhelming force is involved, then accuses *me* of deceit. If you weren't raised to all that entitlement, you would allow me to leave."

Droplets sparkled in her hair and among the folds of his draped cloak. Like a princess abducted by pirates, as if he saw her through glass, she glimmered with desire and dishevelment. His heart turned an odd little somersault. Had he seen her somewhere before, somewhere glittering and bright, with her hair swept up and diamonds at her throat?

"No gentleman worth the name would allow you to leave without insisting on offering further help," he said.

"You obviously know very little about men, my lord."

"You're afraid," he insisted. "Why?"

She shook her head and leaned toward the flames as she peeled away her ruined stockings. A naked foot curved. Blue shadows lurked in the hollow of her anklebone and in the tiny trace of veins beneath the white skin. His attention riveted on the erotic, haughty sweep of the arch.

"You need to hide from your husband?"

"I cannot remain here."

"I shall not let you leave—"

"Oh, God!" She tossed her head up. "You're still wallowing in a nicely superior sense of responsibility? You think you must be chivalrous and gentlemanly? Or you think I'm frantic enough to do myself an injury—is that it?"

She pulled her bare feet back beneath the hem. Ryder swallowed hard. Yes, he was afraid for her, that she was more desperate than she knew. "It might be."

"Then rest assured, my lord, I've survived far worse than this. I promise you I will not take my own life without good cause."

"That's supposed to reassure me?"

"Why not? I'm nothing to you. Lend me a few coins, and your duty as a gentleman is fulfilled!"

He crossed his arms over his chest. "The truth might convince me to agree. Nothing else will."

She trembled as if with fear or anger, or both. "You cannot keep me imprisoned here."

"No, but you can hardly leave in your present state of undress, however delightful that prospect might be to the villagers."

A clanging sound echoed from the hallway. Ryder strode to the door and flung it open to reveal Jenkins with the tub, followed by a string of servants carrying cans of hot water.

"Take a bath," he said. "Worry about nothing. No one will find you here. I'll take care of everything."

Without a backward glance, he stalked from the room.

MIRACLE wrapped his cloak about her body and watched the servants prepare the hot bath. She was—against all expectations—still alive, though she felt weary enough to die. She had been rescued by a man with the natural power of a god, and an earthly power not far from that. But not even the son of the Duke of Blackdown could save her, once the truth came out. The only answer was to flee as far from Dorset as possible. The Americas, perhaps?

She swallowed the impulse to mad hilarity. She was still in shock. Her emotions were hardly trustworthy. Lord Ryderbourne probably had the power to do as he had promised: make sure that no one would find her here, at least for the moment. And if they did? Well, she might as well die clean as dirty!

As soon as the men and boys left the room, Miracle shed the wet cloak and stripped off what remained of her ruined corset and shift. She winced as the hot water sought out every contusion, then dropped her head back into the bath, her hair floating about her shoulders.

Angry voices sloshed in the tub and hissed in the crackle of the fire. *When did you develop such fine tastes? In the gutter? Wait until I've finished with that pretty face! No one will ever want you again. Whore! Whore! You let Hanley roger you, but turn up your nose at Philip Willcott? For the last time, Miracle! For the last time!*

She buried her face in both hands. Water streamed from her hair. She spread her fingers to stare at the faint trace of the rings she had torn off earlier that day. With a shrug, she reached for the soap. It was scented with orange and lavender, like a memory of innocence. Miracle scrubbed herself until her skin shone red, as if she could scour away the stain in her soul.

It was still raining outside. She had nothing to wear but Lord Ryderbourne's damp cloak, huddled where she had dropped it on the floor. One problem at a time, perhaps? She was probably safe until morning, though as soon as he discov-

ered what she had done, Lord Hanley would hunt her down.
And when he found her, not even the high-and-mighty Lord
Ryderbourne could save her from a last dance on nothing.

She must get some clothes and some money. She must find
out what ships left from which ports without attracting attention. *She must plan!*

Yet fatigue had spread its corruption deep in the bone. The
bed beckoned, a warming pan tucked within its cozy embrace.
Surely it wouldn't hurt to lie down for a few minutes?

Miracle climbed from the tub and wrapped herself in a
warm towel, then bent to dry her hair at the fire. The inn had
provided a brush and comb, even a toothbrush with paste,
even scented skin powder: everything necessary for a lady's
pleasure—or a man's?

*Worry about nothing. No one will find you here. I'll take
care of everything.*

And perhaps he would, at least for a few hours, at least until the hue and cry arrived, and jeering strangers came to drag
her away to her death.

Miracle dropped the towel on the floor. She hung Lord Ryderbourne's cloak where she could reach it. Then, in a heady
splendor of scent, her hair like warm silk on her shoulders,
she climbed into the waiting bed.

SHE woke with her heart already pounding. The door had
crashed open. Male voices echoed from the corridor. Lights
danced and glimmered in the darkness, blinding her. It was
too late, then! Too late! She would be hauled naked to her
doom.

Well, damn them all!

Miracle grabbed the cloak, spun from the bed, and ran to the
window to wrestle with the casement. The drop to the inn yard
was probably too far to survive, but better that than the gallows!

A hand clamped down hard on her wrist. Hot breath, angry
and fast, seared her cheek.

"What the devil are you about?"

She stared up at Lord Ryderbourne's face, then glanced
over his shoulder. With a great clanging of buckets, menservants were hauling away her cold bath water. Another procession of servants had lit candles and set a table and chairs in

front of the fire. Maids were bringing in trays of hot food. Miracle closed her eyes against fierce tears: the mad up-welling of relief, and her unholy mirth.

The door closed behind the servants, leaving her alone with her rescuer. His dry hair shone with highlights of ma-hogany, like a blood-bay horse, not as dark as it had seemed earlier, soaked in seawater. He wore no jacket, only breeches with a clean shirt and cravat. The linen at his throat formed crisp folds beneath his freshly shaved chin. While she slept, he must have bathed and changed in another room.

"You promised me you wouldn't try to take your own life." His fingers burned on her skin. "Does your word mean nothing?"

Her pulse thundered, but she smiled up at him. "I only said that I wouldn't do so without good cause."

He gazed down at her with a kind of ironic bewilderment, honed to a knife edge. He was obviously aroused. Though she had held together the front of the cloak with one hand, it must have offered glimpses of her naked body as she moved.

"And this *supper* is cause enough?" he said. "You have such particular culinary requirements that the Merry Monarch cannot satisfy them?"

"Not at all, my lord." His scent enveloped her—man and soap and fresh linen. A hint of ocean lingered only in his boots, dried and polished now, though still stained by salt. She inhaled, flaring her nostrils to take his essence straight into her lungs. "Indeed, something smells heavenly and I'm ravenous."

His eyes shone as keen as kingfishers' wings. The mood shifted, as if sunlight suddenly flooded a dark courtyard.

He lifted his fingers and released her. "So am I."

"Then we should eat," she said, answering the hidden mes-sage in that green gaze, "if you believe it is safe to do so?"

"Everyone in this village is sworn to secrecy about your ar-rival. No one will dare to gainsay me."

Miracle walked away a few paces. Hot shivers ran up her spine. Keeping her back to him, she reached up to take the hooded collar of the cloak in both hands.

"Yet perhaps there's another kind of danger?" she asked. "I could quite easily allow this cape to slide from my shoul-ders. Then I'd stand naked before you, inviting you to satisfy quite another appetite."

She heard him inhale. His boots echoed on the floorboards. The door latch rattled under his fingers. He stopped.

"That thought has obviously occurred to me, but I shan't act on it. I'm not such a cad."

She glanced at him over her shoulder. Yes, he was still erect. Magnificently so! "Perhaps your body wouldn't agree?"

He leaned his shoulders back against the door and crossed both arms over his chest. "The body has no conscience, ma'am. However, I was raised in a thicket of scruples."

"So was Sir Lancelot."

"The most painful example of infidelity in literature?"

She couldn't quite read his expression. A sardonic impulse to mirth? A ruefully gracious withdrawal? She walked to the fireplace, offering him nothing but her cloaked back and the dark waterfall of her hair.

"Painful?" she asked. "Why?"

"Because Lancelot's weakness haunted his conscience. It made him less than he had wanted to be."

"He was still a perfect knight."

"Not in his own eyes. He had believed he was perfect only as long as he remained chaste."

"Then he was in thrall to obsolete teachings about chastity and sin," she said.

"Obsolete?"

"You don't think so?" She turned to face him and smiled pointedly at his obvious discomfort. However much he tried to behave as a gentleman, he was alone in a room with a woman who was naked except for a cloak. Her nipples rose against the soft lining. "Are you also sworn to chastity, my lord?"

"I'm not a member of the Round Table."

"No, you St. Georges enjoy a quite different reputation: one of duty and power and privilege, just like the knights of King Arthur's court, but it's also one of self-indulgence, as typified by your brother. Lord Jonathan is notorious for sin, I believe?"

His eyes burned as if she had just lit a fuse in his heart. "Who the devil says such nonsense?"

"Ah," she said. "So your little brother has *not* adventured all over the world?"

"Jack's not the heir. He can do as he likes."

"Goodness!" She poured open scorn into her voice. "And *Lord Ryderbourne* cannot?"

"You think I'm doing exactly as I want right now? Maybe. But with power comes the responsibility to use it wisely. I'm not without conscience."

"No, my lord, I believe your conscience is very fine!"

He stood in silence for a moment, as if digesting this, then he pushed away from the door to pace across the room.

"Do you want me to flee? It would seem that I'm not quite such a coward, after all." He stopped, his head bent, then he flung up his chin and inhaled. "I would like you to trust me. Is that unreasonable?"

"I don't know. Perhaps it's not a matter of reason?"

"For God's sake! Any gentleman would rescue a dog from drowning without expecting anything in return."

"Then why insist on keeping me here against my will?"

"Because a great deal lies within my authority, and I have judged it best that you eat and sleep before you make any further decisions. I brought clothes. There! On the bed. Something should fit." Intensity streamed from him as light streams from a lamp. "No one from outside will find you here—not even your husband."

Miracle swallowed. "I have no husband."

"Not in your heart, perhaps, not after what he's done. If you wish it, I can make that a reality in the world, as well."

It was a statement of raw power. Very possibly it was true. Yet he could not, of course, help her. Stifling her reaction to the absurdity of her predicament, Miracle walked across to the bed. Dresses, petticoats, underwear lay on the covers. She formed a double drape in the cloak so that she was entirely modest, and turned back to face him.

"How can you be so sure that I'm married, my lord?"

"Only a husband could possibly have sufficient hold over you to create this much fear. You were wearing several rings until recently. Any single lady beaten by a stranger or mere acquaintance would run straight to her family for protection. Or has a foolhardy elopement estranged you from your family?"

She raised a brow. "And if it had, you can order Parliament? You can dissolve marriages simply through the power of your name? Or perhaps you would challenge any wife-beater to a duel, so that you could kill him? Is that your solution?"

The ocean wave turned in the depths of his eyes, as if her words were deadly serious, which perhaps they were. "Which would you prefer?"

"I don't know," she said. "I'm overwhelmed by so much gallantry. Have you ever fought a duel, my lord?"

"I'm perfectly confident of my ability with a pistol."

"That's not what I asked. No doubt your daily life is a dreary round of obligation that leaves you little time to fight duels."

He looked uncomfortable. "I have responsibilities, certainly."

"And can you afford to renounce all that weight of duty to risk your life for a stranger?"

"There's no need to assume that my life would be risked. There are other paths."

"Ah, so you would solve all my problems through the courts! Wouldn't that be a considerable burden on your time, my lord?"

He smiled at her, but it was the smile of the sun-touched clouds that ran ahead of a storm. "Any legal issues you need settled—divorce, annulment—could be delegated to my secretaries. Whatever your problem, I can solve it with negligible cost to myself. Why reject that?"

"Perhaps I don't wish to be any more deeply in your debt, my lord."

"Any such debt is irrelevant and freely forgiven. What can it matter?"

She bit her lip. "It matters to me."

"There's no debt that counts in this," he insisted, "except what's owed to honor. Whether either of us likes it or not, you're my responsibility. I insist that you not leave here without either allowing me to help you, or clearly explaining why I should not. You will agree to that?"

She wrapped his cloak more tightly about her shoulders. "It seems that I must."

He stepped closer, splendid in his masculine intensity. "You give me your word on it?"

Miracle glanced up into his eyes. Beneath the natural arrogance that came with so much power lay a very genuine concern. He probably wasn't aware of what else that intense green gaze betrayed. But she was.

"Yes, I promise, Lord Ryderbourne. I won't leave this room without either telling you the truth or letting you help me."

"Then we have a bargain," he said. "I will hold you to it."

"And tonight? Your family isn't expecting you?"

"The weather's turned foul. I've sent a message to Wyldshay that I've been delayed."

Miracle turned her back. She allowed the cloak to slip just a little from her shoulders. "You intend to spend the night here?"

Lord Ryderbourne sucked in a long breath and strode away. She heard the shutters clang shut. "I certainly intend to have supper."

Her pulse leaped with the hot thunder of awareness, tinged just a little with an oddly wry disappointment. So he was no different from any other man, after all?

"Then if you'll allow me a few moments to get dressed, my lord, I would be honored to join you for a meal. Then by morning you may have either truth or challenge—or perhaps both."

RICH and thick and lustrous—colored like starlings, like blackbirds, like iridescent rooks—her hair spun dark skeins over her white skin. The cloak slipped a little more. Such tender, fascinating bones and flesh, the curve of a woman's neck and spine and shoulder blade!

His heart hammering, Ryder turned his back and locked the shutters in place with their iron bar.

His mystery swooped up the clothes and stepped behind a screen that stood in a corner of the room.

She had been naked beneath the cloak! Her every movement had offered shadowed glimpses of smooth legs, elegant ankles and feet. And perhaps a breast? A curved thigh? He had tried, a little too desperately, not to look.

I'm not such a cad!

Not by conscious intent, perhaps! Yet her movements behind the screen mocked his composure. He stared at his fingers—spread on the shutters like starfish—as his mind arrowed in on the sounds. The shush of silk petticoat. The slide of laces. The snap of buttons. The little rap of shoes. At each rustle his arousal only grew stronger.

For God's sake! Was his body so blind to conscience? She had been beaten and cast adrift. If her husband knew that she'd survived, he would no doubt hunt her down to complete his punishment. Fate had placed her instead into the hands of the one man who could help her, whatever her predicament.

Ryder inhaled and turned around. Light flickered about the room, washing color over the tapestry screen. He had already secured another bedroom, of course: the room where he had washed and changed earlier.

Duty and discipline had always defined his life. He had absolute faith in his self-control and in the rightness of his insistence on gallantry. Yet he also felt this bright surge of courage, the response to adventure, the temptation to take just a few hours for himself with a beautiful woman who owed him her life. Why not? What harm could there be in it? Perhaps, if he could only win her confidence, she would yet allow him to help her?

She stepped out from behind the screen.

Dark hair framed her face to stream in a shining waterfall over her shoulders and back. Loose strands curled at her throat and shoulders and white neck. She had made no attempt to put it up or secure it with ribbon. Instead, where a necklace might lie, she had tied a narrow black velvet ribbon around the base of her throat.

The effect—when she was otherwise formally dressed—seemed outrageously wanton.

Thunderously hot blood pounded into his groin.

Her ivory silk dress buttoned at both shoulders. A gown that had belonged to the innkeeper's daughter, the silk no doubt bought from smugglers, the result purchased by Ryder at a premium earlier that evening. An overdress of thin black netting rippled over the silk, emphasizing every curve of long thigh and waist.

The net sleeves of the overdress disguised the marks on her arms. The bruising on her cheek had disappeared into the shadow of her hair. Nothing hid the glorious swell of her breasts, her skin soft as cream above her low neckline. As if she needed to find solace in his admiration, nothing hid the sheer, breathtaking beauty of his captive, wrapped in mystery and courage and dark wit.

She walked forward, her slippers almost silent: white satin

dancing slippers, just a slip of fabric with the thinnest of soles, and ribbons that laced up the ankles.

"I've been ungracious," she said. "I didn't mean to be. Your Lordship has been most generous and I am grateful. I owe you my life. I've not forgotten that."

"The gratitude is all mine." Perhaps he really meant it. The idea left him feeling oddly defenseless. "If I seemed imperious—"

She laughed. "Ah! Are most ladies *so* demoralized simply by your thunderous presence, my lord?"

He took a deep breath. "Yes, I suppose many of them are." He held out a chair for her, then seated himself opposite. Desire mocked like a third guest at the table.

The black-velvet gaze met and held his. "Yet I've never felt safer in my life."

"Thank you. You cannot know quite how precious a gift that thought is to me at the moment."

"As are your assurances that no one can find me here. So perhaps we may enjoy our mutual comfort and forget all of that mad world out there?"

"Yes, why not?" He smiled, though his heart pounded as if she had flung open a door leading to an unknown destination. "Are you hungry?"

"Ravenous!" She glanced up at him beneath her lashes. "Aren't you?"

Ryder thought he might simply disintegrate, so he grinned at her. "Quite desperately so!" He poured wine and lifted the covers off the dishes. "Do you see something to your taste?"

Her pupils opened like the heart of a pansy, offering infinite depths. "There's very little that I don't enjoy tasting, my lord."

He swallowed hard. "I'm afraid we have only this limited selection, based on what our landlord happened to have on hand: oxtail soup, bread, vegetables, rabbit stew, cold beef pie, roast chicken, a couple of fruit pies—one cherry; one rhubarb and ginger, I think—and a jug of thick cream. Such simple country fare is to your liking?"

She played idly with the trailing end of the ribbon at her throat. His attention riveted on her white skin, where the black velvet tickled over her cleavage in sensuous invitation.

"I like everything, my lord, from the simple to the exotic.

Perhaps I have a fondness for dishes that you've never even had the chance to try?"

He glanced down to fill her soup plate, then looked up again as if her gaze were a magnet.

"The duke employs one of the best French chefs in the country. You think food exists anywhere that's more interesting than what's served at Wyldshay?"

"Oh, I'm sure of it!"

She dipped her spoon in her soup and sipped, though she never took her eyes from his. Her mouth was ripe, delectable, and smiling at him. His pulse hammered.

"I've also dined in London. At the King's table upon occasion."

"No doubt. But the King is so very respectable these days." Her tongue licked over her lips. "Have you never risked truly unusual fare, my lord, indulged every whim of appetite, however wicked?"

"Can food be wicked?"

"When it sits impiously in the mouth, certainly."

"The very thought makes me giddy."

She broke open a roll to split it down its length, her fingers caressing.

"Because a man needs solid sustenance? Something to sink his teeth into?" Her white teeth tore off a small piece of the bread, then she snarled at him, grinning, like a dog worrying a bone. "Or to wrap his tongue around?"

He laughed aloud and poured more wine. Yet in spite of his thundering blood and unruly private reactions, the very outrageousness of this conversation set its own limits. Why not just relax and enjoy himself?

Perhaps—after what she had just survived—she simply needed to be reassured that a man could respond to her with kindness rather than with his fists? How could he be cruel enough to turn that down?

"You're too solicitous of my comfort, ma'am, though I think I'd better keep my tongue between my teeth."

She dabbed a little butter on the bread before biting off another small piece. "But doesn't that make it rather hard to enjoy such a feast when it's offered? How do you expect to indulge yourself in its splendors if you never allow your tongue free rein?"

"But which splendors appeal most, ma'am? Chicken, rabbit, or this noble beef pie?"

The turn of her wrist was stunningly lovely as she picked up her wineglass. Ardor resounded in dark, hidden depths.

"You invite me to partake in the king of meats?" she asked. "Alas, the noble beef would appear to be hiding its desires beneath some very respectable trappings of pastry."

"Beef has no desires."

"Yes, it does," she replied, mirth lighting her eyes. "But if you're so determined to deny them, perhaps you should begin with this white meat and the smoothly innocent potato? Pray, take these two, my lord, deliciously round and dripping with butter—and perhaps this carrot? So very upright and solid!"

He almost choked, then he threw his head back and shouted his laughter. He had not allowed himself such pure joy in as long as he could remember. He felt sharp and hot with desire, but she laughed back, as if she really were carefree, as if all her dark shadows had been forgotten, which only made him fiercely glad.

"And what will you have?" he asked.

Still grinning, she topped up his glass, then laid open the savory pie with her knife.

"I'll have the most noble food offered, of course," she said.

Ryder tossed back more wine, filled with wonder that she seemed to have shed her fears so easily—and that she so obviously felt no apprehension at all at being with him?

"But you're not afraid of the fearsome beef pie, ma'am?" he asked, just to make sure. "You don't think it too formidable?"

She raised a brow, as if gently mocking him. "Do other ladies find such noble pies so terrifying, my lord?"

"A great many of them do, ma'am, I regret to say!" He had begun to feel very pleasantly foxed. "Too damn many!"

"Why? Should beef intimidate simply because it's a superior member of the aristocracy?" She leaned forward over the table to tap the meat pie with her knife. "Arise, Sir Loin!"

He was thunderingly aware of the shadowed cleavage between the magical swell of her breasts. He drained his glass again, knowing it was past time to retreat.

"Yet you can't deny that such an aristocrat among meats makes for a cold pie, trapped within its grand flutings of pastry."

"But it's not cold," she said. "Why should you think so? I

believe it's a pie of great depth and generosity, and very hot indeed at the core."

He took his own knife and plunged it into the heart of the pie, laying it open. "No," he said. "As you see, it's a cold pie."

"There's enough fire in this room, though, to warm it."

The wine burned into his overheated blood. "Dare I risk it?"

"Dare you not? You might otherwise always regret dismissing the poor beef pie as a cold fish, and wonder how succulent things might have tasted with just a little more flame added."

"Mustard by itself won't do?"

"Oh, I'm very fond of mustard," she said, "as long as it's very hot."

He lost himself in hilarity. Candlelight danced and spun, sparking infinite promise in the lovely turn of her throat. Her skin rippled as she tipped back her head to drain her wineglass. Every nerve in his body leaped in response. He was hard and hot and feeling far too reckless.

"Then you don't think we should reach for a little cool detachment?" he asked when he had caught his breath.

"Not at all," she said. "I think we should go directly to the sweets."

"You know that I am filled with desire for the fruit, but these sweets aren't for me, are they?"

"Why not?" Her fingers, elegant and supple, stroked the fluted stalk of her glass.

"Because, however strongly tempted, a gentleman learns to restrain his appetites."

It sounded pompous even to his own ears, but she laughed and speared a single cherry with her fork. Her lips gleamed moist and ripe, her mouth pursed for a moment as if kissing, while she sucked in the red fruit. Desire ricocheted to his groin.

"Then you dislike cherries? Most men claim to prefer them to any other fruit. Or do you prefer a spicier, more experienced flavor, like this rhubarb and ginger?"

Wine buzzed in his head. His body flamed with yearning. His mouth was so dry that he thought he might have to drag his voice over gravel. "I don't know. Tonight I shall go without either."

"You will? Why?" She sliced into the rhubarb pie, then dipped a forefinger into the spilled juice. The tip of her tongue curled as she tasted it. "Ah! It's very sweet. You should try some. It won't harm you."

Ardor flickered about his head in a flaming aura. He could no longer find words. Only this reckless longing as he watched the flick of her tongue over her fingertip. He reached for a last shred of sanity.

"No," he said at last, his voice thick. "However delicious it appears, honor demands otherwise."

She speared a piece of candied ginger with her fork and held it out to him. "You really don't need to fear the bite of the ginger, my lord. The balance between the flavors is perfect."

"I'm not afraid," he said desperately.

"Yes, you are. Your diet has been restricted far too long by all that bitter fruit from the thicket. I think it past time that you indulged yourself a little."

"No! It's not that." He closed his eyes. Otherwise, he thought he might simply lean over the table to kiss her.

"Then you prefer humble pie?" she asked gently. "There's no need for that, I assure you."

Ryder glanced up. Her smile was open, welcoming. No shadow lurked in her eyes. The temptation was overwhelming: to take her up on her invitation. The less noble parts of his anatomy clamored the argument: *Why not? Why not?*

"Though I've been accused of many faults," he said, "humility is not among them."

With his last ounce of willpower, he pushed his chair back from the table.

He meant to make his bow and leave the room. Any debt he owed gallantry was fulfilled. She could be in no doubt now that he found her breathtaking, that he desired her with stunning intensity, and that he intended her no harm. She most certainly would not take her own life: not a life that was so vibrant and witty and alive to sensual pleasure. He could safely leave her in this room and retreat back into his own life.

"No one will find you here," he said. "But I believe I should ride back to Wyldshay tonight, after all."

"In this storm? To have been raised in that brier patch of scruples must have been damnable. Do those harsh principles never allow you to taste any of life's riches, my lord?"

She dipped her spoon into the cream pot and twirled it together with sweet juice from the pie. Taking a little of the mix-

ture on the tip of one finger, she brushed it over his lips: rich
cream, with the sticky undercurrent of sugar and ginger and
fruit.

Her supple fingertip caressed his flayed nerves. His blood
flamed. His eyes closed. He knew nothing but honeyed sensation. Silk rustled as she moved around the table. Orange and
lavender and musk.

His mouth opened to the soft pressure of her lips. She tasted
of cherries and cream, sugared rhubarb and candied ginger, all
vivid with the sweet overtones of woman and wine. Drugged
by need, he met her delicate tongue with his own. She caught
his hands in both of hers to hold him pinned in his chair. Their
shared pulse thundered between them, palm to palm.

It was a heady, willing surrender, though he reached for
one last safe limit. Only a kiss! Just that! One kiss! Yet he
kissed blindly, passionately, aching with tenderness at the
supple generosity of her mouth.

Still kissing, she released his hands to run her fingers up
his arms. She caught the back of his head in both palms.
Pulling his mouth down with hers, she knelt in a crumpled
spread of skirts between his spread knees. He ran his fingers
through her hair, then his palms found her naked shoulders
and smoothed up the long column of her throat above the
black ribbon.

When she broke the kiss at last, he was laughing and
groaning and desperate. Her fingers strayed over his back,
pushed beneath his shirt, just as his palms found the swell of
her breasts. He cupped them in both hands, the sweet weight
through the silk, her nipples hard, thrusting beneath his
thumbs.

A small moan fluttered from her lips as he pleasured her,
then she kissed him again. While their lips sought and found,
her fingers opened buttons to fold down the front of his
trousers. Desire flamed, concentrated on that one throbbing
center as she freed him and took his hard shaft in one hand.
With sure strokes she rubbed up and down, tickling below the
head with her thumb. His brain pulsed with colored lights. His
whole body throbbed with exquisite sensations.

Ryder threw back his head to break the kiss—the last few
brambles of the thicket catching at his conscience—but she
seized both of his hands in hers once again and thrust them

out to each side, before she lowered her head to take his hot organ into her mouth.

Intensity enveloped. Silken, exquisite. Her tongue danced. She played wicked games with her teeth. He knew only the sensations, as concentrated as lightning, as rapturous as orgasm—yet prolonged and prolonged as if she knew how to take him to the brink and keep him there, hovering in ecstasy.

He heard groaning as incoherent sounds of pleasure dragged up from his shaking lungs. His hands gripped hers convulsively. Her mouth plunged him into white oblivion. The ecstasy built, almost to climax. His head fell back, his muscles straining, her palms crushed in his. Yet with a last swirl of her tongue, she abandoned him. Frantic, throbbing, he opened his eyes.

She stood up and stepped back. He gazed up at her beneath heavy eyelids as she unbuttoned her dress at both shoulders. In a sweet shush of silk, it slid down about her ankles. Her eyes were huge and dark and compelling, her smile an enchantment of seduction. Dressed in nothing but her shift and corset, she leaned down to kiss his mouth once again. His breath burned in his lungs as she lifted her petticoat to straddle his lap. While they kissed and kept kissing, she impaled herself on his erection.

Ryder almost came back into his mind then, but not to draw back or deny her.

He was not, after all, such a saint.

Instead he buried his face in her shoulder and thrust hard, seeking to know her deeper, to explore all of her sweet mysteries. As he plunged and withdrew and thrust again, she caressed him inside with exquisite subtlety. He had never known such a feeling. All sweetness. All heat. All pleasure. When he drove up one last time with mind-shattering intensity, her muscles clenched and rippled until the rush of his seed stunned him into ecstatic oblivion.

A fine sweat broke all over his body. He dropped his head back, still cradling her in his arms, and fought for a calm breath. She entwined her arms about his neck, dropping small kisses on his face and hair.

"Ah, my sweet Sir Lancelot," she whispered in his ear. "Not so humble, after all!"

"No, my friends call me Ryder—" He struggled for a coherent thought. "But I thought you wished to be rid of me?"

"Did you?" Her voice purred. "So what did you expect me to do when you insisted on staying?"

"I planned to go home."

"No. You thought you shouldn't leave me alone."

"I didn't trust you not to do something desperate."

She snuggled closer, still balanced across his thighs. "You were right."

He raised his head and looked into her eyes, wide and dark, filled with mystery and humor. His heart thundered.

"Who are you? I don't even know your real name."

"Ah, not now! Morning is soon enough for our reckoning. After all, you've bound me by oath—I won't leave without either telling you the truth about my predicament or giving you a chance to help me. In the meantime, perhaps it just seemed simpler to act on a need we both shared so very plainly?"

Ryder studied her face. Yes, she had needed it just as much as he had. To reaffirm the desirability of her own existence? To recover her power and identity after her husband had so brutally betrayed her? If so, perhaps there was no sin in it. Nothing but the pure flame of passion, burning away hurt. Burning away doubt. Burning away duty and class expectations.

"Yes," he said, a new awareness pulsing in his blood. "But wasn't it still a sin when Lancelot gave in so easily to Guinevere?"

"No." Her eyes were fathomless. "She'd have died if he'd been less than generous. And now your need is for sleep, my lord, not to ride home through the storm like a madman."

"My need," he said, "is most certainly not for sleep."

"Then you would like some more debauchery? The bed is really quite comfortable. Shall we retreat there?"

He was Blackdown's heir, the man responsible for thousands of tenants and dependents, a man of conscience and honor, a man who did not make love to other men's wives. Yet he felt more alive than Lord Ryderbourne had ever felt, as if Laurence Duvall Devoran St. George had suddenly been reborn. He groaned like a man whipped, picked her up with her legs still wrapped about his waist, and strode across to the bed.

He set her down on the sheets. As lovely as starlight she shuffled back against the pillows.

"And your need?" he asked.

"My need was only for a bright memory of my knight in shining armor."

Ryder tugged off his boots, then wrenched his shirt away over his head.

"Not just one memory," he said. "A whole night of them."

CHAPTER THREE

*H*E HAD REFUSED TO MAKE HER A LOAN. HE WOULD NOT let her leave. There was only one way to redeem the debt she already owed him and the further one she'd be forced to incur. It was not, of course, any sacrifice. Lord Ryderbourne was beautiful, firm and smooth, muscled like a racehorse. His nails, his hair, his skin, his teeth, all gleamed with vigorous youth and a lifetime of meticulous habits.

Yet the set of his mouth also betrayed a lifetime of control and responsibility. His eyes haunted her. The intelligence and natural joy burdened with all the trappings of position and conventional morality. Did he never escape? Did he never know indulgence?

Now he was just a little foxed, but he was far more deeply intoxicated by the pleasure she had given him. It went some way to redress the balance, that she could bring peace to the taut lines of his face. Yet Miracle had no intention of allowing him even a moment for reflection.

"Then, yes," she said. "Come to bed, my lord! Our needs are the same."

Lean, lash-hard, tall, and powerful, he threw aside his shirt. His dark gaze stunned in its intensity.

She knelt and set both hands on his chest, then leaned forward to suckle one male nipple, then the other, as she tugged away his trousers. His breathing shattered. His hands sought her naked shoulders. As he pushed down her shift, his fingers outlined the curve of her breasts. Something in the natural courtesy of his movements struck her to the heart.

His hands were so careful and gentle and tender! When he bent to kiss her nipples, his mouth was as sensitive as if his own flesh lay at the mercy of his fascinated tongue, as if he knew in his soul exactly what she would like, as if he cared passionately for her pleasure even more than his own.

Yet he was not noticeably skilled. He might not be a virgin, but he could not be especially experienced. It wasn't expertise that moved her so profoundly: nothing clever or original or wicked, none of the tricks that any rake would have at his fingertips.

Instead, Lord Ryderbourne stunned her heart. An aching sensitivity offered without cynicism. A piercing innocence coupled with an exquisite generosity of spirit. It was the one thing she hadn't expected, couldn't have been prepared for. Miracle quaked as she realized the risk she was inadvertently taking: This one man threatened to melt her to the soul.

Even in the darkest throes of his passion, long after he had peeled away her corset and petticoat, long after they had both ceased to want delicacy and gentleness, she had still never known anything like it. He carried her sweating and crying and laughing and shouting to the brink of delirium and once again into the endless plunge over the edge.

She wept at the power of it and despised herself for being so weak.

Yet she used every skill she had ever learned to bring him more pleasure, more intensity. How could she have known that she would receive more than equal measure?

"Is lovemaking a duel?" he said at one point, his eyes dazed, his voice jagged.

The last few candles guttered on the table, casting untrustworthy shadows.

She lifted her head from his shoulder, aware of the slow stroke of his fingertips down her flank. No man had ever touched her like that before—as if he found her more beautiful than life. Just that one simple caress moved her more profoundly than she could fathom.

"Why a duel?"

His gaze shone as dark as the ocean at midnight. "Because the result may be death, perhaps."

"La petite mort?"

"No," he said, smiling up into her eyes while candlelight glimmered deceptively over the planes of his face. "Not just the little death of climax, but the death of the soul, of the person who once existed."

Goose bumps spread over her skin as if winter had eased into the room. "You're wounded so seriously by a little lovemaking, my lord?"

He laughed and rolled her onto her back, then took her chin in his thumb and forefinger, playing softly with her lower lip. "I am slain, sweetheart. I'll never be the same again."

Another candle flickered out as he lowered his head to kiss her again, burning away the cold.

Yet something very deep, something frangible and precarious, seemed to crack in her heart. Had she made a terrible mistake to think that she could pay her debt to him this way and have done? Of course, nothing that had happened between them would harm him. She knew men. She knew how they really viewed sex, whatever flowery phrases they might use at the time. She knew that he'd be glad enough never to see her again, once she told him the truth.

But for now he was warm and vital and here. Morning was many hours away. Miracle kissed back, ravishing his mouth as she ran her hands down his spine to cup his strong buttocks and pull his body into the core of her heat.

SHE woke later to reach for him and knew a moment of stark panic when she thought he had gone. But he had only left their bed to throw open the shutters and stand silhouetted against the night sky. A faint glow gleamed along the outline of a muscled arm and the firm shapes of his naked shoulder and back: a silver glimmer that highlighted the beauty of his young male body, careless and certain in its magnificence.

As if he sensed the instant she was awake, he turned and strode back to the bed. He slipped between the sheets, then cradled her once again in his arms. Miracle relaxed into his embrace and leaned her head against his shoulder. Her palm lay over his heart. She felt mesmerized by the steady pulse of his strong life.

The rain had stopped. Framed by the open shutters, a handful of stars hung in a velvet sky. She gazed up at a hazy yellow sphere, as if her mind floated in a haven of peace, as if his embrace were a fairy-tale harbor of safety reached after a long and perilous journey.

"That must be Jupiter," she said.

"You know the planets?" His voice breathed husky and warm against her ear.

"Jupiter takes eleven years, three hundred and thirteen days, eight hours, thirty-five minutes, and four seconds to revolve around the sun."

"How do you know that?"

"I was almost exactly that age when I first learned it, so I remembered."

His fingers smoothed over her hair, feather-soft strokes at the temple. "You read books about astronomy before you were twelve?"

"No, but I saw the sky through a telescope and was told all about it. Jupiter has four moons. Saturn has seven. To learn about the stars was like a revelation to me, a miracle. Before that the sky was just a spangled quilt holding down the earth. Afterward it was as if I could lose myself in that huge infinity whenever I needed to."

"Do you still wish to lose yourself?"

She sat up, but his hand only slid down to rest loosely on her hip, his fingers dark and strong and gentle against her white flesh, the bones gleaming in the faint sheen from the window.

"There are over a thousand stars," she said. "Every one of them is a sun and each lies at the center of its own system of planets. I've always taken comfort in that."

"In the perfection of Creation?"

"No, not that. In its infinite indifference, perhaps. When I was little I thought the universe must be perfect, but even our sun has dark stains on it. The marks grow and shrink as if cinders were being randomly tossed up from a furnace."

His palm stroked up her spine as if he would shape her back in his memory. His fingers began to play idly with her hair. "That doesn't detract from its perfection."

Miracle tipped back her head and closed her eyes. "Did you ever look at the stars when you were a boy?"

He hesitated for only a moment before he replied. "I used to creep out alone at night sometimes to stand on the roof of the Fortune Tower at Wyldshay. Not only to look, but to listen."

"Listen?"

"My ears strained for the thin, high music that the planets sing as they revolve in their orbits. Some nights I even thought that I heard it."

"Perhaps you did."

He reached to take the brush from the bedside table. "Or perhaps the wind sang just so in the wires on the flagpole, or the breeze simply echoed its sighs around the gargoyles and battlements."

"No. You heard the music of the spheres. It's a lonely enough melody."

"I was hardly lonely. I had a brother and sisters and lived in a house full of servants."

He began to smooth the tangles from her hair. Long strokes flowed from her scalp to her waist. Little tingles of pleasure danced after them, as if she were melting under his care.

"Yet you still strained to hear that forbidden song," she said. "Your soul reached for the harmony of the cosmos. It's our best escape from chaos."

"I wouldn't have put it quite like that, but perhaps all children make time for such things, even when life demands otherwise."

"You were born the heir to a dukedom," she said. "They must have demanded a great deal."

He brushed her hair in silence for a few minutes. Tingling with pleasure at his touch, Miracle stared at the little rectangle of sky and the remote majesty of the king of the gods.

"Were you lonely as a child?" he asked at last. "When you learned about the stars?"

"Ah!" she said. "Never mind about me."

He set aside the brush and began to braid her hair in careful fingers, then unfastened the ribbon at her throat to use for a tie. "You're perfection," he said.

"Don't say that!"

"Why not? The curve of your back glimmers flawlessly in

the starlight. Your skin seems almost translucent, as if you were a spirit of beauty sent merely to torment me."

She turned to look down at him, at his dark eyes and tumbled hair, the broad chest and lovely male throat. With one fingertip he slowly traced the profile of her breast and nipple, as if he painted her in starlight. The sensitive tip puckered as sensation plummeted down to her groin.

"I torment you?" she asked.

"Only with the promise of more bliss."

Miracle gazed down at him, his splendor blurred by starlight and the wavering haze of sudden tears. She took the ribbon from his fingers and caught his face in both hands to whisper against the loveliness of his mouth.

"I'm no wraith, my lord, just a woman—"

He stopped her words with his kiss. Miracle met his tongue with her own, then slid her thigh over his as she pinned his hands above his head in both of hers. His arousal reared hard against her belly. Slowly, exquisitely, she retreated from the terrifying chasm that had begun to yawn at her feet, and began to ravish him again.

RYDER woke with the bedclothes wrapped about his legs like a shroud. He fought free of them, only to grip his pounding head in both hands. Daylight flooded the room. Not the pearly light of early dawn. Bright, broad daylight. A clatter of activity floated up from the inn yard.

Though the light assaulted his eyes, he forced himself to look around the room. Harsh yellow beams bounced around the walls to illuminate the cold grate and the cheap furnishings. The fire had gone out. He sat up.

She was gone.

A fly buzzed lazily over the cold food on the table.

I like everything, from the simple to the exotic—

She was gone. For a moment he didn't know if he could bear it.

He dropped his head back against the pillows and pressed both palms over his eyes. Memories swirled, a whirlpool of colored sensation. His tongue, his legs, his back, his whole body ached sweetly: a deep physical exhaustion, as if he had

been drained of his soul. His head ached—not sweetly at all—
as if a steam hammer had been set to push his brain from his
skull.

Devil take it, how much wine had it taken? How many bottles to find the courage to make love to a stranger against all of
his better judgment?

She had seduced him. Yet in the end the responsibility had
been his. He had mouthed platitudes about honor and duty.
Then he hadn't hesitated to exploit the vulnerability of a
woman who had barely escaped drowning only a few hours
before, a woman whose husband had beaten her and abandoned her to die.

In a blind search for comfort she, too, had made love with
a stranger and even shared a few painfully deep personal in-
sights. Obviously she regretted it. And so she had left.

Though she was right, of course. To wake together would
have presented them both with the awkwardness of facing
what they had done.

His hands shook as a rush of pain dampened his palms.
Not the pain of too much wine. The pain of self-disgust. She
had asked him for a loan. She had been desperate to leave.
Claiming it was only for her benefit, he had insisted that she
spend the night with him.

Had he known in his heart of hearts that he was trapping her
into sharing his bed? If so, then he despised himself for his duplicity. Yet how could he regret the bliss he had experienced?

He had told her that he wasn't a virgin. True enough as far
as it went. He knew now that he'd had no more knowledge or
skill than any callow boy. She had used her mouth to take
him to the brink of madness. She had used her hands. Her
tongue. Her legs. Her breasts. Her body. She had hesitated at
nothing, done things he had never dared imagine, taken him
to places he hadn't known existed—and kindled an insatiable
potency.

That, perhaps, was easy enough to understand: the irre-
sistible demands of the body. Yet they had also talked, like
lovers or soul mates, lost in shared dreams of stars and childhood.

God! Why had he told her about those naive boyhood vig-
ils on the roof of the Fortune Tower? He had not thought about
any of that in years. He never went up to the rooftops at Wyld-

shay any longer. Yet he remembered as if it were yesterday when he had first thought that he heard Mercury's high singing and the base note of Saturn thrumming in harmony. That had been the very tail end of his boyhood, before he had fully realized that there was no place in his future for fantasy.

But she had woken to regret everything and so she had fled. Tearing his heart from his chest and carrying it with her?

Perhaps he had gone mad? For even in the height of his passion, his intellect had coolly recognized the level of his fool-hardiness: Lord Ryderbourne, fascination and bane of society, had allowed a chance-met stranger to lay open his soul.

Was this obsession? Was this what had driven Sir Lancelot to betray his country, his king, his best friend?

Ryder forced himself from the bed and walked naked to the window. Dried sweat salted his skin. His hair was stuck to his head. He was sheened with musk and the scent of orange and lavender.

His clothes lay stacked neatly on a chair. The clothes he had bought for her were gone. She had taken them, at least—and his cloak, apparently.

She was, of course, forsworn. He would never know the truth about her now, nor be able to help her. Yet as neatly as if she had tied it up in her black velvet ribbon, she had made him a gift of his inexperience and his hypocrisy, instead.

What the hell had he given her in return?

Ryder strode back to his abandoned trousers and felt in the pocket. His purse was still there. He tipped coins onto the table. She had taken nothing, except the clothes and his cloak. So she was penniless. Was she fleeing back along the coast straight into the hands of a husband who had already tried to murder her?

He filled his glass with the remains of the wine from the previous night. Wealth could buy almost anything. Alas, that it could not buy a man sense! It could not even buy him honor. Ryder tossed back the wine, tugged on his trousers, strode to the door, and flung it open.

At his shout a man came running: Jenkins, who was taking care of his gelding, but who also owned the inn.

"Send up hot water and my riding clothes," Ryder said. "Send the maids to clear away all of this mess and bring breakfast. Saddle my horse to be ready for me in half an hour. You may send the reckoning for everything to me at Wyldshay."

The man tugged at his forelock. "Yes, my lord."

Ryder turned back into the room. Something small and white caught his attention. He stared at it: One white satin slipper lay curled at the edge of the bed.

"My lord?"

He looked up. Jenkins still hovered at the door. "Yes?" Ryder said. "What is it?"

"And the lady's reckoning, my lord? We'll send that as well, shall we?"

"What reckoning?"

Jenkins stepped back, visibly anxious. "For the horse and saddle, my lord. For the victuals. For the extra clothes and the lady's riding boots and the gloves and the hat and all—and the saddlebags to carry everything. For a guide to take her straight to the London road. The lady said it was all by your orders."

"A *horse*?"

"She said she couldn't use a hired nag, my lord, and be certain of it being returned. She purchased my daughter's saddle outright, too. She said it was all right, whatever it might cost, saddle horses for a lady being so hard to come by now that we've lost all our trade to the landslide."

Ryder stared at him, almost incredulous. "What the devil horse did you sell her?"

"The very best I had left, my lord: that big chestnut with the bald face and the white patch like the map of Ireland on his rump. Though the lady said she didn't quite like the look of him, that horse'll go many miles without tiring and he's gentle as a lamb. Then there was the decent plain habit, the nice brown wool with the black trim that my daughter had new just last winter, and all the other necessities to go with it. But now—what with our business mostly gone—it's not easy for us to replace, my lord. Yet the lady said not to worry, just to charge it all to your account, even the rope hobbles."

"Hobbles?"

"Yes, my lord. Like the Gypsies use. So the horse can't run away when he's turned loose to graze."

Hilarity caught him like a punch from an unseen assailant, doubling him over. Lord Ryderbourne, son and heir to the Duke of Blackdown, stood half naked in a tattered bedroom in the most run-down inn in Dorset. It was as obvious as daylight what had happened in the bed.

Nevertheless, the minions of the Merry Monarch had, as always, leaped to obey his orders—even when conveyed by the unknown woman with whom he had shared the wildest night of his life.

He threw back his head and laughed till he ached. No word of any of this would ever leave the village, but who could blame an innkeeper if he charged that duke's son an arm and a leg for his silence and his services?

None of the servants looked at him askance as the room was cleared, the table cleaned, the bed stripped of its tangle of sheets. Alice and Mary brought copious amounts of hot water and his own riding clothes, cleaned and pressed. Knowing she would be generously rewarded for her labors, a laundry woman must have been up half the night.

As soon as Ryder had washed and dressed, his hair still damp from its plunge into warm water, Jenkins brought in a tray with coffee, eggs, beef, and bacon. Thirty minutes later, free of any visible trace of his night's adventures, Ryder sat at the window and stared out over the village to the beach.

The boats were gone, taken out for the day's fishing. A million tasks awaited him at Wyldshay, a burden of work as great in its way as that of the villagers, perhaps greater. Jenkins walked the black gelding up and down in the inn yard. Yet Ryder sat as if paralyzed, while thoughts swirled in his head.

She had left him one satin slipper.

And memories—

He stood up with a curse and strode to the door. Even if he went after her, she had several hours' head start. If she had wished for further help from him, she would have stayed and asked for it. Instead she was forsworn. She had broken her clear promise.

The episode was over. He would very probably never see her again. He had a life of his own that demanded all of his time.

He stalked out into the yard, where the sun shouted for his attention and his horse lifted its head and nickered. Jenkins relinquished the reins. Ryder swung into the saddle. As soon as he was clear of the village, he urged the gelding into a ground-eating trot, then a flat-out gallop, only stopping when he reached the first tollhouse.

The keeper stepped out and touched one finger to his cap.

For a moment Ryder was tempted to ask after a chestnut with a map of Ireland on its rump. Instead, he reached into the pocket of his waistcoat for a coin. His fingers encountered a folded slip of paper.

Shock raised the hairs on the back of his neck. He took one glance at the front of it—at his name, *Lord Ryderbourne,* inscribed in black ink in a woman's flowing hand—then crushed the note in his fist before thrusting it back. He found some pennies in another pocket and dropped the correct money into the toll collector's hand.

With her crumpled message burning against his heart, he rode home.

The walls of Wyldshay soared from their lake: that magical fortress of stone and water. His destiny.

Just before he left the trees to ride along the final approach to the arched bridge, Ryder pulled up his horse. He reached into his saddlebag. The ivory satin slipper lay mute in his hand, empty of her erotic white foot. Why the devil had he felt he must keep it?

The gelding moved restively, anxious to return to its stable.

Ryder slid the slipper into his coat pocket, then reached for the note still lying over his heart: the memento that he had not set there himself, that must have been slipped where only he would find it, while his clothes were still hanging to dry in the kitchen.

It seemed like a terrible temptation, to read what she had said: excuses, apologies, pleas, lies?

The St. George banner flew from the highest tower of Wyldshay, the wind whipping the distant fabric. Swallows wheeled over the island that held his childhood home and his future inheritance. This was his reality and his life. The slipper and the note were both irrelevant. He would throw them out as soon as he reached his own rooms. One night's madness with a married stranger would sink eventually into his distant past, to be mused over, then forgotten.

Leaving her note where it lay, Ryder dropped his hand back to the reins and rode his horse home.

MIRACLE dismissed her guide and watched the man ride away, back toward the coast, back toward the Merry Monarch and the fishing village. Dawn cast its long shadows through the faint mist that lay over the fields and cliffs. She had left the duke's son deeply asleep in their disordered bed—the loveliest man she had ever known.

The memory burned in her heart. Would he feel betrayed and abandoned? Would he think that she had robbed him? Probably of his honor, at least. He had tried so hard to play the gentleman. He had not really wanted to become her lover. Though she had never met anyone like him before, she could guess how he would feel.

He would be angry, of course. Angry, or disgusted, or even a little humiliated. But she knew men. He would soon dismiss their encounter as an irrelevant episode, a sweet memory destined to fade into nothingness.

She did not think he would persecute her, even after he read the note, thrust into his waistcoat pocket where he'd find it at the first tollbooth. Neither did she think he would try to intervene any further to save her from her fate. He might even accept that he had made a lucky escape, once he knew who she was.

And that was definitely for the best.

In a blind reach for optimism, she turned her horse's head and rode on. Not toward London. Hanley must be on her trail by now, and the capital was too obvious. Instead she rode north. She would lose herself in a tangle of byways, where she still had a chance.

In the meantime, she owned a horse and saddle, a warm cloak, a change of clothes, and food. When Lord Ryderbourne had refused her a loan, it had seemed fair enough to trade him her favors for what she so desperately needed. To take his money without his permission would simply have been theft. If Miracle had other reasons to feel uncomfortable about trading coins for what they had shared, she did not want to face them.

For several hours she saw no one but farm workers. Curious glances and the occasional open stare followed her. A lady in a brown habit riding alone with no manservant. To be so noticeable was a definite risk, but to travel on foot would have been worse. On foot she'd be too slow and too vulnerable. And though she had supplies for a few days, she had no money for a coach fare.

She would find abandoned barns or odd nooks where she could spend the nights wrapped in his cloak, the horse turned loose to graze in the rope hobbles. She would use the least public of roads. When she arrived at Dillard's house in Derbyshire, she could collect her savings and buy passage from Liverpool.

If she was lucky, she would stay one step ahead of pursuit. If she was lucky, she might yet escape.

Miracle had ridden hour after hour, steadily covering the miles, when she heard it. She halted her horse. The gelding threw up its head. She circled, her heart thundering, before she let her mount feel the cut of her whip. In a spray of mud, the horse leaped forward.

Yet the sound followed her like a nightmare, coming and going at each bend in the road or break in the hedge: the baying of hounds.

RYDER trotted his mount over the bridge and beneath the portcullis. He swung down as a groom ran out to take the gelding. Without a backward glance, the duke's son strode into the Great Hall at Wyldshay, throwing aside hat and gloves as he did so.

Servants bowed and scurried. "My lord!"

He took the stairs two at a time, then strode down the endless hallways to the Whitchurch Wing, the set of rooms reserved for his personal use ever since he'd left the nursery. The house shouted his identity: St. George fluttered on tapestries, stared arrogantly from paintings, butchered writhing dragons carved into stone. Beneath lintels and beams, across ceilings, in the carved turn of balusters, the family motto or the name of St. George stamped its way into every inhabitant's consciousness.

Lord Ryderbourne, the castle insisted, *Laurence Duvall Devoran St. George. You are home!*

One of his secretaries looked up as he stalked into the estate offices that lay near his private rooms.

The man scrambled to his feet. "My lord!"

"We had an appointment this morning at ten, Mr. Davis," Ryder said. "I was delayed. Was it anything urgent?"

It was urgent, of course. All estate business was urgent, always. The Blackdowns controlled over twenty thousand acres in Dorset, and countless acres and estates in other counties. The duchy employed stewards and secretaries, agents and housekeepers, yet someone in the family had to hold all of those reins together. Someone had to make the final decisions.

As he had grown older, the duke had delegated that task piece by piece to his eldest son. Now Ryder ran almost everything.

He worked straight through the afternoon and evening, only stopping when he realized that the secretary's face was gray with fatigue.

"I didn't intend to drive you so hard, Mr. Davis," he said. "Take off what's left of the day. Tomorrow as well, if you like. I can finish this."

"It's my pleasure to work with you, my lord," the secretary said. "I'll take a rest when we're done."

Ryder smiled at him. "No flattery, sir. Take a break. Get something to eat, for God's sake! There's nothing left here now that can't wait until later."

"It's not flattery, my lord," Davis said. "I meant it. It's both an honor and a joy to work with Your Lordship."

The man left the room. Ryder sat back and stretched, a little bemused. Davis might even be telling him the truth, though that would—always and forever—be impossible to ascertain. It was simply part of Ryder's life that he would never be able to distinguish flattery from friendship with any certainty.

Probably, he thought with a wry smile, why he had so few real friends!

When the door opened again, he looked up, expecting to see Davis. Instead he scrambled to his feet and bowed.

"Your Grace!"

Tiny, exquisite, his mother walked into the room. She gazed at him with his own eyes, green as glass. From her blond hair to her shoes she embodied perfection. It was a perfection that Ryder had always longed to encompass, yet knew he never could.

"Are you mad, Ryderbourne?" she asked. "What are you doing in here?"

"I'm managing our properties," he said. "That's what I do. Though not somewhere Your Grace normally visits, this room forms part of our estate offices."

She raised her fair brows as if he had said he were studying slugs. "We employ stewards to see to the estates. You are my eldest son. You left home yesterday morning to offer marriage to Lady Belinda Carhart, a pretty girl of little brain but much consequence. However flawed a judgment about the fair sex that choice may have demonstrated, you claimed to be in love with her. Fortunately, Lady Belinda is qualified by birth, if nothing else, to become my successor one day. It may or may not have occurred to you that the results of that interview would be of interest to others besides yourself."

He felt dumbstruck, but he told her the simple truth. "I apologize, Your Grace. I had forgotten."

The duchess walked away to study a print on the wall: the classical facade of Wrendale, one of the duchy houses in Derbyshire. Her straight back was eloquent with exasperation.

"*Forgotten?* That you are affianced, or that you are not?"

The smallest curl of amusement, along with real surprise at himself, forced him to smile. Lady Belinda and the humiliation of her refusal had not crossed his mind since—Ryder took a deep breath. Not since he had seen a small boat foundering in the ocean. It was almost as if his proposal of marriage had happened in another lifetime, one now entirely irrelevant.

"She refused me," he said.

The ribbons on his mother's dress wavered slightly, as if in an invisible breeze. "Did she say why?"

"I frighten her. She's going to marry Asterley."

The duchess stood in silence for a moment, keeping her back to her son. When she spoke again, her voice was as fine as a sharpened steel blade. "Asterley? How very squalid of her! Yet you do not seem to care so very much."

"I thought that I did."

She turned. Her eyes searched his face. "But now you do not? What has happened in the meantime to change your mind?"

He stood his ground, smiling down into her green gaze, his arms crossed over his chest. The crushed slip of paper lay over his heart, scalding into his awareness. It had been smoldering there, like a volcano, during all the long hours he had spent poring over papers with Davis. He had forgotten Lady Belinda. He had not forgotten his mystery lady.

"That's rather my business, Your Grace."

"Because you stopped for the night at the Merry Monarch in Brockton to drown your sorrows," she said. "If you remember, you sent a message that the storm had delayed you. Yet drink is a coward's way out."

It rankled. "You would not call Jack a coward to his face."

"Because, whatever his other faults, my younger son has the courage of a dragon."

Ryder took another deep breath. Why the devil hadn't he already destroyed the note? He had no intention of reading it.

"That's true, but the real reason is that you love Jack better than life and always have. It's all right. I came to terms with that fact many years ago. I'm sorry that my brother has broken your heart by leaving England for India with his new bride. That does not give you the right to insult me."

"Nor you the right to resent it, if I choose to upbraid you. I am your mother, sir."

"How could I ever forget, Your Grace? But my message last night told you only half of the truth about why I was delayed. There was far too much wine, of course, but I also drowned my sorrows in the embrace of another man's wife."

The duchess did not hesitate. "Then at least you behaved like a man."

He threw back his head and laughed aloud. His mother would never cease to amaze him. Of course, she amazed everyone, slaying hearts and gathering sycophants wherever she set her daintily shod foot.

"You're not surprised?" he asked at last.

A quirk appeared at one corner of her mouth. "I am shocked to the core. My virtuous firstborn son! How fortunate that your sisters are away, touring the Lakes with their aunt!"

"You would rather I were not so virtuous, Your Grace?"

"I would rather that you were engaged to marry. Though I may not have been too impressed by her brilliance, Lady Belinda Carhart would have known how to behave as a duchess, at least. You had better tell the duke that he is once again obliged to delay his hopes for a legitimate grandchild."

"Jack and Anne will have sons," Ryder said. "The line is perfectly secure, whether I marry or not."

"There are other issues at stake."

"Because freedom suits Jack so much better than the burden of being my heir? Even though you cannot bear it that he has always refused to stay by your side, you don't want my brother to be hampered by the duties of the dukedom, do you?"

The curve of her neck seemed almost deliberately vulnerable beneath her blond hair. "Don't blame me for loving him too much, Ryderbourne! Though you were as robust as a bull from the beginning, I was afraid for the first five years of his life that your brother was too delicate to survive. He almost died when he was born. Did you know that?"

"I'm amazed. I thought you loved Jack better than me simply because he blazed such a brilliant path through all of our hearts."

She set her hand on the jamb, the elegant fingers glimmering with rings. Her knuckles shone white. "There is that, too, of course. The whole world is in love with him. But you are my eldest son and the heir to one of the greatest estates in England. Whatever Jonathan's gifts, you will make a better duke. You must wed wisely and it were better if it were soon. Go to London! Take up an invitation to visit some of the right families at their country homes this summer. Find a child who's so impressed with your prospects that she forgets to be afraid of you."

The idea repelled him. Yet he had offered for Lady Belinda Carhart. What the hell would he have done if she had accepted his suit?

"I cannot spare the time right now to leave Wyldshay. Unlike Jack and my little sisters, I have responsibilities here."

"Nonsense! What you call duty, my dear boy, is only a way to escape the other half of your destiny."

"To marry wisely?"

"To dazzle society—in a wave of scandal and disrepute, if need be. Then you must marry your future duchess, of course. But why not try a little rebellion and outrage first?"

"I cannot become Jack, Mother," he said. "I'll never match him."

"No, of course not." She smiled, almost as if she loved him, too. "Your brother is unique. So, of course, are you. However, if you have trained the staff as you should, there is nothing to keep you here that cannot be delegated. And now, if you would be kind enough to dress for dinner to join the duke and myself in the dining room, we may all pretend once again to be civilized."

* * *

THE horse shook and sweated beneath her. Miracle allowed it to drop to a walk, then she dismounted and led the tired animal by the reins. She had outrun them, whoever it was. Perhaps just a farmer with a couple of dogs. Perhaps just the local Master of Foxhounds exercising the pack, or even a foxhunt in full cry. She could not remember clearly enough now to interpret what she had heard with any certainty. She had just fled along lane after lane into a maze of unknown countryside.

The track ahead of her cut up through a miniature gorge. High above, trees overhung the banks, shutting out almost all of the remaining daylight. The surface underfoot was as wet as a streambed. She had no idea where she was, but she struggled on, her boots sliding in the mud. At the top of the gorge the lane broke out into open fields. A thick wood lay a small distance away to the right.

Fighting exhaustion, Miracle opened a gate and led the horse along a dirt path toward the trees. At the edge of the wood she found a small hut, the roof half fallen, the clamber of ivy over the ruined walls rustling with mice and small birds. A pile of old straw lay heaped in one corner.

She crouched to put the rope hobbles about the horse's pasterns, then unbuckled the girth and pulled off both saddle and bridle. The faithful animal dropped its head to crop at the turf as she rubbed it down with a twist of the straw. Still grazing, the horse moved away with constricted little strides, and Miracle entered the hut.

Some leaf litter in the outer corner was cleaner than the straw. She propped the saddle there so that the leather skirts and the pad made a nest. Leaning back against it, she ate some cheese and bread, then chewed an apple down to the core. Every muscle ached, not only from riding and walking, but from the blows that Willcott had given her. A small shiver ran down her spine.

Miracle tossed the apple core to the horse and blinked back the foolish sting of tears. Whatever happened now, she was determined to regret nothing—not even last night!

The darkness deepened. She took off the brown habit to hang it from a nail and slipped on the ivory silk dress—

without the black net overdress—to use as a nightgown. Whisper-soft fabric caressed. Oranges and lavender.

Dismissing the images, she wrapped herself in his cloak and curled up to sleep. The scent of man and sea enveloped her: another heartbreaking reminder of that heady encounter with a duke's son.

Somewhere not too far away running water trickled over stones. An owl hooted softly in the woods. Its long, mournful cry mingled with the gurgling brook, as if the bird called the name that would haunt her dreams for the rest of her life: *Lord Ryderbourne. Lord Ryderbourne.*

THE Whitchurch Wing had been remodeled some fifty years before. Nothing much remained of the stark reality of ancient stone beneath the smooth plaster walls. Yet Ryder stood now in his bedroom—surrounded by the elegant simplicity of cool green, warm tan, and white—and stared from the window. Wyldshay lay enveloped in darkness.

His younger brother, Jack, in stark contrast, had chosen one of the oldest parts of the castle for his own. The round rooms of the Docent Tower stamped their unmistakable mark that Wyldshay was still a medieval fortress at heart.

Even as a child, Jack had been a romantic. As a younger son, he'd had few responsibilities other than his own amusement. So Jack—Lord Jonathan Devoran St. George—had cut a brilliant swath through both society and the world, then wed with stunning disregard for family tradition.

Anne Marsh—the new Lady Jonathan Devoran St. George— was a commoner, a dissenting minister's clever, generous daughter. Jack had married her in the beginning from necessity, but in the end he had whisked her off to India with him simply because they loved each other so profoundly.

Ryder turned from the window and began to shed the evening clothes he had worn for dinner. The garments he had ridden home in earlier had been taken away to be cleaned and pressed once again. The contents of his pockets were arrayed neatly on a table.

He tugged open his cravat as he looked at them: his watch, some coins, her silver slipper. Her still-folded note had been ironed.

Ryder smiled a little grimly to himself. The fire beckoned. Yet he picked up the slipper and set it in a drawer before he took the note and held it to his nostrils for a moment.

Would it carry her scent?

Nothing, of course. Just paper and ink.

It took only the flick of his thumb to open it.

The four sentences burned into his heart as if she had written them in flame:

My name is Miracle Heather.
I am London's most notorious harlot.
When you found me in the boat, I had just murdered a man.
Thank you for all you have done or offered to do for me, my lord, but you are well rid of me.

CHAPTER FOUR

$\mathscr{B}$LACKBIRDS WOKE HER. MIRACLE OPENED HER EYES. IT was barely light. Dried leaves rustled in her hair. She sat up and brushed them out with her fingers, then sorted through her saddlebags for a comb and some food. Running water burbled beneath the birdsong, laughing as it rippled over stones.

She put on her boots, then—still wrapped in Lord Ryderbourne's cloak—she followed the sounds to a stream that cascaded through the woods. She crouched to splash cold water over her face and arms.

A blackbird eyed her as she sat on the bank to comb out the night's tangles and pin up her hair. Miracle winked at the bird and unwrapped a little bread and some cheese. When she rinsed her fingers again in the stream, the bird flew away.

"Here's a fly turnabout for a brace o' Jack Puddings!"

Miracle froze. Drops splashed into the brook from her fingers, but the tumble of water swallowed the sounds. The voice had drifted down through the woods from the direction of the hut: a man's voice with a hint of nastiness beneath the rough accent.

"Well, well, you old dog," a second man said. "When a nag droops about like a lobcock waiting for the next likely coves to 'appen along, I say ask no questions and you won't get no wrong answers."

"There's a moll about," the first man said. "Lookee, here! A mort's saddle and dress!"

"A bracket-faced hedge whore, most like! No bother to us—"

For several painful moments, silence invaded. Miracle strained to listen above the thump of her heart.

"Heave ho, then, m' lad! A nacky setup, right enough! Worth the risk of a morning drop with Jack Ketch!"

Hooves struck hard as if a horse circled nervously. Rage instantly conquered fear. As if freed from a trance, Miracle raced up the slope. She broke free of the trees just as her gelding cantered away. The two thieves clung together riding double, perched absurdly on her sidesaddle and bouncing like ducklings on a pond.

As they disappeared from view, it started to rain.

LONDON was dirty and loud. Even the most fashionable houses wept streaks of soot down their faces. Ryder stepped from his carriage and glanced up at the facade of his townhouse. The duchy also owned a mansion—the duke's official town residence—overlooking Green Park, but Ryder preferred the simplicity of this terraced set of rooms in Duke Street. No one in the family used them but himself.

Rain splashed and puddled. A footman ran out with an open umbrella.

"Ryderbourne?" some newcomer said in his ear. "By Jove! Didn't expect to see you in town, my lord!"

The footman jerked to silent attention beneath the umbrella as Ryder turned to face the interloper. Hurrying head down against the rain, a bedraggled young gentleman in a wet greatcoat had almost bumped into him.

With a flick of the wrist Ryder raised his quizzing glass, pinning the fellow in place.

The man flushed scarlet. "Ah, my lord! I was just—Well, I—"

The footman tipped the umbrella to better protect His Lordship. Small waterfalls ran straight from the ferrules onto the head of the impertinent young gentleman.

"We have met before, sir?" Ryder asked. "Over a practice blade, perhaps? Mr. Lindsay Smith, I believe."

Mr. Smith tried and failed to swallow his grin. His faced glowed like a gas lamp. A cascade now splashed straight onto his nose, but he seemed glued to the pavement.

"Honored to fence a few times with Your Lordship. Flattered Your Lordship would remember. Trounced, of course. But, well—Best be on my way! Your Lordship will forgive— Didn't mean to offer any disrespect—"

"Not at all," Ryder said. "I've just returned to town for a few days and would welcome a little convivial company. Later this evening, perhaps? A glass of wine and a hand of cards with a few other gentlemen?"

Lindsay Smith's face shone like a polished apple above his drenched collar. Speechless, he managed to nod.

"Then that's settled." Ryder lowered the quizzing glass and turned toward his front door. "Ten o'clock?"

With the footman trotting beside him Ryder strode up the steps, leaving Mr. Smith beaming in the rain.

There were many compensations to being a duke's heir. The ability to command lesser men was one of them. Lord Ryderbourne had remembered a plain Mr. Smith and had not cut him dead, even when that foolhardy young man had shown the temerity to accost His Lordship so rudely on the street. Lindsay Smith would be talking about this coup for days. If he had had any other plans for the evening, he would cancel them.

Ryder tossed his outer garments to the footman and walked into his study. A fire glowed in the grate. His preferred brandy sat waiting. His favorite armchair offered its respectful embrace. The room gleamed an immaculate welcome, as if His Lordship had just stepped out for a moment, though he had not been in town since the end of the Season.

In the hallway behind him, menservants thumped his luggage upstairs. The kitchen would produce any meal he desired, but they already knew his tastes so well that no one need ask. The smooth machinery of his life, where his every desire was anticipated and fulfilled.

He had always taken it for granted, as if an army of invisible elves existed only to wait on him.

Ryder filled a glass and sipped the rich liquor, frowning thoughtfully into the flames.

Where the devil was she now?

Like a madman he had brought her white slipper to London with him. He took it from his pocket and stared at the delicate satin, slowly pulling the ribbon through his fingers. Should he go from whorehouse to whorehouse, looking for the slender ankle and foot that belonged to the one woman it would fit? God! Such footwear might fit any of a thousand!

With a curse Ryder threw the slipper onto a table. Of course, she was not any of a thousand. She was—What? His obsession? And, now that he had read her note, his responsibility?

Since arriving back at Wyldshay, he had barely slept. He had even found himself striding up the spiral stair to the roof of the Fortune Tower to stare like a mooncalf at the stars. Jupiter hung caught in the net of constellations, staring back at him with a jeering yellow eye.

She had made love to him in *payment*, already planning what she would do the next morning. The idea burned and hurt, driving a desperate rage. He had refused her a loan, so she had purchased what she needed from him with her body.

It had taken several days of hard work before he could walk out of Wyldshay, but he had left all his ongoing business in the hands of Mr. Davis. If any emergency arose, the steward would send for instructions. Her Grace the Duchess of Blackdown thought he had come to London to pursue a little vice. Meanwhile, every mama in the home counties already knew by now that Lady Belinda Carhart had settled on Asterley, and that Lord Ryderbourne must still be looking for a bride.

The excitement would be intense. Myriad invitations would follow.

Too bad that he intended to disappoint them!

His butler entered like a ghost, seeing to His Lordship's every last comfort and arranging the room for the party later that evening. Ryder barely noticed him. He ate alone in the dining room, leaving half the dishes untasted, then lingered over brandy as he waited for Lindsay Smith and the others to arrive.

He had sent his invitation to a select group of young rattles not generally so honored. His summons would be promptly obeyed, even if he offered them nothing more than a convivial game, some excellent wine, and his own company. No doubt every one of them had canceled other engagements and been thrilled to do so.

The clock struck the hour. The front knocker rapped, followed by the tread of shoes in the hall. Ryder set himself to be witty, to be welcoming, and to listen. His butler had seen to everything else, especially the unending flow of fine wine from one of London's best cellars.

By midnight half a dozen young men shouted over the latest town gossip—the wagers, the races, the duels and entanglements, the latest crop of marriageable young ladies.

Lord Dartford, more sober than the rest, raised his glass. "A toast to Virtue, sirs!"

"Let's toast Sin, instead," Ryder said gently. He had hardly touched his own wine. "Her charms are surely more interesting?"

The guests roared with laughter. "To Sin!" the men bellowed. "To Sin!"

"And to the most glorious Sinner of them all!" someone yelled. "Miracle Heather!"

Heads tipped back as every man drained his glass once again—a hint of envy or lust or frustration in each drunken face.

His blood burning, Ryder forced himself to relax and signal for more wine. He had invited the men here for this. It would hardly further his cause if he threw over the table and punched out his guests. Yet he felt as if he were holding back a storm.

"Damned unlikely name, if you ask me." Lindsay Smith had slumped back in his chair and was staring into his glass. "Who was ever christened Miracle?"

"Harlots don't need *christened*," a wit said. "Just rogered!"

Every man there guffawed without noticing the storm cloud gathering around the head of their host.

"I don't recall the lady," Ryder said. "She is pretty?"

"Gad, my lord! A raving beauty. Your Lordship must have seen her around town?"

"I couldn't say," Ryder replied. "I've been in the country."

Smith leaned forward with conspiratorial intimacy, his focus blurred. "Alas, she's too toplofty for the likes of me! Never kept company with less than a peer's son. Went off to Dorset with the Earl of Hanley just recently—the damned rogue!"

"A relationship of long standing?" At the mention of Hanley's name, Ryder's fists had clenched beneath the table.

"A few months," Dartford said. "Hanley was besotted. Yet he came back to town a few days ago without her."

"Perhaps Miracle Heather has found a new lover?"

"If she has," Smith responded, "the man better look out for the earl. They say he's fit to be tied. To be so publicly embarrassed by a whore? Damme, sir! This game's yours, as well."

Dartford swept up the coins. Ryder stood up. The party was over. Dartford had emptied everyone's pockets, including those of his host. Of course, unlike some of the others, Ryder could afford it.

In ones and twos the guests lurched onto the street, praising the best damned evening any of them could remember—not counting the time six naked women had served the drinks at Lord Asterley's, of course. Ryder watched them go and wondered briefly how Lady Belinda would feel about that.

The only sober man among them, Dartford was the last to leave. He hesitated for a moment as he pulled on his gloves. A keen intelligence lay behind the man's bland gaze.

"Rumors are already on the fly about the cause of Hanley's comeuppance," he said.

"I barely know the earl these days," Ryder said. "It's no concern of mine."

"Then you've been out of circulation too long, Ryderbourne. If you'd ever met Miracle Heather, you wouldn't soon forget her. They say Hanley went up to her rooms and smashed furniture, then raved at the maid like a madman." Dartford took up his cane and smiled. "Were the rooms rented furnished? You should know. They were in Blackdown Square."

The front door swung shut behind him. Ryder closed his eyes for a moment, then he threw back his head and laughed till it hurt. Blackdown Square! For God's sake! She had rented rooms from the duchy?

Somewhere, in the interminable records of his affairs, her name might even appear as a tenant—though it was more likely that Hanley had used an agent to rent the place for her.

It was late. Almost morning. Ryder strode straight up the stairs to his bedroom, abandoning the foul ruins of his study to be scrubbed clean by the servants.

The slipper gleamed on his bedside table.

Whatever it took, he would turn London upside down until he found her—and damn Lord Hanley to hell!

It rained on and off for three days. Miracle walked steadily north, finding thick hedges or empty barns—and once a hollow oak tree—where she could curl up in his cloak when darkness finally descended after the long summer evenings. It was damp, but not particularly cold, yet sleep came fitfully, or not at all.

Whenever the clouds parted, she gazed up at the indifferent heavens. Jupiter spun like a top, taking nine hours and fifty-six minutes to revolve about its own axis, at a huge distance from the sun. The sun was eighty-one million miles from the Earth. If she walked twenty miles a day straight up into the sky, she would take over ten thousand years to reach it. Yet the distance to the stars was immeasurably greater. More in miles than the number of grains of sand on all the beaches of the world, more than all the threads of cotton ever spun in all the mills of Derbyshire.

And she, Miracle Heather, was just an infinitesimal speck in all that infinite universe. A rather damp, undignified speck, with no money and almost nothing left to eat, absurdly clad in a silk dress. The thieves had taken everything else: horse, saddle, saddlebags, her spare clothes and supplies—even the riding habit—everything except a comb, a bit of bread and cheese, and the few contents of her pockets.

In comparison to the universe, of course, all that was splendidly insignificant. She hugged his cloak more tightly about her shoulders and laughed up at the vast, starry sky.

The maid scraped a deep curtsy, her face shining like a beet. Her hands, too, were red, as if she had just finished scrubbing something.

"It's all right." Ryder smiled at her. "No one's going to turn you out onto the streets."

The girl mumbled something inaudible. A pretty and sadly insignificant creature, who had probably come up to London fresh from the country.

"Your mistress left for Dorset with Lord Hanley and didn't return. The earl came here looking for her. When he didn't find her, he lost his temper and threatened to dismiss you without a reference. However, this house is mine to administer. You have nothing to worry about."

She fumbled with her apron. "Yes, m' lord."

"What's your name?"

"Izzy, m' lord."

"Then sit down in that chair like a sensible girl, Izzy, and tell me everything that you know about Miss Heather."

The girl collapsed as if punctured. She perched on the edge of an elegant chair and stared at her red hands. There was no sign of broken furniture, yet only one of what should have been a pair of vases still stood on the mantel, and the wall was marked here and there, as if the plaster had been damaged by a blow.

"I don't know nothing, m' lord. She never told me nothing about herself."

Though strangely reluctant, Ryder strode over to an interior door and opened it. It was only a simple, white-painted bedroom with a pale-green carpet. Delicate gilt tracery ran around the ceiling. Not exactly the bedchamber the world might expect of a notorious courtesan.

He stared for a moment at the dumb sheets and ivory coverlet. Had she shared that bed with Hanley? As if his mouth and throat had just been seared by a flame, it felt painful to swallow. He closed the door and turned back to face the maid.

"Miss Heather never said anything about her family or her childhood? Where she came from?"

"Nothing, m' lord."

"When she left here with Lord Hanley, did they travel alone?"

"I couldn't say, m' lord. I don't know nothing about that."

"Never mind. What about her personal possessions?"

A second door opened on a small study with a shelf of leather-bound books. Some of the spines were scored, as if a blade had been dragged diagonally across them. Others were haphazardly piled, as if they had been thrust back too hurriedly after being flung from the shelves.

"She took some of her things with her," the maid said. "But

the rest of her clothes and the things in her dressers, Lord Hanley ripped up like a demon. He broke some of the china, too. I didn't know what to do. I mended what I could and put a fresh cover on the bed."

"He attacked the bed?"

The maid nodded, her face on fire. "Even the mattress—it was all cut up with a knife."

Ryder choked down the flames that seemed to be searing his throat. "What about her jewelry?"

"She took all of that with her, m' lord. Lord Hanley didn't find anything valuable."

A little shock, like a light blow, paralyzed him for a second. "Did he seem to be searching for something?"

"I don't know, my lord, I'm sure. He was very angry, like a bull just let out of a barn. Shall I pack up what's left of her things? Do you want the rooms for another lady?"

"No. Leave everything here! I'll keep the rooms as they are. You're a good girl, Izzy. You may stay on here."

"Very good, m' lord."

Her pale eyes watched him as he tugged on his gloves. He strode to the door to the hallway, anxious to be gone. Had that pristine set of white sheets and ivory coverlet not been her choice, at all—simply the maid's attempt to put things to rights after Hanley had rampaged through the bedroom? Had she and her lover slept in red satin or black silk? He didn't want to know.

Yet he did want the answer to something that seemed to make very little sense: *Lord Hanley didn't find anything—*

"I did think that she might have come from Derbyshire, m' lord."

His heart lurched. He stopped and turned back. "Derbyshire? Why?"

"She said once that even London was not so noisy as a Derbyshire mill. That's all."

"Here," Ryder said, reaching into his pocket. "Take it! It's all right. It's a sovereign. For you."

Tears rolled slowly down the maid's face as she bit at the coin and watched Lord Ryderbourne stride back out of her life.

*   *   *

THE Earl of Hanley occupied his usual place at his club. They had first met as boys at Harrow and avoided each other ever since. Ryder studied him for a moment, trying to see him through a woman's eyes. The man was handsome, he supposed: lean and tall, with a firm chin and blond hair, silver gilt at the temples.

Lady Hanley was a pale, meek creature, who mostly stayed in the country with their growing brood of young children, while her husband lived in town.

There was nothing unusual in the earl's slightly uneven attitude to his marriage vows, nor in that schoolboy relationship.

Hanley folded his newspaper and glanced up as Ryder approached.

"You've come to ask me about my mistress?" he asked with a curl of the lip. "So very tiresome! The whole town is abuzz with speculation. Did I murder her in a passionate frenzy and dismember that delectable body? Or did she run off with some princeling from Bohemia?"

"Do tell," Ryder said as he sat down. "Which is it?"

Hanley drummed his fingers on the table beside his chair. "Neither, of course, is the case. Though of the two, the image of the black-hearted assassin leaves me looking a little less the fool."

"Though you did not, of course, murder her."

Something flickered in the blue gaze for a moment. "What do you think?"

"I think it possible, but unlikely. So—for whatever reason—she must have run away from you. Humiliating, but hardly momentous." Ryder picked up a newspaper and idly scanned the headlines. "I assume she will eventually return to her rooms in Blackdown Square?"

"I've no idea," Hanley said. "I'm no longer paying her rent."

"But I am. You must know that the rooms belong to the duchy."

Fingers still tapping, Hanley stared at him for a moment. "I wash my hands of the wench. When she returns to town on the hunt for a new protector, you're welcome to her."

Ryder let his voice turn to ice as he set down the paper. "If she'll have me, I hardly need your permission."

The earl laughed, a bark like a startled dog. "If she'll have you! She's a professional whore. You're Blackdown's son and heir. Of course she'll have you. She'll take the first man that offers."

"Then you can recommend her company?"

The earl leaned back in his chair, but his fist closed on the newspaper, crushing it. "She's a vixen between the sheets, of course. When you find her, ask her to try that little trick she does with a ribbon. Something rather thrilling about being tied up like that, don't you know?"

The impulse to kill and do a little dismembering of his own washed hotly through Ryder's blood, yet he stood up with studied unconcern.

"There's also the small matter of some damage to duchy property—some furnishings, the minor defacement of some plaster. Trivial, but annoying."

Hanley threw aside the paper and rose to look the younger man in the eye. "I'm sure you can understand that no gentleman appreciates being made to look the fool by a harlot. She's a gutter creature, Ryderbourne. Corrupt as a rotten peach. If you can find her, take her. Meanwhile, if you wish to dabble in home repairs, pray send a statement to my man of business. Now, if you'll excuse me?"

The newspaper slipped to the floor as the earl bowed and stalked out.

Ryder inhaled several deep breaths. He was a St. George. He stood at the heart of the world's greatest empire. He was as helpless as the most pitiful of the king's subjects in his search for this one woman.

Yet if Hanley had beaten her and discarded her in that boat, the man had better start practicing his aim with a pistol.

He strode out onto St. James's Street and walked blindly across the park. The Houses of Parliament bulked beside the Thames. At Westminster Bridge he stopped and gazed at the span of white arches over the river. Every week some poor wretch ended a miserable existence in those fast-flowing waters.

But not Miracle! Surely life burned too brightly, too vibrantly, in her soul for such a desperate step? Yet she was obviously not in London, and meanwhile he had learned this single clue about where she might have gone.

If she rode as much as forty or fifty miles in a day, she could be halfway to Derbyshire by now, but at some point she must have crossed the London to Bristol road. If he could once pick up her trail there, he could follow it. It was his only hope.

Ryder spun about and stalked back to his townhouse.

As dawn rose hazily over London the next morning, Ryder's fastest carriage drove him west out of town. Once he passed Marlborough, he would ask after the chestnut gelding at every tollhouse and inn where she might have been seen. If it took him the rest of his life, he would find her.

THERE was solace in the night sky, but she could not eat stars. There was comfort in Lord Ryderbourne's cloak, but it was not a warmth that soothed her heart. The imprint of sea and man disturbed her like a haunting shadow that she could not quite focus on.

It was foolish. Fatal. Wrapped in his scent every night, she could not forget that one encounter with this one man. A duke's son! Had she at least also given him a night to remember? Or had he already dismissed her from his mind and his life, and returned undisturbed to his daily round?

There had been a time when she would have leaped at the chance to take such a powerful protector. Yet something had happened between them that she could not afford. The thought of it terrified her. Something that threatened her almost as deeply as the threat of Hanley's revenge.

But life had surely taught her to have courage and faith and perseverance. She would not give up now.

The next morning Miracle struggled through endless fields and along boggy lanes that ran into quagmires of mud. Farm workers shot curious glances at her as she passed, but no one harassed her or asked where she was going. At last she climbed up a small rise and sat down on a fallen tree trunk to survey the countryside ahead.

Beneath her lay a broad stretch of road, busy with travelers: the main Bristol turnpike from London. Carriages and coaches were turning in and out of the arched entryways to several grand inns on the edge of a sizable town.

Several miles farther west a green path crossed the road. A drover's track, running northwest. Another building, small and low-slung and fenced about with animal pens, lay beyond

the crossroads between the turnpike and the green track. She
shaded her eyes and stared. Though she couldn't see it, she
could guess the name of this smaller, shabbier inn: the
Drovers' Arms.

Miracle pulled a little knife out of her pocket, one of her
small remaining treasures purchased so dearly at the Merry
Monarch, and hiked her skirts up over her knees. Her boots
were mired in mud, but the meadow in front of her glimmered
with wildflowers. She would cut ribbons from her petticoat to
tie posies to sell to travelers. Her heart ran cold at the risk if
she was discovered, but she had to buy food now, or starve.

RYDER's coach pulled into the yard of the White Swan. Ostlers
looked with envy at his outriders' smart livery and his splendid team of horses. Wherever he stopped, the business of the
inn was deformed by his arrival, like tiny satellites falling under the gravitational sway of a large planet. Once again he
stepped down into the center of a whirlwind of service and re-
peated the litany he had been intoning since London.

"A lady in a brown habit riding a bald-faced chestnut gelding. The horse has a white patch like a map of Ireland on its
rump."

Grooms shrugged. Servants tugged at forelocks. The host
hurried out to wait in person on such a distinguished traveler.
Ryder swallowed brandy while the horses were changed. No
one had seen her. No one had seen the horse.

He had just spun about to step back up into his coach, when
another traveler stepped forward. The stranger glanced at the
crest on the coach panels—the writhing dragon dying beneath
the spear of St. George—and saluted him.

"Kenneth Blake, my lord, at your service! I was unable to
avoid overhearing your inquiries. You will forgive my pre-
sumption, I'm sure? It may be another animal altogether, of
course, but I could swear that I saw just such a gelding earlier
this afternoon at the horse market in the next town, some ten
miles farther up the road."

Ryder's heart began to pound. "Ridden by a lady, sir?"

"Alas, no, my lord. Offered for sale by a couple of ne'er-
do-well characters—out-and-out ruffians, I would say—but
the horse carried a sidesaddle and was marked exactly as you

describe. I took a quick look at the nag for my daughter, but the man selling it didn't seem to know much of its history. I thought it rather odd at the time."

Rank fear made Ryder physically ill for a moment, as if steel pincers had closed inside his gut. He thanked Mr. Blake and issued orders. His coach swung from the inn yard. The fresh horses plunged on toward Bristol at a gallop.

EVENING was closing in, cloaking the overhanging balcony in its gray veils. The painted swan on the sign curled its head back over one wing, as if to wink at passing travelers.

Miracle swallowed hard and walked up to stand in the arched entry to the inn yard. She curtsied and kept her head down as she offered her flowers to everyone going in and out. "For your lady wife, kind sir! For your daughter."

She had already sold enough to buy a supper and a length of ribbon. Tomorrow she would make more posies. Perhaps wildflowers would take her all the way to Derbyshire. Meanwhile, she had only a few bunches left for sale and it was getting late.

"Odd thing that," a man said to his companion as he strolled out into the street. "One wouldn't think that any member of the peerage would go to such lengths to hunt down such an ordinary animal."

His friend grinned. "Unless the peer in question was Irish, with a sentimental attachment to an animal with a map of his homeland on its rump—"

"—or an even deeper attachment to the missing lady in the brown habit?"

Both men laughed and walked on.

Her last few bunches of flowers fell at Miracle's feet.

Another gentleman had walked out of the inn door. Tall and blond, he stopped to pull on his gloves as he glanced up at the gathering darkness.

"My horse," he said to a passing groom. "I fancy a ride before supper."

"Very good, my lord."

She did not need to see the face beneath the gilt hair. The sound of his voice was enough. Backing rapidly into the shadows, Miracle slipped out into the street and walked fast out of town. A stile took her from the main road onto a footpath. Terror beat hard, robbing her of breath. She could not risk traveling so slowly any longer. Whatever it cost her, she must secure another horse. Then she must disappear completely, before Lord Hanley caught up with her.

RYDER'S horses steamed as four fresh animals were run out, ready to take His Lordship wherever his whim might demand next. His servants stood stoically as Lord Ryderbourne told them to take their supper in the inn, then strode off alone into the town.

The Market Square was littered with dung and straw, where horses had been bought and sold earlier that day.

Ryder accosted the first man that he met. "Good evening, sir. I'm looking for a bald-faced chestnut gelding—"

The man scratched at his head and shook it. Ryder asked three more strollers and a lad with a dung cart and shovel. In vain. Yet the fifth man nodded and pointed with one finger.

"Why, Mr. Pence, our apothecary, purchased that very nag this afternoon, my lord, along with a saddle and bridle. Said he needed a good mount for his wife. . . ."

Ryder shook the man by the hand and strode off in the direction he had pointed.

Mr. Pence came to the door in person and immediately insisted that His Lordship step into his humble parlor. The knife in Ryder's gut twisted again as the man only confirmed what Ryder had already learned at the White Swan. Ghostly in the twilight, the gelding's white face peered over the apothecary's stall door. A lady's saddle hung in his tack room.

"I also purchased some saddlebags and their contents, my lord. If Your Lordship would care to come back inside to take a look?"

A brown riding habit, a fresh petticoat, all the little bits and pieces that Miracle had taken with her from the Merry Monarch. The fabric moved softly under Ryder's fingers. Grief and anger surged in a floodtide. The apothecary's face seemed to disappear into a dark mist.

"Thank you, Mr. Pence," he said at last. "I'm most obliged to you, sir."

"You wish to recover the horse and these things, my lord?

Did I purchase them in error? Alas, I'm afraid the men who sold all this to me are long gone by now."

"No," Ryder said. "It doesn't matter. Keep the horse. You bought him in good faith."

He strode blindly back through the town to his coach. She had been robbed. The horse. The saddle. Even the riding habit she had been wearing, and the pitiful little necessities that she had carried in the saddlebags.

There was little doubt what must have happened to her.

The bitterness of his grief filled his mouth with ash.

NIGHT was falling by the time Miracle arrived at the Drovers' Arms. Fatigue rang in her bones from her tramp over the fields, climbing stile after stile, occasionally losing the path in the dark, only to stumble into the edge of wheat fields, or startle a lumbering cow.

A gaggle of boys crouched outside the inn, keeping watch by the light of wavering torches over herds of sheep and cattle and pens full of ponies. Bulky shapes shifted, permeating the night with their animal odors. The boys glanced at her without interest as she passed, then huddled back inside their coats.

She hesitated for only a moment on the doorstep, listening to the dull rumble of men talking and their occasional laughter as she unpinned her hair. Then she looked up one last time at the pure night sky, before she pushed open the door.

It was even darker inside the inn, the air thick with the reek of tallow candles, oil lamps, and tobacco. In the few islands of light, men in travel-stained coats stood about or sat on benches, tossing back tankards of ale and eyeing each other, some with camaraderie, some with veiled suspicion.

Many of them were no doubt armed. In spite of their shabby clothes, some of the drovers might be carrying large sums of gold in the deep pockets of their coats, though most would have bought and sold their herds on credit. Yet they were all working men, far from home after weeks on the road.

And there were other travelers here—drifters, old soldiers, men hunting for work—less honest than the sober Welsh drovers, and less faithful to wives and families left behind.

She took a deep breath. Lord Hanley was already at the White Swan. She could not walk any farther in the dark. So instead she must risk this: a room full of rogues and traveling men, some of whom might simply take what she had to sell before parting with a penny.

Heads turned as she entered. Miracle slipped her cloak from her shoulders to let it drape from one finger. Every eye in the room focused on the low neckline of her gown. Only one kind of woman would enter here alone dressed like this.

"Is this a merry company," she asked, "that might like a song for the road? Name your ditty, gentlemen, and if I don't know it, I'll throw in another for free."

Booted feet shifted in the sudden silence, then a man laughed.

"Keep your ditties, sweetheart," he said. "How much for a private moment with me?"

"More than you can afford," Miracle shot back, "and if a moment is all that it takes you, I'm surprised you would boast of the fact before all these jolly fellows."

Some of the men laughed, but the tension remained as thick as smoke in the foul air.

"Suppose we all shared, share and share alike?" another voice asked. The man glanced about, gathering the others' attention and perhaps their approval. "What the devil's all this talk of pay for what a man may take for free, if he pleases?"

"And there's maybe twenty of you, so at three seconds each, it wouldn't take more than a minute for all of you." Though her pulse raced, Miracle stalked up to him and lifted the tankard from the man's hand, then leaned down to stare into his eyes. "If you'd not spent the last hour drowning your manhood in ale, sir, you'd know the difference between a woman and a song."

Applause echoed about the room. "She's got you there, Tom!" someone shouted. "The lady's a wit."

"Aye, but Tom still had an eyeful," another man said.

Miracle handed back the tankard and winked at Tom. "Drink up, sir," she said. "An old soldier must pay for his drink and his songs, but at least he can look for free."

The wave of mirth was better humored this time.

Tom grinned. "How d'you know I was ever a soldier, missy?"

"Because you're a brave man, sir, and you've seen the world."

Open laughter swept around the room, accompanied by whistles and clapping.

" 'Greensleeves,' " a man with a white beard called out. "Or 'Barbara Allen.' Sweet songs for an old man, darling!"

She swallowed her surge of relief. "You'll have them both, sir, if you'll pass around the hat for me."

"Damnation," Tom said. "If you'll give me a kiss, sweetheart, I'll pass the hat myself."

"And fall flat on your face?" the bearded man retorted. "You'd do better to feast those sore eyes from right where you're sitting, my lad."

Tom thumped his tankard on the bar. "Then let's have 'Greensleeves,' sweetheart."

" 'Greensleeves' it is." She winked at him again. "A ditty about a man who can't get his lady to stay. Then we'll try 'Barbara Allen' and hear about a man who dies from the loss."

"I believe the lady dies, too," a new voice said quietly, but Miracle had already started to sing.

She chose tunes designed to evoke home and longing and love, nothing bawdy, nothing too arousing. A group of Welsh drovers soon joined in, offering an exquisite harmony even when they didn't know the English words.

The bearded man passed his hat when she finished, chivying the others to pay more. There was not a man left in the room who would molest her against her will now, though a couple of the travelers surreptitiously felt in their pockets. In a few minutes one of them would no doubt approach her privately to try to strike his bargain.

"There you are, darling," the bearded man said. "Here's enough raised from the lads for a mug of ale and a supper."

She glanced into the hat. "Then I'd better sing some more. I've higher ambitions than that, sir."

"The lady wants fine wine!" Tom shouted. "And a feather bed, most like!"

"No," she replied. "The lady wants a horse."

"If you'll sell this one night to me," someone said, "I will buy you a horse and a saddle to go with it."

Miracle froze in her tracks. An echo tickled in the back of her mind—*I believe the lady dies, too.*

The speaker was almost lost in the shadows of a dark corner and wrapped from head to boots in a plain cloak. A broad-brimmed leather hat hung low over his forehead. His quiet voice had seemed almost cultured, that of a gentleman, though it was muffled by the tankard he had just raised to his mouth. She could see nothing of the man's face, only the glimmer of long, clean-knuckled fingers, clutching the tankard as if he would crush it.

Her heart began to pound. The other men glanced sharply at the stranger.

"I'm worth more than that for just another ditty," she said. "Come, sir, name your song!"

His hat and high collar still shielded his features, yet his eyes shone like flint. "No more singing," he said. "I want the rest of this night, ma'am, from now until cockcrow. If you please me, you may have your saddle horse and whatever price in gold you care to name."

A black-and-white dog growled low in its throat. Indulgence fled the room. The bearded man thrust one hand into his pocket, where he no doubt kept a weapon. Several drovers reached for knotted staves and clutched them in hard fists.

"Here, now," Tom said, rising unsteadily to his feet. "The lady sings for all of us. If it's to change to something else, share and share alike is our motto."

"But it's not mine." With a grace that spoke clearly of danger, the stranger stood up to loom over the other men. Light glanced off the barrels of a pair of pistols held in each steady hand. "No inventive ideas, gentlemen," he said into the sudden silence.

Staves fell with a clatter. Tom collapsed back to his seat.

The stranger slipped the pistols out of sight beneath his cloak and stepped forward. "Well, ma'am? Do we have a bargain?"

Miracle lifted her chin and faced him, though her blood beat fast in dark, terrified rhythms. "Yes," she said. "Yes, sir, we have a bargain."

"With all of us here to witness it," the bearded man said. "And to seek retribution on behalf of the lady, if your boast proves empty."

"You may tar and feather me in the morning, if I don't keep my promise," the stranger said. "But will she keep hers?"

The drovers fell back as he strode up to take Miracle by the elbow. She felt almost faint, as if the thick air had closed around her face, suffocating her. The lamplight wavered. The sea of faces blurred.

The man slipped a hand about her waist to pull her into the circle of his arm. Like a memory of pain, her nostrils imagined the heartbreaking drift of sea and horse, brightened with overtones of orange and lavender. Yet it was too late to demur or run away. She had made a bargain.

"A private bedchamber." The tall man tossed a handful of coins onto the counter.

The innkeeper hurried to throw open a door at the back of the room. It led to a staircase.

The man thrust Miracle ahead of him up the stairs and into a bedroom beneath the rafters, lit only by a thin glimmer through dusty glass. He slammed the door closed and turned the key in the lock, then strode to the window. Starlight shimmered, its faint glow outlining his hat and long cloak, shaping a figure composed entirely of darkness.

"Get undressed," he said.

Anguish uncurled deep in her belly. "Just like that?"

He spun about, his cloak sweeping behind him. "This situation hardly encourages subtlety. Remove your clothes and lie on that bed. On your back. I would like to get my money's worth—or are you already regretting our bargain?"

"I cannot afford to regret it," she said, reaching for calm, though her veins ran with cold trepidation.

"The terms are quite clear: your body for my use; my gold for you to squander. Or do you first wish to find out just how much gold I have with me?"

"I agreed to give you what's left of this night. I did not agree to either humiliation or revenge."

"Revenge?" He threw aside his hat and dropped the cloak to the floor, then strode up to her as if arrogant power was his birthright. "But what if I wanted only another ditty? Would you sing it for me?"

"No, I have sung enough." Miracle swept her hair back from her forehead with both hands. "You have purchased my body for the night, that's all. Do with it as you will. You'll get nothing else."

She started to open the buttons that secured her dress at the shoulder, but his hand seized her wrist, stopping her.

"Your vocal cords are part of the bargain," he said. "And I want a song."

Miracle stood rooted, staring up at him, his palm burning onto her skin. Rage and hurt shone harshly in his dark-ocean gaze, yet he opened his hand and released her.

"Which song would you like?" she asked.

His boots rang on the wooden floorboards as he paced away to stand once again at the window. His shadow stretched, black on gray, to the opposite wall. She felt an inexplicable fear, though not of him.

He tipped his head back against the glass, as if his eyes had closed to shut out the night. "Sing me the song that the planets sang when they were first set in their orbits," he said.

CHAPTER FIVE

*M*IRACLE STUMBLED AWAY TO SIT ON THE EDGE OF THE bed. She dropped her head into both hands. She did not really think that he was here for revenge. Yet an icy terror petrified her soul.

"I can't," she said at last, looking up. "I know neither the tune nor the words."

"But when you sang 'Barbara Allen,' and the Welsh drovers added that haunting harmony, I thought for a moment that I was hearing the music of the spheres, after all. Why not sing me the song of Jupiter, or the refrain that Orion chants as he marches across the heavens?"

"I don't know any songs like that."

"So not even the stars are cold and distant and inhuman enough for you? Aren't the heavens your element, where every pinprick of light is perfect and unchanging—not vulnerable, not prey to human warmth, or mistakes, or even empathy? Is that my misfortune, Miss Heather?"

The chill fear raced like a flood in her veins. "I'm so very sorry, Lord Ryderbourne."

He stood in silence for a moment, as if spun from black glass. "You had no idea who I was when we first struck our bargain downstairs, did you?"

"Not then," she said. "Not immediately. No."

His shadow leaped as he flung out one hand and pointed. "You'd have shared that bed with any stranger that offered?"

"For the price promised, yes."

Silence enveloped him again, while her heart beat hard in her chest.

"Why did you run away from me in Brockton? Why the devil wouldn't you let me help you?"

"You did help me," she said. "There's nothing more you can do for me now."

"Except to pay for your favors this time with gold?"

"If it would help you to know that I'm glad that this latest pact turned out to be with you, Lord Ryderbourne, then know it."

He spun on his heel to pace the room again, his boots striking a hard rhythm of distress.

"Of course," he said. "Because you know that I shan't force you to keep it. You may have my gold and return nothing. What you offer in exchange is anyway valueless to me."

"It didn't seem so at the Merry Monarch."

"I didn't know then that your only motivation was money."

A welcome anger unfurled beneath her inexplicable fear. "What a grand, self-serving statement! Only those who take wealth completely for granted ever claim that money's an ignoble motive. Other men have paid very well for what I gave you that night. I offered what I thought was a fair exchange for what I needed. I didn't cheat or steal from you."

"Didn't you?" Even in the dark she could see the gleam of white teeth as his lip curled.

"Why did you come after me? How did you find me?"

"God! The simple questions? I suppose we can hardly begin with the difficult ones. Your gelding with the pretty map of Ireland on its rump has a new owner. This honest fellow purchased him from two rogues who've already been swallowed up by history, along with your saddle and everything else you possessed, even your riding habit. That knowledge was burning a void in my gut when I returned to the White Swan, only to discover that a dark-haired woman in a silk gown had been selling flowers to travelers."

"That could have been anyone."

"Exactly."

"Then why did you come here?"

"Because, if it was you, where the hell else were you likely to go on foot in the dark? Where else was the nearest alternate route toward Derbyshire?"

She wrapped her arms about herself and shivered. "Who else knows?"

"My coachman and two menservants. One of them discreetly secured that hat and cloak, then my coachman dropped me off half a mile down the road, where my other man was waiting with a horse."

"So you rode here in disguise. After which you brooded in your corner until I arrived, then you propositioned me as if you were a stranger. It's horrible!"

He stopped pacing as if he'd run into a tree. "For God's sake, until you walked into that room downstairs, I thought you'd been killed."

She bit her lip and glanced away. "No," she said. "Not yet. But you shouldn't have come here like this."

"Should Lord Ryderbourne have pulled up in his coach and four with the Blackdown arms emblazoned on the panels, instead?"

Pain fought with the anger in her heart. "Now that His Lordship knows the true nature of his fantasy, he should not have come at all."

He reached into his pocket. Ribbons trailed from his fingers in long glimmers of silver. Miracle stared in silence at the white satin slipper as he held it out to her.

"This is all I have left of our previous encounter," he said. "Your carriage had already shriveled into a pumpkin, your horses were twitching their little mouse noses behind the wainscot, your silk gown was shredding into rags, while you fled headlong back to the ashes. Yet, true to form, you left me one slipper. How the devil did you expect me to react?"

The depth of his rage and anguish threatened to drown her. "I'm not Cinderella. I'm a harlot. Once you knew the truth, I thought you'd forget about me."

He crushed the slipper in his fist. "For God's sake! You think you can present a man with such an experience, enigmatic and unexpected, and expect him to simply ignore it?"

"Yes. I thought so. What can a duke's son want with a woman like me, except to buy another night in my bed? Unfortunately, I'm no longer selling."

He tossed the slipper onto the bed and stalked back to the window. "So you break another promise!"

"Not *another*. I kept the first one: I left you a note."

His back seemed rigid, frozen in starlight. "I remember."

Long shudders raked up her spine. "I expected you to be disgusted," she said. "I expected you to curse me."

"Even though I'm the only witness you have that whatever you did—or believe that you did—it was done in self-defense?"

She jerked upright. "You cannot know that."

"Before you were left to die in that boat, you'd been beaten." Power and frustration built in his voice, like water behind a dam. "I—and only I—can testify to that in court."

Her angry sense of the ludicrous forced her to laugh, though her heart felt like breaking. "Lord Ryderbourne would stand up before the King's Bench to tell the world about the night he spent at the Merry Monarch with a notorious harlot? How many bruises did he count in the throes of his passion? In which interesting locations did he spot all those charming contusions? The innkeeper and the maids would certainly make splendid witnesses. It would be the richest scandal London's enjoyed in years—"

"You have no idea of the power that my family holds in society."

"Yes, I have!" She stalked up to him. "It's a position that would allow you to make an even bigger fool of yourself than you already have, and your family would never allow it. Poor, besotted Lord Ryderbourne—tricked into taking the whore's part! His Lordship wishes to tell the court in every detail all the naughty little things that they did together that night? Explain why he's prepared to drag his noble name through the mud? You think there's any court in the land that would let me walk away free after that? One word from your father, and the judge would know exactly what to do."

He seized her by both arms. "How do you even know what you did? No one is missing. I talked to Hanley—"

"Lord Hanley? Why? Where?"

"In London. At his club. It wasn't hard to learn the name of your latest protector."

"So now the nasty earl is wondering why Lord Ryderbourne is so interested in his missing mistress? Did Lord Hanley follow you here?"

"Follow me?"

Miracle stared up into his eyes. "Yes! Back and forth up the turnpike after that honest fellow who bought my horse and saddle? To the White Swan, where so many witnesses saw me take my one risk?"

His hands crushed. "Why the devil would Hanley come after me?"

"To find me, of course. To bring me to justice. He was at the White Swan. I saw him there, though he didn't see me."

"Hanley seemed both unharmed and disinterested when I last saw him in London. You're certain he was at the White Swan?"

She wrenched free. "You think I wouldn't recognize my own lover?"

His face blanched. He dropped his hands and turned away. "That was a foolish question. I'm sorry. But why do you think he followed me there?"

"Lord Hanley is very interested in my fate, but of course he's not harmed. He wasn't the victim. He was the witness."

"Of what?"

"Does it matter?" Miracle laughed, not caring if the memory of that night was poisoning her laughter with bitterness. "I felt obliged to express my opinion to a friend of his. When words seemed insufficient, I used a knife. You may say it was in self-defense, if you like. But whatever her reasons, a whore's attack on a gentleman is enough to stretch her neck. You cannot save me in the courts, my lord. Your theories and your passion would never stand against Lord Hanley's account."

"Nevertheless, I'm offering you my protection. I could take you to any of the duchy properties. I could keep you hidden—"

"And what a pretty accomplice to crime you would make! You're a duke's son, so they won't hang you, only gossip about you as you watch my last dance at Tyburn. Or would you squander your honor to challenge Lord Hanley to a duel and hope to dispatch him, so that he cannot bear witness against me? Or perhaps, once I'm found guilty of murder and condemned, you could become the court jester and petition the King for clemency? For whose sake? Mine or yours?"

He strode across the room, bouncing blows with one fist off the plaster wall. "Just tell me this: If I had seen what Hanley witnessed, would I have wanted to stop it?"

Miracle was surprised into the truth. "Oh, yes!" she said. "Very definitely!"

Starlight silvered his cheekbone, the skin smooth as satin, as he stared out at the night. "Then Hanley deserves to die for not doing it."

Ice seemed to crack and splinter across her vision. "Oh, God! You *want* to fight a duel over me? Forget him! Forget me! You have a life of your own, full of obligations. Go back to it!"

His boots echoed on the floor. "Devil take it, Miracle, don't faint on me!"

He caught her as she swayed. For a moment she was too weary not to lean into his strength—not to listen to the steady beat of his heart, not to inhale his night-dark scent straight into her lungs—yet she forced herself to push him away. His hands fell to his sides as he stared down at her.

Miracle sat down on the bed and hardened her heart to tell him the one more lie that would send him away forever.

"I don't want to be with you. I never did. I made a trade, that's all. Anything else that you believe happened between us was only playacting on my part and foolishness on yours. Go home, Lord Ryderbourne! I don't want you."

Silence flooded the shadows. Absolute quiet flowed over the rug on the floor, eddied up into myriad tiny crevices, filled the jug on the washstand. As if pain had been poured like liquid crystal into the air, the hush filled her ears until she heard only the unbearable beat of her own heart.

"No, of course, you would not want me," he said at last. "I apologize if I assumed otherwise." He bent to pick up the drover's hat and cloak. "So what the devil do you plan to do now?"

"Disappear, if only you'll let me."

"How?"

"I shall walk to Derbyshire, where I have other resources, then leave the country."

"Doing whatever it takes?"

"Yes. Whatever it takes. Unless you're prepared to call in the law right now and see me hanged, you cannot stop me."

"I can," he replied. "But I won't."

Clouds had spread over the sky outside, blotting out the faint starlight. Miracle groped for the tinderbox on the bedside table and lit a candle. An illusion of warmth flickered over his face. His long shadow stretched out behind him. Her heart pounded heavily.

He strode back to the table and set down the hat. Coins clinked, sparkling in the candlelight as he spilled his purse onto the wooden surface. "Here's my gold. Though—as you so correctly surmised—you don't need to earn it. Buy a horse. Ride to Derbyshire like the Queen of Sheba visiting Solomon."

"I don't want your money," she said.

"For God's sake!" His gaze pierced as he looked up. "Rogues already stole your first mount. You were lucky not to be killed or raped into the bargain. You were desperate enough after that to be willing to prostitute yourself to any stranger, even when there was every chance that some of those travelers downstairs would have appropriated your favors for free— *share and share alike!*"

"Yet they didn't," she said. "I know men. Didn't you notice?"

"Only too clearly." He strode toward the door. "You played with those drovers' emotions as if they were your fools."

"All men are my fools."

"So take the money! If you need further help, send a message to Wyldshay. I assumed a responsibility for you when I dragged you from Brockton Bay. That's not your choice. It's mine."

Shadows rushed as she stood up, as if flocks of vultures swooped about her ears. "How dare you hunt me down like this and try to bully me? I will not be obligated to you. I will not take your gifts, nor your money."

"But you will!" The cloak swirled as he turned back from the door. "Though, if you insist, you can earn it!"

His boots pounded as he flung aside the cloak to stride up and seize her by both arms. His eyes raged, without tenderness, without caring, as he pulled her against his tall body. Miracle snarled up at him and laughed.

His mouth ground down onto hers in genuine fury. His tongue plunged without mercy, as if trying to force her to reject him. Anguish and loss scorched from his lips.

An answering rage at all of her hurts fired as if canisters of grapeshot exploded behind her eyes. She wrestled with tongue and teeth and lips, biting, crushing, until pure carnal lust roared its mean triumph. Kissing, kissing, hot and moist, like a demon. His erection reared against her belly, heavy and demanding. Heat flooded her groin.

Yet he pulled away, his eyes like pits, and opened his hands. The flush of desire still glossed over his cheekbones, but he dropped his head to stare down at his clenched fingers.

"I must beg your pardon," he said. "I've never done such a thing in my life. I didn't mean—"

Miracle stopped his words with one finger. Hot tears scalded down her face—as if she were being purified in a crucible, leaving nothing but a core of pure gold. His scorching desire and agony plummeted into her soul. Without making any conscious decision she reached up and kissed him again, allowing her lips to open under his as a flower opens, welcoming and tender, allowing him full measure and returning it.

He succumbed in a heartbeat. She knew it in her mouth, in her bones, in her ache of regret at the inevitable anguish of it. His kiss eased and caressed, like a seductive whisper rippling over her lips. With ever more delicate flicks of her tongue, she deepened her surrender, until the pain in her heart melted like crystallized honey liquefying in the sun.

Lord Ryderbourne was the loveliest man she had ever met. He would not hurt her, even if she deserved it. He could not easily abandon her, even if she drove him away. She could not fight him with her body. Neither, obviously, could he fight her. The bed waited behind them. Yet he was far too ready for self-sacrifice, and she had suffered men's obsessions before.

Gently, gently, she broke the kiss, then touched his swollen lips again with one fingertip.

He took a deep breath, the power of the deep-night ocean shining in his eyes.

"I promise that I will never again trade either gold or anything else for your professional favors," he said. "I did not come here intending to importune you or seduce you, and certainly not to force my attentions— That's not the bargain I would strike."

"I never thought for a minute that it was."

The candle guttered. He strode to the table and began to gather the coins into neat little piles.

"I will not be like all the others," he said.

Miracle walked away to the window. A soft rain pattered on the glass. Outside was nothing but darkness and damp.

She set her palm against the cold glass. "You were different, Lord Ryderbourne. You *are* different, though it changes nothing."

"If that's true," he replied, "it changes everything."

"Because we were such perfect lovers for one strange night out of time?"

"If you like. I certainly think that should allow you to call me Ryder, at least."

"As your friends do?"

"Yes, why not?"

She digested this in silence for a moment, before she turned back to face him. "At least you understand now why I cannot take your money?"

"You cannot travel to Derbyshire alone and penniless."

"Yes, I can." Miracle forced gaiety into her voice. "After all, I've been alone and penniless before."

"You imply quite correctly that that's something I can hardly imagine." A wry self-derision crept into his voice. "But what the hell's the point in tearing out a man's heart if you won't even accept his protection?"

She could not bear it, though she owed him her life. "Whatever we shared," she said gently, "it wasn't love."

"Ah! Very probably not. What the devil do either of us know of love?"

"Not much, perhaps, which is why—though we may seem to have a talent for invoking the splendid ache of lust—we shan't complete the bargain that we made downstairs, and why you are now going to go home."

His heels rapped as he paced the room, from the bed to the shabby dresser and back. He would realize in a few minutes that she was right. With regret, perhaps, with a soft grief at the ways of the world, but he would know that there was nothing more he could offer her—and then he would leave.

Yet he stopped by the bed to pick up the slipper. The ribbons flowed like water through his fingers.

"You believe that Hanley followed me to the White Swan?"

"I don't know. After I left you in Dorset, I could hardly travel unseen. He would have received reports—"

He flung up his head, nostrils flared. "You think he's sent spies after you?"

"Yes, I'm sure that he has."

The slipper folded like a crumpled white rose. "And you still expect me to go home?"

"If you refuse to leave now from some misplaced sense of gallantry, I'll reject it. There's no earthly reason why you should stay for yourself. You have no real duty toward me."

He strode off again, back and forth, like a caged lion. "No, of course not. My clear duty is to find a suitable bride. Throughout the last Season, London was filled with fleets of young ladies in full sail, all flying every flag for my attention. I'm expected to choose the most tolerable of them and marry her."

"Then you should go back to finish courting whichever lady most takes your fancy."

"No," he said. "I should come to Derbyshire with you."

She was incredulous, stunned into silence, though her pulse leaped into startled life, like a pheasant whirring up from a hedgerow.

"But you can't," she said at last. "You can't simply walk out of your life."

"Yes, I can."

"You're mad," she said. "A madman! There are a million other answers."

He dropped into the chair, arms on thighs, hands clasped between his knees. Candlelight smoothed his skin to warm bronze. His shadowed jaw betrayed where he needed a shave.

"Yes, I know."

"You wouldn't survive for a day."

His eyes gleamed, as a cat's gleam green in the dark, as he glanced up. "Are you offering me a challenge? I promise to keep up with you."

"On the drovers' roads and packhorse trails? On foot?" Panic began to flutter in her gut. "And what happens every night?"

"That's not why I want to do this."

"Then why?"

"I don't know. Perhaps I need to do it, before my life is given up entirely to all those inescapable obligations. I had already realized it in London during the Season, I think. The yearning for something unknown has been like a fist crushing my mind. If I cannot save you from your fate, perhaps you can at least save me from the horrors of my immediate future."

"From all those young ladies who'd like to become duchesses?"

"I'll still return to marry one of the handful who's qualified to become a duchess. It would be disastrous to any female to marry me otherwise."

"You'll find the right lady. There's no sin in being young and untried."

"Of course not. Yet there's something so brutal in the game. How can I even trust my own judgment when I'm such a damned golden prize that even the most innocent of females will deceive and scheme just to ensnare me? The rest is . . . I don't even know. Perhaps you represent the means for something else entirely—for an escape without associations of cowardice, since I've told myself that your care is my duty? I don't know. Only know that I'm not doing this from lust."

"Then you will do it to demonstrate how very little you know yourself? You are indeed doing it from lust, Ryder, but you intend to nobly suppress your desires. Meanwhile, I find you—"

"No! Don't!" He cupped both palms over his ears in mock outrage. "Don't! Of course, I desire you! But why the devil must we act on that? Men aren't beasts."

"It didn't seem so just now," she said dryly, "when you kissed me like a savage."

He stood up and strode closer to her. "Which is only grist to my mill. That won't happen again."

"So now you reject what happened between us at the Merry Monarch?"

"I don't reject it. I just want my memory of that night to remain unsullied, with no past and no future. I didn't know then why you felt you had to seduce me. Perhaps that ignorance lent a certain purity to our exchange. I don't know. But I wouldn't trade that memory for the base coin inevitable between a courtesan and a gentleman."

She brushed both palms over her cheeks. "You were only the recipient of my professional services."

"Yet I would prefer not to be so again in the future." He

turned away to pick up the slipper. The ribbons entwined about his long fingers, as if they would knot themselves into mysteries. "Does such restraint seem absurd to you? You think this simply the romantic impulse of the moment?"

She felt as if he were slowly tearing her in two, like tissue rent inch by inch in careful, precise little movements. To have been offered the protection of a duke's son at any other time in her life would have seemed like the answer to a prayer. Now she knew only that she owed him his freedom.

"I don't know," she said.

"Then understand this: I'm telling you something truly fundamental about myself. I've never been promiscuous. I've never frequented bawdy houses, or dodged from bedroom to bedroom in my friends' country houses. In spite of the expectations inherent in my position, I would prefer to marry a lady I could love. You've told me what you are and what you expect. Now I'm telling you what I am and what I expect. I will escort you to Derbyshire. I will prevent Hanley from doing you any harm. But not because I want your sexual favors in return."

"Then why?"

"Because you're my responsibility and because I want to go."

"So insanity runs in your family? I've heard many things about the St. Georges, but I've never heard that. Yet I can't prevent your coming with me, can I?"

"No, you can't." He thrust the slipper into his pocket and retrieved his cloak from the floor. "That bed seems clean and free of fleas. I suggest you climb between the sheets and go to sleep."

"While you keep celibate vigil?"

His lips curled with a very faint derision, but only at himself. "In purity, in holiness, in prayer?" He wrapped himself in the cloak, propped himself in the hard chair, and crossed his arms over his chest. "Of course. Yet if Hanley breaks into this room, I shall shoot him."

She gulped down her fear. "In spite of all your precautions, you think he might find us here?"

"No, but two of my men are watching the place anyway. We're certainly safe here till morning. Then I'll go back to the White Swan to make sure of him."

"So you'll shoot him there?"

He laughed. "I shall simply bump into him in the hallway

to tell him that the trail has gone cold and that I'm going back to Wyldshay. He'll find me a bitter and disappointed man. A few stray hints will then send him off on a wild-goose chase. Meanwhile, my coach may travel home without me."

"By then I'll be gone," she said.

"I'll catch up with you—and not on foot. That makes no sense at all. I'll buy you a pony before I leave, then the drovers will accept that our pact was fulfilled." His grin made him seem younger, almost merry. "To be tarred and feathered sounds like a most unpleasant procedure."

"You don't know which route I plan to take."

"There's another drovers' inn about ten miles north of here: the Duke of Wellington. Wait for me there."

She did not believe that he really meant any of it. Or at least, he might think that he meant it now, at this moment, but in the clear light of day, once he had returned to his own world, once he had tasted again all the luxury that he was used to—

"Very well," she said. "I'll wait till midday, but no longer."

"Then let's get some damned sleep!"

His eyes closed. His long legs stretched out in front of him. His boots alone were worth a small fortune.

Miracle snuffed out the candle, stepped behind the screen, and slipped off her dress. The sheets smelled of soap and sunshine. The innkeeper's wife must be a proud housekeeper. How would that worthy lady react if she knew that the Duke of Blackdown's heir was sleeping in the hard chair and not in the bed with the harlot he had purchased?

Ryder could probably throw Lord Hanley off her trail, at least for now, and her heart eased at the thought. Yet she had no faith at all that—if he really came with her—he'd be able to keep the rest of his promises.

His dark figure had almost disappeared into the shadows, though a faint luminosity glistened on his thick hair. His breathing became steady and even.

A small, insistent pulse of pleasure beat in her blood as she watched him beneath her lashes. He had seized her in his hands to burn ferocious, angry kisses into her mouth. Then they had exchanged kisses of exquisite delicacy. She had known him naked and erect and feral with passion. They had talked about the stars. They had laughed and flirted over a dining table. He had saved her life. He did not intend to ever touch her again.

Yet the craving and the desire were not only his, they were hers, too. Whatever happened, it was going to be a difficult journey, with an ending full of pain.

The base coin inevitable between a courtesan and a gentleman—

Hugging the blanket to her chin, Miracle turned away to face the darkness. She had been right to begin with, though the idea gave her no joy at all.

Not Sir Lancelot, the unfaithful. Sir Galahad.

SHE turned in her sleep, her face shadowed like an ivory carving. Thoughts raced—thundering herds of duties and preconceptions and only half-understood motives, flocks of impressions beating sharp wings of yearning—while Ryder's blood drummed in his veins.

What did he know of professional courtesans? His affairs with women had been few and discreet, mostly with society's most glamorous widows, where money was never exchanged, only nice little droplets of guilt. When he married—as of course he must—his wife would eventually become a duchess. Once she had produced an heir, they would not expect to be faithful to each other, though appearances must always be maintained. Whatever happened, he must marry a lady who had been raised and trained for such a role, someone like Lady Belinda Carhart.

But not yet!

Not yet!

There are a million other answers. God! The heavens glittered with other answers, like stars.

So why had he just chosen the dark path directly into the unknown?

Laurence Duvall Devoran St. George, heir to the titles of Duke of Blackdown, Marquess of Ryderbourne, and Earl of Wyldshay—with all the duties and obligations and privileges they implied—had no idea how to survive on the drovers' roads. He had never spent a day without menservants to wait on him. He had never before traveled without an entourage. The efficient machinery of the dukedom had smoothed his way forward since the day he was born.

Which was one reason why he was going to do this.

He was also going to travel with the loveliest woman he had ever seen—a woman who inflamed his blood, seduced him from his principles with a glance, maddened him like a burr beneath a saddle—yet not make passionate love to her every night?

That part, surely, would not be beyond his power? If he failed in it, then he doubted he'd ever be able to trust himself again.

He was obviously going to do it for her, because no one else could protect her from Hanley's wrath, and because every other man had only ever wanted her for her body.

He was also going to do it for himself, because only she had ever offered him such a clear opportunity to follow the will-o'-the-wisp straight into the void.

MIRACLE woke knowing that he was already gone. The room echoed, barren without his vital presence. She lay still for a few moments, staring at the ceiling. Lord Ryderbourne—Ryder—wanted to escape from his life for a few weeks and lose himself in the perceived romance of a journey to nowhere. Yet he did not intend to make love to her again?

Whatever his motives, he seriously thought he could do it. It touched her, stirred something vulnerable and lost deep in her heart, that—in spite of all of his power—his approach to life was so innocent. After what they had already shared, did he know himself so poorly?

She swung her feet to the floor. A bundle sat on the hard chair. Miracle padded over to it: a new riding dress and a clean petticoat, wrapped in a cloak. She rubbed a finger over the soft cotton stockings and the fresh linen. When had any man last taken such careful thought for her needs?

A tray with rolls and cheese and a jug of cold milk beckoned from the table. As soon as she was dressed, she tore into the warm bread and thought she ought to weep tears of gratitude.

Thirty minutes later she walked out into the yard of the Drovers' Arms. Clouds hung heavily over the fields. The drovers had already left with their flocks, or were riding home with their letters of credit safely folded in a pocket.

The innkeeper was leaning on the fence of one of the pens,

chewing idly at a straw. A saddled white pony stood tied, head drooping, fetlock deep in mud, next to him. The man looked up as she approached.

"Your friend already left," the innkeeper said. "He paid for your breakfast and that dress, and left you this pony, before going back to his pretty habits on the highway."

"What habits? The careless use of such accusations could get a man hanged."

"Your gentleman of the road, then, shall we say? Who else carries two fine pistols and is so free with his gold? And who else arranges to meet his moll in an out-of-the-way inn like this, where they can play their little games at the expense of more honest patrons? Though I've never seen nor heard of him in these parts before."

"He was just passing through," Miracle said. "Your trade is in no danger."

"That was the consensus in the taproom this morning," the innkeeper said. "That and a general desire for discretion when confronted with such a man, along with some little regret that you were already spoken for, as it were. Else he might not have been allowed to ride away from here quite so freely."

Miracle untied the pony and led it to the mounting block against the wall. She stepped up into the saddle and arranged her skirts.

"You should forget it."

"That was his suggestion, too. Gently made, mind you—and all the more dangerous for that!" The man looked up at her, eyes slitted against the first rays of the rising sun. "So you're to meet up with him again in Bristol? Not to worry, my lamb! The Drovers' Arms is blind, deaf, and dumb. No one will learn a word of that from me."

Miracle gave the innkeeper the full force of her most dazzling smile.

"How very wise of you!" she said.

RYDER strolled into the breakfast parlor of the White Swan. He had luxuriated in a hot bath, a fresh shave, and clean linen. Yet the call to adventure sang hosannas in his blood. Why not do this? Why not travel north into nowhere? Wyldshay—with all of its beauty, with all of its obligations—would still be waiting for him when he returned.

The host hurried up to wait on His Lordship. Whatever Lord Ryderbourne might want, the White Swan would be honored to provide. There were strawberries. There was excellent roast pork.

Ryder ordered his meal and sat down facing the door. Miracle had been deeply asleep when he left her, her hair like a raven's wing on the pillow. Desire pulsed through his veins. Not only desire for sex—though that was real enough—but desire for the unknown, for the way ahead to take a fork where both paths led to mystery.

A few moments later, elegant, deadly, the Earl of Hanley stepped into the room. Genuine surprise seemed to flicker in his eyes for a moment, then he bowed, a barely adequate nod of the head.

"Ryderbourne? An unexpected pleasure!"

"Mine host recommends the roast pork," Ryder said. He indicated the seat opposite. "Pray, join me, sir! You're known to be a connoisseur of sensual pleasures. Let me have your opinion of the cuisine. You're traveling to Bath? Or Bristol, perhaps?"

A servant pulled out the chair and the earl sat down. "Neither. I came to find you."

"Really? I can't imagine why. Should I be alarmed?"

The older man leaned back. His ice-blue gaze offered nothing. "Miracle Heather. You've been searching for her."

"Have I?"

"When we last met in London, I neglected certain obligations that one gentleman always has to another in such circumstances. If you will allow me, I would rectify that now."

"You came so far out of town to do so?" Ryder signaled the waiter.

"Why not? After all, we knew each other as schoolboys."

"Indeed. You would enjoy eggs with your pork?"

A small flicker of annoyance disturbed Hanley's gaze for a moment, like the dark shadow of unseen wings flitting over a blue sky.

"I came here to warn you, Ryderbourne: You're in deadlier peril than you can possibly imagine."

CHAPTER SIX

"I'M IN DANGER?" RYDER ASKED, LIFTING BOTH BROWS. "Of what? You have me quaking in my boots."

The earl's gaze swept him up and down, irritation plainly stamped in the set of his mouth. "I doubt that. Nevertheless, I recommend that you abandon this search."

"I'm most flattered by your concern," Ryder said. "She's a femme fatale, I take it?"

"Miracle Heather eats men like you for breakfast."

"A delightful thought!" Ryder laughed. "Alas, to my chagrin, the lady has disappeared."

The earl's knife cut savagely into his meat. "How do you know?"

"How do I know my own disappointment, sir? You've lost me."

The angry quirk deepened. "How do you know that she's disappeared?"

"After you abandoned her in Dorset, a lady was seen riding alone through Blackdown lands. From what I learned of Miss Heather in London, that lady answered her description. She's a remarkable beauty, I understand, and she had acquired a rather distinctive mount. Your gift to her, perhaps?"

"No, but I have learned the same. Several farmers and field hands were able to describe her horse to my agents—"

"Your agents, sir? You've also been trying to track her down?"

"I have. Pray, go on!"

"She disposed of the horse. I spoke with its new owner—as you did, perhaps?"

The earl's gaze was intense enough to drill through steel. "One Pence, an apothecary. He was out when I called."

"Alas, the trail ends there." Ryder nonchalantly sipped coffee. "Though you may be able to winkle more from the man than I could. I spent yesterday riding up and down the turnpike, searching like a hound. The general opinion seems to be that she caught the stage to London, or that she's gone off to Bristol with a highwayman, or that she met an old sweetheart and went with him to Reading."

"You have no opinion on the matter?"

Ryder set down the cup and curled his lip. "Though the strawberries were very tolerable, this coffee leaves a great deal to be desired. Don't you agree?"

Hanley leaned forward, his eyes almost black. "Miracle Heather?"

"Ah, yes! The delectable mistress you so carelessly lost. My own suspicion is that the lady came to a foul end and is buried in a ditch. You're welcome to follow any of those leads, sir, but I'm bored with the quest and I'm going home."

The older man grimaced. "Home?"

"To Wyldshay. Tiresome, but necessary."

Hanley's chair scraped as he abruptly stood up. "A wise decision, Ryderbourne!"

"Yet, alas, I'm afraid I've forgotten exactly what should so terrify me?"

The earl's nostrils flared as he turned toward the window. Carriages and horses moved outside. The racket of hoofbeats and the grinding of iron-shod wheels echoed into the room.

"It's nothing," he said. "The issue is obviously moot."

Ryder pushed back his chair and rose to his feet. "I thought the pork overrated, also. Didn't you?"

Hanley's upper lip bent—it was almost a snarl—as he shook hands briefly and stalked from the room.

THE hook-nosed face of the Duke of Wellington wavered as the sign creaked. A thin layer of vapor was shredding against the solid gray cloudbank above it. Miracle sat on the edge of a stone trough, holding her pony by the bridle while it sucked in water. Slimy drool dribbled back into the trough.

"Well, Jim," she said to her mount. "It must be close to one o'clock. What do you think we should do now?"

The pony plunged its nose down and splashed. Miracle laughed, though an odd grief had settled around her heart.

You were right. He's not coming!

No doubt it was for the best. No doubt he had thought more clearly about his mad pledge and gone home. She ought to be glad. She knew enough of men—and more than enough of the more privileged members of the peerage—to know that there was nothing he could offer a woman like her except heartbreak.

Yet she had promised to wait for him, though only till noon.

A regiment of geese marched past on tarred feet. Three strings of pack ponies—baskets laden with pottery, or iron work, or in one case with live poultry—trailed through the village.

The breeze died. The clouds stilled. The Iron Duke fell silent, glaring beneath painted eyebrows along the track that led south. Jim lifted his head and stared after a flock of sheep as they disappeared down the empty green way, followed by three drovers on fat ponies.

He's not coming!

Miracle led Jim to the mounting block and pivoted into the saddle.

So men were, in the end, all the same. There must surely be some relief in the thought!

One trail ran off to the northwest through a stand of birch, the entrance thick with dung. She dodged to avoid a couple of overhanging branches, then broke free onto an open path worn deeply between high banks. Jim plodded on, snatching at convenient weeds. When the path climbed up at last into the Cotswold Hills, the clouds began to weep their cold rain.

That night she found a huge half-ruined barn, tucked into a sheltered spot at the edge of a meadow, where a fold of hills dropped down into a small dell. The roof had fallen in at one end, so grass grew through the cobbles in a thick mat. Miracle barred what was left of the door and turned her pony loose inside to graze. The remains of the hayloft at the opposite end of the building still seemed sound enough, so she climbed up and pulled the rickety ladder after her.

Wrapped in her cloak, she snuggled down into a pile of dry straw. He had taken back his own cloak and given her this new one. It smelled of nothing but damp wool.

Damn him! Damn all men! *He's not coming!*

SOMETHING tickled her nose. Miracle brushed it away. It tickled again. She was instantly awake, her heart alive with hot trepidation. Nothing but straw, caught in the thick fabric beneath her cheek. She turned lazily and gazed up at the rafters. Dawn gleamed watery sunshine over the barn ceiling. Cobwebs glistened in a filigree of silver lace. Hooves clopped about downstairs. Otherwise the new day had arrived wrapped in a reassuring peace.

She sat up, then froze in place.

A long shadow flowed from the east end of the loft, cutting a dark path across the floorboards. A leather saddlebag lay crumpled against the wall nearby.

Panic cascaded through her gut, accompanied by wrenching recognition. Ryder sat perched on the windowsill, gazing out through the unglazed opening, one knee drawn up to his chin. His long cloak was wrapped about his body, cocooning him in isolation.

Miracle gulped down the panic. A searing awareness also thundered for her attention: the surge and exaltation of desire—for the strong curve of his spine, for his long, long legs, for his lovely hands, for his smile. She knew in her bones that he had watched her as she slept, sharing that need and that awareness, but that—like Galahad—he thought himself too perfect and too controlled to act on it.

"Did you sleep well?" he asked without looking around. A hint of humor colored his voice. Humor and perhaps an odd reluctance, as if he must force himself to find mirth in his own desperate choices.

"Too well, obviously." Miracle propped her back against the trusses of straw stacked behind her. "How long have you been sitting there?"

"Most of the night."

Ryder dropped from the windowsill to the floor and sat

with his shoulders pressed against the wall and his arms folded over his chest. Shadows swallowed his face as morning poured in through the unobstructed opening, half-blinding her.

"How did you find me?" The ladder was still lying where she had left it. "And how did you climb up to this loft?"

He glanced up, ignoring her question, his profile ghostly against cobwebs and dust. "Why didn't you wait for me at the Duke of Wellington?"

"I asked my question first."

"Then the answer is that you call to me like a Siren. The scent of wilderness and autumn that haunts your hair leaves a trail a man can follow like a bloodhound. I would slash my way through a brier hedge, I would scale a tower one hundred feet high—"

"You have the wrong fairy tale," she interrupted.

His smile creased both cheeks as he looked back at her. "You certainly slept as if enchanted, so the Sleeping Beauty seemed more appropriate for our present circumstances."

"Then you should have woken me with a kiss."

"You haven't been asleep for long enough yet." He retrieved the leather bag, then knelt to rifle through it.

"You weren't really tracing the scent of my hair," she said.

"Wasn't I? Then believe, if you wish, that I followed your pony's tracks and climbed in by way of the window."

Miracle hugged her arms about her shins and rested her chin on both knees. "But it must be at least twenty feet from the ground!"

He looked around and smiled. "I was raised in the labyrinth of Wyldshay. Jack and I scrambled up the outside wall of the Fortune Tower once, hanging onto the stone like lizards. The duchess had us caned."

"I don't blame her." Sunlight sparkled in her lashes, scattering his image into a dance of darkness, though blood-bay highlights gleamed in his hair. "And you knew the pony, of course. You bought him."

"Fortunately, his front shoes are quite distinctive. My own mount has joined him downstairs. Beauty isn't too proud to graze from the cobblestones." He held out a leather-covered flask and a small package. "Are you hungry?"

She grinned. "You asked me that once before with apparently disastrous consequences."

He crouched down to face her. Sunlight burnished the tiny crinkles at the corners of his eyes. "I don't claim that our appetites have changed, only require that we not act on them again so precipitately."

"So we're both doomed to remain forever hungry and thirsty, like Tantalus?" She met his ocean-green gaze as she took the food. "Though, of course, appetite is a secret, private, and personal attribute. So go ahead, my lord, and tell me what lies you will."

A wash of color stained his cheekbones, maddeningly vulnerable, maddeningly attractive. He stood up abruptly and moved away.

"I don't need to lie," he said. "You already know the truth. However, I see no need for either of us to voice it."

"Then why did you really come after me? I felt so sure you would not."

He leaned both fists on the windowsill, his back tense. "But I gave you my word!"

"Yet there are so many reasons why you should have gone home, instead."

He seemed grave suddenly, as grave and solemn and as lovely as Paris, when he foolishly gave the apple to the Goddess of Love, and thus slighted both Wisdom and Power.

"Among all the other reasons," he said at last, "is this: I have a younger brother, Lord Jonathan Devoran St. George. Jack has adventured all over the world, sometimes following chimera, sometimes acting the knight errant in tasks that might shake the very foundations of our world."

Miracle swallowed watered wine and nibbled at the bread and cheese, hungry for something else entirely. "I don't know that I see the connection. Do you envy him that?"

"Envy? No." He leaned one shoulder against the frame to gaze at the bright morning outside. "I love my brother with such a deep, strong, absolute faith, it leaves no room for pettiness. Yet Jack left England again recently to return to India, taking his new bride with him." He thrust away from the window and paced back across the loft. "Everything I said yesterday is still true, but it's partly because of Jack that I can't simply go home."

"I don't understand."

"To begin with, Jack would always drop everything to follow the wildest, least expected answer to a problem, whatever promised to expand his view of the world."

"He's a younger son. He doesn't have your responsibilities."

"No, but for the first time in my wretched life, that's what I'm going to do, too. I told you that I wanted to walk out of my life for a few weeks, but I *need* to do it—to better understand my brother, perhaps to better understand myself."

"So to gain this mysterious new understanding, you'll go gallivanting up the spine of England with a whore who's wanted for murder?"

He seized the ladder and slid it over the edge of the loft. The feet hit the stone floor below with a thud. Hooves clattered as the horses startled and jumped away.

"*Was* it murder, Miracle?"

"I don't know what else you'd call it." She looked down at the wine flask, the contents delicately flavored, a perfect match for the cheese. "I stuck a knife into a man's chest. He was Lord Hanley's dearest friend, one Philip Willcott."

"Why?"

"For all the obvious reasons. I didn't like him. He didn't like me. It was ugly and sordid and there's no use at all in talking about it."

"You don't regret it?"

She made a face at him, though her heart thundered and her palms felt clammy and cold. "I only regret that I didn't stab Lord Hanley, too, when I had the chance."

"Why?"

"You don't need to know."

"Yes, I do." Every inch his father's son, Ryder stood squarely by the top of the ladder, his arms folded. His eyes burned with green fire. "Before we leave this loft, you will be pleased to tell me everything that took place before you were set adrift in that dinghy."

"No." She stood up to gather her few possessions. "I shall not be pleased to do any such thing. Perhaps you've forgotten that I'm not your minion to do as you bid. Whatever I've done—even if I'd killed a hundred men—I'm still a free agent, at this moment, at least."

Everything about his stance was intimidating, probably more than he intended, his mouth set, his jaw hard. "He abused you?"

"What difference does it make?" She lifted her chin and walked close enough to inhale his scent: man and night and whispers of clean linen, far more heady than the wine. "Now, if you'll kindly stand aside, my lord, I need to go outside."

"I shan't stand aside until you tell me what happened."

"No." Taking a deep breath, Miracle stepped forward as if to brush past him.

One booted foot kicked back at the top rung, sending the ladder flying. The horses careened into a gallop as it fell to the floor below and shattered.

"We shall not leave this loft," he said, "until you tell me the truth."

She laughed defiantly up at him. "You would blackmail me with the pressure from my own bladder?"

Deeper color flooded his cheekbones. "If that's what it takes."

"Unless you wish to embarrass us both beyond repair, my lord, you should know that I can't wait that long."

"Very well." His boots resounded as he strode to the window. "Of course. But then you will tell me?"

"I don't see that it's any of your business. However, I need to go outside and now there's no ladder."

"I'm aware of that." A tall silhouette against the brilliance of daylight, he seemed rigid, inflexible, but he tipped his head back and laughed, as if suddenly amused at himself. "However, its loss isn't an insolvable problem, just an uncomfortable one."

"Ah," she said. "The walls of the Fortune Tower? You now intend to carry me down from that window?"

"It seems that I must." He turned to grin at her. "You will understand—after what I said—that I face that prospect with a certain reluctance?"

She walked up to him. "If you hadn't been so precipitate, my lord, you wouldn't now be forced to touch me."

Heat flared as if a fire had been lit beneath his skin. "But I long to touch you, though I didn't intend it. I didn't expect the ladder to break."

"In your world nothing gets old or worn out, does it? Nothing breaks, and if—by some mad audacity—something has the nerve to crack or splinter, some invisible elf repairs or replaces it instantly."

"I'm not quite so removed from daily reality, Miracle."

"Yes, you are," she said. "Yet now I'm becoming quite desperate to get down from this loft. I'm happy to accept whatever means present themselves, even those that you face with such dismayed self-derision. So how shall we do it? You'll need both hands free in order to climb. Do you wish to sling me over one shoulder, or shall I cling to your back like a monkey?"

His eyes were as green as glass. "Whichever you prefer."

"Then the monkey method will probably inconvenience my person a little less, considering my present bodily needs."

"I'm sorry," he said.

"For kicking away our ladder? Don't be!" She moved closer and slid both arms about his neck. "We've launched into an adventure, you and I, my lord. Why not include a little derring-do? I'll do my best not to choke you, while you endeavor not to drop both of us into a pile of broken bones. Shall we go?"

He didn't know if he could bear it. Her fingers strayed; her palms lay serenely on the hot flesh of his neck. Wisps of straw still decorated her hair, as if promising gilt opulence and harvests of plenty. She was laughing up at him, her eyes pools of darkness and wicked mirth, her skin as cool and perfect and inviting as a pan of thick cream in the dairy.

He wanted to kiss her, ravish those red lips, delve deeper into her wicked, knowledgeable passions. Yet it seemed imperative that he refrain, as if she were Calypso tempting him to seven years' forgetfulness.

"You must get behind me," he said.

"Like Satan?"

He laughed openly then. "Like the witch that you are. But even without your enchantments, I won't let us fall."

"My dear Ryder, I didn't think for a minute that you would."

One fingertip trailed fire along his jaw as she slipped around him. His pulse beat hard, filling him with more wild, self-deprecating amusement. *Men aren't beasts?* Circe's enchantment had turned men into swine. For the first time in his life, he thought he understood why.

She slipped both arms over his shoulders and wrapped them

tightly about his chest, then jumped onto his back, embracing his waist with her thighs like a child playing pickaback.

The stone wall was rough and half-tumbled where the entire building had settled sideways, so it was an easy enough climb offering plenty of footholds, even with his burden. Easy, and foolish, and mad!

She clung tightly against his back—all delectable softness and heat and sweet scents—as he swung down hand over hand. Unnerving images swarmed into his mind. Hot images that aroused, followed by memories that disturbed and tormented. Ryder shook his head in a vain attempt to drive them away. Surely he could at least control his own thoughts?

As soon as they reached the ground, Miracle jumped down.

"Well done," she murmured in his ear. "But now you're torturing yourself because you cannot remain indifferent when a female presses her breasts into your spine and wraps her naked thighs about your waist?"

Ryder pressed his forehead onto the cold stone wall between his spread hands, thinking he might yet dissolve into painful hilarity. "God, Miracle!"

"And you claim that men aren't beasts? What were you thinking about just then? I wager that—in spite of what you demand of me—you won't have the courage to tell me."

He choked back his misplaced mirth and stared down at the crushed weeds. "You really want to know what flashed into my mind?"

"Yes, absolutely."

"It was just a memory—nothing to do with you."

Her fingers strayed over his shoulder, firing importunate need, forcing him to spin around to break the contact. The bruises marked her face with yellow stains and indigo shadows. Yet she seemed ever more lovely to him, as if she were lit from within with a white light.

"Though you insist that I tell you all the facts about my shabby past," she said, stepping back and grinning up at him. "Surely I can demand at least one insight into yours?"

"It's not the same thing."

"Yes, it is."

"If you insist that we exchange truths," he said, "you'll

learn things that I've never told a living soul. But I thought you were desperate—"

"For the bushes? I am. Though I wonder what the duchess would think if she could see her elder son at this moment?"

"My mother?" He was genuinely taken aback. "I don't know. Her Grace would probably raise one elegant brow and wonder at my lack of good manners."

She winked. "Or perhaps she'd be amused at the sight of her virtuous elder son panting like a stag in rut for a woman he's sworn never to molest again?"

He was surprised into laughter. "Why the devil do you care what my mother thinks?"

"I just wondered where you learned your strange ideas, my lord. Would the duchess understand that Lord Ryderbourne thinks he may have unwittingly begun a sacred quest, without even knowing what hallowed object he seeks? Would she then agree that abstinence is necessary, lest the Grail slip away before Sir Galahad can grasp it?"

"Her Grace is a subtle and complex lady, but I doubt that she's ever given the intricacies of my conscience that much thought."

"Ah, then perhaps that's why I think that I must taunt you: to see if your claims to nobler motives are just hypocrisy?"

Before he could reply, she picked up her skirts and ran for the edge of the nearest woods.

Laughter fled. *Just hypocrisy?* Ryder leaned back as if he might simply become part of the cold stone. Dumb, blank, rooted to the earth. He stood in silence for a few minutes, then with a sudden longing for solidity, he sank down to sit on the damp ground. With his legs extended and his back against the wall, he watched the sun break over the trees. The meadow flooded with brilliant light.

She was enchanting. He was enchanted. In spite of what he had told her, was there truly no good reason for him to be here, except that? She had killed a man named Philip Willcott. She was fleeing for her life. If he really cared about nothing but duty, he would turn her over to the nearest magistrate and walk away. Was he, like the enthralled travelers in *The Odyssey*, in danger of forgetting all of his other obligations?

He watched her through narrowed lashes as she returned, the sun bright on her hair, her skirts rimmed in gold. Her movements seemed carefree, wanton, as free as if this walk over the buttercup-spangled meadow were enough by itself to bring her untrammeled joy. Every now and then she bent to pluck a poppy or a cornflower from the tall grass that bordered the path. As if she had no past and no future, she seemed complete in the moment.

No past, no future: like that one night they had shared at the Merry Monarch?

"Here," she said, walking gracefully up to him. "I've no pennies to spare, but I always pay my own way, so here are some petals for your thoughts."

Scarlet and cobalt rained from her hands to scatter over his lap.

He squinted up at her, silhouetted against the bright sky. She was more than lovely. Even damaged, even bruised, she shone as if she were nothing but gold at the core, pure and upright and clean as a knife blade, as if her very bones had been stolen from the angels.

"Which thoughts?" he asked. "At this moment my mind is filled only with uncertainties."

The remaining flower stems dangled from one hand. Sunlight framed her fingers in gilt. "I thought that was the main reason you came."

He laughed. "I suppose it was. Yet such uncertainty is a bit more uncomfortable than I'd imagined."

Miracle crouched down, crushing scarlet and sapphire against her skirt. She tipped her head to one side as she smiled at him. "Adventure is meant to be uncomfortable, Ryder. Didn't your brother tell you that?"

He plucked the wilting poppies and cornflowers from her grasp. "Of course mountains and deserts are uncomfortable. I wasn't referring to that."

"Yet if Lord Jonathan told you about rocks and sand—"

"—and snow—"

"—and snow, that was only half of the story. The challenge of adventure isn't physical discomfort. Anyone can put up with that. The challenge of adventure is change. And change is always uncomfortable, if not downright terrifying, even when it's been chosen with both eyes open."

He gazed into the black core of a poppy, the stamens thick with pollen. "Is this pounding in my blood caused by terror, then? Or is it just that poppies are known to bring headaches and thunderstorms?"

She wrinkled her nose at him and stood up. "I've no idea, though the bulge in your trousers is caused by something else entirely. You know, we really ought to make love again, just to disabuse you of your romantic absurdity."

"No," he said, grinning up at her. "The romantic absurdity is more fun."

Miracle glanced up at the sky. The remaining wisps of cloud were burning away in a suspiciously bright bowl of blue.

"Well, if you want a challenge, I think my poppies may bring headaches and thunderstorms quite soon." She leaned down to take the flowers from his fingers. "In case you've forgotten, my lord, my neck is forfeit if I'm caught, and the world seems very precious to me right now. I'd rather my last image in this life wasn't of jeering crowds and obscene comments."

"Then you want to die old and alone in your bed?"

She thrust a wilting poppy into her hair. "Not necessarily alone, but definitely a good deal older than I am right now."

"Then let's get the horses," he said. "We can talk as we ride."

Her skirts rustled as she walked away toward the door. His pulse still unsteady, his mouth dry with longing, Ryder watched her go, then sprang up and strode after her.

The heavy planks groaned as she dragged the door open just enough to slip inside.

"Good Lord!" she said. "What's this?"

He peered over her shoulder at the two horses now standing quietly nose to tail. "What? I see nothing wrong."

Miracle pointed and spun back to face him. "*That* is your mount?"

"Yes. Why not?" He stepped past her to take his bridle from the hook on the wall where he had hung it the previous evening. "Beauty's an excellent mare. I had her sent up from Wyldshay." He strode toward his horse. "Are you jealous?"

"*Jealous?* You left your black gelding behind, then brought that dazzling chestnut mare, instead?"

He slipped on the bridle. "Why not?"

Miracle slumped back against the door and gestured her exasperation with both hands. "Because if Beauty lifts her head, she shouts quality. If she flares those sensitive nostrils, coins clink and ring. One dainty step of her delicate feet, and her noble breeding calls out as loudly as if the town crier rang a bell in the market square. We're supposed to be slipping unnoticed along the packhorse trails, my lord, not advertising our progress to the world."

He rubbed the mare's nose. "I don't agree."

"You don't agree to what?"

"I don't agree that we should travel only as you planned, or that Beauty will make any difference. Anyway, I may need her."

"With her stunning silver stockings and flaming red mane that anyone would instantly recognize anywhere?" Miracle sat down on a large stone by the barn door and tipped back her head. "Heaven save me from the romantic idiocy of duke's sons! I thought you might be a holy fool. Now I know for certain."

"You think if we travel as peasants, we'll succeed any better? I cannot agree to become that vulnerable to chance, and I'm damned if I'm going to either walk all the way to Derbyshire, or ride some short-pasterned pony that'll rattle my teeth out."

"You didn't have to come."

"No, but since I have, I might as well ride a decent horse."

"I suppose it was a vain hope that a duke's son could simply blend into the armies of unemployed wretches that trudge the countryside looking for work?"

"It's absurd and unnecessary. There are places where the drovers' roads blend with the turnpikes. No one is really looking for us, and if they are, we should concentrate on making better time."

"Lord Hanley is looking for us," she said.

"Why should I believe that, when you won't even tell me why he cares?"

She closed her eyes. "Very well. We can argue about this later. In the meantime, the excellent Beauty is the only mount that you have, so by all means saddle her and let's go."

"I'm so glad you see reason," he said. "Allow me to saddle Jim for you, also. He may look fat and lazy, but he has some decent enough breeding of his own."

"Unlike me," she said.

He glanced around from buckling the girth. His gaze pierced. "I don't know that."

"Ah, but I do."

He raised a brow, then handed her Beauty's reins to hold while he went back to fetch Jim. "Are you sure?"

Miracle plucked out the drooping poppy and tossed it aside. "Did you think me an orphan who never knew her real ancestry? The long-lost last scion of a noble house, perhaps? Or the natural daughter of a local aristocrat, accidentally misplaced at birth, but soon to be reunited with her loving father, who'll shower her with wealth and social acceptability?"

He was startled into laughter. "Who are you, then?"

"Ah, that's asking for too many secrets at once." She stood up. "But I probably know as much about my lineage as you know about yours."

"I doubt it." He set her saddle on Jim's back. "The St. Georges trace an unbroken line of descent all the way back to the Norman Conquest."

"And my family boasted pure Saxon blood long before yours even thought about wading onto the English beaches to steal a land they didn't own."

"The Saxons were fair-haired," he said. "Whereas you're as dark—"

"—as sin?"

He led Jim up to her. She climbed onto the stone and shredded the last of her poppies to rain their shining petals onto his boots.

"I think the thunder promised by these petals will very soon become a reality," she said. "This isn't a game, my lord, not for me."

"Because you're in genuine fear for your life? Don't be! Though I wish you would tell me exactly why the descendant of all those upright British yeomen decided to incur the wrath of the Earl of Hanley by murdering his friend."

"You would force me to do so?"

"No. I would prefer you to tell me of your own free will, simply because you've decided without reservations that you can trust me."

Miracle swung onto her saddle. "Then perhaps I will tell you, my lord, once you've explained exactly why carrying me down that wall like a sack of grain brought back such disturbing memories."

CHAPTER SEVEN

EVESHAM FORBES FROBISHER, THE FIFTH EARL OF HANLEY, drummed his fingertips on the sill as he stared down from the window. Streams of horses and carriages were still coming and going from the yard of the White Swan. A boy raked away dung, but the smell of ammonia was almost overwhelming.

He turned to face the man who stood, cap in hand, on the carpet in the center of the inn's fanciest bedchamber, and raised a brow.

"Miss Heather was definitely here," the man said. "Half a dozen of us scoured up and down the turnpike without learning anything more. The apothecary, Pence, bought the horse, but he knows nothing."

Hanley's gaze snapped back to the window. "Ryderbourne said the same."

"Ryderbourne—?"

"The Duke of Blackdown's eldest son, Lord Ryderbourne. I knew the man when he was still puling like an infant."

"My lord?"

"Never mind." The earl spun about to glower at his servant. "So the woman vanished and Ryderbourne left?"

The man stared blankly at a spot just past his master's left ear. "Several witnesses saw him leave, my lord. He was heard to mention that he was going home to Wyldshay."

Hanley tapped the servant under the chin with the brass head of his cane. "Then I believe I shall pay a visit to the Duchess of Blackdown. I've a fancy for ancient castles afloat in their rivers and for seeing duke's sons in their native habitat—if, by any chance, he is there, after all. Meanwhile, you will discover where they've really gone."

"*They*, my lord?"

"God! Do I employ idiots? The woman and—very possibly—her noble companion! You're short and dark with a nose like a rat, Mr. Lorrimer, as are most of your associates and half of the travelers on this turnpike. Your new quarry is more than six feet tall with the unmistakable manner of a St. George, and the woman's a raving beauty. You will find them. You will follow them. You will ascertain where they're going. Without being seen or suspected. You will send that information back to me."

Mr. Lorrimer gripped his hands together behind his back. "Very good, my lord."

"Very good indeed for you, Mr. Lorrimer. For when you find them, you may collect twice the purse that I originally promised." The earl smiled. "You may also get to witness a hanging."

THE way ahead was marked with the imprint of innumerable hooves. Skylarks and meadow pipits showered song from a blazing blue sky. Yet clouds massed on the horizon, as if an invisible giant piled whipped cream into fantastic mounds, then stained them with ink.

They had trotted away fast from the barn, passing through woods until they climbed back up here onto the open hills. For the first time they were able to ride side by side. As if by unspoken consent, the horses dropped to a walk.

Miracle glanced at her companion. Ryder sat easily on his mare, looking straight ahead. Dark hair danced fretfully on his forehead, casting shadows. A faint sheen marked his skin, drawing her attention to the perfect sculpting of cheekbone and jaw.

She had known so many men, yet this man moved her in a way that she could not quite understand, something far deeper than her visceral reaction to that masculine beauty. *The romantic absurdity is more fun?*

"Why were you called Miracle?" he asked.

"My mother feared I would die. When I refused to do so, and instead kicked lustily in my basket, she thought I'd been born under a lucky star."

"You were a frail baby?"

"My brother, Dillard, says I bawled like a calf right from the start. But he's eight years older than I am."

"You have other siblings, also?"

"Five others were buried: stillborn, miscarried, found cold in their cradles."

"I'm sorry," he said. "That must have been terrible for your mother."

"She died when I was three, so I don't really remember her."

"And were you born under a lucky star?"

"Of course! Otherwise, I certainly wouldn't be alive now and riding with a duke's son beneath this hot blue heaven."

"Which is scorching my back like the fires of Hades." He pointed with his whip. "I see succor in the form of a pool of clear water. In that little valley just below us. It beckons."

"Like the Sirens?"

"Exactly!" He winked at her. "It most definitely sings out its mystical, silent songs of longing—"

"—tempting travelers into dangerous detours?" she finished with a deliberately exaggerated flourish.

Mirth still flickered in his eyes. "I'm in the habit of bathing every day."

"So am I, but I'll forgo a bath to save my neck. Desperate men wish to string me from the nearest tree, yet you suggest we succumb to the habits of luxury?"

"A cold pond is bracing, not luxurious."

"And so it will cool your fevered humors? Very well. By all means, bathe in your mystic pond, if you must."

She halted her pony. A stream tumbled over the edge of the limestone escarpment into a small pool, its dark surface partly obscured by rocky outcrops. Ancient trees stood in picturesque groups in a deer park that stretched several furlongs to the facade of a great stone house. Carved chimneys smoked silently.

"It's in the grounds of someone's country home," she said.

"So it is."

"There are fires in the kitchens, which means that the owner is very probably in residence."

"Almost certainly."

"Furthermore, he's not likely to encourage trespassers. There may even be mantraps in the undergrowth."

The breeze tossed his hair as he corrected his sidling mount. "So there may. If you're afraid, we'd better resist temptation and ride on, though at the moment I'd probably give half my inheritance for a bath."

"Even if there aren't steel teeth in the long grass ready to take off a man's leg, there may be fences with spikes to disembowel the intruder."

"I doubt there are any barriers in the way too great for someone bold enough to attempt them."

"Then never let it be said that we weren't bold enough!"

Miracle cantered her pony down off the ridge. Ryder followed, holding Beauty back just enough so that the mare would not overtake. They pulled up only when the way was blocked by a tall iron railing, topped with spear-shaped spikes.

"As I suspected," she said, spinning the pony back to face him. "His Lordship—whoever he is—has fences to keep out hoi polloi like us."

"Then damn His Lordship's beady eyes!" Ryder glanced about. "Yet he's forgotten to trim his own trees."

One large oak grew close to the other side of the fence. Several stout branches had spread over the top, though the lower spurs had been sawn off, leaving their stumps protruding between the railings.

Ryder halted his mare beneath the oak and threw the reins forward over her head to catch over a cut stub. Too well trained to pull back, Beauty nevertheless rolled her eyes. Yet as Ryder kicked his feet free to stand up on the saddle, the mare swung her haunches sideways, forcing him to balance on one foot with outstretched arms. At this grotesque new shadow, Beauty ducked and shied, but her rider had already leaped up to catch the spikes on the top of the fence. Moments later he sat comfortably on an overhanging branch. Freed of her mad burden, the mare dropped her head and relaxed.

"Come!" Ryder reached down with one hand, grinning like a schoolboy. "Let's invade!"

"You want me to stand on Beauty's saddle? She'll dump me."

"So she will, but Jim won't." He locked his feet around the branch and reached down with his hands. "Like any other lovesick male, the pony won't leave the mare. Come, ma'am, a grotto awaits its nymph!"

She secured the reins, tugged her skirts out of the way, and scrambled up to stand on the pony's back. Jim flicked an ear, but stood quietly next to the mare as Miracle stretched. Ryder caught her hands and lifted her to sit on the branch beside him. The climb down into the deer park on the other side was simple.

He led her across a short stretch of grass. Against the base of the cliff, huge boulders formed moss-covered stacks, leaving a network of secluded fissures, which led the intruders to a waterfall splashing down into the pool, dark and cold in the shade of the trees.

Ryder crouched to splash water over his face with both hands.

Miracle perched on a limestone outcrop and wrapped both arms about her knees. She was determined not to let him see how afraid she was.

"This place was carefully enhanced, wasn't it, to be more picturesque?" she asked.

"Absolutely! Nature no doubt created the cliff and the waterfall, but she never designed these pretty stacks, nor planted them with all those exotic alpine flowers. I imagine the judicious use of explosives produced both the spare rocks and a pool with enough depth to evoke mystery." He dashed more water over his hair. Drops sluiced down over his face. "It's a folly. My grandmother built some similarly charming fancies at Wrendale."

"Wrendale?"

"One of the smaller of the duchy properties."

"Ah, I see. If I weren't here, you wouldn't hesitate to strip off and bathe in that mysterious water, would you?"

"I'll content myself with a little splashing like a wagtail, instead. I don't fancy riding in wet undergarments." He glanced up at her through his damp lashes. "And I can hardly bathe naked in front of a lady."

"You keep forgetting," she said. "I'm not a lady."

Water dripped from his outstretched fingertips. "But what

if a gardener, or a bevy of guests from the house, or a nurse-maid with her charge, or His Lordship himself, should happen to take a stroll and discover my frolicking in his pool?"

"Then you would meet the intrusion with an arrogant stare, which would cow the gardener, terrify the guests, thrill the nursemaid, or reassure His Lordship. No one would ever mistake you for anything but a duke's son: even stark naked, even standing on your head, even when you've chosen to keep company with a murderous harlot."

"I'm not planning," he said dryly, "to stand on my head."

She rose to her feet, her heart battered by his smile, by his carefree assurance, by the wicked curve of his ear. "Yet it must be very fine to know that you may make free with the whole world, even when it belongs to someone else."

"It's not always that simple, Miracle."

"Nevertheless, being of humbler stock and possessing fewer watery skills, I think I'll stroll away by myself and allow you the lonely delights of the pond."

"You don't swim?"

"I don't swim."

He stripped off his jacket. His back flexed as he set the garment on a flat rock, then glanced up at her. "I can teach you."

She smiled down at him. "It's too dangerous."

His eyes seemed very dark, almost black. "I wouldn't allow you to come to any harm."

"No, but I think that my joining you in a state of nature in that pool might be a little perilous to our recently agreed equilibrium, my lord, even though that chivalrous abstinence is all your idea, not mine. So while you take the plunge, I'll paddle about discreetly downstream. It will be just as refreshing, but much safer."

She marched away, leaving him staring after her. A labyrinth of shaded paths wound between the rocks. Tiny flowers nodded on slender stems in every crevice. Mosses and ferns hung dripping from the cliff, the sun firing every droplet.

Miracle trailed one hand over the rocks, alarmed by her unsteady pulse and mad longings, then stopped to laugh at herself. She had always tried to live in the moment. Life had never offered her a past that she much wanted to remember, nor a future that she much wanted to contemplate. Guilt and fear were her daily companions now, but Lord Hanley could never find her here, and what could be more magical than this strangely bright morning?

She leaned her back against a dry slab of limestone and stared up at the sky. She longed to grasp this beauty and hold it in her heart. If she were alone, that was all that the grotto would be, of course: a lovely, magical place, discovered unexpectedly.

Instead, the presence of this duke's son charged it with hidden meaning, as if Oberon cast his enchantments of power on every last living thing, including Miracle Heather: courtesan to the less respectable scions of the nobility, a fallen woman who had tumbled so far from grace that there was little choice left now, except to keep sliding.

In which case, she might as well do it with as much mirth and defiance as she could muster. A harlot's final fate might be inevitable, but that didn't mean that she couldn't still meet it with audacity.

Just ahead of her, a fork in the path led up a set of rough steps. Miracle climbed them and found herself on a small ledge. A rustic bench, green with moss and overhung with imported aspens and red maples, framed a view of the pool. She sat down, just as—in a flash of white—Ryder dived naked into the water.

He swam strongly, his hair slicked to his head, his shoulders and buttocks glimmering like marble as his arms cleaved the surface. Entirely unaware that anyone could see him, he turned a somersault and emerged to float on his back, his arms thrown wide, his ribs arched, his genitals bobbing in the water.

Miracle felt pinned in place as if pierced by an arrow—*Ah, but he was beautiful!*—then she buried her face in both palms in a vain attempt to destroy the vision that was already burned into her brain.

He looked so strangely innocent and pure—the cold green water flowing over his white skin, the smooth bones and muscles and tendons carved with unearthly perfection—as if he were a creature from the far side of the moon, or from heaven, tumbled unexpectedly to earth.

Yet she could so easily recall the scent and feel of that male loveliness in her arms, in her body, and remember that he was ashamed and—in some deeply buried place—probably still angry at how she had used him.

Miracle turned her back, clambered down the steps, and followed the other fork, away from the sound of a man playing like an otter in a grotto, away from his communing with the water as if he had been conceived in the curve of a dark ocean wave.

The path soon looped back to the stream. She crouched and splashed water over her face, drowning out all awareness except that of her own thundering heart.

Ryder really wouldn't care, of course, if he were discovered by a gardener or a nursemaid, and certainly not if he were discovered by the owner of this place: probably a peer who was related to the St. Georges in some way. All the great families married each other. Whatever he did, he was invulnerable. No one could ever touch him. It was unfortunate that such immunity would not extend to any less noble females with whom His Lordship might choose to keep company, especially when those females had committed a capital crime.

Miracle made a wry grimace at the sky and laughed at herself. Some things, perhaps, couldn't be prevented, but all things could be faced with optimism.

She unlaced her boots and paddled her bare feet before she slipped off her clothes and washed herself all over. Then—as if drawn by the vision of Ryder's silent cleave through the water, of the silvered droplets sluicing over his powerful shoulders—she dressed and walked back to the pool.

He was floating with his eyes closed. His clothes formed a tidy little pile on a rock, his boots standing next to it. Without making a sound, Miracle sat down next to his discarded garments. She smoothed her hand over his jacket and stroked absently at the collar of his shirt. When she looked up again, he had already turned to swim toward her.

Silver streamed over his shoulders as he stood up, the water lapping around his waist.

"You were watching me?" He wrung one hand over his wet head. "What about your maidenly modesty?"

Miracle grinned at him. "I told you that I wasn't a lady."

He grinned back. "Obviously not! But how am I supposed to maintain my modesty and retrieve my clothes, when you're sitting on them?"

"I'm not sitting on them. I'm sitting beside them. And

whatever chivalrous nonsense you've chosen to believe, you're not completely chaste yet."

"Yet I'm balanced like the Lorelei on this submerged rock, contemplating the demands of circumspection."

"I don't believe for one moment that you're so bashful, but I promise not to look, if you like. Tiny rainbows are dancing in the high spray from the waterfall behind you. I'll happily study them, instead."

"Not bashful," he said. "Just wondering if perhaps I ought—in my present state—to be considering a little rectitude, at least."

Miracle laughed as she seized his shirt and held it out. "So nature asserts herself once again, in spite of all that cold water? Here, my lord, come fetch your shirt to cover your shame."

He plunged back into the pool to swim the few strokes to the shore. Sunlight glittered over his shoulders as he vaulted up onto the bank, water slicking the sprinkling of dark hair on his skin, sparkling on his arms and buttocks and the proud length of his erection.

Without hesitation he strode up to her. Miracle glanced up into his eyes as he bent down to take the shirt.

As if arrested, he froze, unmoving, unblinking, meeting her gaze. His eyes darkened as he studied her face. Her heart began to thump.

"We've talked of debts and ransoms," she said. "But no more are owed."

Water fell in fat droplets from his hair to burn, blissfully cold against her fevered skin. He brushed the moisture away from her cheek with a thumb. "Not even for a shirt?"

"No," she said. "Along with everything else, this shirt's already yours."

He crouched beside her, still erect, and slipped one hand into her hair, cradling her head as he tipped it back. A dark green fire burned, precariously banked, in the depths of his eyes.

"I think this is a very bad idea," he said. "I should have stayed in the pool."

His shirt fell from her fingers as Miracle reached up to take his shoulders in both hands.

"No," she said, smoothing her palms over his firm, chill

flesh, feeling the flame that scorched just beneath the surface. "Not if it's just a celebration of a bright swim in a magical place."

He exhaled as if punched, and closed his eyes. "Then I'm defeated. God help me!"

She slid her fingers into his wet hair and met the fire of his mouth with her own. He seized her around the waist and half lifted her in his damp arms, until she knelt between his spread thighs, her breasts pressed into his chest. The kiss deepened. Her lips searched, sweetly, sweetly, for the honeyed firmness of his. Her tongue found hot, rough velvet. Her hands strayed over his shoulders and strong spine. His erection caught against her skirts.

Mad sensations plummeted down to her stomach. If his arms weren't supporting her, she knew she would fall, trampled by desire. Yet she kept kissing, allowing the splendor and the excitement and the stunning magnetism of his naked body to enthrall her.

He pulled away at last to draw breath, still holding her by the waist. His eyes were wide and opaque, as if he absorbed his own shadow.

"No," he said, grinding out the word and opening his fingers. "This is a very bad idea, especially when we're not intending to make love again."

Miracle took his hands and lifted them unresisting to kiss each one in the center of the palm. Denying all of her own desires, she called on self-control.

"But when the opportunity presents itself, a woman of easy virtue must steal whatever she can get. Now, get dressed, my lord, before I ravish you on the spot. It would definitely disturb His Absent, Beady-Eyed Lordship of the Spear-Topped Fences, if he discovered us here in flagrante delecto. Because, if you kiss me again, that's exactly what will happen."

He laughed, sitting back on his heels, still splendidly rigid, as she scrambled to her feet and stepped back.

Miracle marched away into the maze of little paths, her body in flames and her mind reeling. As soon as he could no longer see her, she stopped to stare up at the sky through a bright blaze of tears.

More than beautiful. Entrancing!

For as long as she lived she would treasure this memory of

this man—slick and wet and aroused, kneeling beside the dark pool like a pagan deity of the deep water—on fire for her, but opening his hands and letting her go.

THEY rode back up onto the ridge track. Thunder boomed and rolled, far away as yet, but coming ever closer. Hot oppression still hung heavily in the air, though a cool wind gusted now from the west. Near where their path turned, a tall spire broke above the treetops at the head of a valley.

"See that church?" he said. "Thanks to our detour to the grotto, this storm is about to break onto our heads. We'll take shelter there. We can rest the horses and have a bite to eat. Are you tired?"

"Not really," she said. "Just brimming with trepidation."

His glance was sharp. "Why?"

"Because we'll be trapped together in a holy place during a storm."

"And you think pagan grottoes better suited to our circumstances?"

"To mine at least. Unlike you, my shining lord, I'm very much a sinner."

"God, I'm no saint," he said.

"Then perhaps that church will be where you'll tell me what memory was imprinting itself so strongly on your mind when you carried me down from the loft."

A shadow flitted over his face. He frowned for a moment. "I will, if you like. It's certainly nothing to cause you any grief."

"Yet it's a grief to you, isn't it?"

"It was at the time. It's not any longer. There's no reason for my not telling you."

"Yet perhaps it will be a test of your faith in me. After all, I might hear your revelations and still refuse to give you mine."

"No, you won't."

"You think that I'm too honest to cheat you? Or simply that I know better than to risk it?"

Beauty sidled and pranced at a fresh gust of wind. Ryder corrected the mare without apparent effort. "Something like that."

Lightning crackled across the clouds. The thunder rumbled

closer. The birdsong stopped abruptly. The sky was growing ever blacker, as if they were being surrounded by demons. A few cold drops of rain spattered into Miracle's face.

"Come," Ryder said, glancing up. "We just ran out of time. Ride!"

As Jim galloped after the mare, the horses carried both riders straight into a driving downpour.

They arrived at the church soaked. Ryder swung down from Beauty and led her clopping into the porch. Keeping her head down against the pelting rain, Miracle followed, leading Jim, then she stopped. Her companion had pushed open the heavy door to the nave and was leading his mare inside.

"We can't take the horses inside the church!"

"Why not?" The stone floor rang as Beauty spun about behind her master. "Where better to shelter them than in a house of God? You don't think He created the dumb beasts? He doesn't care like a Father for their welfare?"

The pillars supporting the ceiling flashed into stark relief as lightning hit somewhere nearby.

"We may find out," Miracle said. "If the tower is struck and falls through the ceiling, would that be a sign of divine disapproval, do you think?"

He grinned. "No, it would simply mean that there's no proper lightning rod on the spire. Come, you're wet through, and we can't risk the horses being hit."

He took Jim's reins from her hands and tied both mounts to the handles of a large chest that sat near the door. Miracle pulled off her sopping cloak and looked about. There were no seats or pews, just one solitary bench at the base of a pillar, so she draped the wet fabric over the time-worn stone font. At the far end of the nave, an elaborate wooden pulpit boasted of a more prosperous past, yet the altar stood empty except for a single large cross.

Beauty and the pony stood quietly, heads drooping, as Ryder unsaddled them. The empty spaces echoed with hollow booms as more thunder rolled. Their human voices seemed to disappear into whispers.

"There must once have been a village here, as well," she said. "I imagine a few tumbled remains could still be found out there in the woods, long covered over with brambles."

He glanced around. "Yes, abandoned after the Black

Death, perhaps, or diminished little by little when ever fewer men were needed to extract the wealth from wool."

"So the houses returned to the earth."

"And the church, being solid stone, still stands." He propped the saddles at the base of a pillar. "Not used regularly, perhaps, but even now a place for an occasional funeral or maybe a wedding. Someone left flowers in the graveyard quite recently. It's still hallowed ground."

Miracle strolled away, glancing up at the traces of paint clinging to the arches. "When I was a young child, the Sunday walk twice a day back and forth to church was often the only time I ever saw the outside world."

"You never went out except on Sundays? Why?"

"It doesn't matter. We've promised to exchange more immediate confidences than that, haven't we? So, are you ready to tell me your secret remembrances?"

"They're no secret." He offered her some bread and cold meat, unpacked from his saddlebag.

She walked back to take the food. "Thank you. Then why did the memory so disturb you?"

"Because of what I believed I had seen." He sat down on the bench. "Because of the way it made me feel."

She perched on the opposite end of the wooden seat and tore off a piece of bread. The atmosphere seemed to have changed, as if charged with the darkness of the storm.

"Don't tell me if you don't want to."

"There's no reason—other than a lingering discomfort that will probably seem ridiculous to you—why I shouldn't. Almost everyone at Wyldshay, except my sisters, soon learned exactly what had happened. And I think perhaps I should tell you. After all, I've been pressuring you for your secrets. Why shouldn't I offer you one of mine?"

"Not if it's something that causes you distress—"

"I'm not that much of a coward," he said. "It happened at Wyldshay. My cousin, Guy Devoran, was with me. He and I had just walked into one of the enclosed gardens in what was once the outer bailey. We were deep in conversation when I happened to glance up."

She bit her lip at the mention of his cousin's name, but it would not help to complicate this tale any further. "And you saw something that shook you to the core, or outraged you?"

"Outraged? Yes, I suppose so. I was certainly angry and appalled and bitterly disappointed." He wrung wet hair from his forehead. "Jack and Anne were together on the edge of my grandmother's fountain. It was before they were married, or even engaged. Anne was a dissenting minister's daughter. She was a commoner, desperately unsuitable to wed a St. George. Yet they were oblivious to our presence, until Anne looked up—"

"Ah! They were making love?"

"Yes, it was love, but that's not what I thought I was seeing."

"Because you thought you saw something else in her face?"

Ryder seemed to have forgotten his food. "What I saw was guilt and shame and a kind of blind horror, mixed with an indescribable ecstasy. I stood frozen in a mad agony of grief as she turned her face into Jack's shoulder and started to weep."

Miracle stared at her cold meat. She was hungry, yet she also seemed to have lost her appetite. "Because she was a virgin?"

"She'd certainly been so, when they'd met only a few days before. It was obviously terrible to her to be discovered like that. Then Jack's eyes met mine. I'll never forget his face. He knew right away how I was stricken, yet he seemed filled with defiance and something almost close to mockery."

"Your distress over this isn't ridiculous at all." Miracle crumbled her bread, then made herself swallow a piece. "He's your brother and you love him. You thought he had betrayed that love, along with his own honor and Anne's."

"Betrayed *my* love?"

"Yes, certainly!"

"Perhaps, but that didn't matter. What mattered was what it did to my mother—"

Miracle laid aside the remains of her meal and hugged herself. "I have no one in the world besides my brother, Dillard. The love for a sibling is surely the most important of one's life? Why did you think that your love for your brother didn't count?"

"Because the true disaster came after Guy dragged me away, insisting it was none of our business, and we ran straight into the duchess. She guessed immediately what had happened—"

"How could she?"

"Because what she saw in my face confirmed exactly what she had most feared all along: that Jack had lost all claim to norms of morality, that he defied her and everything she had ever wanted for him. With Anne his pawn, caught in their cross-gambits. My mother and I didn't exchange a word. I simply left her there among her roses."

Tension radiated from her taut fingers. Her shoulders ached. Miracle tipped her head back against the wall. "Because you knew that was what the duchess would want?"

"She needed to be alone. Jack had always been her favorite. She had nothing to say to me."

"You didn't mind that?"

"What? That she loved my brother the best? No. My mother's obsession with Jack has always seemed nothing but a cruel burden, one I've been relieved not to have to carry myself."

"Have you always been so lonely?"

He seemed genuinely puzzled. "What? This isn't about me!"

Miracle glanced down. A lonely elder son in the midst of a large family? Even lonelier than she had been? "No, of course not. Though you had burdens of your own."

"Mine are simply part of who I am, not something I've ever questioned or doubted."

"Yet Lord Jonathan took the weight of your mother's love very hard?"

He seemed almost relieved to have moved the focus back to his brother.

"Yes, I think so. Jack escaped into travel and into the arms of countless women. He sought out courtesans throughout the farthest reaches of the East, where he indulged in every possible erotic experience. Anne was entirely innocent of all that esoteric knowledge and—as I wrongly thought—simply a victim of his heartless seduction. It seemed that he had no compunction about corrupting her. My own brother!"

A flash of lightning seared across the nave, flinging grotesque shadows. Brasses blazed suddenly in the stone floor: knights in armor, ladies wearing dresses like shrouds. Ryder leaped up to stride away, then stopped to gaze up at a plaque on the wall, a memorial to some sixteenth-century baronet.

Miracle stared at her wet boots. Her pulse beat heavily. "And so he broke your heart?"

"I wanted to kill him."

Silence filled the church, haunting against the storm's drumming outside. Cold seemed to sink into her bones. For men like Lord Ryderbourne there were only two kinds of female: the innocent, like Anne—the untouchable virgins whose honor any gentleman must defend to the death—and the fallen, who existed only to satisfy that same gentleman's baser needs. Women like her.

"I'm not a priest who maintains that there's virtue in confession," Miracle said. "Why are you telling me all this?"

He spun about. "Because you insisted on knowing."

"No, I didn't!" She shot to her feet. "Are you trying to tell me that you understand the impulse to murder? The impulse, but not the act, of course!"

"No, but for that one moment—" He took a deep breath. "I was determined to punish him, at the very least. He'd brought me back an exquisite jade horse from the Orient. A little carving, with every detail perfect. I smashed it. Then I went back to find him."

Her boots rapped as she marched to the font. Water streamed down the church windows as if the sky were a lake bed, suddenly ruptured. "Because you were furious and wounded and horrified. Yet what recourse did honor leave open to you? To challenge your own brother to a duel?"

"That never occurred to me. I found Jack standing alone, his back toward me, gazing at my mother's roses. I tried to break his jaw with my fist. It was the most dishonorable thing I've ever done in my life, to strike at another man—my own brother—without warning. Yet Jack had learned more than just eroticism in the East. Before my knuckles connected with his face, he whirled and kicked out like a demon. He knocked me out."

Miracle stared at the heavy church door, every nail bleeding its small trail of rust stains. She wanted only to escape. Why did this story make her feel so frantic? Did he think that a harlot's experiences hardened her for anything? That nothing would shock her? Perhaps he was right. She swallowed the panic and walked back to face him.

"Yet you've forgiven him now?"

"I forgave him almost immediately." He gave her a wry smile. "It was far more difficult to forgive myself."

"Why?"

"Because I'd misjudged him so profoundly. That error was a terrible failure of faith, and of love, I suppose." He leaned his shoulders against the pillar and gazed up into the shadows. "Jack worships Anne as the stream worships the riverbed. She is deeply and forever in love with him. She always was, even when my cousin and I surprised them at the fountain, and so—though he didn't quite know it then—was Jack. My brother didn't hesitate to defy all of us to marry her. So the only real sin was mine: the sin of doubt."

Miracle shivered. Her pulse wavered as if its rhythms had been permanently distorted by the storm. "I don't know why you told me this. It's such an intimate story to tell to a stranger."

He didn't move, only pinned her with his dark gaze. "Our relationship seemed intimate enough at the Merry Monarch."

She glanced away toward the windows, the little panes blurred with rain, hating the storm that had trapped them both here.

"You're such an innocent in the ways of the world, my lord, in spite of all that glory of power and position. No wonder your brother met your outrage with defiance! He knew you could never understand him. You still don't, do you?"

Angry color washed into his cheeks. "What do you mean?"

"You said he'd indulged in every possible erotic exploit as he'd traveled through the East. Your brother knows in his bones that sex with a professional has nothing to do with intimacy. Yet you can't tell the difference. You thought only that he'd become dissolute."

"He did nothing to disabuse me of that impression."

"Why should he? Unlike a woman, a young man who makes such choices isn't a harlot, he's a hero. Yet you could judge him only through your Galahad eyes, and so you blinked at the sight of two lovers between the shutters of all your respectable English uprightness. And thus you can only comprehend what happened at the Merry Monarch through the lens of a fairy tale."

His mouth set, as stubborn as a wayward child's. "I only know what I experienced."

Miracle walked up to him. "You experienced good sex

with a courtesan, that's all. And now you stand there in all your shining armor, prating your ideals of chivalry, and try to demand intimacy?"

He spun about and strode away, his boots echoing harshly. "I doubt that intimacy is something one can demand, but if you deny that any semblance of it exists or ever existed between us, then how the devil is it won?"

Distress beat at her heart. "I don't know! Intimacy isn't something I pursue. I know only how to charm a man into parting with money and jewels and the provision of a roof over my head and food on my table. I do it by satisfying his desires, by fulfilling his fantasies, by sweetening his bad tempers, by making him feel more powerful and alive and infinitely more potent than his friends."

He strode off down the nave, speaking over his shoulder. "You asked for the truth and I gave it."

"Then I didn't know what I was asking."

"And it would seem," he said, spinning about to face her, "that your judgments are just as rash as any of those of which you would accuse me."

"Perhaps they are! I owe you my life, but I don't owe you any particular accuracy of judgment."

"Accuracy? No, I don't expect that. But I think I might lay claim to a little more generosity."

The temptation to simply trap him into becoming her lover again was almost overwhelming. Miracle clenched her fists and fought against the longing. Had any saint ever fought harder to drive away a treasure in order to avoid mortal sin?

"I am being generous. I don't forget what I owe you. But it's no kindness to pretend to offer more than one can give. Yet why did your memory of this scene with your brother intrude into your thoughts so forcefully when you carried me down from the loft? What the devil did it have to do with me?"

The large cross framed him, the altar standing cold and hard at his back. "I've no idea."

"Because you understand nothing of your own carnal desires, do you? Yes, you were shocked when you saw your brother and his wife-to-be making love at that fountain, but you were also aroused by it, weren't you?"

"For God's sake!" Beauty threw up her head as her master's voice echoed through the cavernous spaces.

Miracle crouched down at the base of the font. She wrapped both arms about her knees and stared up at the soaring arches, the pure lines of an architecture of devotion: quiet and awe-inspiring and filled with an ancient awareness of the transcendent.

"Why deny it? I don't mean this harshly, Ryder, and no doubt your feelings were overlain very bitterly by your sense of betrayal, by your gallant concern for Anne, by your disillusionment in your brother. But have you ever tossed up a woman's skirts in a garden? Have you ever made frantic love on the edge of a fountain—simply from the urgency of that overwhelming need—while water cascaded unregarded over your head? Or has Galahad only given way to impulsive lust just one time in his life: when a professional seduced him into a haze of forgetfulness, and let him think for a moment that he'd fallen in love?"

"Do you want to make me regret telling you?" His boots rang as he strode back down the aisle toward her.

"No, I want us to be honest."

"I'm not Galahad. But if I did think for one moment that I might have fallen in love with you, devil take it, then you've just disabused me of any such absurdity."

"Then don't try to claim that what we shared was true intimacy. I used you. I paid with my body for a horse and a saddle. That's what I do. It's how I survive. And I'm very skilled at it."

Beauty shied as another drumbeat of thunder rolled across the church roof.

Ice had invaded her bones, freezing the marrow. She must strip him of his romance and his quixotic ideals, and, if she could, she must send him away as soon as possible, for his own sake as well as hers. Yet he stopped in front of her, his boots splattered with mud, his thighs powerful and lean, and his energy hit her with the force of a wave.

"That may be true, yet perhaps I felt that you ought to know that—while I may have misjudged my brother—I won't judge you, whatever you've done. I'm capable of impulsive action in the face of extreme provocation, but I still try to do what's right. I pulled you from the sea with the signs of a beating fresh on your skin. Those bruises still mark your face. Whenever I look at you, they fill me with fresh rage at your attacker. Whether we share intimacy or not, honor makes its own demands."

She glanced up at all that arrogance and power. Though his force was now blunted by distress, she thought that if she held up her palms, the passion of his soul could warm them.

"And so you felt you must offer me something painful of your own, before you could demand that I tell you what really happened in Dorset? You're more generous than I am, Ryder."

"Am I? If there's any truth to that at all, perhaps it's only because life has been more generous to me. I have less at risk. Yet there's no kindness in forcing your confidences in exchange for mine. When you wish to tell me the truth, then do so."

"Don't you see, my lord, that I wish you were not such a good man? For however I might shrink from telling you the truth, now I very definitely owe it. But why do you really want to know?"

"Perhaps you're just a mystery to which I want answers."

"Mystery? What mystery?"

His ocean-green eyes betrayed only anguish, intense and passionate. His mouth, made for kisses and laughter, was pressed into taut lines of concern. "For God's sake, Miracle! You don't need to be afraid."

She laughed in open defiance of her own feelings, then picked up the remains of her bread and walked away to give it to the horses. "Why shouldn't I be afraid? I'm trapped between two mad lords and the hangman!"

Jim gulped the crusts from her palm. Beauty took hers with delicate velvet lips, while watching her master from a liquid brown eye.

Ryder strode up to stand behind Miracle. He draped the cloak about her shoulders, holding the fabric close on each side of her chin.

"Hanley isn't mad. Far from it. He calculates everything he does."

She turned to look up at him. "And you? The perfect knight, hiding his seething passions beneath a frigid coat of shining armor?"

"It doesn't matter what I am." He gazed down at her as if he looked into the depths of a well. "What matters is what Hanley is. Yes, he'll be remorseless in his quest for revenge over the death of his friend. Yet, though he wouldn't shrink from personal violence if it suited him, at heart the earl's a cold fish."

Miracle studied his face. "You know him that well?"

"He and I went to the same school."

"But surely he's some years older than you?"

The chill light cast blue shadows beneath his jaw, glimmered coldly over his cheekbones. "Three, to be precise. Yet we have reason to despise each other. Whenever social occasions force us together now, it's very much the way one cat might acknowledge another."

"With a certain chilly disdain?"

He turned and walked away. "It's a little deeper than that: more of an intense animosity."

A bright spark of rage and fear flared beneath her ribs, radiating pain. "You and Lord Hanley are *enemies*?"

"In some sense, yes, I suppose so."

"Why didn't you tell me this before?" She grasped a handful of Jim's mane to steady herself. "God save me from white-clad knights!"

"What difference does it make?"

"Oh, only a little! Of course, you were bound to know him. The peerage consists of a limited number of great families, after all. Yet this particular peer is a personal enemy of yours, though you simply forgot to mention that before."

"I didn't think it was important."

"Not important? When you've given Lord Hanley yet another reason to hunt me down: not only to take revenge on the mistress who murdered his best friend, but also to have it out with an old antagonist—yourself!"

He strode back, holding out both hands. "Hanley doesn't know that we're together. Even if he finds out, it would only be to discover that the quarry is now more dangerous than the huntsman."

"Why? Because you outrank him?"

"No, because he has reason to appreciate that I'm not so easy to intimidate."

"And this is meant to reassure me?" She hefted her saddle onto Jim's back. "God, I thought you so upright and honest. Now I learn that you've been keeping secrets from me all along."

"I just told you something that I've never told another living soul."

"Yes, yes, and it breaks my heart as your brother broke yours. Yet you also neglected to reveal that you're not a disinterested party in all this. It simply slipped your mind to inform me that you've a feud with Lord Hanley. Which—whether you like it or not—makes for a damned dangerous game for the pawns, caught openly on the board as a duke's son masses his snow-white knights against the red men of an earl. It would seem that every man I ever met only wishes to play me for a fool—even Sir Galahad!"

"That's not true!"

She tugged the pony forward and opened the door. The bright scent of wet grass and damp earth poured into the church. The headstones sparkled as if sprinkled with silver. Miracle scrambled into the saddle and turned the pony's head to the north.

Beauty neighed and tossed her red mane. Ryder set his saddle on her back and buckled the girth. The mare's hooves rang as he led her out of the church.

"That's not true!" he insisted.

"Then what is true, my lord?" Miracle asked. "That you fell in love with a mirage just before midnight, and will try every scullery maid in the kingdom to find the one female whose foot fits your imaginary glass slipper?"

CHAPTER EIGHT

WYLDSHAY CASTLE ROSE LIKE A MAILED FIST FROM THE broad waters of a lake. The Earl of Hanley gazed up at the towers as his coach horses trotted over the arched stone bridge and beneath the portcullis. He stepped down into a courtyard. A pair of tall oak doors were immediately flung open on silent hinges by two bewigged footmen.

Wyldshay was excruciatingly well run.

"Is Lord Ryderbourne at home?" he asked as a more senior servant came forward. "Or perhaps the duchess?"

The man led him into the Great Hall, where he was kept waiting. Stone dragons leered at him from the fireplace. On another wall St. George wrestled with a rearing white horse as he speared a green serpent to the heart. Yet when he was eventually led into an elegant parlor, the Duchess of Blackdown walked up to greet him with both hands extended, as if he were a long-lost son.

"Hanley? How very charming! To what happy chance do we owe this unexpected visit?"

The earl bowed low over her rings. "The happiness is all mine, Your Grace."

She sat down in a rustle of skirts and waved him to a chair. "Yet handsome young men do not pay surprise calls on their mother's friends without good cause, do they? No doubt you really came to see Ryderbourne. Alas, he is not at home."

He buried the small rush of triumph. "Alas, indeed! Yet when I met him on the road, he expressly said he was driving here. Perhaps I misunderstood? He has returned to London, instead?"

Her eyes were brilliant, like those of a pagan idol. "You met my son on the road?"

"We enjoyed breakfast together at the White Swan on the Bristol turnpike."

Her smile seemed a little bored. "Then he must indeed be at Wyldshay. Perhaps he has gone down to the coast, or is making his rounds of the farms. I have no idea. I do not keep track of my son's movements, Lord Hanley. By all means, go in search of him, if you wish."

He stood up. "Alas, Your Grace, I have pressing business. I can't stay. I wished merely to pay my respects before traveling on."

She called a servant to see him out. Hanley strode back to his waiting carriage. His man was waiting to fold up the steps and close the door.

"Well?" the earl asked.

The servant touched his hat with one finger. "The duchess already knows that Lord Ryderbourne isn't in London, my lord. She sent a servant up to town with a message for him, but the man returned empty-handed this morning. And the groom says his carriage returned here several hours ago, but His Lordship wasn't in it." The man grinned. "You might say he's disappeared, like."

"Then we return to the White Swan as fast as these damned nags can carry us!"

The duchess watched from a window as the carriage rattled across the bridge. Her mouth curved when it turned north.

"Ah, my dear boy," she said to herself. "So where are you? Wherever it is, I rather hope you are having an adventure."

RYDER allowed Miracle to ride away alone. The white pony cantered up the wet path toward the hill track. Beauty fretted, eager to follow, yet he held the mare in check, fighting memories.

If the earl had appeared on the horizon at that moment, Ryder would have been tempted to shoot him down without mercy. Not with the confused rage that had once made him try to hit his brother without warning, but with an ice-cold desire for justice.

Apart from his fury over Hanley, it was almost impossible to sort out his feelings about Miracle. He knew only that he could not let her slip away into disaster. Whether she wanted his help or not, he would pursue her to the ends of the earth. Though what he would do when they reached the world's end, he had no idea.

He was under no illusion about sharing any real future with her. Wyldshay was not just his duty. It was his love and his passion, and had been since the day he had first opened his eyes and seen the great inheritance into which he'd been born. He glanced down at his hands, clenched too hard on the reins.

Miracle could enslave any man with her sensual beauty and she knew it. For perhaps the first time in her life she was trying not to do it, instead. That perhaps could've been seen— in a rather backhanded way—as a compliment, even when she was so obviously failing.

Ryder eased his fingers and choked back a kind of mad, frustrated mirth at his own impotence in this.

Even if he thought he could somehow clear her of the charge of murder, what could he offer her? To install her in a townhouse in London as his mistress? Perhaps in the very same rooms where she had so recently been welcoming his enemy? The idea repulsed him. In the face of that, even his burning desire seemed only tarnished and sordid.

The wealth and power of the Blackdowns was almost infinite. Ryder outranked every man in the kingdom, except for the handful of dukes and marquises. That knowledge had both haunted and enthralled him all of his life. As long as he could remember, if he reached out a hand he could have almost anything he desired.

It was a little disconcerting to realize that this time he had no idea what he wanted.

Miracle was almost out of sight before he allowed Beauty to follow.

SHE rode blindly, tears coursing down her cheeks. Surely he could not follow her now, not after what she had said to him. She would ride on to Derbyshire, recover her valuables from her brother, take a ship to America, and never see or think of her white knight again. Every scullery maid in the kingdom understood perfectly well how any real prince would treat her, whatever fantastic promises he made at the ball. And perhaps it was a kindness, too, to remind the prince of that, before he made too great a fool of himself.

At least the storm had blown itself out. A bright breeze blustered from the west, drying out her sodden clothes and promising a dry night. Still, it would be miserable to camp too near the track that hugged the exposed hilltops. As the night drew in, she rode Jim down into a little valley. Before long she found a sheltered spot where a spring bubbled out of the rocky escarpment. The place seemed hidden enough to risk a small fire.

She hobbled the pony and turned him loose to graze, then hunted under the trees for some dry sticks. Once she had them burning, Miracle lay for a long time wrapped in her cloak staring up at the sky.

The same cold stars glimmered down on every hamlet and village and town, every great country house, every field and factory and workshop in England. Their thin light sparkled on the Channel and the Severn Estuary and the Irish Sea. Those identical stars sent their faint phosphorescence to haunt the sails of His Majesty's navy and every flotilla of small fishing boats, flung far across the sea, until at last they disappeared over the curve of the horizon to discover new oceans sparkling beneath the Southern Cross.

Many, many years ago the wonder of it all had enchanted a young girl who had once been allowed to stare up through a telescope, after so many years of sleeping in darkness. How could she have imagined that the same starlight was beating down onto the dark head of a lonely young lord, who listened with heartbreaking intensity for the music of the spheres?

She closed her eyes and buried her face in her arms.

So he had robbed her even of this: the chill comfort of infinity.

RYDER found a perch among the roots of a great tree, where he could see into her little clearing without being seen and keep watch as she slept. When her fire burned down, he gathered more wood with infinite caution, his boots easing into the damp ground with each careful step. Burning with frustrated desire, he added more fuel to the fire. When she turned in her sleep, he tucked the cloak back around her shoulders without waking her, then crept away.

The night creaked and rustled with small sounds—a mouse nibbling, a stoat hunting—then quavered with the long-drawn cry of an owl. Ryder wrapped himself in his cloak and stared at the sky. How many years had it been since he had allowed himself to sit and do nothing like this?

A strange mixture of elation and unease tickled at the back of his mind. For the limited duration of this adventure, he had no truly weighty responsibilities, only the simple demands of a journey without his usual entourage. No ducal carriage. No liveried servants. Just himself, a sleeping woman, and the vast, rustling world.

He felt as if his life were temporarily stripped to an unknown essence that he couldn't quite grasp, while he busied himself with the mundane tasks that his real existence never demanded: gathering firewood, taking care of a horse. Perhaps if he allowed himself to truly comprehend the wheeling silence of the heavens—perhaps if he managed to penetrate the real mystery of this woman—he would learn something so vital it would change him forever.

As soon as dawn glimmered, Ryder walked back through the woods to the spot where Beauty grazed, hidden in a hollow. Before any farmhand could find that his neglected patch had sprouted such a jewel—like a pearl in an oyster—Ryder saddled her and led her back to Miracle's camp. Holding the mare by the bit, one hand in readiness over her nostrils lest she whinny, man and horse remained lost among the trees.

At last Jim started down the path. Before pony and rider were too far out of sight, Ryder swung into the saddle.

He followed her the same way the next day as the hills gave way to the broad vale of a river, and the stone escarpments of the Cotswolds slipped abruptly into half-timbered prettiness. The drovers' road now turned west toward Wales. Miracle picked a lane that ran north and slightly east, straight into the heart of England.

Ryder rode steadily after her, dog tired from lack of sleep. They were traveling now through the rich pastures and woodlands of Warwickshire, where every track led in and out of a village, and every road led straight to a town. Ryder made necessary detours for supplies, then followed Jim's prints, cantering where he had to, so that he would not fall too far behind. If Miracle was not going to disappear down one of a multiplicity of lanes, he had to stay close on the pony's heels.

The third evening she turned down a narrow track through thick woods. It led to a ruined farmyard. The remains of a cattle barn lay open to the sky. Young trees had set up camp like an invading army among the broken pigsties. Locals had obviously been robbing the place of dressed stone for decades. The ground beneath the shattered walls was soft with moss.

Throughout the drizzly night Ryder kept his vigil with his back propped against the wall of a wrecked granary. The abandoned platforms for the ricks showed gaping holes where some of the stones had been hauled away. A fox trotted by on silent feet, his sharp muzzle testing the air. Ryder met the animal's questioning gaze for a moment, before the fox raced away into the undergrowth.

Dawn had begun to dilute the shadows when the sound of heavy breathing ruptured the quiet. A shiver of alertness shocked down Ryder's spine. Caught on the edge of dreaming, he had almost drifted into sleep.

Two men were tramping up the path. They were neither masons nor woodsmen.

The small glow of Miracle's campfire burnished their ragged clothes and desperate faces. One of the men whistled softly between his teeth and nudged his companion with an elbow.

"Aye, and there's a pony, too," the other man hissed.

His companion pulled out a long, wicked knife, and stepped forward.

There wasn't time to stand. Ryder leaned forward, sitting with both forearms on his knees, and spoke quietly, so that Miracle wouldn't wake. "Not so fast, my lads!"

Four eyes swiveled toward him, trying to focus in the half light.

"Well, if it ain't a sparrow squatting on a stone," one man said.

"A sparrow with pistols," Ryder replied. "Speak softly, if you please."

"I see two empty hands." The second man stared with obvious belligerence, yet his voice dropped to barely more than a whisper. "Sure you have a gun, mister?"

The duke's son raised a brow. "You doubt me?"

The men looked at each other, then shifted nervously from one foot to another. "No harm meant, m'lord."

"I believe you gentlemen have taken a wrong turn. Your path lies to the southeast. I prefer not to waken the lady with any sudden noise, but if needs must—"

"Of course, m' lord. Of course." One of the men doffed his leather cap. The knife had disappeared. "No harm meant, Your Lordship. Jeb and I didn't mean no harm at all, didn't mean to trespass on Your Lordship's lands. We was lost."

"Just decent, hungry folk, looking for honest work," the other man said. "If Your Lordship would happen to be in need—?"

"No." Ryder reached into a pocket and tossed a couple of coins. "But here's something for your trouble."

The ruffians grabbed the money from the air, then turned and hurried off down the path.

The innocent sounds of the woods trickled back into the sudden silence. Miracle turned in her sleep. A deep satisfaction flowed through Ryder's blood.

HE was trotting Beauty along a well-worn lane that meandered along a stream bank, concentrating on picking out the pony's odd-shaped shoe print, when a pheasant burst from the undergrowth. The bird whirred up beneath Beauty's nose. Ryder's balance adjusted automatically as his mount twisted and ducked. He gathered reins, annoyed only that he had given her enough slack to allow it to happen. He must be more tired than he knew.

"Ah," Miracle said. "So you ride like the god of horses, even in your sleep! Of course, any son of the Duke of Blackdown has spent half his life on horseback."

Jim and his rider were blocking the way ahead.

The mare threw up her head and whinnied. Ryder allowed it, all his concentration riveted on Miracle. His pulse hammered. Broken sunlight cast entrancing shadows over her face as she gazed at him.

"I've always had horses," he said.

Miracle patted the pony's white neck. "Yet you sit your sweet mare like a ghost of the dead. When did you last sleep soundly for an entire night?"

He stared at her in silence as the question whirled in his head, then he grinned. "Not since before I met you."

She bit her lip. "Damnation! Then if you fall to the ground and expire, it'll be my fault. Meanwhile, wherever I camp, I wake in the morning to find hot embers. Every day I saddle a pony mysteriously groomed by pixies in the night. My food is magically replenished, my bottle refilled. The wee folk, apparently, have been very busy taking care of me."

He walked Beauty forward. "Does that annoy you?"

Miracle turned her pony, and Jim fell into step beside the mare. "No, it amuses me. Or perhaps the truth is that it touches me to the heart."

The shattered sunlight made him squint. His eyes burned as if rubbed with ash.

"I don't know if you appreciate quite how bloody dangerous this is," he said. "England is full of desperate men who will turn to anything to survive these hard times. You were already robbed once. No woman is safe traveling alone."

"And thus we have Sir Galahad, still keeping vigil?"

"I wish you wouldn't call me that."

"No, because it was Lord Ryderbourne who faced down those rogues this morning, as calmly as if he were dismissing two grooms who'd mismeasured the oats, or spilled tea onto His Lordship's boots." She glanced up at him beneath her lush lashes. "It was really rather splendid."

"You saw that?"

"I did. Though it seemed wiser to pretend to continue to sleep, at least until I could ascertain whether you might need my assistance. You didn't, of course. You reinforced all that lordly hauteur with such absolute confidence that they thought you owned all those woods and probably the surrounding several thousand acres."

"I hoped they would believe something of the kind, and thus that I had armed servants within earshot."

"Exactly. But you didn't have anyone within earshot except me, so you took a hell of a risk to face them down like that.

Though I imagine Sir Galahad would follow a damsel into Hades, if he thought she'd become his responsibility."

"Hades isn't necessary. If you will only relent enough to allow me to help you openly, I can hire a carriage to take us both straight to Derbyshire."

"You're tired of riding?"

He laughed, though it made his head ache. "No, but I am tired to the bone."

"Then we have two choices," she said. "Either you turn around now and go home—"

"—or we abandon this whole crazy venture and ride straight to the nearest town to hire a coach and four."

"At the risk of being discovered at the first tollgate. I thought you were rather enjoying yourself riding alone through the countryside?"

He smoothed one palm down Beauty's mane. "Yes, in an odd way I am. There's a rather enticing freedom to traveling on day after day without ever turning back. For the first time in my adult life I have no responsibilities other than staying in the saddle."

"Which you can obviously do in your sleep. So you'll pursue your mysterious quest all the way to its unknown destination?"

"Sir Galahad can do no less," he said.

She laughed. "I feared as much. But in the meantime, you need to eat and rest. You're a ghost. Should that process become complete, your wandering spirit will haunt me for the rest of my days."

"I'm tired, but I don't plan to expire."

"Neither do I. Though, alas, if I end up on the gallows, there won't be that many days left for me to be troubled by your ghost." She turned the pony to splash through the stream. "An exhausted knight errant is more of a danger than a help in these taxing times," she said over her shoulder. "So let's chase the roebuck into the thicket!"

Feeling slightly bemused, Ryder followed.

The horses clambered up the opposite bank and pushed through a stand of willows to emerge into a little clearing. On one side it was bordered by the stream where it had looped away from the lane. On the other, short turf ran from the water's edge to the base of a grassy bank thick with vetch and germander speedwell.

Miracle slipped from Jim's back to the ground, tied the pony to a tree, and pulled food from her saddlebags.

"I discovered this spot quite by accident," she said. "Something ran across the lane in front of me, so I followed it."

"Thus the sacred roebuck leads the wanderers into the magical glade?"

She sat down on the grass and began to unwrap a meat pie. "The roebuck makes for a better tale, though I think it was actually just a fox."

Ryder slid from the saddle, tied Beauty and loosened her girth a notch, then walked up to join Miracle.

Damsel flies dodged above the water, disturbed only by the occasional jewel flash of a dragonfly. The clearing was cut off from the lane by the stream, and entirely screened from passersby by the intervening undergrowth and trees.

"Sit," Miracle said. "Have some wine. The fairy folk also gave me this pie last night. They must have gone into a village bakery somewhere and raided the shelves, though I think that the wine was bottled by Titania herself, aided by Cobweb and Peasblossom."

He stripped off his jacket and dropped onto the grass next to her, then lay back with his hat pulled over his eyes and the jacket pillowed under his head. Something plopped into the water: a vole, perhaps, or a frog. Doves called somewhere in the woods. The pungent scent of water mint permeated the air. The sense of peace was almost tangible.

"Go ahead," he said. "I'm not hungry."

Miracle said nothing.

Ryder lifted his hat just a little and gazed at her through slitted lashes. Her hair was looped into shining plaits, hiding most of the bruising on her cheek. As if carved from stone, she was staring at the food in her hands, not moving.

"You're not eating?" he asked.

She looked away. "It's hardly polite to eat alone."

He sat up and took her by the shoulders to turn her to face him. "Miracle—"

Tears spilled over the dark lashes, over the fading marks on her exquisite skin, past the corners of her brave mouth.

Desire seared his heart. Desire and tenderness and heartbreak. He tossed aside his hat and gathered her into his arms, then pulled her down to cradle her head on his shoulder. He brushed the moisture from her cheeks.

"It's all right," he said. "They won't hang you. Hanley can never get past me to harm you. I'll do whatever it takes, but no one is going to haul you in front of any court in this land to charge you with murder."

Miracle pulled away just enough to stare down at him, one hand cupping the side of his jaw. Her fingertips strayed softly into his hair. Her lips curved with poignant courage.

"No, for the wee folk have also sent me a knight in shining armor for my succor."

"If you knew me better, you wouldn't say such things."

She stared away into the trees. "Why? Because at the end of this journey, you'll return to your real life, enriched, perhaps, by this temporary escapade, but with nothing fundamental changed? You don't need to feel guilty about that."

"Yet perhaps there are some things I'd like to change—"

"Only small things. Certainly nothing that would prevent your settling back into the well-loved path of duty. For you do love it, don't you? The levy exacted by your inheritance is in truth the deepest joy of your life."

"Wyldshay is part of me. Perhaps I know that all the more clearly from having temporarily left it behind." He stretched and gazed up into the leaves. "Sometimes it's as if the River Wyld taught a song to my blood that resounds against the bone. I wish I could show you the castle and the estates—"

"Duke's sons don't take females like me home to meet their mothers," she said.

"No, I suppose not. Yet are we really so different?"

"Ha! I was born without even a wooden spoon to my name. My father was a laborer. My brother makes shoes. When I was six years old, I was apprenticed into the local cotton mill."

"The cotton mill?"

"Ay, laddie! 'Appen tha' ma'es nowt of t' way folks talk, back in t' mill?"

He swallowed his shock. "I'm sorry?"

"So, even though you have property in Derbyshire, you can't understand your own people? Which only goes to prove once again that between you and me, my lord, lies a gulf greater than the Milky Way."

"Because you know the local dialect?"

"Language shapes us. The aristocracy are fluent in both English and French, while the serving classes switch between a language that their betters can understand, and the private tongue of the cottage where they were born."

"Which is still English."

"Is it? My childhood speech was so broad that it might as well have been another language, but even if I'd been born in a castle, I'm still a lady of the night, Ryder. Not someone you can introduce to your family."

"I don't know what I thought," he said, the shock still reverberating, "but it was never that you had worked in a cotton mill."

She brushed her fingertips over his eyelids, gently closing them. "Go to sleep," she said, breathing the words into his ear. "If you don't rest, you'll be of no use to me, nor anyone."

Her palms stroked over his temples, brushing his hair back from his ears. The sun beat down on his closed lids, filling his mind with red light. He tried to relax, his hands flung out to each side, drifting on the edge of sleep.

A cotton mill? How had she escaped such a life? Would she tell him, if he asked? Or would she think it was none of his business?

If he were not here beside this stream with a courtesan named Miracle Heather, he might be at Reversham, or Tilling Hall, or Templeford, walking in manicured grounds with a succession of ingenues. He had met most of them at Almack's during the Season. Almost any of them would make a suitable bride, attractive and accomplished. Some even sparkled with wit and intelligence. Yet he had wanted none of them.

Had he ridden to Monksford Leigh as summer burgeoned over Dorset and proposed to Lady Belinda simply because her home was the closest to Wyldshay?

"You're thinking of things that distress you," Miracle whispered. "Don't think! Just be."

Her hands massaged the tight muscles of his arms.

Yet thoughts erupted in incoherent little snatches of anguish. A laborer's daughter . . . a cotton mill. He'd had no idea . . . no idea . . .

"You'll never sleep, unless you let it all go," she murmured. "And you must sleep, Ryder, or you'll fade away. Then I should indeed be bereft."

Sheer exhaustion at last wiped the thoughts from his mind. The stream gurgled. Doves called softly. Her clothes rustled as she moved, easing his buttons, untying the harsh knots of his cravat, loosening the ties of his shirt, tugging away his boots. He allowed it, grateful to rest beneath the hot sun.

Though the touch of her fingers fired little explosions of desire, he kept them banked and let his mind float.

A gulf greater than the Milky Way—

He had almost begun to lose awareness, not even quite sure where he was any longer, when her salt mouth pressed softly against his. Immediately his lips parted, as if fatigue had purged him of everything but tenderness.

Her tongue touched his with fleeting little strokes, as gently as the demoiselles alighting on the bent river grasses.

Ryder's resistance dissolved. Mind and conscience had finally flitted beyond reach.

Warm honey coursed in his veins. Still supine, still relaxed, he kissed her back, reveling in the growing intoxication of arousal, the delight stirring deeply, the flames licking along his hot bones. Her lips feathered over his, her tongue dancing wicked little dances, then she began to kiss him more profoundly.

Still kissing, she slid one hand inside the loosened waistband of his breeches. The heady ecstasy of desire launched its imperious demands. He groaned into her mouth as need thundered in his groin.

Her fingers strayed, stimulating, maddening, exquisite, up and down the length of his erection. Her palm smoothed, cool on his hot flesh. He gasped in a breath, then another, absorbing her kisses deep into his lungs, conquered simply by the longing for fulfillment.

When she straddled him, a knee on each side of his hips, his hands closed without thought on her waist. His mouth only knew that she was still ravishing his tongue. His mind no longer cared for anything except the luscious feel of her, all suppleness, all female, all curves.

His palms slid up to cup her breasts. Their soft weight filled his hands. Through the fabric of her dress, her nipples pressed into his palms. He raised his knees and rubbed one nipple gently with the ball of his thumb. The peak tightened into a hard pebble and she moaned into his mouth. Erotic pleasure pulsed straight to his erection.

She pushed clothing out of the way. Her nakedness, moist and hot, pressed against his. Knowing only that sweet, urgent need, he raised his hips, groaning like a man wounded. She had no need to guide him. Passion knew its own need and its own path. And she was slick and hot and silk velvet, ready for him.

MR. Lorrimer chewed thoughtfully at his pipe as he lounged in the doorway of the bakery to stare up the village street.

"Was that what you hoped to learn, sir?" the shop girl asked, wiping her hands on her apron. "The man was dressed simply enough, but he sure acted like a duke, I thought. Yet he's probably one of those traveling players on his way to a show, since real dukes don't come around these parts very often."

He met her eager, starstruck gaze. "What traveling players?"

"You know! 'When mine eyes did see Olivia first . . .' Um—oh, I remember!—'that instant was I turned into a hart, and my desires, like cruel and . . . and fell wild dogs, pursue me ever since. How now! What news of her?' That's from *Twelfth Night*. I saw it performed a few weeks ago at Miller's Barn. That duke was called Orsino."

"This man was alone, you say, and on horseback?"

"Aye, and I did think that part odd. You never saw such a fine chestnut, sir. She was all fire and flash. Lovely! That mare was almost enough to make me think that maybe he was a real lord, after all."

"Yet no one was with him? A woman? Or perhaps a boy?"

"No, sir, but he bought enough food, and he took his time picking it out, as if he had someone besides his own self that he wanted to please."

"Ah!" Mr. Lorrimer said. "Did he, then? Well, I've also someone besides myself who's cooling his equally noble heels not ten miles from here, who'll be very pleased indeed to hear this."

"Then you'll take the bread and the mutton pies, sir?"

"I'll take a kiss, if you like."

She struggled and tried to kick him in the shins as he

kissed her. He bit her lip, then laughed down at her angry face, before he swung into his saddle. The baker's daughter scrubbed away tears and shouted a curse after him as he rode away.

Mr. Lorrimer laughed again. Quarry almost found. Purse almost secured. And then there was the little matter of the hanging.

His arms flung wide on the grass, Ryder slept like the dead, though he smiled like an angel bestowing a blessing. He barely stirred as Miracle tidied his clothes. He only groaned a little in his sleep when she kissed his mouth one last time, then he turned over to pillow his face in his jacket. Her mad knight errant was relaxed at last, lost in the deep slumber of abandonment.

She washed in the stream, then untied her pony to lead him back through the willows. Beauty tossed her head as Jim left, but fortunately the tired mare did not whinny.

Miracle's heart felt heavy enough to break, but she also knew a little free-floating anger. At Ryder, because all men were, in the end, so easy to manipulate—even her knight errant? Or at herself, because she only knew one way to be—and that was to steal the virtue from a good man, or outwit the vice of a bad one?

Whatever romantic fancies Ryder thought that he believed, surely now she had destroyed them. She had told him the truth about her birth. She had reestablished the truth about their only possible relationship.

Without looking back she rode fast along the lane that they'd left just over an hour before, then branched off on another path. If she was going to lose him—if she was going to bury Jim's telltale hoofprints among a mass of others—she must either find a large drove of cattle, or risk the turnpike.

Miracle emerged not more than ten minutes later onto a sizable road, probably not the main toll road, since no carriages were in sight, but obviously fairly heavily traveled. She turned her pony's head to the north and trotted on. A handful of walkers and the driver of a wagon examined her, a few exchanged pleasantries as she passed, but no one molested her. The other travelers on the road simply assumed that a woman traveling unaccompanied on horseback must be local.

Yet the pony, though tough, was not tireless. After several hours she was forced to stop to let Jim drink from a village water trough. Some of the laborers and tradesmen coming home at the end of the day cast curious glances in her direction. She stared into the far distance, trying to look as if she belonged.

By the time she rode on, the long summer twilight was already drawing in. Shadows stretched over the muddy road. The traffic thinned out and disappeared as night eased into the hedgerows. At a crossroads she rode past a gibbet. The indescribable contents of the iron cage creaked in a small breeze. Instinctively dodging away from the sight, and having no idea where she was, she took a narrow lane that ran off to the right.

Soon she must find a place to shelter for the night, and this time there would be no faithful follower to make sure that no one disturbed her. Though it was her own choice, though she had left him deliberately lost in sleep in the clearing, that loss hurt like a burn.

At least the night promised to be warm. She would not need to risk a fire. She never would have done so before, of course, except that she knew that Ryder would be there to keep watch and would care if he thought she was cold.

That idea was terrible to her: that she had ensnared a fundamentally good man in the disastrous web of her misfortunes. She had tried to repay him in the only way that she knew and only woven the snare more tightly. Now she had compounded it. In a last desperate bid to get free, she had deliberately taken advantage of his fatigue and his desires to trample on his honor.

Yet it had been necessary. He would sleep now for hours, probably till well after dark. He would wake to find her gone. He would remember what she had admitted, something she had never told any of her previous lovers: *When I was six years old, I was apprenticed into the local cotton mill.*

He would wake to think about it and be dismayed. Any fantasies he might have woven about her must collapse under the weight of that reality: She was a scion of the ignorant laboring masses. Her brother was a shoemaker. The brilliant society courtesan was a fraud.

And she knew men. As quickly as they developed their obsessions, they tired of them. There was always a new woman:

younger, prettier, less trouble. If she was lucky, Ryder might have come to that conclusion already.

An odd kind of luck, of course, when it made her heart numb with dread at the loss.

Jim flicked back an ear. Miracle stopped the pony and glanced over her shoulder to listen. A carriage was driving up behind her. There was no obvious place to get out of the way. Each side of the lane was bordered by high banks topped with hedgerows. Fortunately there was a wider spot just ahead, where a five-barred gate stood open in a gap in the hedge. If she could reach it in time, she would simply ride off into the field beyond.

She urged Jim forward. The pony balked.

The approaching horses were obviously fresh and galloping too fast for safety. Some gentleman, eager to get home after a day's drinking with cronies, perhaps, or late for a dinner engagement?

Her heart beating hard, Miracle pressed Jim up against the bank as the coach and four sped past and—in a flash of red and gilt—she saw the crest on the door panel.

The sickening jolt of panic made her clumsy. She frantically tried to turn the pony around. Jim backed his rump into the hedge. The carriage pulled up, blocking the road ahead. It began to turn, using the gateway.

Miracle hauled Jim about with the brute force born of terror, but the pony stubbornly snatched at some grass. As if she rode in a living nightmare, she tried to kick him into a gallop, knowing that Jim could not outrun the carriage horses, knowing that she was trapped, even when the tired pony finally lumbered forward.

The carriage rolled back at a mocking, almost leisurely pace. When the postilion drew level, he simply leaned down and seized her pony's bridle. Mutinous now, Jim balked, then reared. Miracle slid from the saddle. The carriage door was flung open, cutting off any last hope of escape.

The coachman grinned down at her from the box. A liveried servant who had been clinging behind the carriage ran to the horses' heads. The postilion winked at his comrade.

Lord Hanley slid forward on the plush seat inside the coach to stare at her. His hair gleamed like silver.

"So I was looking for a hedge whore! What a comedown

for the glorious toast of London! Rats seem to have taken up residence in your hair, ma'am. Most distasteful!"

Miracle extricated her skirts from the thorns and stood as upright as she was able in the space encompassed by the bank, the carriage door, and her own pony.

"If my appearance so distresses you, by all means drive on, Lord Hanley."

"Drive on?" He smiled. "Oh, no, I don't think so. You really shouldn't have stabbed Philip Willcott. You've put me to some considerable inconvenience."

"No more than you've put me."

The earl took a pinch of snuff, then dabbed at his nostrils with a pristine white handkerchief. "Yet here you are, neatly netted like a perch. Though not quite as neatly as that corpse we just passed, rotting on the gibbet. A fell warning to ill-doers."

"Then perhaps you should take the lesson to heart, my lord?"

He leaned back and laughed. "Pray, step inside, ma'am. Your idiotic flight has just come to an end."

Miracle curtsied. The intensity of her fear hammered hard beneath her ribs. The stifled rush of frantic energy threatened to choke off her breathing. "Your Lordship is kind. However, I prefer to remain here in the hedgerow."

Ice congealed in Lord Hanley's gaze: the cold blue stare of a blinded reptile.

It was almost impossible to believe that she had ever been his lover. Yes, he had always been distant, his caresses perfunctory, his tastes uncaring—though that had made it easier, of course. Her aim had always been to fulfill a man's needs, while leaving her heart unscathed.

"Turn the bloody pony loose," the earl said. "Throw the saddle and bridle over the hedge."

"How very mean of you!"

"Nowhere near as mean as I intend to be very soon. You will kindly step up into the carriage. Or shall I have my men lift you, kicking and squealing?"

"While I have the free use of my limbs?" She climbed into the carriage and sat down opposite the earl. "Certainly not. I'll save the kicking and squealing for the scaffold."

He grinned and snapped closed the lid of his snuffbox.

"Yet perhaps we may first kick and squeal a little together? Though it pains me to think that afterward you're still destined to hang by your pretty neck until dead."

She heard a slap—a man's hand on her pony's rump, no doubt—and hoofbeats as Jim trotted away. The carriage jostled and started forward.

"Nothing would possess me to share anything more with you ever again," she said, though the choking fear still ran and ran, like a never-ending river of ice in her veins. "Better a fast end on the scaffold than the slow torture of your bed."

His chin jerked, though his gaze was still veiled. "You won't goad me with petty insults, Miracle. I seek only justice. However, you owe me something for my trouble."

"Really? I thought that any debt that remained in our relationship was yours. We had a bargain. You broke it."

A muscle twitched in his jaw as he stared from the window. "What the devil do you think that I owe you? The baggage you left behind on my yacht?"

"Good Lord! I can't imagine that you still have it."

"No." Something intense flickered in his eyes as he glanced back at her. "I threw all of your trash into the sea. After all, your valuables weren't there any longer."

"You searched my bags? Why? Wasn't that a little undignified?"

He seized her arm, passionate interest burning in his gaze. *"What did you do with it?"*

"With what?"

He released her and stared from the window again, his expression suddenly bland. "Surely you had jewels? A little money?"

"I fail to see how that's your concern, my lord. I took nothing of yours."

The earl leaned back against the squabs, drumming his fingers on the window frame, though he continued to stare out at the passing night.

"You will tell me," he said at last. "However, I have other needs at the moment."

"Which are not my concern."

He glanced back at her and smiled as he opened his jacket and waistcoat. He began to undo the buttons at his waistband.

"No? I've never been fellated by a condemned woman before, but the idea has a certain appeal. Imminent death is said to intensify sexual gratification."

For a split second the absurdity of her predicament overwhelmed her fear. "Hardly relevant to our situation, when it's my death, not yours, that's at issue."

"You refuse me?" Already aroused, he tugged down the flap of his trousers to free himself.

Miracle laughed. "Oh, I think so, though I'm also rather tempted—"

His teeth flashed white. He took her by both wrists to jerk her forward onto her knees. "You nasty slut! So I tempt you, do I?"

"—only to bite, if you force me." She smiled up at him, though his grip hurt, and the strength of fury washed through her blood. "After all, I have nothing left to lose, and you have so very, very little to offer."

The earl released her left wrist to swing back his hand. She was determined to defy him, but—as if her body refused to forget Willcott's earlier blows—her eyes flinched shut.

The blow never landed. Lord Hanley rocked back as the carriage jerked to a halt.

Miracle wrenched free and scrambled sideways. A blast reverberated into the night and another shot cracked past the window. Cursing, the earl fumbled to secure his trousers. In that one free moment Miracle dived for the pocket and grabbed the coach pistol.

A highwayman's cool tones cut through the night air outside like a blade.

"Stand and deliver!"

CHAPTER NINE

THE CARRIAGE ROCKED AGAIN. SOMETHING HIT THE ROAD. Without compunction, Miracle jabbed the pistol barrel under Lord Hanley's jaw.

The earl's fingers stiffened in place, leaving his shirt hanging from his waistband. "For God's sake! You wouldn't shoot me?"

A mad bravado soared in her heart. "Oh, I might. After all, what's one more murder, when a woman's already doomed to hang for the first? Leave your shirt alone! Keep your hands where I can see them!"

He raised his hands above his head and glared at her. "I'd never harm you."

"You already have."

Springs creaked as the coachman and his companions climbed down into the road.

"You refer to that business on the yacht? God! I intended—"

"Oh, hush, my lord! You would try to tell me that you were only playing games again just now, when you threatened me with your fist? Alas, I don't think the gentleman who's about to rob us is playing any games—and neither am I."

"For God's sake, let me have the pistol! Or do you want to be raped in a hedgerow by a ruffian?"

"Since I was about to be raped in a carriage by an earl, I

fail to see the difference. So I think I'll take my chances with the ruffian."

She flung open the carriage door and jumped down into the road, though she kept her weapon pointed at the earl's chest. The three servants stood grouped in a huddle by the hedge with their hands up. The coachman's blunderbuss lay in the road, as did the firearms that had probably been carried by the other two men.

A single horseman held them all at bay with two pistols. A black scarf covered his nose and chin. Beneath the shade of his hat brim, his gaze pierced like a knife point.

His horse pranced forward and stopped beside Miracle. He leaned down to gaze at her. "You seem very concerned about keeping the gentleman in the carriage in your sights, ma'am. Are you sure you're not about to change your mind and shoot me, instead?"

"That depends," she said, "on what your intentions are."

"My intentions are honorable, of course: a little theft, a little entertainment." He glanced into the carriage. "You will step down, my lord, still keeping your hands above your head. Pray, don't hesitate! My fingers are regrettably damp with nerves. Only too easy to squeeze the trigger accidentally."

His face like thunder, Lord Hanley climbed down from his coach.

"Your watch and purse, my lord. And that pretty cravat pin? Your rings? No, pray don't reach for them." The highwayman nodded to Miracle. "The lady will no doubt oblige. If she does not, I might shoot her, as well."

Her heart throbbing with a dizzy madness, Miracle relieved Lord Hanley of his valuables and handed them up to the horseman. He jerked his chin. She picked up the blunderbuss and pistols and threw them over the hedge.

"Thank you, ma'am. A very pretty watch, my lord, with a chain of gold, no less! And a pleasantly heavy bag of coins!" He thrust them into his pocket, then studied the earl's cravat pin. "I do believe this is a real diamond! Which makes me wonder: Why are His Lordship's trousers not buttoned up correctly? Is his valet that incompetent? Or has he hidden something even more valuable in his underwear?"

"You already have my watch and purse and jewelry," the earl said. "I've nothing else hidden."

"Except evil intentions toward this lady, perhaps? You will be pleased to remove your shoes, my lord."

Hanley's face turned black. "This is an outrage!"

"Well, so it is!" The mare backed a step as the highwayman gestured with a pistol. "You will still do it."

The earl sneered up at the rider. "Make me, sir!"

With the cadenced moves of a dancer, the mare side-stepped to pin the earl against the carriage door. The horse-man pressed the pistol barrel against Lord Hanley's temple.

"You don't know quite how close you are to losing your brains, my lord. As soon as this mare backs a step, you will do as I say."

The mare edged back. Shaking with rage, the earl kicked off his shoes. Mud squelched beneath his stocking feet.

The highwayman's aim remained steady. "A good start, my lord! But pray don't try anything foolish! My hand is beginning to shake at my own temerity. Any sudden, untoward moves and I'm afraid this pistol will fire. Your trousers, if you please."

His eyes glued to his tormentor, Lord Hanley snapped open his buttons. At a gesture from the highwayman he raised his hands above his head once again, and Miracle tugged his trousers down over his feet.

"Perhaps you would oblige me by checking the pockets, ma'am? Then you may toss His Lordship's shoes with his un-mentionables over the hedge."

Swallowing laughter, she did as he suggested. "There's nothing else."

"What, no more gold? No pocket pistol?"

"Nothing."

The horseman tipped his head. Lord Hanley's stockings were now soaked. "Perhaps your treasure is secreted in those nice linen drawers, my lord?"

"Devil take it, sir! Have you no decency?"

The highwayman laughed. "Not much! Though now that we've established that you have no hidden weapons, you may keep your undergarments. But only for the sake of the lady's outraged modesty, you understand."

One of the menservants sniggered, then bit his lip and stared off into space.

"You, sir!" The highwayman pointed one pistol at the servant. The man snapped to attention. "You will unhitch the horses and encourage them to leave."

A few minutes later the harnessed team careened away up the road, leaving the carriage behind.

The horseman bowed from the saddle. "So sorry to discompose you, my lord." He gathered his reins, as if about to ride away. "May I wish you and the lady a safe journey?"

Miracle stared at him with her heart in her mouth. *He would leave her here?*

The mare turned. Lord Hanley dived toward the coach and reached inside. He spun back with a pistol in his hand. Powder flashed. The mare reared. Shots reverberated in the lane. As Miracle's attention riveted on the horseman—his rearing mount, the smoking pistols in his hands—the earl whirled and hit out. The barrel of his discharged gun hit her hard on the wrist. The carriage pistol spun from her grasp.

She dived after it, but the earl rammed her aside and swooped to recover the only weapon that was still loaded. His fingers closed on the butt.

Spinning on her hind legs, the highwayman's horse knocked him aside. The earl scuttled for the safety of the coach as a shod hoof stamped down, pressing the gun into the mud. Dancing in place, the mare trampled it into uselessness.

"Come, ma'am!" The rider thrust his empty pistols into his saddlebags and reached down with an open palm. "You would appear to be at odds with your protector. Why not try your chances with me?"

Her heart thundering, Miracle stretched up to grasp his hand. The highwayman swung her onto the saddle in front of him. The mare sprang forward, spraying mud as the earl's servants ran to help their master.

The highwayman galloped his mount up the lane, then turned to dive into thick woods. Hoofbeats thundered as the mare dodged fast through the trees. Darkness enveloped. Branches whipped past. Encompassed in the highwayman's sure embrace, Miracle gasped for breath, then laughed.

They came out onto another road, then cantered across a field to pick up a narrow track that led them at last to a towpath. It was almost entirely dark now. The canal reflected a scattering of stars in a surface like ink. Miracle clung to the saddle as they thundered on into the night, then scrambled up a bank into another lane. At last the horse dropped to a walk.

Framed at the end of the hedgerows, Polaris shimmered like a faint white diamond in the northern sky, where Ursa Major, Cassiopeia, Cepheus, and Draco marked the seasons with their stately dance. Miracle tipped her head back into a warm, broad shoulder. More brilliant still, yellow Arcturus and luminous Vega marked the summer heavens high above like a blessing.

The night air washed over her face and eased deep into her lungs, carrying a poignant, bittersweet knowledge. She was rescued and in the same moment entrapped again. But surely her rescuer must now realize the reality of their relationship?

The mare arched her neck and pranced as if she were playing.

"I told you I might need a decent horse," Ryder said. "Are you all right?"

"I'm a great deal better for your rescue. Thank you."

His arm tightened around her waist. "Did Hanley hurt you?"

"No, though he was thinking about it. But didn't you notice? I had the pistol."

"Yes, I noticed and I'm very glad."

Miracle relaxed back against the warmth of his body and tried to dismiss her misgivings. "Though it was a close run thing—"

He seemed exuberant, filled with masculine power. "If I thought he'd laid a hand on you against your will, I'd ride back right now to beat him to death."

"Beat him to death?" Before she completely unraveled, she reached for levity. "You couldn't simply shoot him?"

"I've already emptied both pistols."

"Ah, the holes in his coach!"

His sudden laugh eased her heart. "When he took those shots at me, I was very tempted to further wound his self-importance, I admit. But since his aim went so wide of the mark, I let mine puncture his carriage door, instead. Those grand crests are very expensive to replace."

"Which will annoy Lord Hanley no end."

"That was—partly—the idea."

Miracle smiled up at him. She wanted to make amends to him for his stunning generosity, recover something of his mirth and his quixotic gallantry, whatever the cost to her heart.

"Stand and deliver?"

His dark eyes met hers. "Devil take it, I've wanted to say that ever since I was a boy."

"But to make the earl strip off his trousers and shoes, so he stood in his shirttails! How could you?"

He laughed again. "I was angry enough, in truth, to do a great deal more than that. However, my primary motivation was simply to delay his pursuit. Though his team is probably no more than a quarter mile up the road, it'll take time for Hanley to recover everything that you threw over that hedge."

Her personal misgivings paled in comparison to another reality. Miracle forced herself to voice it. "Yet he'll have the hue and cry out after Beauty, and she's very easy to recognize."

"Unquestionably. Even with my disguise, he must have known it was me."

"And his servants were witnesses to everything that happened. I know no one can touch a duke's son, not even for highway robbery, but surely it would still prove awkward?"

"If Hanley did anything other than demanding satisfaction over this escapade, he'd be a laughingstock. Yet it's a problem, of course, since—though I did my damnedest to make it look as if you were innocent of complicity—capital charges can still be pinned on you."

"Yes, and for previous crimes, as well as for aiding and abetting a highwayman." She shuddered as she remembered the earl's eyes. "You've saved me for now, Ryder, but we really should part company before Lord Hanley—"

"Nonsense!" he interrupted. "I don't give a damn for Hanley, and he has to catch us first."

"Then I surrender to your superior judgment."

Miracle said it lightly, but perhaps she really meant it. She was so tired of fighting: for survival, for trying to keep intact a core of compassion that was too often proffered in vain. All of her adult life she had struggled to protect the vulnerable emotions of some men, while suffering the callous disregard of others: something that Lord Ryderbourne, with his honor and gallantry, could never understand.

"Excellent," he said. "Then my judgment is that we travel on together for now, and devil take the hindmost."

She took a deep breath. "Where we are? We seem to be heading due north."

"Physically we're somewhere in Shropshire, I believe, though I've no idea where else you and I may be."

"Ah!" She glanced up at him. "So it comes to that!"

His gaze searched her face, as if he sought answers to a problem he could barely articulate. "I should have remembered that you never make love unless you want something. And thus I awoke to a fretting horse and nothing but another memory. Should I be annoyed at your flighty habits, or flattered to be the recipient of your professional attentions yet again?"

Her heart began to beat heavily, as if with an awareness that none of the answers she might ever give him would be enough. "If it's your choice to pursue, may it not be mine to flee?"

"Not when you fall straight into the hands of your persecutor."

She stared blindly at the sky and tried to strip her voice of emotion. "You're trying to protect a harlot who's murdered a gentleman. It's an endeavor that's bound to fail. Perhaps I wish to avoid your further entanglement in that inevitable final reckoning."

"What if I've decided the entanglement is worth it?"

"It's not."

"That's my decision to make." His voice had cooled, also, though obviously that control cost him some effort. "Though you used your seductive skills only to escape me, I can hardly claim not to have enjoyed them."

"Then I've been pursuing the wrong strategy, for now my debts to my knight errant are getting so deep that they can never be repaid."

"There are no debts." His arm tensed. The heat of his buried rage scorched over her body. "After all, you've been paying as you go."

The mare broke into a trot, heading uphill toward the stars, then back down into a hollow where a ford slicked like black ink over the road.

Miracle bit her lip. Why did she feel as if her heart were

breaking? Women like her didn't fall in love. They couldn't afford it. Meanwhile, this heir to a dukedom was trying to offer her his friendship and his protection. He would do so in vain, of course. But it was indeed his choice to make.

"You would prefer us to travel just as comrades once again?" she asked.

"God! My body derides the very idea, but I will not take part in this adventure simply from lust."

"Does your lust offend you so very much?"

"Not really, but I'm damned if I want your favors as payment. We share a mutual enemy. That alone is enough to justify my being here."

"Then you think I'm entirely mercenary?"

"Even if you are, perhaps I can simply purchase your time instead of your body, to be paid in cash when our adventure is over."

She stiffened. "I haven't asked for your gifts or your condescension. May I not take pride in my own autonomy? My brother Dillard has invested my savings for me for years. When I reach him, I'll have plenty of money. Travel on with me, if you like, but owe me nothing. I'll accept your company on those terms and no others, at least until the end of this journey."

"What if I decide that our journey never ends?"

"You won't. Like a magnet to a sword blade, Wyldshay will draw you home, and there's no escaping who I am and what I've done. So I'll throw in my lot with you until I reach my brother's house, but no further."

"Are all of your relationships with men negotiated clause by careful clause, like contracts?"

"Of course. What else would they be?"

He rode in silence for a moment, though she still felt the heat of his buried rage.

"Then you have my word on it," he said at last. "We're comrades. Now, since I have no desire to have Hanley catch up with us right now, perhaps we should give some thought to our present predicament." He eased Beauty back to a walk as they approached the black water. "We need to disappear."

"Yes, I agree. Lord Hanley went to some pains to remind me that he's feeling very much the avenging angel at the moment. And there was something else—"

"Something else?"

"He wanted to know what I'd done with my valuables. He seemed disproportionately concerned, as if he thought that I'd stolen something from him."

"And had you?"

"No, I—"

Beauty shied, then jolted to a halt, snorting. Ryder stiffened as if immobilized by ice, his spine rigid. Miracle clutched a handful of mane.

A man had materialized from the darkness to grab the mare's reins near the bit. The pistol in his other hand pointed at Miracle's heart.

A second footpad blocked the ford, light glinting faintly from the barrels of two guns clutched one in each fist.

A third man stood close by Beauty's rump, where Miracle couldn't quite see him.

"Sit tight," Ryder murmured to Miracle. "One of our new friends is pressing the point of a knife into the small of my back. We are, regrettably, surrounded."

"Get your hands up!" the man at the ford said. "No funny business."

Ryder let the reins slip through his fingers, surrendering control of the mare, and held both hands above his head. "Good evening, sir," he said calmly. "You would seem to have the advantage of us. You will, however, stand aside."

Doubt shimmered through the night air at the cool, crisp command in Ryder's voice. The footpad clutching the mare's reins seemed to shrink into himself, almost as if he might simply lower his weapon and leave.

But the man at the ford laughed. "Well, if it ain't His Fake Lordship! You never owned them woods and all them ruined pigsties, did you? You had no one there within earshot to help you, at all! You're just a scarecrow like us. Though you had me and Jeb fooled for a moment. What are you, an actor?"

"Something like that. But even though you're as bristling with weaponry as if you'd sprung fully armed from dragon's teeth, you will allow us to pass."

"Listen to him, lads!" The man stepped forward with belligerent bravado. "Name's Bruiser. You want to offer me a fight for the favor, Miss Molly?"

"If you like. However, I strongly recommend that you do as I suggest, Mr. Bruiser."

The ruffians' laughter betrayed a dangerously nervous edge, as if they privately feared that Ryder might hold some secret weapon to wreak terrible retribution.

Bruiser set his jaw and gestured with one pistol. "Get down! I won't say it a second time. Nice and easy, and keep your hands where I can see them."

"And if I don't?"

The man spat. "I'd shoot a fancy fellow like you, as soon as look at him."

"In that case," Ryder said, "we surrender."

Miracle glanced once at his face before she slid to the ground. Flat rage burned in his eyes. Yet he smiled at her, then with both hands still in the air, he kicked one leg forward over the mare's withers and dropped to the road. Beauty jibbed, but Jeb yanked the reins forward over her head and jerked her to a standstill.

"Get the valuables, Tom," Bruiser said to the man with the knife. "Jeb and I'll keep you covered, so this pretty cove don't try anything foolish."

"My dear sir," Ryder said. "I may have made mistakes in my life, but I've never done anything that foolish. You'll find my watch in my inside pocket, along with another that's not quite as fine, but far better than you deserve."

He stared impassively into space as Tom took his watch and small bag of coins, then Lord Hanley's watch and purse. The thief whistled when he discovered the diamond cravat pin, then he quickly dropped it into a pocket.

Meanwhile, Jeb had looped Beauty's reins over his elbow and was rifling about in her saddlebags. The mare stood quietly, only showing a little nervous white in her eyes as she surrendered to the clumsy handling. Ryder tried to send his mount a silent apology. The mare was just a lovely riding horse, athletic and sound and honest. She knew no more fantastic tricks with which to defend herself from these footpads than Ryder did.

Tom finished his search of Ryder's clothes, patting down his legs and checking his boots. Keeping the knife at the ready, he leered at Miracle. "And what about you, miss? Any pretty baubles hidden under those skirts?"

"A waste of time," Ryder said. "There's nothing else to be found on either of us, except more nails in your coffin."

The ruffian thrust the point of his knife beneath Ryder's jaw. "You want me to carve your heart out, Miss Molly?"

Miracle gave a dramatic sigh. "Then you're not going to search me, after all? Oh, sir! That's so very gallant!"

Tom lowered the blade to smirk at her. "Hark at that, lads! The lady don't know that Tom always saves the best for last."

"Stand still," Miracle hissed to Ryder. "Do nothing! They want only our money."

Ryder was hardly aware that he'd moved. Yet he had started to step between Miracle and Tom, only to stare into the barrels of the pistols. One more stride and he would have been either stabbed or gunned down.

He smiled casually and stepped back, though his hands clenched into fists as Tom began an unnecessarily thorough exploration of Miracle's clothes. Fire emanated from his bones to burn intensely in his veins. Afraid that his face must be marked by black lines of impotent rage, Ryder forced himself to gaze away into the darkness.

So much for his vaunted offer of protection! He was just a bloody useless aristocrat, after all, whose fighting experience had been limited to an occasional bout at Gentleman Jackson's, and a little practice at the firing range. Yet Miracle bore the groping fingers with a show of supreme indifference, somehow diffusing Tom's leering pleasure. At last the thief shrugged and turned away.

"Nothing on the mort!" he called to Bruiser. "A fair haul from the cove."

"Especially that diamond pin?" Ryder asked loudly. "The one that slipped into your pocket?"

Tom spun back, knife raised.

"Stop it!" Miracle hissed under her breath. "You'll not set them against each other. It won't work."

"If that oaf touches you again—"

"He did me no harm. Meanwhile, you're a keg of powder, almost too dangerous to be around."

"You've no idea how bloody dangerous I feel."

"Then take a deep breath," she whispered back, "and think about buttercups."

"Shut your traps!" Bruiser shouted.

Ryder almost laughed, though the tension threatened to lift off the top of his head. Whatever Miracle claimed, there was nothing to stop the thugs from shooting their victims and leaving them to die. There was nothing to stop them from first raping Miracle. The thieves had not bothered to conceal their faces. Why would they leave witnesses who could identify them?

Yet Ryder's brain was racing now. His only truly reliable attribute. He took a deep breath, but he did not think about flowers. He concentrated on his mare, her fine nostrils, her delicate ears.

Beauty had raised her head to stare back up the road. As Ryder focused on that bright sensitivity, he began to feel almost supernaturally alive, as if he could see in the dark, or hear the silent hum of the planets wheeling overhead. His rage began to dissipate as he seized on their one chance of survival.

The mare pulled back as Jeb spun about from his search of her saddlebags. "Look at this! The cove had pistols." He waved one at Ryder and laughed. "You're a pretty Cock Robin, ain't you? To travel along a road like this at night without bothering to reload 'em? Robbing a gabey like you is like taking a bottle from a baby."

"What else would you expect from a poor thespian?" Ryder asked. "As a certain gentleman of Verona once said: ' 'Tis the mind that makes the body rich.' Words, not action, are our gift."

"Then you'll have to sing for your next supper." Jeb guffawed at his own wit.

Ryder raised his brows in the exaggerated grimace of a fool. "Alas, although robbed of my paltry savings, I'm far too fine to arouse the sympathy of a crowd. Appearances are everything." He pressed one hand to his chest. " 'What, is the jay more precious than the lark, because his feathers are more beautiful?' "

"Hark at him go!" Jeb said.

Tom tossed his knife in his hand. "That's a damn nice jacket, ain't it? Nicer than mine."

"Then I'd be happy to give it to you, sir."

"You ain't doing the giving. We're doing the taking. Strip it off!"

It allowed Ryder a little free movement. It allowed him to delay a little longer. The music of the planets had begun to sound tinny, as if faraway brass pans were banging against iron pots. The sound was accompanied by a much deeper drumbeat in a oddly dislocated rhythm. Beauty quivered with alertness.

"You would *take* my jacket, sir?" Ryder asked. "But what's the virtue in a gift, if it's forced?"

"We ain't talking about virtue, Miss Molly! We're talking about theft."

Her brow furrowed, Miracle glanced sharply at Ryder's face. As the men laughed again, he bent his head to hear her frantic whisper: "I know you can fence and box, but for God's sake don't try anything against three loaded pistols."

He brushed her ear with his lips. His new alertness sang in his blood, as if Orion blew a distant trumpet. "Then you would be sad if I were shot?"

Her eyes widened, but only to reveal a cold, hard core of determination. "Very. You will not intervene, even if they rape me. I want your promise on that!"

"I won't promise any such thing, except that it won't come to that."

"Stop that whispering!" Bruiser said. "Take off the bloody coat!"

Ryder slipped off his jacket. "Here you are, sir, though I must warn you that this humble item of clothing will almost certainly prove the death of the wearer."

"Soaked in poison, is it?" The footpad laughed again, before he tossed his own ragged coat into the hedge and shrugged into Ryder's jacket. "Well, if that ain't a nice fit! Don't look half so humble on me!"

"What is this?" Miracle hissed. "Do you know other ways to fight—as your brother does?"

"Not at all! But listen hard! I don't believe I will need to defend your honor with my life, after all."

The jangle was closer now, accompanied by a distinct rumble and an arrhythmic trotting. It might mean succor, or it might mean more trouble, but it shifted the balance, at least for a few more minutes.

Beauty whinnied. Jeb jerked his head, then turned to stare back up the road. "Someone's coming!"

Still covering Miracle and Ryder with both pistols, Bruiser

retreated toward a gap in the hedge. "Come on, lads! That's enough. Bring the nag! She's worth more than all the rest put together."

"If you take my mare," Ryder said, "she will kill you."

The footpads glanced at each other as if shadows reached from the sky with the fingers of death.

"We ain't aiming to ride her, Your Fancy Lordship," Jeb said with open bravado. "We're aiming to sell her."

"I cannot impress this on you strongly enough," Ryder replied, his mind clear as crystal. "If you take that mare, you will hang."

"Oh, Miss Molly is fond of his pretty horse," Tom said in an odd singsong. "I'll bet he's even more fond of his pretty whore. What say we have a little fun, lads, as we go?"

The light of two lamps appeared like the eyes of a dragon at the top of the hill. The rumble differentiated into the sound of wheels and horses trotting fast. The metallic clanging grew louder, like the clash of a medieval battle.

"If you want the moll, bring her!" Bruiser shouted.

Tom tried to grab Miracle by the wrist. With more speed than he knew he possessed, Ryder grabbed a handful of gravel from the edge of the ford and threw it. The thief staggered back, roaring curses. Jeb spun around and raised his pistol.

Ryder seized Miracle around the waist and dived with her into the bank. The bullet roared past them to splash harmlessly into the stream, sending up a spurt of white water.

"Leave the wench be!" Bruiser raced up the bank. "Let's get out of here!"

Still cursing, Tom sprinted after him. Dragging the mare by the reins, Jeb smashed behind them through the dark gap in the hedge to be swallowed by the night.

His pulse rapid, Ryder stood up and offered Miracle his hand. "Not much of a knight errant, I'm afraid. You're all right?"

"Yes! Yes, of course." She scrambled to her feet, but she immediately turned away, as if to gulp in a clean breath of air. "I'm sorry about Beauty."

Ryder stared at her silhouette, as pure as a knife blade, then retrieved the footpad's jacket from the hedge and thrust his arms into the sleeves. "They won't hurt her. She's too valuable. And if Lord Hanley finds them—instead of us—because of her, our footpads are dead men."

"Yet your mare was your last link with home, wasn't she? Now you have no money, no weapons, and nothing left that identifies you as anything other than a wandering vagabond—and it's my fault."

Except for her assumption of blame, her perception was, as always, stunningly accurate. For the first time in his life he was entirely at the mercy of fate. It was a bloody uncomfortable feeling.

"It doesn't matter," he said.

"They almost shot you. It was madness to risk that."

"You really think I should have done nothing to prevent your being raped?"

She spun back and gestured angrily with both hands. "Rape isn't the end of the world, but do you think I'd have found it any easier to bear if you were already lying dead in the road?"

The light from the approaching lamps washed over her face. Ryder's heart contracted as if he had been struck. Long runnels of moisture tracked down her cheeks. With one furious sweep of her hand, she brushed them away, then she laughed at him.

"Yes, I'm weeping for you, you brave fool!"

For a moment it paralyzed him. He had no idea what to make of it, for now she was smiling as if she had never had a moment's disquiet.

In a grand cacophony of noise, a wagon came up and stopped. Another jangled up behind it.

Miracle curtsied to the newcomers, holding her skirts as if she wore a silk ball gown.

"How now!" The driver of the first wagon whistled between his teeth. "What have we here, lads? I thought I heard a shot."

The mouth of a blunderbuss yawned in the hands of the man who sat beside the driver. Both men's faces were shielded from the lanterns by a canvas awning stretched above their heads.

"I'd say this ford's a bad spot for footpads, Mr. Faber."

"And I'd say you were right, Mr. Faber."

Ryder swallowed a grin as he studied the wagon. Castle walls flickered in front of a fantastic forest. An entanglement of wooden swords, spears, and a barrel full of pikes thrust up toward the sky. As the horses shifted, the painted trees and stones rippled like images in a dream, and a row of silver shields and helmets jangled against a dozen swinging tin plates and some cooking pots.

Yet the strangers were well armed, and other heads had jostled up among piles of trunks and cases. Every pair of hands bristled with an assortment of weapons. With a series of clicks, the guns were cocked.

For the second time that night, Ryder raised both hands above his head.

"Our game has just taken an entirely unexpected new turn," he whispered to Miracle.

"Why, so it has!" She also raised her hands. "So let's play on and face the music! If they'll take us with them, I think we can hide very well in plain sight."

"You don't think Hanley would look for us among a troupe of traveling players?"

"Never!"

"What do you suppose the play is?"

"Apparently something that involves a great deal of martial bravado."

The wagon driver leaned forward into the light. Three turkey feathers impaled the crown of his hat. White hair fringed out beneath the battered brim like the petals of a daisy.

"Well, answer us, sir: Are you vagrants or villains?"

"Not villains—Mr. Faber, is it?—victims." Ryder lowered his hands and bowed. "You're quite correct about the footpads, sir. We've just been robbed of all we possess. Even my grandfather's watch: a loss that burns to my heart, though the wretched timepiece never kept very accurate time."

Mr. Faber's jacket seemed to have been pieced together from the trimmings of a quilt. "Left you nothing, eh?"

"Just our wits and our lives, sir, for which we are duly grateful."

The black gaze pierced as the driver squinted beneath his bushy white brows. "You've the voice of a gentleman, though I'd say that coat has seen better days."

"Perhaps not as interesting as the days seen by your own, sir?"

A woman laughed. "You may not be a thief, laddie, but I believe you're a damned rogue."

Ryder grinned at her. "A rogue who'd be grateful for a ride with your merry company, ma'am. And a meal, perhaps?"

The driver pulled his mouth into a lugubrious crescent. "We'll be hard pressed to feed our own mouths for the next few days. We've missed tonight's performance of *Hamlet* and we'll be canceling tomorrow's."

"After we already went to the expense of the posters," the woman said.

"—which will leave us as penniless as yourselves," a younger man commented from farther back in the wagon. "Worse, it'll leave us in bloody debt and selling up our horses, most like. We only have one night at each stop. For most of our audience, it's a once-a-year chance to see a play."

Ryder walked up to the team—two heavy draft animals with foreheads like blocks of limestone—and rubbed a shaggy gray neck. "Yet you seem to have most of Denmark on that wagon. What's the problem?"

"We're short three of our best players," the woman said. "I'm the queen, but we've no Ophelia."

"Horatio languishes in the cellar of an inn, where the innkeeper locked him up."

"And Fortinbras, who doubles as assorted other parts, broke his arm. He and Horatio got into a fight."

"And Ophelia?"

"Just had her seventh baby," the young man replied.

Ryder choked back his reaction, which was entirely inappropriate for the circumstances. "A lady in her ninth month was playing Ophelia?"

"Peggy makes a grand enough Ophelia when she's not in her cups, however many nippers she's had. The costume has plenty of drapes. But now we can't double up enough parts. Sam there"—the driver nodded toward the young man—"is the only one of the lads who can play a girl's part in a pinch, but he's Hamlet. So, no play and no pay, and another long stretch till the next square meal."

Miracle walked around the horses to stand directly beneath one of the lanterns. She smiled up at the driver with shining brilliance, the bones of her face as pure and clear as if she were very young.

" 'But, good my brother, do not, as some ungracious pastors do, show me the steep and thorny way to heaven—' "

"Good Lord!" the man with the blunderbuss said.

Her expression changed to betray a heartbreak so real that Ryder felt the cold touch of dread. She pulled a few odd leaves and stems of grass from her hair—acquired in her recent encounters with hedges and banks—then began to quote lines from another speech.

" 'They say the owl was a baker's daughter. Lord, we know what we are, but know not what we may be.' " She curtsied again, with every eye riveted to her face. "If you will help us, Mr. Faber, I can play Ophelia."

"Well, I'll be—!" the wagon driver said into the sudden silence. "That's better than the London stage."

"Which is where I learned it," Miracle replied.

"And your husband?"

"We're not married," she said. "This is my cousin, Mr. Devon. He could help with the props and—"

"—play Fortinbras, certainly," Ryder said. "And possibly some assorted other gentlemen, though Horatio might be a bit more than I could manage on such short notice."

Several members of the troupe clapped their hands.

Hiding his appreciation for the absurdity of the moment, Ryder managed to recall a few words spoken by Fortinbras at the end of the play.

" 'For me, with sorrow I embrace my fortune—' "

The wagon driver whistled again. "You'll make a damned fine Prince of Norway, sir. Anyone would think you were born to the part."

Miracle glanced up into Ryder's face, an odd quirk at the corner of her mouth.

He leaned close to answer the unspoken question. "Jack and I used to perform the plays for fun when we were boys. I can probably study up enough to remember most of the lines."

Hamlet climbed from the wagon and extended his hand. The youth was handsome, with bright blue eyes and a knowing smile. "Then it's our lucky day, sir! That innkeeper won't hold Horatio past tonight, so we expect him back in time for tomorrow night's performance."

"Then you'll take us with you?" Miracle asked.

The youth grinned at her, then turned back to Ryder. "But will I be allowed to kiss your pretty cousin, Mr. Devon?"

Ryder stared down at the younger man in genuine surprise. "I don't remember Hamlet kissing Ophelia anywhere in the play. Does he?"

"He does the way we perform it. The audience likes it."

"We don't play in theaters for the gentry," the woman explained. "Our performances are for country folk, in barns and inns and on village greens. They like something to take them out of themselves."

"Then why pick *Hamlet*?" Ryder asked. "Why not one of the comedies?"

"Because *Hamlet* has everything," Miracle said. "Passion, tragedy, buffoonery, love, insight, and a ghost—and almost everyone is dead at the end. So, of course, I'll be happy to kiss Hamlet. For a bed and a meal and a ride north, I'd kiss the ghost himself."

The young man laughed, seized her around the waist, bent her back in his arms, and kissed her. Miracle wrapped her arms about his neck and kissed back.

Ryder's gut clenched as if he'd been punched. He forced himself to relax his hands and look away, but cold fury boiled in his blood.

"Come on up and join us, Mr. Devon," the driver said, his shrewd eyes watching Ryder. "You've an honest face, sir, and your cousin will have the audience queuing in the streets."

It would never do to beat Hamlet to a pulp. Calling on as much ducal hauteur as he could muster, Ryder turned his back on the faithless Ophelia, and strode up to the wagon.

The driver thrust out his hand. "Robert B. Faber, sir, pleased to make your acquaintance. This fellow with the blunderbuss is my brother, William B. Faber. Bill plays Polonius to my Claudius." The dark eyes twinkled. "I like to play the villain, you understand. Hamlet there is my son, Sam: Samuel B. Faber." He jerked one thumb over his shoulder. And that's my wife, Mrs. Faber, back there, but all the lads call her Gertrude."

"You're very kind, Mr. Faber." Ryder shook the proffered hand and climbed into the wagon. "Larry Devon, at your service."

The driver glanced back at his son and Miracle.

"Come along with you, Sam!" Mr. Faber called. "Let the lass be!"

With the practice of a lifetime, Ryder feigned absolute in-difference. Yet anguish seized him by the throat when Sam took Miracle by the hand and led her back to the second wagon, where they disappeared from sight.

CHAPTER TEN

ℳR. Faber's traveling players camped in an open field on the edge of a village about five miles farther up the road. With practiced efficiency, the troupe set up tents and awnings. Ryder was offered a nook with part of the canvas castle for shelter. A snoring actor slept beside him. Though the players had already eaten, Mrs. Faber—otherwise known as Gertrude, Hamlet's mother—had earlier found some bread and cheese and handed him a mug of ale. Ryder suffered the generous hospitality in a hurt rage.

For God's sake! He was *jealous*? Of what? That Miracle was free with her favors? She was a member of the muslin company. She had never pretended anything else. She had been Hanley's mistress, and perhaps Dartford's and . . . God! The list was probably endless. Asterley? Lindsay Smith?

A knife slowly scored along the inside of his belly and carved a path of dull pain through his gut.

To resent it was insane, yet he was damned if he could sleep, knowing she was with the bright-eyed Sam.

As the camp settled into quietness, Ryder crawled unseen from the wagon and stalked away. Dark trees loomed, sheltering the inky eye of a small pond. With a similar blackness in his heart, he paced along the muddy bank.

He almost walked right into a wooden stile that blocked an opening in a hedge. His mouth full of bile, and the blade still gouging, he clenched his hands on the top rail and stared up at the remote brilliance of the night sky. Cloud veiled the horizon, but directly overhead a few stars glimmered brightly enough to penetrate the haze. The most brilliant must be Vega, heart of the Lyre.

Ryder stared blindly at its remote purity for a few moments, then closed his eyes. Was he simply putty in the hands of a ruthless temptress? For whatever high-minded reasons he kept concocting for this flit like a renegade across England, there was really only one: his fascination with a woman.

"I think I can just make out Altair," Miracle said softly. "The star that marks the eye of Aquila, forever flying home along the Milky Way. And see, there in the wing, is a star that grows brighter and dimmer every week, as if it smiled and frowned at us in turn. I don't know if it has a name of its own."

He spun about, choked. She stood in the shadow of the hedge, her face a pale glimmer surrounded by a cloud of black hair, as lovely, as treacherous, as any dryad from myth.

"Damn you!" he said. "Damn you!"

"Ah," she replied. "Condemned unheard, like Desdemona?"

"The wrong play. We're acting out a farce, not a tragedy. But if I'm to be cast as the fool, may I not play a little, as well?"

"Only at the risk of getting burned."

Rage flared painfully in his skull. "You're the one pouring oil on the flames."

"Am I? Then, by all means, let's burn!"

She laughed in open defiance as she stepped into his arms, all softness and welcoming female curves. Her back bent, pliant beneath his hands. Her neck and jaw slid perfectly into one open palm. Mad with grief, Ryder tipped back her head and crushed his mouth down onto hers, as if desire could negate the void of resentment.

Her tongue met his in a velvet embrace, hot and generous. He groaned into her mouth and thrust her up against the stile. Her arms wrapped about his neck. He ground his pelvis against hers, his erection mocking his resolutions. Her fingers strayed into his hair. Her scent tormented. When he broke the kiss in an agony of self-reproach, she sighed as if her heart were breaking. *Ah, Miracle!*

"It's all right," she said softly. "It's all right to be consumed by fire. I know that you think you're in love with me."

"Do you?" Desperately he searched her face. "But what if it's true, Miracle?"

Her gaze was soft, and open, and candid. "I know. Men often think so. But this time perhaps I think I'm in love with you, too, my dear fool. It's all right. We'll get over it. But now we are here and hungry and we want each other. There's no need to deny ourselves."

He was past argument. He was perhaps past quite comprehending everything she had just said. She wriggled back to prop herself on the stile with her feet supported by the steps, then pulled him forward between her legs.

Ryder dropped his head to nuzzle her warmth through the thin fabric of her dress. Buttons snapped open beneath his seeking fingers. Cotton and linen slid away. Her naked breast, warm and round and smooth, exactly fit his palm. Her nipple hardened, responding to his hungry tongue.

Almost frantically he tugged up her skirts. Her thigh was satin delight, female and soft beneath his palm. His thumb strayed over curls and dampness. The intensity of his arousal almost overwhelmed him: that pulsing surge of desire and pleasure and hot anticipation.

He raised his head to kiss her again, little kisses over her collarbone, all the way up her long throat to her ear, over her lovely jaw to the compliant promise of her lips. Kissing back, she wriggled against him and unfastened the flap of his trousers. Her fingers cupped his naked flesh with blissful honesty, unambiguous and skilled. Her tongue ravished his. Her arms slipped about his neck. He lifted her in both hands so that her thighs wrapped about his waist. She rocked her pelvis against his, and moist, indulgent heat encompassed his erection.

He moaned against her mouth. She tipped her head back and slid down. He thrust hard, dropping his head to her shoulder as his arms supported her weight, suckling the fascinating curves of her neck and earlobe. He felt scorched by her stunning generosity, that she was brazenly working for his pleasure: the male ecstasy, impetuous and direct.

Miracle felt so right! So damned, bloody *right*! He reveled in her loveliness and her munificence, every fiber and sinew dedicated to loving this one woman with all the confusion and tenderness that was tearing him apart.

He cried out when his powerful contractions obliterated his awareness. Strong tremors ran through his blood like aftershocks. Gasping for breath, he laughed for sheer joy.

He opened his eyes to see a matching rapture flood Miracle's face, transforming her for that instant into the embodiment of everything he longed for. Carrying her with him, he sank to both knees, then lay back on the grass. Warm and soft, she sprawled on top of him, panting gently in his ear.

Her lips pressed tiny kisses over his jaw. Almost as if she loved him. Almost as if she was moved, as he was, to the soul.

An aching tenderness burned in his blood, as if this intensity of contentment could scorch away all doubts. He smoothed her hair away from her ear, then ran a hand down her fluid spine, reveling in each curve of soft flesh.

Slowly, slowly, the world eased back into focus. The haze had thinned. The Milky Way cast its long silver net across the heavens, catching stars like fish.

"Did you make love with him, too?" he asked at last.

She pushed up on one elbow. "With pretty Hamlet?"

Ryder nodded, unable to articulate more. She rolled aside to rearrange her skirts. Swallowing the agonizing sense of loss, he sat up and put his clothes to rights, also.

"Would it make any difference, if I said that I had, or had not?" She scrambled to her feet and stared down at him. "Would you believe me?"

A sudden bitterness threatened to wipe away all memory of joy. "Of course, Sam could never have afforded your fee, could he? So I suppose you did not."

Miracle longed to smooth the thick hair back from his forehead. She wanted to massage his broad shoulders, hunched now in reproof. Instead, she looked away, before she, too, touched him with overwhelming tenderness as well as passion.

She had never made love like this before in her life. Physically, yes, of course. But to feel that a man had flooded her barren womb with gathered starlight? That a lover cared so deeply for her pleasure? That he might really believe that he loved her?

God help her that she was so desperately, painfully in love

in return! Even angry, even hurt, Ryder was only passionate and caring—and more magnificent than he knew. She felt terrifyingly vulnerable, as if fate must demand an inevitable retribution for her foolishness. She no longer knew how to protect him, or herself. She no longer knew any way to save them both from disaster. Meanwhile, it was doing him no kindness to pretend to be worse than she was.

"I don't always get paid," she said steadily, even if it wounded him. "If I choose, sometimes I have sex with a man simply from fancy."

He stiffened for a moment, but then he stood up with arrogant carelessness and stretched. "Then why have you insisted all along on my paying you?"

She was shivering, though she wasn't cold. This was, perhaps, more than she could bear. "Maybe because you can afford it."

To her immense surprise, he laughed. "Not anymore, Miracle. The footpads took everything, remember? I was proved to be a veritable Miss Molly, as charged."

"It was an insult, that's all."

"Of a particular kind." His voice was dry, almost amused, with no self-pity, though colored by a certain inherent self-condemnation.

"They meant nothing by it," she said.

He sat down on the stile steps, his expression lost in shadows. "They meant something very exact by it, as you well know."

She spun about. "Is that what you tried to negate just now? The charge that you're effeminate, a sodomite? It's obviously nonsense!"

He tipped his head back, throwing his profile into perfect relief. "I'm just stating the facts as I see them and drawing the rational conclusions. This wasn't the lesson that I hoped to learn from this journey, but it's hard to avoid. Stripped of the power of my position and judged as men generally judge each other, I have very little to offer. I don't resent it, but Jack could have fought off those footpads with his bare hands and laughed while he did it."

She wasn't even sure where to begin. "They had pistols and knives and the advantage of natural brutality," she said. "I would rather you were a live man than a dead hero, Ryder. I'm traveling with you, not your brother."

"Not by choice!"

"Why do you think your brother's prowess—or lack of it—matters a damn to me? When you provoked Tom into taking your jacket, do you think I didn't realize that you were delaying deliberately? That I didn't hear the horses coming and guess exactly what you were doing? You saved our lives!"

"Yet Jack would have stopped to reload his pistols at the first opportunity and thus avoided all the rest before it even began."

"You couldn't reload right away. It was vital to escape Hanley as quickly as possible."

"I was careless. Which brings home another truth that I've been rather desperate to avoid. As you surmised from the beginning, I've never traveled before without an entourage of armed servants. No footpads or highwaymen would ever try to stop a St. George's coach. If—in spite of my warnings to you—I felt invulnerable, that shows an insufferable arrogance, doesn't it?"

"Perhaps. Or perhaps you're just in the habit of too much analysis."

He reached out to catch her by the hand, then spun her to sit on his thigh—like a lover. "No, don't try to diminish the importance of this, Miracle. I was staring death directly in the face. Not only mine, but yours. I hadn't realized quite how much this adventure had begun for me simply as something of a game. When Tom threatened you, it became only too real. I owe you an apology for that."

"Yet you outwitted them in the end, and you rescued me from Lord Hanley." She laid her head on his shoulder and leaned back into his arms. "At that moment I knew that you wore three stars at your belt. I knew Sirius the Hunting Dog might run up from the hidden sky to trot forever at your heels. I don't care if your brother has two heads and five arms and the strength of Hercules himself. You're my Sir Galahad."

His lips pressed softly on her forehead. "If I am, what this stile witnessed just now has certainly cost me the Grail. Not a very good example of godly purity! Yet it was only chance that I wasn't entirely helpless against those footpads. And as a lover, I'm doubtless less skilled than any of the men in your past—"

"No," she interrupted. "Don't say that! That's not what's at issue."

"Yes, it is."

She reached up to kiss him again, quickly. "I didn't make love with Sam, Ryder. Not because he couldn't pay me. Not even because he in fact shares his bed with Rosencrantz. But because I've pledged myself only to you since this journey began, even if I break my heart over it."

He sat in silence, rubbing his cheek against her hair. The small rustles of the night whispered across the field.

"And mine," he said at last. "Jealousy would seem to be another surprise gift of this journey. I felt almost mad with it, another sin caused by lack of faith."

"It was natural enough in the circumstances."

He drew her close, keeping her warm and safe in his embrace. "You think I had any rights to such an ugly emotion?"

"No one has a *right* to jealousy, though all of us feel it eventually. People don't own each other. Just as duke's sons don't fall in love with ladies of the night, females who have neither hearts nor souls."

He buried his face in the curve of her neck. His lips touched just below her ear. "That's a bloody barbaric statement, Miracle. Though I've no idea what to do about it, I'm in love with you. It's neither minor nor trivial for me to say that."

She pulled away from him and stood up. If a woman ran full tilt toward a cliff, how could she complain when she plunged over the edge? Every bit of fluff knew exactly what her protector's protestations of love really meant. After all, she had heard them before.

"But even if it's true, you can only be in love with a fantasy. You don't really know me."

"That can be rectified."

"What do you want to know?"

He leaped to his feet and strode off a few paces. "How you can say that you have no heart, when it's so obviously not true?"

She glanced up at his careless male beauty, trimmed in starlight. "It is true, because it has to be. We ladies of the night content ourselves with a farce, a play at love, a clearly limited barter of the body's natural bounty in exchange for room and board, a few gifts, and perhaps a little educated company."

"Yet what a cold-hearted arrangement for something so profoundly warm and human! I want to give you so much more than that."

"Yes, I do believe that you think that you love me at the moment, Ryder. But in the end, every protector tires of his mistress and walks away. 'I'll give her a pretty bauble,' he'll say to his friends, even when it's a damned diamond necklace."

"I'm aware, of course, of the social expectation in such situations." His tone was restrained.

Miracle spun away, determined to hammer at the truth. "And of course she takes it, which allows him to salve his conscience—if he has one—with the belief that she was only after his money all along. After all, she's a fallen woman, a soiled dove—ugh, what an obnoxious expression!—so obviously she's mercenary and heartless at the core, without morals or values or even any real desire, except for money. That's what your friends say and what you believe, too, Ryder, in your heart of hearts."

"I've never kept a mistress. I don't know."

The force of his male power beat at her defenses, as if she stood unprotected in the path of a storm. "Yet you thought you simply felt jealousy? Deny, if you will, that the thought of my past repels you, however much you keep trying to ignore it. At heart you esteem only purity and innocence. Thus you agonize over your desires and drag guilt and moral superiority in equal measure into every erotic encounter."

"Perhaps." He folded his arms and leaned back with careless arrogance against the trunk of a tall elm. "However, I began this journey prepared to learn something new. Did you?"

She turned her back to gaze out at the dark, sleeping world. It was easy for any gentleman, even one so profoundly honorable as Ryder, to fancy himself in love with the lady of the moment. It was an absolute disaster for a harlot to allow herself to fall in love in return.

"Why should I change? I've learned the truth about men throughout many bitter years."

"You would condemn all of society? And half of humankind?"

"Yes, on the whole—simply for the hypocrisy of it all."

Ryder walked up to set both hands on her waist. She allowed him to do it, to use his warmth and strength to shield her from the cool air rising off the night grasses, even if he could not shield her from herself.

"If a female trades her body for money," he said in her ear, "she can hardly complain when the world sees her as mercenary."

Miracle dropped her head forward and closed her eyes. "No, she can't. So she'd better secure every bauble she can get, for one day she'll no longer be pretty enough to attract another protector. Then, if she's been too fine in her scruples, she'll be an old woman begging at the side of the road. She may even watch as the man she once loved passes in his carriage, taking his respectable wife to the opera, where he once noticed a girl dancing and fancied her in his bed."

His breath faltered, as if his heart stopped for a moment. "Did you love any of those men, Miracle?"

Her fingers gripped the damp wooden rail. "One or two of them, when I was younger. But believe it or not, there haven't been that many. Even a member of the muslin company can sometimes pick and choose. I've been lucky."

He tipped her face up to his with one hand. "I think I understand—most of it, anyway. Yet, if the choice was yours, why did you pick Hanley?"

Miracle turned her head aside, letting his fingers slip down to her neck, knowing that this duke's son would condemn her in the end, knowing that he would then leave her, just like all the others.

"Precisely because I knew that I would never fall in love with him. And, of course, he promised to be generous."

"You'll never have to face poverty again," he said. "I promise!"

She pulled away and laughed. The summer night was too seductive. Because she loved him, she had told him the truth. It wasn't fair to either of them. Time to retreat, to find a safer basis for their relationship.

"And perhaps I'll never have to face old age, either, if Lord Hanley catches up with me."

"He won't. But there's something else that's been bothering me. Before our journey was so inconsiderately disrupted by Bruiser and his friends, you were telling me that Hanley had just accused you of stealing from him?"

"Well, not exactly. But after I left the yacht, he searched my bags and I can't imagine why."

"Neither can I. He also ransacked your rooms in Blackdown Square."

She stared up at him, stunned. "He searched my rooms? When?"

He gazed down at her beneath contracted brows, an angry tilt to his mouth. "After you left him in Dorset. What the devil was he looking for, Miracle?"

"I've no idea! Are you sure?"

"Hanley cut open your mattress, ripped into your dresses, smashed vases, tore the books from their cases. Your maid tried to put it all back to rights, but yes, I'm certain."

Deep tremors shook their way up her body. "He was very angry with me, even before I left. That morning in Exeter he seemed consumed by jealousy—"

"Which was how it looked at first glance, or was meant to look. Yet it was not simply the work of a man hurt and enraged at the loss of a mistress. He was searching for something that he thinks you have, or had, perhaps."

"But I have nothing of his, except for the jewels he gave me. Surely he would not want to take them back?"

"I don't know. God, it's late! We both need our sleep. Yet, if you can bear it, I think you must tell me exactly what happened in Dorset, before you were cast adrift in that dinghy. Tomorrow?"

"Tomorrow," she agreed, grateful for the consideration that allowed her a night's reprieve. The image of Lord Hanley slashing up her bed with a knife was going to haunt her dreams. "And, yes, I can bear it—though I doubt if I'll sleep much tonight after what you've just told me."

"Neither will I," he said. "Though perhaps for different reasons."

Miracle thrust her anxiety aside and smiled as she gestured toward the camp. "Meanwhile, Mr. Faber's company is sleeping like a baby, in spite of the disaster of missing tonight's performance."

"Thanks to Ophelia's fecundity! But they'd anyway planned

to stay here tonight. In the morning the troupe heads north toward Buxton, and tomorrow night the play will be performed in a barn near a village called Hulme Down. You still wish to play Ophelia?"

"Why not? We might as well travel north with the Fabers as far as that, at least, and if they give us their food and their protection, we must do our best to save their play for them, as well."

His gaze was disturbingly perceptive, but he laughed. "You think the play can be saved? I have certain misgivings about *Hamlet*'s being performed as a farce."

She struck a dramatic pose. " 'Oh, what a noble mind is here o'erthrown!' "

"Instead, I could borrow a horse from that farmhouse down there to ride into the nearest town to demand all the rights and considerable privileges of my position."

Her renewed fear made it tempting: to let him fetch a carriage and horses to speed her to Dillard's house—and straight into another encounter with Lord Hanley?

"We can't let the Fabers down."

He raised a brow. "You would risk discovery, simply for the sake of one more bad performance of *Hamlet*?"

"We gave our word, Ryder."

"Yes, I'm aware of that."

She felt frantic to convince him, though she knew she was only trying to find rationalizations for herself. She had always tried to live by a code of honor—yet this time it might indeed be at risk of her life.

"It would anyway take you some time to arrange other transportation, and meanwhile, Lord Hanley will never think to look for us among the traveling players. There'll be no one in the audience tomorrow night except locals, and we'll be in costume. Obviously we'll do as little as we can to attract attention otherwise."

"Which is the only reason why I'm agreeing to this insanity."

"I'll put myself at your disposal after the performance to travel in any way that you wish. I promise."

He took her hand and turned it up, then traced the curves and hollows with one finger, as if he might find the secret of the Gordian Knot written in her palm. Heat spread from his touch, as if her veins soaked up sunlight.

"And meanwhile our play will go on?" he asked lightly.

"I don't think we can escape it," she said. "You've certainly made plenty of dramatic entrances and exits in my life so far."

His pulse throbbed against hers as he closed his fingers. "It's not only the play that I can't escape, but the passion. Whatever the consequences, I cannot fight that any longer, Miracle."

She searched his dark gaze, pinned by her heartbreaking need to be honest—simply because he was too fine to be lied to?

"No, a dark thread of desire binds us at the moment. Yet you mustn't forget—in fact, I promise it will be the only thing that matters in the end—that I'm a lady of the night. I'm good at it. That's what I am."

"No," he replied with absolute certainty. "That's what you've done. It's not who you are."

She slipped her fingers from his and walked away. "Whereas you're exactly what your birth made you. You were wrong when you said you'd be nothing if you were stripped of the power of your position. That power is who you are. You can't shed it, any more than you can shed your skin."

"I'm going to be a duke, whether I like it or not."

"And you like it."

"I'd better," he said. "A title isn't something one may renounce. I have responsibilities to thousands of people besides myself. Material assets come with the position, of course, but only if I husband them."

"Whereas my destiny was to scrabble for every penny from the day I was born. If we'd met under different circumstances, you wouldn't have hesitated to set me up as your mistress. You'd have done so expecting to tire of me eventually. And since you're an extremely wealthy man, I'd have driven the hardest bargain I could manage."

"So what's happened instead?"

A fox ran, loping across a far hillside, head turned for an instant as if the animal looked directly into her heart.

"Nothing that can be allowed to matter," she said.

He caught her hand again and spun her to face him. "We shan't solve it tonight. Come, let me escort you back to Hamlet's wagon!"

"Alas, he and Rosencrantz like their privacy. So I'm sharing with the Fabers, who are past the age of any such nonsense."

Ryder brought her knuckles to his mouth and kissed them. "Really? I don't believe there's any male alive who would agree to that statement."

She laughed and kissed his fingers in turn. Hand in hand, they walked back across the dark field to the camp. Miracle stood on tiptoe and kissed him once again on the mouth, using every ounce of her control to keep it light and friendly, though contact only fanned the flames. Before he had time to regret his resolutions, she slipped inside the largest tent.

Ryder stood for a long time staring up at the Milky Way, before he strode away to his wagon and crawled back into his empty bed.

His hot craving for the gifts of her body would sear him for the rest of his days. He had never before lived every moment of every day with this crackling erotic spark charging every breath. Yet Miracle possessed an extraordinary strength of mind, as well, along with a bright intelligence and audacity that had allowed her to survive, even flourish, in a world he knew to be cruel.

She knew she was taking a risk to take part in the Fabers' play, yet she would do it simply because she had given her word. And—God! It must have taken all the courage she possessed to be so honest with him.

The obvious solution—if he could only somehow clear her of the charge of murder—was, of course, to make her his mistress.

Yet something in him still rebelled at the thought—that to use her in such a way would inevitably demean her? The dread that she was right in her judgment about men and would prove him to be no different from all the others, after all? Or simply that she would in the end demonstrate that she was more honorable than he?

Meanwhile, what was he really risking? The Duke of Blackdown's privileged elder son with all the wealth and power of the St. Georges at his fingertips?

Whatever he wished to the contrary, Miracle was right: He could guarantee her nothing, not even himself.

THE next morning's journey allowed them no privacy at all. Miracle laughed and joked with the other players in the second wagon, while Ryder rode with Mr. Robert Faber in the first one. It was some time since he had read *Hamlet*. If he was to play Fortinbras and other assorted gentlemen, he must learn his lines. Yet he kept looking up from the book in his hand as other characters' words burned in his mind.

Doubt thou the stars are fire; Doubt that the sun doth move; Doubt truth to be a liar; But never doubt I love.

As they crossed into Derbyshire, the landscape began to look familiar. If he strode into any bank in any of the nearby towns, Lord Ryderbourne could replenish his empty pockets. If His Lordship sent a message to Wrendale, he would have a carriage and servants immediately at his disposal to take Miracle straight to her brother's house.

Yet he said nothing. He agreed with Miracle that they were temporarily safe from Hanley's pursuit. They certainly owed the Fabers that night's performance. And these might be his last days and nights with the woman who had turned his world upside down.

It was as if she had lit a slow fuse in his heart. Whenever he glanced at her, his pulse quickened. If he allowed himself memories of their lovemaking, the explosive flames of passion would consume him. Yet images of her face and her quicksilver laugh stirred him just as profoundly, and sent a deeper, hotter fire burning into his soul.

He tried to force himself to see reality.

Miracle had purchased not only a horse and saddle with her body that first night in Brockton. She had also purchased his silence and his cooperation. Why else had she seduced him with such stunning expertise? She had known that once he had shared her bed, he could never allow himself to become the agent of her destruction.

Give me that man that is not passion's slave, and I will wear him in my heart's core—

How seriously, even now, was he fooling himself? After all, as soon as she'd no longer needed him, she'd only wanted him to leave.

"Cousins," Mr. Robert Faber said, his eyes twinkling. "It's none of my business, Mr. Devon. But cousins?"

Ryder looked up. *Lord Hamlet is a prince out of thy sphere. This must not be.*

"Ho hum!" Mr. Faber scratched at his chin. "I've seen

much of the world in my day, sir, and I know when a man is in love with a woman. Yet he doesn't usually pretend that they're cousins."

Ryder closed the copy of *Hamlet.* "You wish to offer any other observations, Mr. Faber?"

"Ha! You won't browbeat me with that haughty air, sir! You're no more Mr. Devon than I'm the King of England. In fact, I'd say you're the kind of man who could normally crack open the world like a nut to take whatever he wants. And so I ask myself: Why not this time—and with a woman as lovely as Aphrodite? But then, I suppose—if she can slay the audience tonight as well as she's slain you—it's not my concern."

"Exactly," Ryder said. "Though I shake in my boots at your perspicacity, sir."

Mr. Faber winked and whipped up his team. "You never shake in your boots at anything, if I read you aright, Mr. Devon. But whatever your secrets, they're safe enough with this company."

The horses broke into a ponderous trot. Ryder laughed and returned to his study of the play.

By late afternoon the wagons had begun the climb up toward the heart of Derbyshire. A small drizzle eased away across the hills. A watery sun sparked gilt highlights in the rattle of shields and pikes and helmets. As the horses leaned into their collars, most of the younger players jumped down from the wagons and started to walk.

Ryder strode back to find Miracle. She glanced up from her conversation with Sam. They were talking about the play. The actor smiled at Ryder as he joined them.

"There's a shortcut," Sam said, pointing. "That path over the hill up there cuts off a couple of miles. We'll rejoin the wagons on the other side at an inn called the Jolly Farmer. See you there!"

He ran off after Rosencrantz, who had already set off up the path. Miracle and Ryder dropped behind the rest of the troupe, where they could be private.

"You want to know about Dorset," she said after a moment.

"After what we discussed last night, I think I have to know

now." He took a deep breath and looked away, before he should be tempted to touch her.

Damp had soaked into her hair, tied back carelessly in a ribbon, so that small wisps rioted about her face. Sunlight smoothed over her cheek, where the bruises had faded to a soft shade of ocher. Though her sensual loveliness fired his most primitive cravings, something in the depths of her eyes radiated an extraordinary compassion and serenity. Was that the source of his deepest yearnings? That she seemed to know exactly who she was and accepted it?

"Why have you refused to tell me before?" he asked.

"Because whatever you think you understand about me, what I'm going to tell you now will only further upset it."

"No, it won't," he said. "Try me. Just begin at the beginning and don't stop until you get to the end."

She stopped for a moment, gazing up the path. The dull shadow of distress darkened her eyes and settled at the corners of her mouth. A distress that kisses would not cure.

"Lord Hanley had been my protector for some months when I agreed to accompany him to Exeter. He'd bought a new yacht there. Not just a small sailing boat, but a seagoing craft that was fitted out to rival the King's. We were to sail together to the Isle of Wight, where he'd promised me a house for the summer. Yet when we reached Exeter, we were joined by Philip Willcott."

He tried to keep his voice dispassionate. "You'd met Willcott before?"

Picking up her skirts, she started back up the path. "Occasionally. Lord Hanley sometimes brought him to my house in London, though I made no secret of my dislike of the man. Something about him made my blood run cold."

Ryder followed, staying one step behind her. Her neck seemed very fragile beneath the weight of bundled hair.

"I've never heard of him. What kind of person was he?"

"Not the kind one would expect to be the bosom friend of an earl, certainly." She stepped around a small puddle. "A lump of coal trying to be mistaken for a diamond, and filled with resentment that his fate was always to be fuel for someone else's fire, when he longed to decorate tiaras, instead. Perhaps he hoped that intimacy with Lord Hanley would give him enough superficial shine to impress, though he would always remain black at the core."

"I know the type. Why did he come to Exeter?"

"I don't know. I was barely civil to him. I went up to bed. He and the earl sat up late in a private parlor in the inn, drinking together."

"You've no idea what they were talking about?"

She glanced back at him with a kind of wry bravado. "Only that in the depths of some wine-soaked discourse, Lord Hanley promised Willcott that they would share my favors later that night. The earl sent me up a message to that effect, so that I could make myself ready."

"To *share* your favors?" His step faltered. "For God's sake!"

Her lips curved in a kind of painful, ironic mirth. "It's never been your fantasy to share a lady's bed with a friend?"

"No!"

Her head turned away as if she swallowed laughter. "Ah, Sir Galahad! The innocent abroad! Perhaps you prefer the idea of two ladies sharing your bed, instead?"

Heat flooded his body, as much discomfort as outrage. "Is this what it means—?"

"To be a courtesan to the English aristocracy?" She marched ahead, her skirts lifted in both hands. "It often enough means things that you obviously can barely imagine."

"I'm not quite such an innocent," he said. "Much to my regret, my imagination is in perfect working order."

She shaded her eyes with one hand as she turned to look back at him. He couldn't read her expression, but her stance was defiant.

"Then don't imagine too much. Within certain obvious limits, I've always dictated my own terms. I'd already made it clear to Lord Hanley that Willcott was never to be part of our bargain. When I received the earl's message, I dressed, came down, and said so."

Relief was too mild a word. Something very close to elation surged in Ryder's blood. In three strides he had joined her, and they started up the path again.

"I can certainly imagine that Hanley was . . . annoyed?"

"I felt some annoyance of my own."

"In fact, you were furious?"

Miracle nodded. "A little righteous anger always helps one to be brave. Yet Lord Hanley simply shrugged and told his friend to leave. Willcott bowed and called for his horse. The earl and I went up to bed. That should have been an end of it. Yet I felt—I don't know—this bizarre intensity in their exchange. I was unnerved. Then when we reached our room, I thought the earl seemed—"

He kept his tone as gentle as he could. "You were afraid of him?"

She shivered and hugged herself. "At that moment I was terrified. Though he'd pretended not to care when I rejected Willcott, Lord Hanley was very deeply angry about it. I was afraid of what he might do in the grip of that rage, so that night I pretended that nothing was wrong."

His fists closed involuntarily. Ryder felt as haunted as any man facing martyrdom. "You made love?"

"What we did in bed together isn't relevant."

"But Hanley was still your protector."

"Yes, of course. However, I never share with other gentlemen what happens in the bedroom."

He felt as if he had been kicked in the belly: wretched that he wanted to know, wretched that he had been cad enough to ask, wretched that she was having to relive this.

The path just ahead led past a cluster of ruins: the remains of a small keep, abandoned hundreds of years earlier. The stone walls perched on a rocky outcrop, where water coursed down through a deep gorge from the sudden swell of the Peaks just ahead. Miracle spun aside from the path to run under an arched doorway into the grassy inner bailey. A spiral stair led up to the top of the ruin. She raced up to the crumbling battlements.

Ryder stared up at her for a moment, her slim figure silhouetted against the wash of clouds and blue sky. She shook as if she were being buffeted by a strong wind. He took the steps two at a time.

"I shouldn't have asked," he said. "I'm sorry."

She shook her head and sat down on a chunk of stone, then wrapped her arms about both knees. Her profile was pure steel as she gazed out across the countryside. Filled with distress at his helplessness to change the past, or to save her from having to remember it, Ryder propped his hips on a broken merlon.

"The next morning the earl barely allowed me out of his sight," she said. "His mood was very black. I'd never seen him like it before. I didn't dare to defy him openly. He was a man enraged, taking solace in a favorite possession, holding on to my arm with a death grip. To have tried to leave him then would have meant making a public scene in that grand inn in Exeter. I thought he'd never forgive me for that."

"So you boarded the yacht together?"

"Yes. Before sailing to the Solent, we were to make a detour to spend a few days in Lyme Regis. I thought I would escape him more easily there."

"After dulling his suspicions?"

"If you like. Yet before we reached Lyme, Willcott came aboard secretly in the middle of the night. I went up on deck to see the stars and discovered him there, drinking with Lord Hanley. I knew then that I should have walked out in Exeter, whatever the cost, but it was too late."

Ryder dropped down beside her. Almost blindly she reached out to seize his hand. Her pulse echoed the broken rhythms of his, as if they weathered a storm together.

"Hanley was drunk?"

"I don't believe so. Yet Philip Willcott was, certainly. They'd already decided to go forward with their original bargain, whether I was willing or not."

Fear and pain for her ached in every muscle. "I wish I didn't have to ask this, Miracle, but I must know what happened next."

"Ah, don't worry! It's not so very bad." She squeezed his fingers and turned to smile at him. Her dark eyes were filled with courage and defiance at the world. "Probably nowhere near as bad as you've been fearing. Willcott tried to rape me, but he didn't succeed."

"You fought him?"

She released his fingers and rose to pace along the battlements. "Like a demon! He dragged me down to the cabin, but I was filled with cold fury and a blazing determination to outwit him, or at least to give as good as I got."

"And Hanley?"

"Lounged in the doorway and watched. His eyes were as sharp as needles as Willcott tore away my dress, but he seemed otherwise turned to stone. I don't think he was even particularly aroused by it."

"*Aroused* by it? For God's sake!"

Miracle spun about to face him. Revulsion marked every line of his face. Ryder was so fundamentally decent and honorable. Had he never—living next to the stars in his ancestral towers—known just how ugly the world could be? Yet now she had begun, she could no longer spare him—nor herself.

"The earl must have had some reason of his own for wishing to so gratify Willcott," she said. "Though it may be an alien thought to you, there are plenty of men who find the idea of witnessing rape exciting, even though they might shy away from it themselves."

He regained his icy control with an obvious effort. "You think that's true of Hanley?"

Memories crowded in. Swallowing her fear, she closed her eyes so that she could describe exactly what she recalled.

"No, not really. Yet his expression was . . . It was as if he wore a steel mask—a complete indifference. I despised him more at that moment than I hated Willcott. I managed to tear away—I'd lost my shoes by then, and my hair had come down—but I snatched a shoe from the floor and struck Lord Hanley in the crotch. He doubled over, retching. That's when Willcott began to hit me in the face. The earl simply turned and left the cabin."

No one will ever want you again. Whore! Whore! You let Hanley roger you, but turn up your nose at Philip Willcott?

"Miracle!"

The voice seemed to come from very far away, but it was only the faint impression of an anguished concern that she'd perhaps once imagined, but never really experienced. Far more frantic emotions surged, threatening to overwhelm her in darkness. She pressed both hands over her closed lids and let the words pour out.

"Willcott bent me back over the table. He was leaning over me, biting my neck, but he had to use one hand to unfasten his trousers." The fear and nausea began to swarm, buzzing behind her eyes. "I flailed out and my fingers closed on a knife handle. He fell to the floor. There was blood. Such a lot of blood!"

"Miracle!"

Firm hands caught her by the shoulders. She opened her eyes and the nightmare cleared. His dark lashes stark against his pale skin, Ryder stared down at her, his eyes desolate.

"You almost fainted," he said. "I'm sorry. I had no right to force you to tell me this."

"I'm all right." She laughed unsteadily and reached for the strength of defiance. "Why shouldn't you know? My mad knight errant, bent only on my salvation? Or have I given you enough information now to see me hanged for murder, after all?"

CHAPTER ELEVEN

THE WORDS HUNG BETWEEN THEM. SHE WOULD GIVE AL-most anything to have left them unsaid. But he did not reel away in disgust. He merely gazed at her steadily and helped her to sit down.

"Nothing you say to me will ever be used to harm you," he said gently. "You must know that."

Miracle smiled up into the storm-green gaze. "Ah, of course! Not even torture would make Sir Galahad break a confidence."

He strode away a few paces, saying nothing.

She leaned her shoulder against a taller part of the stone wall, where a higher tower had crumbled away. It seemed an apt enough metaphor for the state of her defenses. Tall and forbidding, Ryder gazed out across the distant hills. The shadows of drifting clouds moved over the short turf like giant shoals of fish.

"I've no idea how the knife got there," she said, "but there was blood on my hand. A dark pool was spreading beneath Willcott's body from a wound in his shoulder. I tore off my rings and stumbled out onto the deck. I wasn't thinking . . . I wasn't thinking very clearly. Lord Hanley was sprawled in the bow. He'd drunk himself into a stupor. No one paid any attention as I ran to the stern, climbed down into the dinghy, and cut the line. I threw the knife into the ocean and escaped."

"Into a boat with no oars?"

"I discovered that when I was swept out to sea," she said dryly. "And yes, I think at that moment I wanted to die."

A profound silence settled over the ruined keep. He turned and pulled a small flask from his pocket. His eyes seemed as gray as the stone outcroppings in the distance.

"Here," he said with a grave smile. "On loan from Mr. Faber. Brandy. Would it help?"

The liquor burned in her throat. She coughed and made a face at him. "Thank you. And thank you for not offering a litany of hackneyed condolences over my outraged modesty. My primary emotion was fury."

"I'm stunningly relieved that it wasn't worse. I had feared—"

"That I was raped?"

He took back the brandy flask and swallowed some himself, tipping back his head to reveal his strong throat.

"Yes. Though now I know what really happened, it's going to take a little time to think through all the implications."

"What implications? It's a sordid enough tale, but a simple one: Willcott tried to force me, so I killed him."

Ryder sat down next to her. He dropped his head to gaze at the flagstones beneath his feet, his hands clasped together between his spread knees. "God! You had every right."

"Yet it's a terrible thing to have done, Ryder, and there's no court in the land that would agree that a harlot *can* be raped, so what right does she have to defend herself?"

He dropped his forehead onto his closed fists for a moment. Miracle gazed longingly at the taut lines of his back, at the mahogany highlights in his dark hair. There was no sense at all in wishing for a different reality, yet—

Ryder leaped to his feet and paced away. At the end of the battlements, where the wall had collapsed, he stopped and stared down into the gorge. "I'm glad that I didn't know all the details before, or Hanley might no longer be alive. Yet none of this makes any sense."

He spun about and walked back with rapid, decisive strides. "Why the devil would Hanley make such a pact to begin with? Why—after displaying such extraordinary possessiveness— would an earl arrange for another man to ravish his mistress, then drink himself into oblivion? Why was there a knife ready to hand? And why the hell did the dinghy have no oars?"

A numbing exhaustion had seeped into her bones. Miracle stood up and walked back to the head of the spiral stair.

"I don't know. I can't think about it. We must go, if we're to get to the Jolly Farmer in time not to be left behind by the others."

He caught up with her in three strides. "Hanley's pursuit is far more dangerous than I'd realized, Miracle. To play Ophelia is too great a risk."

"But I can't break my promise to the Fabers."

"Whatever money they'd lose by canceling another performance, I'll double it."

All the uneven, painful emotions of the last hour surged in like a red tide, swamping her. "Not everything can be solved with money! There's also a question of honor. I gave them my *word*!"

"I understand that," he said quietly. "It doesn't mean that you must also give them your life."

Miracle ran down the stairs and away up the path. He caught up to stride along beside her.

"Even if Hanley were in the audience—and he won't be—he'd never imagine it was me," she said. "There's a whole neighborhood of working people who've waited all year for this. There's a troupe of players needing to fulfill their art and express their talents. There's the Fabers' professional reputation, if they're to maintain any future business. There's a farmer who's rearranged his entire schedule to accommodate this one annual event. How can money compensate for the loss of all that?"

"It can't, obviously."

"I won't back out now, especially when I doubt there's really very much danger in fulfilling my promise."

"Very well," he said. "We'll be as unassuming in Hulme Down as church mice. No one who matters will see us. But afterward, I insist—"

"Afterward, you can do whatever you like." She stopped and faced him, desperate to make him understand. "I can't handle anymore just now, Ryder. Once I've collected my savings from my brother and taken ship for America, none of it will matter, will it?"

The path had brought them to the top of a small ridge. It wound back down to a cluster of buildings along a wooded stream. The walkers from the troupe were already gathered there at the Jolly Farmer, waiting for the wagons.

Ryder stood for a moment, gazing down at the trees and the sparkle of sunlit water, then he turned back to her and smiled.

"Then let's help the Fabers put on the best production of *Hamlet* in their entire careers," he said.

HULME Down was dominated by a small mill. Cottages clustered along the stream to the door of the church, then strayed along a muddy lane that led west to the farm that was to host the Fabers' play. For most of that day the audience had been streaming toward the village in various primitive conveyances: wagons, carts, traps, and on foot.

The barn hulked beside a large farmyard, not unlike the place where Ryder had warned off Jeb and Bruiser during their first encounter, except that this time every building bustled with pigs, sheep, and cattle. It was a threshing barn, temporarily empty, awaiting the harvest. The floor would serve as the pit, a high platform at one end as the stage.

Miracle climbed from her wagon and helped with the costumes as the Faber brothers began to prepare for their play. Ryder carried castle walls, stacked wooden weapons, moved trunks, and saw to the horses with quiet efficiency, as if he understood at a glance what needed to be done and how to do it.

She was alert to his every movement. The long strides. The easy strength and obvious intelligence. She was very painfully in love. It was an emotion she neither wanted nor understood, yet this terrible heightened awareness—this throbbing, dizzying excitement in the blood—accompanied her like a drumbeat.

Ryder had said nothing more about Lord Hanley, or the incident on the yacht. Yet he had offered a wealth of tacit consideration, allowing her to come to terms with what he had so instantly discerned: *It made no sense.*

In her blind desire to put it all behind her, in her blind fear of the consequences of what she had done, she had not allowed herself to really think about it before.

But Ryder was right: Why had there been no oars in the dinghy? And what was Lord Hanley looking for?

But what was she to do, a bird of paradise in love with a duke's son, when her life was forfeit and every hint that he returned her feelings only meant that she would break his heart in the end?

"Don't believe we've ever set up so fast, sweetheart," Mr. William Faber said, sitting down with a thump on an upturned barrel. "That cousin of yours is a clever chap. Perhaps even a bit too clever for the likes of us?"

She looked up from her unfocused exploration of a trunk of costumes and tore her mind back to the problems at hand. "Why do you say that, Mr. Faber?"

The actor gave her a shrewd glance. "He's not throwing his weight about, now, is he? He's not interfering, nor asking stupid questions. Yet I figure that young man could take over this whole company with a snap of his fingers and we'd never know what hit us."

"Then he'll make a very good Fortinbras," Miracle said with a smile. "The prince who offers salvation, in the end, to Denmark."

DARKNESS dropped over Hulme Down, collecting in the damp shadows of the trees and buildings. The yard and the fields surrounding the barn jammed with carts and wagons and horses. An enterprising couple were selling hot pies. Someone else broached a barrel of ale.

An ever larger crowd of pedestrians, jostling and merry, arrived to swell the floodtide. Ryder walked here and there making casual suggestions that seemed to translate—as if by magic—into commands that reduced the chaos. He was deliberately inconspicuous, slipping through the throng like a shadow. Yet wagons and carts lined up to leave clear passageways to link road, stream, farmyard, and barn.

Miracle watched him do it, steadfast and imperturbable. Another surge of longing suffused her bones.

At last the audience packed into the dusty, echoing space inside and gawked up at the illusion of Elsinore, wavering behind a row of lamps.

Horatio had turned up just in time, though his face was as bruised as a bad apple, which caused a general shout of mirth and several rude comments. Fortinbras was to escort Peggy and her new baby to rejoin the company the next day. It was generally agreed that the wounded man could play the Prince of Norway tomorrow, even with his arm in a sling, as long as he was no longer inclined to fight Hamlet's friend.

Ryder and Miracle would be needed for this one night only, then they could be on their way.

It is almost time, she thought with a stab of pain. *It is almost time—and then I shall never see him again.*

In his rich costume with its silver-painted breastplate and helmet, Ryder found a place in the makeshift wings, where he could wait for his first cue. He had done what he could to bring order from anarchy. The Fabers had been too overwhelmed setting up for the play to pay much attention to their surroundings. The farmer, Mr. Hodgkin—already counting his share of the night's proceeds, no doubt—had been celebrating with a bottle of brandy.

Ryder had collared him and bluntly stated his fears, but Mr. Hodgkin was oblivious to peril.

Yet the danger was real. Not everyone was inside watching the play. Courting couples were stealing the chance to escape their parents. A gang of boys raced about among the farm buildings. There was a scattering of lanterns. Glowing pipes had flitted about in the darkness, like sparks in the soot at the back of a grate.

Yet, unless Ryder abandoned his role as Fortinbras, he could do little more, except to trust to luck and hope that his earlier tour of the farm would bear fruit, if the worst happened.

An ominous roll of thunder sounded from behind a screen at the rear of the makeshift stage. The crowd rustled into an expectant silence. Two soldiers tramped into the gleam of the lights. One took up his post by the painted castle walls. The other thumped his wooden pike on the boards.

"Who's there?"

The play began.

The audience groaned and laughed and clapped and cursed, raw emotion on every face. Both men and women shrieked at the ghost and moaned aloud when treachery was revealed. As if they could alter the course of the drama, they shouted out warnings to the characters. Ryder had never seen anything quite like it.

Shakespeare's words had become strangely bawdy and direct, as if peeled open by naïveté to reveal their essential power.

Yet when Miracle drifted onto the stage as Ophelia, silence fell as if a blanket of darkness had been cast over the barn. Her hair lay unbound over her shoulders. A vaguely Grecian dress—white muslin, with a gilt cord bound beneath her breasts—draped lovingly over the curves of her body.

Men sighed. Women began to weep quietly into their handkerchiefs. Sam seemed to blossom in her presence, until Hamlet became stunningly real. When he cursed Ophelia, farm workers leaped up to shout and shake their fists, as if the Prince of Denmark had spurned one of their own sisters.

When Miracle walked on again later in the play, the white dress had disappeared beneath a fantasy of flowing rags. Strings of flowers wrapped around and around her body and up into her hair, piled now like a magpie's nest on top of her head. Yet she was still achingly beautiful, as if light shimmered from a pure, bright soul to illuminate the shredded muslin with brilliance.

Ryder stared at the floor, afraid of what his face might show to the other members of the troupe. His blood coursed too warmly in his veins. His body ached with desire. The memory of making love to her—her soft breasts, the long, sweet curves of her flank—haunted him far more deeply than any ghost ever haunted a prince of Denmark.

He must never allow her out of his life. He must somehow clear her of Hanley's persecution and set her up in London. Long evenings in her company. Long nights in her bed.

Her voice enthralled: *"There's rosemary, that's for remembrance; pray, love, remember!"*

Listening, entranced, he almost missed the first sign of trouble: a faint reek, sharper than the pipe smoke rising from the audience.

"And there is pansies, that's for thoughts."

The audience sighed, spellbound. Yet a faint bleating began to murmur outside, followed by the low rumble of a bull and the nervous whickering of horses. Ryder wrenched his mind back to reality. Tossing aside his helmet, he swung hand over hand into the high loft of the barn, where he could see clearly into the rick yard. It was already too late.

"Fire!" someone shouted outside. "T' hayricks 're on fire!"

Screams echoed as men surged back from the stage, then began to shove and elbow toward the doors. Women shrieked as they tried to grab their children.

Miracle dropped the dry stalks that had served her as Ophelia's herbs and flowers. There was no way out for the players, except through the crowd, and several hundred people were about to pile up against a door that was closed, trampling each other in their terror. Two more seconds would produce full-fledged panic.

But from somewhere above her head, Ryder leaped down onto the stage.

"Stop!"

His clear voice carried absolute command. Everyone froze in place. Heads turned to stare up as Ryder strode forward into the lights.

"You will each remain exactly where you are." The certainty and reassurance of natural authority spread into the sudden silence. "This barn is in no danger. The ricks are far enough away and the ground is damp. Now! Each man will help the woman nearest to him to secure her children. The four men who are closest to the doors will open them. Once that is done, every man who is sufficiently able-bodied will make his way quietly through the crowd to join me outside. Then we'll put the fire out."

He jumped down into the audience and strode through its center as if he were—Ah! Miracle swallowed hard. This was exactly who he really was, of course: Lord Ryderbourne.

The crowd split before him. Ryder picked out the tallest, strongest men and beckoned them to follow him. The door was now creaking open.

"You, sir! You will choose and direct a bucket brigade to fetch water from the stream. Buckets hang on the west side of this barn and in the milking shed on the south side of the yard. And you, sir, will take five men to fetch hooks from the shed at the north end of the yard to pull down any brands that threaten to spread the fire. You, and you, and you, will take charge of this crowd, delegating as necessary, to make sure that anyone who wishes to leave does so in an orderly fashion. You, sir, will make sure that no spectators get in the way of those putting out the fire."

The crowd stirred itself into new patterns. Younger men

moved quickly but calmly out to the rick yard. Some of the women followed. Others settled down to wait with their children clinging to their skirts. Mrs. Faber, dressed in a blond wig and paper crown, marched up onto the stage and waved both arms.

"Come!" she cried. "Let's tell the little ones a pretty tale!"

As the women and children gathered around to listen, Miracle slipped outside. She found a vantage point at the top of the stone stairs that led up to the loft of an apple store. Ryder was easy to pick out. He was a head taller than most, and the glare of the blaze flamed on his fake breastplate. She bit her lip and laughed at her wretched new vulnerability, but she could not bear not to watch him.

In the same unruffled tones, he was issuing more orders: for some of the wagons to be moved; to make sure that a second chain of buckets flung water onto the ricks that weren't yet burning—as well as the two that were—so the fire could not spread. In spite of the bellowing of the livestock and the natural threat of any feral fire, a determined efficiency dominated the scene. Men ran, but they did so without panic, almost like a well-disciplined army.

The flames began to recede, then die away into smoke. Runnels of water traced among blackened trusses of hay, tossed here and there on the ground, then thoroughly doused. The frantic pace of passing bucket after bucket slowed, then stopped. The fire was out.

"The job's done, gentlemen." Ryder smiled at two of the men who had headed up the bucket brigade. "If you, sir, and you, will stay here to watch for any stray embers, the play may resume. And perhaps Mr. Hodgkin will allow every man who tossed a bucket a free draft of ale for his trouble?"

A cheer went up as the farmer staggered forward. He stared at the smoldering ruins of two of his hayricks, then walked up to lay his hand on the untouched bulk of one of the three that remained. Tears ran openly down his face. Miracle couldn't hear what was said, but another cheer resounded around the yard. Ale flowed down thirsty throats, then the crowd began to stream back into the barn.

Ruthlessly reining in her confusion of emotions, she ran down the steps to go inside to finish the play.

Ryder suffered the farmer's bleary, effusive thanks with as much good nature as he could muster.

"I remember as how you warned me tha' there was too many folks about with pipes and such, sir," Mr. Hodgkin said, "and as how I ought to set some men to keep 'em out of my ricks. It were lucky there were a clear shot w'out wagons in t' road from t' stream. 'Appen tha'll be expecting a reward, sir?"

"No." Ryder glanced past the man's head to the stone stairs that led up to the apple loft. "No reward."

"Nay? Then I willna' fret mysen about it—"

In her floating costume of flowers and rags, Miracle was flitting down the steps. She seemed so free of all constraints, free to take every moment of every day and make it into something dazzling. He knew that he craved that freedom and grace, as much as he craved the oblivion he could find in her body.

With a last quick comment to the farmer, Ryder strode across the yard to intercept her.

She stopped and turned to face him while he was still several paces away, as if she knew in her bones when he approached.

"Your foresight paid off," she said gravely, her eyes huge in the darkness. "You saved the people in the barn, as well as that drunkard's hayricks. A stampede for the doors would have caused trampling, even deaths. You'd already made sure that there was a way left clear to the stream and knew where to find buckets."

"The threat was obvious. I did no more than any man would, once I discovered that Mr. Hodgkin was blind to his own peril."

She twisted a floating scrap of her skirt in her fingers. "But you're not any man. Evidently it occurred to no one to disobey you."

"I suppose not." His natural satisfaction in successfully putting out the fire and saving the audience began to fade. "Does it matter?"

A wry smile lurked at the corners of her mouth. "Of course it matters. I think you're missing Wyldshay more than you know. I think you're craving the realities of your life and realizing that you can't reconcile all of your desires, and never will. Though you've paid that dilemma little attention up till now, it's going to eat you alive. But there's no real choice, Lord Ryderbourne, and there never was. So perhaps you should accept it and go home."

The young man playing Laertes ran out to collect Miracle to finish their scene. She seized the boy's proffered fingers and smiled at him with dazzling gaiety, before they ran back inside together.

Pain lacerated Ryder's heart. Wyldshay was the center of his life: his very soul. He could never give it up, not even for love. Miracle was right: If he was foolish enough to think that he was truly in love with a bird of paradise—with a woman who sold herself to whichever man promised her the most in jewels and security—he would be making the biggest mistake of his life.

Yet his craving for her burned through his bones, as deep and immediate as any passion for duty and inheritance.

Thought and affliction, passion, hell itself, she turns to favor and to prettiness.

Ryder walked back to the barn. Just as he reached the door, a tingle of premonition made him glance over one shoulder.

A carriage had pulled into the yard, a gentleman's carriage drawn by two horses. It stopped by the farmhouse. A tall, dark-haired man stepped down and glanced about at the multiplicity of wagons and carts. He said something to his coachman, before he turned and began to stride toward the barn.

Ryder made his way to the stage. Miracle's part was done, but Fortinbras was critical to the last scene. The Prince of Norway was one of the few left standing after the general slaughter at the end. The final speech was his.

The play must go on, of course, even when stark reality had just caught up with him.

THE cast took their bows. The audience finally began to stream away. Thanks to the orderly ranking of the carts and wagons that Ryder had arranged earlier, the exodus proceeded without incident. Miracle disappeared to change out of her costume. Ryder stripped off his fake armor in seconds, but the cast crowded around him, wanting to shake his hand and congratulate him on his performance, both on- and offstage.

At last Mr. Faber shooed them all away, so he could express his own gratitude in a speech worthy of a great thespian. Ryder listened as long as necessary, but in the end he cut the actor off in mid-sentence.

"You've been most kind, sir. The pleasure was all ours. However, my cousin and I must be leaving now."

"Now, sir? In the dark of night?"

Ryder gestured over one shoulder. "A friend has come to collect us."

He joked and smiled with Mr. Faber for a few more moments, but somewhere deep inside, the pain had begun to burn. While he had still been trapped onstage by the cast, Miracle had walked out across the empty threshing floor to greet the newcomer, who was now lounging casually in the doorway.

Guy Devoran, Ryder's cousin, held out both hands. Miracle slipped into his embrace, then stood on tiptoe to kiss him on the mouth. From the intimacy of the greeting, it was plain to any observer that he and Miracle must have been lovers once—and perhaps still were.

Ryder knew with crushing and immediate intimacy why jealousy was known as a monster.

Guy glanced up as Ryder approached. Miracle stepped back, her expression guarded. She sat down on the ledge beside the door and stared off into the distance.

"Good God!" Guy said in mock horror as he held out his hand. "Swords or pistols? Or do you wish merely to punch me in the jaw?"

Ryder shook hands, because to do otherwise would be petty, but he could not keep the bite from his voice. "Is there any good reason why my fist should connect so unpleasantly with your face, Guy?"

Without waiting for a reply, he stalked outside. He must move, before his words became a deadly reality. Without further comment, his cousin fell in beside him. The two men crossed the yard in silence until they reached the animal pens.

Guy propped his hip on the wall of a pigsty. His expression was noncommittal as he met Ryder's gaze.

"Obviously this meeting's no coincidence," Ryder said. "So what the hell brought you to Hulme Down?"

"Concern at Wyldshay."

"For God's sake!" In spite of his distress, Ryder laughed. "Mother?"

"Apparently Lord Hanley paid the duchess a visit, and now ducal uneasiness haunts the towers and whispers about the Great Hall. Hanley was unctuous, but Her Grace believes that he wishes you no good. I received her request to find you and deliver that message."

"Then I must apologize for my mother's indifference that you might have a life of your own."

A sow snuffled up to the other side of the wall. Guy leaned down to scratch her ears. "Fortunately I'd already planned to come north, so it was no real inconvenience. Also, of course, I caught the intriguing scent of a mystery—always hard to resist."

"Did the duchess wish to convey anything else?"

"Only that the earl's visit left quite a stink in Her Grace's nostrils—something like this pigpen, I imagine. However, it's pure chance that I found you. I saw the glow and smoke from the fire. It was out by the time I arrived, but I noticed how impressively well-organized everything was."

"At which point you entered the barn and were slain with astonishment to see my strutting about onstage dressed in fake armor?"

Guy glanced up and grinned. "Having known my older cousin all my life as a model of ducal rectitude—yes!"

Ryder leaned his forearms on the top of the wall. Though he and Guy had never been very close, Ryder knew his cousin to be honorable to the core. Guy was the same age as Jack. They had always been like brothers—closer perhaps than Ryder and Jack had ever been—a friendship that had only grown more profound when Guy and Jack had blazed a riotous path together through London society some years earlier.

"I'm taking a holiday from myself," he said at last.

The sow shuffled back into her shed. Piglets began squealing. Guy pushed away from the wall and began to pace.

Ryder folded his arms and watched the younger man: the vigorous, charismatic only son of his mother's sister, who had died long ago when Guy was small. "And you may indeed assume," he added, "that my thunderous expression when we shook hands was because of Miracle."

His cousin stopped dead. "In which case, you're displaying an admirable self-control."

"Perhaps, but you've no idea how very murderous I feel!"

Guy laughed. "I wasn't sure how to broach it, but I trust you'll allow me to be equally blunt? You saw her kiss me and didn't like it?"

"Your life was hanging by a thread. You're lovers?"

"*Were,* not are. For a short while. A very long time ago."

It was a relief, though a small one. "And Jack, as well, I assume?"

"I've no idea! She's never tattled to me about her relationships with other men."

He did not want to have to articulate it, but the thought burned. "Yet it's not unlikely, is it? You and my brother ran together often enough. Jack must have met her, in which case I can only assume the obvious."

"It's possible, of course," Guy said. "Though Jack never intimated any such thing. Does it matter?"

"No, of course not." Ryder choked down his inchoate emotions. "She's never tried to hide what she is."

"And Hanley knows that you're with her now, I assume? Yet it seems very odd that he would care."

Ryder glanced back toward the barn. Miracle was standing in the open door, her dark hair massed in waves about her face. His heart contracted with a desperate longing: for the world to be different, for her to be different, for her.

"I don't think the earl gives a damn about Miracle," he said. "Something else is afoot. If you'll take us to Wrendale—assuming Miracle has no objections to including you—I'll fill you in as we go."

GUY and Ryder stalked back to the carriage like two rival tigers, forced to follow the same track through the dark and only too eager to bound away on their separate paths as soon as dawn broke.

Miracle swallowed a painful dismay.

When would she learn to be less free with her promises? If she had not given Ryder her word, she could have stayed with the Fabers for one more day's journey north, then fled straight to her brother's.

Though Ryder had immediately controlled his reaction when he found her kissing Guy, Miracle knew what it felt like to be hurt by a lover. She had always tried, heart and soul, not to inflict any such wounds of her own in return, but this time she had failed. She did not expect him to understand why she had done it. And unless Guy decided to explain, she could not in honor do so herself.

Perhaps it didn't matter. She had taken lovers for many years. No man could accept her company without tolerating that.

The men separated. Guy walked up to his coachman and gave orders. Tall and commanding, Ryder strode on toward the barn. If he was still angry, it was carefully banked beneath a clear, cold control.

"Guy will take us to Wrendale," he said. "You'll be safe there."

"From Hanley, or from you and Mr. Devoran?"

He gave her a sharp look. "Do you need protection from either of us?"

"Guy's an important part of my past," she said. "I owe him a debt of gratitude, but there's nothing else between us now. I will tell you no more than that, but you don't need to feel threatened."

"Every man I meet may have been your lover at one time, even my own cousin. I accept it. It doesn't matter."

Yet it did. She knew that it did, that the knowledge burned and festered deep in his soul. Lord Ryderbourne might think he was in love, but he would never really give his heart to a fallen woman.

"I trust Guy as I would trust any old friend," she said. "That's all."

"And I trust his integrity as I trust my own. So I think we should include him in our little feud with Hanley. You agree?"

"You want to tell your cousin what's happened so far? Why?"

"Let's just say it might be wise to have an insurance policy. Jack's in India. If something happens to me, it would be up to Guy to bring down the wrath of the St. Georges on Hanley's miserable head."

Darker and more lightly built than Ryder, Guy joined them, a ghost in the dark. "You think the earl would really try to damage you?"

"I think he is desperate. You'll see why when we explain."

Guy opened the carriage door, handed Miracle inside, and

climbed in after her. "My sword arm is at your disposal, ma'am, my lord."

"Then I agree," Miracle said. "A conspiracy of three!"

"I think I'm beginning to feel sorry," Ryder said dryly as he swung up after them, "for Hanley."

The carriage rattled away into the night. Miracle sat beside Ryder and listened to his dispassionate explanation. Blinded by her distress over Willcott, she had not allowed herself to think it all through before, but now goose bumps rose on her skin.

"So what are we left with?" Guy asked at last. "Setting aside Willcott's death for the moment, the salient point would seem to be that the earl is searching for something."

"Exactly. Let's take it point by point. Hanley's not the type to indulge in the wanton destruction of another man's property, yet—even though they were leased from the duchy—he wrecked Miracle's rooms in London. After what happened on the yacht, it makes no sense to assume that he was simply jealous. So he was indeed looking for something. He then directly accused her of stealing from him when they were alone in his carriage. Obviously, he thinks that Miracle has something of his in her possession, and this missing item is far more important to him than Willcott's untimely demise."

"So what the hell was Willcott's role? That entire episode stinks to high heaven."

"The words that come to mind are blackmail, extortion, fear," Ryder said. "Hanley is afraid of something."

"Of something that Willcott either knew or possessed," Guy replied.

"Yet now that Willcott's dead, the earl is even more terrified, not less."

Guy turned to Miracle. "Did Hanley ever hint that he might be afraid of something?"

"No," she said. "He never seemed to be a very emotional man."

"Until Exeter, where everything changed." Ryder stretched out his legs and stared at his boots. His profile gleamed dimly in the dark carriage, but his entire being shimmered with an aura of power. "What happened to your things, Miracle? Your jewelry and clothes. The possessions you'd taken to Exeter with you. Was everything left on the yacht?"

Her heart began to thump as she followed his thinking. "No, not all of it."

Guy gave her an encouraging smile, his teeth white in the dark carriage. He was—he had always been—a lovely man. "Ah! So something was left behind in Exeter?"

"Not exactly," she said. "I'd honestly forgotten about this until now. I wanted to block all of it from my mind. But when I decided to leave Lord Hanley, I managed to send a few things to Dillard."

Ryder's eyes seemed to reflect starlight. "Did the earl know that?"

"No, I'm sure that he didn't. It was that last morning. It was all rather desperate. Lord Hanley wouldn't let me out of his sight. But I couldn't afford to lose my jewelry, and there were some other things that I valued. I doubted that I'd be able to smuggle anything off the yacht when we reached Lyme Regis. So I bundled some items haphazardly into a little bag and hid it beneath my cloak. I thought I might get the chance to give it to the innkeeper to post for me."

"And did you?"

"No, that was impossible. Lord Hanley clung to my elbow the entire time, and—as I told you before—I was afraid to make a scene."

"So how did you manage it?"

"When we'd first arrived in Exeter, I'd fallen into conversation purely by chance with another man who was staying at the inn. I saw him again in the lobby as we were leaving."

Guy sat upright, as alert as a hunting dog. "Who was that?"

"His name was Melman, George Melman. In the few seconds while Lord Hanley's attention was distracted by the arrival of our carriage, I managed to slip the bag to Mr. Melman. I was damned if I was going to leave it behind or take it onto the yacht, so when I saw the opportunity to outwit Lord Hanley, I took it."

"You gave your valuables to a total stranger?"

"He was a Derbyshire man."

Guy leaned back and laughed. "And Derbyshire men are always honest?"

"It seemed worth the risk. He's also a minister. I'd already written my brother's direction on a slip of paper for the innkeeper, so instead I gave it to Mr. Melman with the bag. I couldn't say anything, but I tried to signal what I wanted with my eyes. He understood right away and nodded his promise to deliver it for me."

"This exchange was entirely without words?"

"Yes, but I knew I could trust him."

Ryder smiled, not in mirth, but with a kind of bitter recognition. "What exactly was in the bag?"

"I don't know. Most of my jewelry, a little money. A couple of books that were precious to me. One of my fans, I think. I don't really remember. It was all very hastily done. I had only a few seconds, while Lord Hanley used the chamber pot."

"Yet you sent something to your brother that Hanley wants." Ryder glanced out the window. "In which case, I doubt if he gives a damn about Willcott's death. In fact, I'm prepared to wager that he was thrilled to find the man killed."

"Which explains why he's raised no public hue and cry against Miracle," Guy added. "And why he's so desperate to find her."

Miracle shivered. Why should Lord Hanley think she had stolen something from him? It was absurd. She had rescued only a handful of personal possessions to thrust into her little bundle. Hanley hadn't even known that she'd done it. Yet the thought of the earl tearing apart her London rooms—even her clothes and books, even the bed they had shared—sent cold ripples down her spine.

She remembered with horror his face in the carriage. *I threw all of your trash into the sea. After all, your valuables weren't there any longer.*

"Does Hanley know that you have a brother?" Ryder asked.

Miracle glanced up at him, but his expression was lost in the darkness. "No. No one does. No one except you and Guy."

"Then we have a little time," Ryder said, "before the ax falls."

CHAPTER TWELVE

Even though it was summer and almost morning, Ryder ordered the fire lit. After their journey across the Peaks in the unheated carriage, he was chilled to the bone. He downed a welcoming draft of hot coffee laced with brandy, then leaned back in his chair to stare down through slitted lids at the coals in the grate.

Wrendale, with its elegant rooms and landscaped grounds, belonged to the duchy, of course. Ryder was lord and master of all he surveyed. It was a surprisingly empty feeling.

Miracle, her face ashen with fatigue, had been taken up to one of the bedrooms by a startled maid. Though his blood yearned for her, though the memory of their passion obsessed him, he felt a very real discomfort about sharing her bed with Guy in the house.

His cousin stood at the hearth. He set his empty cup down on the silver tray next to the coffeepot.

"What do you want me to do?" Guy asked. "Waylay Hanley with tales of mayhem in the hills, while you and Miracle escape unnoticed to the Antipodes?"

"Unlike you and Jack, I can never escape unnoticed," Ryder said. "It's one of the perks of my position."

"I never thought of it quite that way before," Guy replied with a wry smile. "I suppose one of the advantages of having no such exalted position myself is that I get to waste my time pretty much as I please."

Ryder poured himself a second cup. "And, for Miracle's sake, you're offering to put that freedom at my disposal now?"

"If you think I can help. I assume you have a plan?"

Now was not the time to think about Miracle, softly dreaming upstairs. The problem at hand needed cold, hard, analytical assessment, not the heated imaginings of a man blinded by lust.

"Part of one, at least. Whatever we do afterward, we'd better recover her missing treasure first and we don't have much time. Hanley's bound to find out about this brother, Dillard Heather. The man's a shoemaker. He'd be no match for an earl."

Guy turned to warm his hands. "You still think the crux of this business is some kind of extortion scheme?"

"Why else would Hanley promise Miracle's favors to Will-cott? Apparently, he wasn't satisfying any deviant interests of his own."

"God, it's foul! I'm not sure how you refrained from killing Hanley yourself."

Ryder sipped at his cup. "I didn't know enough details to justify it when we last met, or I might well have done."

Guy paced away across the room to stare out at the gray hints of dawn beyond the window. "But what the devil could Willcott have been blackmailing him about?"

"I've no idea. But if we're right, he'll go to almost any lengths to prevent our finding out."

"But Hanley knows that you've taken Miracle under your wing. Doesn't that make Wrendale an obvious target?"

"For what?" Ryder picked up the poker and rattled the coals in the grate. "If he came here in person, I'd take the greatest pleasure in shooting him down like a dog—after the proper formalities were exchanged, of course."

"And I imagine he knows that. If it should come to a duel, I'd be happy to act as your second, of course."

Sparks leaped in the soot at the back of the fire, scattering and disappearing like shooting stars. "Thank you. Anyway, I've had enough of skulking about the countryside like a vagabond."

"Yet he's bound to guess that Miracle's going to tell you what happened on the yacht."

"Which makes him doubly dangerous. He's desperate to recover whatever he thinks Miracle stole from him. He's probably equally desperate to silence her."

"And to silence you?"

Ryder set aside the poker and leaned back into the harsh embrace of his chair. "That depends on what he believes my feelings are toward her. If the situation were reversed, Hanley would side with me against a courtesan—purely from gentlemanly solidarity—even though he hates my guts. So if he assumes that she's only a temporary interest, he'll trust that I'll abandon her without compunction, rather than involve myself in a scandal."

"And what are your feelings toward her?" Guy asked.

"That's none of your bloody business."

"No, I suppose not. You're my social superior and five years older, for a start." Guy's boots thudded on the carpet as he strode back across the room. "We've never really been intimate, have we? Yet I spent my boyhood admiring your every gesture and striving to be more like you."

"Good God! Did you?" Ryder laughed. "Obviously you've no idea how I envied you and Jack. From the day you were born, you both had so much more freedom than I did."

"I suppose we did," Guy said. "But we envied your power far more."

"The grass is always greener."

Guy stared down at the fire, as if making up his mind to something.

Ryder studied every perfectly shaped bone, every nuance of shape and texture, with cold objectivity. Guy Devoran had inherited all the fey good looks of the duchess's family: tall and lean, but with the whiplike strength of a greyhound and the graceful economy of movement of the born horseman or swordsman. Women no doubt fell at his feet, if he so much as snapped his fingers.

Had Miracle ever loved him? Did she still?

"Yet perhaps this situation demands the tearing down of fences," Guy said at last. "I happen to care a great deal about Miracle. The state of your heart may be none of my business, but—as you yourself just said—your intentions toward her are an important part of the picture with Hanley."

Ryder poured more coffee, without the brandy this time. "You don't like him, either, do you?"

"We've no personal feud, but he's always made me think of a snake. I told Miracle—"

"Go on," Ryder said with icy forbearance. "What did you tell Miracle?"

Guy dropped into a chair, then looked up, obviously aware of all the implications of what he was about to say. "I warned her not to accept him when he offered her carte blanche a few months ago."

Not only grass was green. Ryder swallowed the ignoble impulse to strangle his inappropriately decorative cousin. "So you were on intimate terms that recently?"

"Not in the way that you think. We're friends, that's all."

Ryder set down his cup and brushed aside the temptation to refill it with liquor. This was far too important to risk dulling his tired mind with more brandy.

"Perhaps you and I have never really been close enough," he said. "Yet you're my cousin and Jack's best friend. I trust your integrity implicitly. I think we are, as you have just so astutely observed, going to have to spill our bloody guts to each other about Miracle."

Guy gazed away across the room. His profile had that same damned angelic purity as Jack's.

"I can tell you some of the facts about how I met her. As for the rest, I don't know. Half of the story is hers. She might not want it told."

"Not so easy, is it," Ryder said, "when the boot is on the other foot? The same reservations apply to her present relationship with me, of course. However, her life is at stake. Hanley can decide at any time to bring a charge of murder against her. In the circumstances we'd better swallow our personal discomfort, and for her sake share all the information we have. Nothing said here will go beyond this room, obviously."

"Very well," Guy said. "I suppose I should start. I assume you know that she's not a lady by birth?"

Ryder nodded. Distaste and curiosity and dread seethed in an unholy mix in his gut. He had avoided pushing Miracle for the truth about her past. Because he didn't want to know? Because it was bound to reveal the impossibility of any real future together?

His cousin leaned forward, hands clasped between his spread knees, head bent as if he studied a speck on the carpet. "What has she told you of her upbringing?"

"Not much. She said she was apprenticed into a cotton mill when she was six."

Guy glanced up to meet Ryder's gaze. His eyes blazed. "Have you ever seen the inside of such a place? The mills are the pride and joy of our burgeoning industrial landscape up here in Derbyshire. The apprentices are properly fed and clothed, and they all go to church every Sunday. Yet the children work unimaginably long hours in indescribable noise and dust. The machinery stops for nothing, not even when a child falls asleep at the job, at the cost of an eye or a hand or a life."

"I thought many of the new mills were built to be models of social care?"

"They are. But it's a harsh life for a child without the comforts, however humble, of a home and a loving mother. That's how Miracle spent five years of her childhood, sleeping on a straw pallet with the orphans in the apprentice house, working long hours in the mill, spending any remaining moments sewing and mending."

"But she wasn't an orphan," Ryder said.

"No, but her father apprenticed her to the mill all the same."

"He sold her?"

"If you like. She never saw him again. The only other activity besides church and work was a few hours' schooling once a week. The apprentices are taught their letters, so they will make better Christians and more useful workers."

"Which is more than one can say for the workhouse, or for the child of the average farm worker."

Coals fell in the grate as the fire died down. Both men ignored the small sound, as if they were caught together in some desperate net.

"Farm life can be physically brutal, also, of course," Guy said. "Yet the villages of England boast their quota of elderly rustics: men who've spent a tough life in the fields, yet are hale enough for all that."

"God! Wyldshay is full of them. We're as dependent on them as they are on us. It would be pretty damned inhuman to turn a man out to starve, after he's labored for the duchy for a lifetime."

"You also provide dame schools, so every child on the estate is guaranteed a decent chance in life. Yet somehow I think we'll never see these mill children grow old. Their lungs fill with cotton dust. Their souls wither in the face of all that relentless machinery. The girls almost never see the sky, except in glimpses. Even the meanest crow scarer in the fields knows what it is to chase butterflies, or stare dreamily at the clouds."

Or the stars—

"What happened when Miracle was eleven?"

Guy rubbed one hand over his mouth as if to brush away a bad taste. "She was seen walking to church with the other children one Sunday by a gentleman named Sir Benjamin Trotter. Her beauty was already quite extraordinary, I imagine, and her intelligence would have been obvious after two minutes' conversation. Sir Benjamin bought out her apprenticeship papers and took her into his house."

Dread uncoiled in his gut. "In what capacity?"

Beneath the flush of reflected firelight, Guy's face was drawn. "What do you think?"

"For God's sake!" Ryder's head snapped up as disgust and rage ripped through his heart. "Did he begin to abuse her right away?"

"You'll have to ask her. She told me only that Sir Benjamin gave her the run of his library. I think she's grateful to him."

"Though he ravished her when she was still a child?"

"I only know that, when he died, she was sixteen and had been sharing his bed for some time."

A deep shudder racked Ryder's body. "He'd made no provision for her in his will?"

Guy shook his head.

"What about her brother?"

"Dillard was still unmarried and living over a master shoemaker's store. He couldn't support her. Yet, whatever his other faults, Sir Benjamin had given Miracle the manners and education of a lady. She was accomplished and extraordinarily well-read. His family allowed her to keep her clothes and some trinkets, and a cousin handed her a few gold coins, so she traveled to London to become an actress. No other occupation was open, except the grinding poverty of occasional farm work."

"Because she refused to go back to the mill?"

"Do you blame her? And having been publicly ruined, she couldn't become a governess, or a lady's companion, or even get work in a haberdasher's."

Ryder leaped to his feet to stride across the room. Unable to pass through the wall, he stopped to stare blindly at the leather-bound spines in the bookcases.

"We talk very glibly of virtue and purity, don't we? I have tried to understand, to imagine the desperation that might lead a woman like Miracle onto such a path. I suppose I expected her to starve?"

"You might say that she triumphed, instead," Guy said.

Ryder punched his fist against the wooden molding at the side of the bookcase. A blind, incoherent rage cascaded, past analysis, at the very edge of his control. "How did you meet her?"

"How does any young blood meet an opera dancer? I went to the green room after a performance and begged her to honor me with her favors."

"And did she?"

"No. She'd only recently arrived in town. She still thought she could live decently enough off her earnings on the stage. That was impossible, of course."

Ryder looked back at his cousin through a black fog of confused resentment. "So she joined the rest of the muslin company and took a lover?"

"Shall we walk in the long gallery? If you don't expend a little physical energy soon, you might murder me yet." It was said with a smile, but Guy's eyes reflected the haunted, bleak feelings that contaminated Ryder's every breath.

The men strode up through the house in silence, their boots resounding on the oak floors. Ryder sucked the dawn air deep into his lungs as they walked. The gallery stretched the entire length of the house, lined with tall windows on the north side. Family portraits ranked opposite them: an endless procession of ladies and gentlemen—his ancestors—who had never known anything but excess. Harsh echoes bounced down the long space as the men paced in silence from one end to the other.

"So she changed her mind?" Ryder asked at last. "And accepted your offer?"

"Yes."

"How old were you?"

"Eighteen. Only two years older than she was. I had very little money to spare, but I shared my winnings at the tables or the racetrack, whenever I could."

"And so you made her into a professional courtesan, after all."

"Yes, if you like."

It hung unspoken between them: Guy had not taken Miracle's virginity, obviously. But had she taken his? Ryder's anguished rage began to dissipate in the face of his deep-seated sense of fair play and justice. Miracle's inevitable path in life was not Guy's fault. Yet he felt a poignant, yearning envy for that love affair, experienced in the first flush of youth, before Miracle had experienced all the casual indifference of her wealthier lovers.

"So what happened?"

"We were children. We fell in love. We quarreled. Neither of us knew how to trust what we thought we had found. Even with my help, she didn't have enough to pay the rent. My lifestyle was too erratic. After a few months, it simply blew apart. One day I walked out in a rage. When I came back, it was too late. She was already under the protection of a much richer man."

"If it counts for anything," Ryder said as they turned at the end of the gallery and began to stride back, "I'm glad that she had those months with you first."

Guy stopped dead. "God! That's the most generous thing any man ever said to me."

"No, I mean it. For her sake. Shall we shake hands on it?"

His cousin grasped his hand and grinned. "I think she won't forgive my telling you all this."

"I think it very likely that she won't forgive either of us."

They turned and began walking again with a new sense of companionship.

"She insisted that she wasn't any good for me, anyway,"

Guy said. "She was wiser than I was, of course. I'd like to be able to offer a whole heart to a wife one day."

The words sank into Ryder's heart like a death knell. Miracle was the kind of female that gentlemen enjoyed, but never married. Each lover had taken her another irrevocable step away from the possibility of a home and children.

"Yet you still see her?"

"She's an extraordinary woman. Occasionally we get the chance to meet and talk. The only limit she's ever put on our friendship is that she won't take a penny from me, not even a Christmas gift."

"Nor did she take your most recent advice."

"Why should she? She's created a brilliant career. In a world where mistresses are discarded with each season's new fashions, Miracle has made herself rare and sought after. Not every relationship she's agreed to has been heartless—"

Ryder struck one palm with a fist. "Then why the hell did she pick Hanley?"

"He pledged to give her enough to retire. She's only twenty-five, but what the devil will the future offer? Can you honestly say that you can sit in judgment of her taking that chance when it was offered?"

The plaster glimmered with gilt. Red silk velvet draped the windows. In a portrait over the central fireplace, his great grandmother wore emeralds and pearls, only a small part of the fortune of the St. Georges.

"No," Ryder said. "I don't sit in judgment, just in grief that she thought it necessary. Tell me about this brother, Dillard Heather. Did she talk much about him?"

"He's her one stable anchor in life, I think. At least, that's the impression she gave me. A year after she came to London, Dillard married and opened his own shop."

"Did she ever visit?"

"I don't think so. Dillard and his wife started a family right away. It was essential to his success in business that he maintain absolute respectability. Miracle thought that a visit from a London courtesan would do him more harm than good. Yet they wrote and exchanged gifts."

"Gifts?"

Guy ran his fingers over the rails of a set of ranked chairs as they walked. "Dillard would send her little pots of honey, and once a purse made out of leather scraps. She treasured it, even though her protector at the time had given her a reticule of black velvet, trimmed with pearls and gold wire."

"I imagine that Miracle was even more generous to her brother?"

"Yes, of course. After all, he had a burgeoning family to support. I don't think she ever received a gift from an admirer without sending something to Derbyshire."

"Dillard's also invested her savings for her."

Guy stopped and raised a brow. "Has he? I didn't know that. What else don't I know?"

Ryder met his cousin's dark gaze and smiled. "You suggest that it's my turn now to spill my guts?"

"Merely the strictly essential information," Guy said. "Whatever's relevant to this problem with Hanley."

"That," Ryder replied dryly, "is all you're going to get, however grateful I am for what you've just shared."

The men strode on down the gallery. Picking his words with care, Ryder gave Guy a broad outline of events since he had rescued Miracle from the dinghy. All the rest—the glorious, painful tumult of emotions that cascaded through his heart as he recalled every moment of their time together—he kept to himself.

Guy listened in silence, then turned into the embrasure of a large bay window in the center of the north wall. The landscape was flooding with color as the sun rose behind the distant hills.

"But other than the lure of her obvious charms," Guy asked, "what the devil made you want to accompany her on such a journey to start with?"

Ryder folded his arms and leaned one shoulder against a life-sized marble sculpture of Hercules and the Hydra. "I think I wanted the adventure of traveling off into the unknown without any particular goal or destination."

"Why?"

"Perhaps because I've never really been tested. Not as Jack has been. Not in circumstances where one's life is forfeit on a daily basis."

Guy sat down on the window seat and stretched his legs out in front of him. Light poured in through the glass to rim his dark hair. "You envy Jack that?"

The Hydra's head beside his knee grinned at him with ghastly stone teeth. Ryder laughed.

"God! It seems that everyone wants to know whether I'm jealous of my own brother. The answer is no. One can yearn to comprehend the experience of a loved one, without being envious of it. I've no desire to suffer through the deserts of China, nor face a slow death in the snows of the Himalayas. Yet perhaps I wanted to taste something of the freedom that Jack found on his travels."

"To discover what forged the pure steel at the center of his being? And did you?"

"No, of course not! There's never a real path into another man's soul, not even when that soul belongs to one's own brother. Anyway, my adventure was just a Sunday excursion. The lanes of England are not the high passes of the Karakoram Mountains, and the eldest son of the Duke of Blackdown always has a safety net available, whether he likes it or not."

"Except when His Lordship is unarmed at night on a lonely road and facing three footpads bent on robbery, if not murder." Guy pushed one hand back through his hair. "That was as real as any threat I'd ever want to face."

Ryder shrugged and paced back into the center of the long gallery. "I was essentially helpless. It was just luck that we escaped with our lives."

"Even good luck prefers a cool head, and bad luck demands it. Don't underestimate yourself, Ryder. Jack and I admire you for a great deal more than any advantage of position. That steel you so admire in your brother's heart shines just as brightly in your own."

"Thank you," Ryder said. "I wish I could be as sure of it as you seem to be."

"God, a certain sterling quality has been obvious for years in both of you, though I rather think that my aunt might have more to do with that than any adventures on the road."

He swallowed a surge of genuine mirth. "Mother certainly believes in holding her sons' feet to the fire on a regular basis. However, the lessons I've learned so far have been mostly those of humility and Christian repentance. Miracle calls me her Sir Galahad, even though I've failed miserably in every test of becoming the perfect, gentle knight."

"You're in love with her, aren't you?"

She has stolen the essence from my soul.

Ryder shrugged, unwilling to voice it: the painful, impossible state of his heart. "Let's just say that if we can win through this business with Hanley, she'll never have to fear poverty again."

Guy stood and walked up to join his cousin. "Will that be enough?"

"I don't know! God, why ask me that?"

"Because it seems the obvious question."

Ryder spun on his heel and paced back toward the west door. Guy fell into step beside him. The portraits passed in a blur, the dance of daylight picking out colors like jewels: emerald green, ruby red, sapphire blue.

"My greatest fear is that it won't be enough, that she'll accept nothing less now than complete independence. Though Hanley broke his word, she has her own savings, and she's sacrificed enough, devil take it, to earn them. She doesn't need my wealth and she certainly doesn't need me. Why the hell would she want me to set her up in London as my mistress, after living at the mercy of so many other worthless lords?"

"Right now she needs you to save her life," Guy said.

"You don't think that awareness hasn't already burned a track in my brain?"

"Yet Hanley's not raised any public hue and cry about Willcott's death. Instead he's hunting her down himself. What the devil is he planning?"

"I wish I knew."

"Will he set minions to watch Wrendale?"

"I imagine that he already has. However, we arrived in the dark and it was raining from blessedly black skies. He'll get a report that a carriage arrived during the night, but he can't know that Miracle and I were in it. It was, after all, yours."

"Ah," Guy said, walking up to another tall window to stare out. "I begin to understand your devious thinking. You would like me to make my lonely presence here known to all and sundry, while you secretly visit Dillard to recover whatever Miracle sent him?"

Ryder remained in the shadows, his hand on the door latch.

Beyond the glass, daylight burnished the treetops. White sheep trailed across the high pastures to the north. He realized with painful acuity that he was tired enough to drop.

"Assuming the honest Mr. Melman didn't run off with it," he said.

"Never!" Guy stifled a yawn. "He's a Derbyshire man."

WRENDALE was radiant. With splendor. With paintings, vases, sculpture. With exotic furniture, dishes, carpets. Breathtaking landscapes jeweled the far distance from every window.

Miracle wandered slowly through room after room. This was only one of the duchy houses, usually occupied for just a few weeks every year later in the summer, when Her Grace the Duchess of Blackdown preferred these cooler northern skies. Wyldshay Castle could then be cleaned thoroughly from top to bottom.

The arrangement sounded positively medieval, conjuring visions of herb-strewn straw, and dogs snatching bones flung from the high table. It was, however, simply time to scrub ceilings, touch up paint, dismantle bedsteads, and turn carpets, without inconveniencing the family.

Miracle learned all this from the maid who had arrived to bring her breakfast, even though it was early afternoon. She had slept for twelve hours. The gentlemen, the girl said, were still asleep. They had finished a bottle of brandy together, then tumbled into their respective beds and asked not to be disturbed.

Yet before collapsing in an inebriated stupor, His Lordship had left very strict instructions: Miss Heather was not to allow herself to be seen by anyone outside the house. She must avoid windows and not step—not even for an instant—onto any of the patios or terraces. The staff were to pretend that she and Lord Ryderbourne had never arrived.

The maid's message sent a little shiver down Miracle's spine, and not only at the idea that Guy and Ryder had been talking together. Lord Hanley knew she was with Ryder.

She walked on through echoing rooms and hallways, then up flight after flight of stairs. The house circled a central atrium with a domed skylight. Sunlight sparkled on marble and rosewood and gilt, and an endless procession of paintings.

Miracle had always maintained a certain style in her rooms in London. Elegance was essential when one entertained viscounts and earls. Yet she had never lived anywhere like this. Sir Benjamin's house had been modest in contrast.

A wide corridor led her at last to a set of closed doors. Curious, she opened one. A brown glass eye gazed at her beneath a long hank of horsehair. Painted red nostrils flared, as if the wooden horse breathed fire. She walked closer and touched the glossy gray-and-white dappled neck. The horse rocked gently, making the iron stirrups swing from the real leather saddle.

A nursery.

Miracle picked up a white shawl that had been flung across a wing chair by the empty grate and sat down. Had Ryder played in here as a child? Had he ridden that horse and laughed with glee as he drove it over imaginary fences, or across the Milky Way to the moon?

A new life alone in America seemed almost as cruel now as the scaffold. She closed her eyes and tried to think about the stars.

She had seen a famous comet once, not long after she had been apprenticed, though she hadn't known what it was at the time. Many years later Sir Benjamin had shown her a drawing of it, the tail stretching between the twenty-third and twenty-fourth stars of Ursa Majoris. Sir Benjamin had thought the tail must be twenty or thirty million miles long.

"Ah," a voice said softly in her ear. "I've been looking for you."

Miracle opened her eyes to gaze straight up into ocean-green depths. Her heart began to hammer, but she tried to smile lightly, as if nothing were wrong.

"My lord," she said with a coy dip of her lashes. "You find me at a disadvantage."

Ryder grinned, but he stepped back to perch one hip on the top of a dresser, his arms crossed over his chest. He was lovely like this: relaxed and easy in her company, though the fire of desire lay carefully banked beneath that dark gaze.

"I'm sorry to wake you. You sleep very charmingly."

"I wasn't asleep. I was thinking about a comet I once saw."

"The great comet of 1811? I watched it through an opera glass all that autumn from the roof of the Fortune Tower. But you can't have been much more than seven years old at the time. How did you see it, if you were already apprenticed at the mill?"

"I'd tried to run away. I thought if I could only get home, my father might want me back. I'd not made it more than a hundred yards, before I was caught. As a punishment, I was locked alone in a small room at the top of the apprentice house every night for a week. There were planks nailed over the window, but I was able to plaster my nose against a crack to gaze out at the night sky. A hazy new star had appeared in Charles's Wain."

"You knew it was a comet?"

Still bemused, she spoke without thinking. "I thought it was my mother, looking down on me from heaven."

He glanced down at his boots. "I hope that was some comfort, at least?"

"When she died, I was told she'd become an angel." She reined in the memory and forced herself to sound matter of fact. "I learned later that I'd seen a famous comet, instead. I also learned that the correct name for the Wain is Ursa Majoris, the Great Bear. Truth is far more comforting than fiction."

As if he understood that she wanted neither sympathy, nor platitudes, he continued to gaze idly at the floor. "How is that?"

"My mother's spirit is everywhere, I think, always available to my heart, not pinned like a dead butterfly among the stars, and certainly not attached to a heavenly body that visits only once in a lifetime." She stretched, then tossed aside the throw. "I've already slept half the day. I thought you were sleeping, too?"

He looked up. "For a few hours."

Miracle leaned forward and smiled teasingly as she met his gaze. "But the games we have afoot are far too interesting to justify wallowing about in bed?"

"Too much so, at least, to justify wallowing about there alone."

She bit back laughter, along with a headily painful recognition of his acuteness—that he had accepted her escape into flirtation, that he had not pressed her about her mother, nor her childhood.

"The maid also told me that you were three sheets to the

wind when you collapsed between the sheets, so I doubt you'd have been much use either way."

He grinned with real mirth. "Which maid was that? I'll have her hide."

"No, she relayed your instructions very faithfully and is in obvious awe of your prowess."

"Then she may stay, of course. Anyway, I suspect the girl in question is the daughter of one of my nursemaids. Thus her position here is secure, even for a lifetime of impertinence."

Miracle glanced about. "Was this your nursery?"

"Yes, for some of the time. I was born in this house. Unfortunately, I lacked the grace to wait until my mother could return to the appropriately grand ducal bed at Wyldshay."

"Was she disappointed?"

He stood up. "To have a son? And give birth for the first time here at Wrendale? No, it was exactly what she planned."

"Planned?"

"The duchess plans everything. No child of hers would dare to be the wrong sex, or arrive at an inconvenient time."

"Then why did she want you to be born here, rather than at Wyldshay?"

He strolled over to another door, opened it, and gazed into the next room. "I believe she thought the clean air of the Peaks would help me to grow into a strapping lad."

"Which it did." Miracle walked up to join him. He was looking into a night nursery with a cradle and three beds.

"One for the wet nurse," Ryder said. "The others for her assistants. Three women to wait on one tiny infant."

"You slept in that cradle?"

He laughed. "I don't know how much I slept. They say that I bawled inconsolably for weeks after I was born. Apparently, the wet nurse's milk disagreed with me. It turned out that she had a penchant for gin."

Miracle walked ahead of him into the small room and gazed down into the cradle. The satin coverlet was embroidered with the arms of St. George.

"I've never understood why a mother would hire another woman to feed her own child," she said. "Was the duchess that vain?"

"No. I don't think so. Not in that way. But it was Her

Grace's duty to produce another baby as quickly as possible, and they say nursing slows a second conception."

"Working people feed their own babies all the time and still manage to have plenty of children."

"So they do. Did you ever want babies, Miracle?"

Her heart contracted in pain, almost as if he had struck her. Since her back was turned, he could not see that she had to blink back a hot rush of tears.

"No, of course not! Anyway, I'm barren."

"Barren? Are you sure?"

She walked away, deliberately filling her voice with scorn. "I miscarried a child when I was fifteen. The doctor said then that I would never conceive again. You don't think that nine years without the embarrassment of a pregnancy has proved him right?"

"I'm very sorry, Miracle."

"Don't be! It's been a very useful attribute in my profession." Something bumped into her thigh. Miracle looked down. "Good Lord! What's this?"

"My baby carriage."

She sat down with a thump on one of the beds and stared at it. "Who the devil would put an infant into such a monstrosity?"

"My family. It's a priceless heirloom."

Miracle ran one hand over the shafts, where a goat or a large dog could be harnessed to pull it. Deeply cushioned red velvet lined the seat, but two gilt-and-green dragons reared menacingly over the hood, fangs bared. Their lashing tails curled around each side. Bizarrely realistic flames ran from the dragons' mouths to meet them.

Any infant placed inside would see only green glass eyes, ferocious metal scales, and an illusion of fire.

"No wonder you cried! Whether your milk contained gin or not, this is enough to destroy any baby's sleep."

"Nonsense! The first son and heir always rides about in the dragon baby carriage. It builds character."

Miracle glanced up at him, not sure whether he was teasing or not. "You would use it for your own sons?"

He glowered down at the dragons. "Probably not."

"Though you must have a son to inherit the dukedom one day."

"I can't exactly guarantee it, though Jack would never

speak to me again, if I saddled him with the title. He's having too much fun gallivanting about the world with Anne."

He opened another door and beckoned to her to follow him. A wasp buzzed frantically in one of the hallway windows. Miracle took off her shoe and quickly swatted it. Ryder glanced back and lifted a brow.

She met his bemused gaze and laughed at him. "You'd have opened the sash to let it out, instead?"

"Not at all! I'd have left its fate to the maids."

"Who'd have swatted it, before it could hide in a duster and sting someone. Wasps can sting over and over again. Unlike honey bees—or half-ravished courtesans—they don't die when they defend themselves."

"You won't die," he said.

"Even Lord Ryderbourne is not above the law. Once I've recovered my money from Dillard, only a ship can save me from the gallows."

"If it comes to that, I'll take you to the port myself."

"Then you agree that I must go straight to my brother as soon as it gets dark?"

"A curricle will be waiting. In the meantime, may I ask you to honor my cousin and myself with your presence at dinner?"

"A formal meal in the grand dining room?" She laughed up at him. "Forgive my speaking in a cliché, but I have absolutely nothing to wear."

"Then ask that meddlesome maid to help you. I give you both permission to raid the house. I'm sure you'll find something suitable in one of the dressers."

"Your mother and sisters leave some of their clothes here? There's not a female in your family who'd ever forgive you, if you allowed a woman like me to wear one of their evening gowns."

"But I won't forgive you, if you don't," he said. "So which is it to be?"

CHAPTER THIRTEEN

S HE WAS LOVELY. EVEN MORE LOVELY NOW THAN SHE HAD
been at sixteen. Guy watched the lift of her lashes as she
looked up at his cousin. The alluring turn of her neck. The soft
swell of white flesh above her low blue silk neckline. Her lips
promised sinful enticements. Poised on the stem of her wineglass, even her fingers were enthralling.

And Ryder—for all the cool grace of his manner—was obviously enthralled.

Guy sipped at his wine, only half listening to their conversation. For the first time in years, memories haunted him:
those early days in London, when he and Miracle had burned
away the last innocence of youth in a conflagration of passion.
The occasional encounters after that, before Miracle had announced that she must stay faithful to her protectors, and that
she and Guy could only be friends.

An intense, viscerally exciting flirtation was natural to her,
of course. Even now, when she and Ryder were exchanging
only dry facts, her sensuality glowed in every gesture, every
glance. Ryder burned as if she had lit a fire in the depths of his
heart.

Didn't they know that they were both tumbling headlong
into heartbreak?

Guy set his glass on the table. He wanted, very badly, not
to have to witness this. Yet he would do anything in his power

to help or protect her, and something in her eyes also spoke of pain and remorse and longing—something far deeper than the delicate regret she had once shown him.

"No, Dillard's been very successful," Miracle said in answer to a query from Ryder. "He moved the family from the rooms over his shop several years ago. They're living in a grand new mansion in one of the best streets in Manchester. He's described every detail in his letters."

"Then if we leave as soon as it gets dark, we'll arrive at your brother's shortly after dawn."

"With Lord Hanley still hot on our heels?"

"Without doubt," Ryder said dryly. "But we'll get there first."

It was a simple enough exchange, yet the air almost crackled between them. Why the devil didn't Ryder just sweep her into his arms and carry her off to bed?

Miracle stood up. Her smile encompassed both men, but the real passion in it was only for Ryder. "Then I'll leave you gentlemen to your brandy, while I go and prepare for another journey."

In a sweet rustle of silk, she left the room.

Guy dropped his head into both hands. Ryder pushed away from the table and stalked across to the fireplace.

"Are you still in love with her?" he asked.

"God!" Guy's head jerked up. "Is it that transparent?"

"No more so than with me, I'm sure. Miracle tends to do that to men."

"Then yes and no." Guy refilled his glass. "I've no desire to revisit that much pain. There's no going back, in spite of those adolescent declarations of undying love. I can offer her nothing now except friendship and she wants nothing else."

"Yet no man can ever look at her and not want—what we both want," Ryder said. "It's a bloody disaster."

"Why?"

Ryder stared up at a portrait of the third earl in his strict Puritan garb. "Nothing can change the facts: Every possible future for a courtesan and a duke's eldest son contains the inevitable destruction of love."

"You want love?"

With the fluid power of any natural athlete, Ryder spun about to face him. "I hope I know better than to waste my life wanting something I can't have, but let's at least save her from Hanley."

"I'll help in any way that I can."

"Thank you."

"For her sake," Guy said with a wry smile. "At the moment, I feel rather like strangling you, but what do you want me to do?"

"Wait here for a day to engage Hanley's spies in useless speculation, then go back to London to resume your normal life—on the surface, at least."

"While you recover whatever she sent to her brother?"

Ryder nodded. "And perhaps while we're gone, you could find out everything there is to know about this Philip Willcott?"

Guy stood up and offered Ryder his hand. His cousin shook it.

"Hanley doesn't stand a bloody chance," Guy said. "It does almost make one feel sorry for the man."

"No, it doesn't," Ryder said.

THEY slipped out of the house into a black world. It wasn't raining yet, but thick banks of clouds hung over the hills to block out the stars. Ryder led Miracle away from Wrendale in absolute silence. Entering the woods was like plunging into an inkwell. For mile after mile she was suspended in damp darkness, his grip on her hand her only compass. Every once in a while he would tug her to his side, so she could avoid puddles of water or the slap of wet leaves in her face.

The curricle was waiting in a lane. Miracle barely made out the dark shapes, but a harness jingled and a hoof clopped once as the horses shifted. Ryder handed her up, then exchanged a few whispered words with the groom. The curricle dipped beneath his weight. Ryder swung into the driver's seat. Hoofs and wheels muffled by the muddy road, they drove off in an eerie quiet, as if a dream carriage carried them straight into the heart of the night.

Dawn arrived as they dropped down out of the hills and into the tidy valley of the Dean River. Not far now to the cotton mill and the apprentice house, where Miracle had spent half her childhood. Somewhere beyond those trees, machines clanked and hammered as the small children tending them slowly went deaf. Whatever happened now, she would never, *never* work like that again!

Manchester was still half asleep under watery blue skies. The scent of baking mingled with the smell of coal smoke and horses. A few tradesmen were already about, carrying goods and opening up businesses.

"The respectable gentry are still snugly abed," Ryder said. "Since your brother counts himself as one of them these days, we'll try his home first."

They turned onto a street of fine new houses, and the horses dropped to a walk. Ryder reached over and clasped Miracle's hand. She had almost stopped breathing.

"It's been years," she said. "I've not seen Dillard in years. I've never met his wife, nor seen his children."

"He's your brother. He'll be thrilled to see you."

"Yes, of course!" She choked down the growing panic and excitement. "Oh! That's it!"

The green-painted railings were as familiar as if she had known them all her life. The symmetrical ranking of tall windows. The fanlight over the door. The brass knocker, shaped like a boot. Her heart pounded, as if she were running. Her only brother! All she had left of her family. The only person in the world who would always love her, no matter what.

Ryder pulled up the horses and swung down. The street was empty, except for a boy with a broom. His dung barrow stood near the railings. Without asking, the boy ran up to hold the horses' heads.

Miracle sat in the curricle and waited in a haze of nervous anticipation as Ryder rapped at the door.

No one answered.

"The knocker's up, so they can't be away." He stepped back to stare up at the facade. "You're sure this is the right house?"

She nodded, gulping down agitation before she could speak. "Perhaps Dillard's already gone to the shop?"

"And taken his staff and family with him?"

Ryder pounded with more force. A baby started crying.

"Go away!" a man's voice shouted from inside. "Go away!"

"Someone's home. You said Dillard keeps his own carriage. There's a mews at the back?"

Miracle nodded. Fists of indiscriminate fear clenched in her gut. She fought to remain calm, staring at Ryder's thick hair and long legs, as if just the sight of him could prevent her falling apart.

The boy scratched at a flea. "Tha'll ta'e nowt f'r a' thy axing, f'r a' tha's mebbe a lord."

Ryder raised a brow.

Miracle swallowed hard. "He says that we'll get nothing, however much we ask, even if you are a lord."

"Perceptive lad!" Ryder reached into a pocket. "Here's a penny for you, sir. However, you must swear to tell no one we were here, or I'll return to take the hide off your backside."

A grubby fist snatched the coin from the air. The boy crossed himself in a solemn promise. Then he grabbed up his broom and ran back to his barrow. Lifting the handles with an effort, he trundled it away down the street.

Ryder swung back into the curricle and whipped up the horses.

"It's all right," he said with quiet determination. "We'll get to the bottom of this soon enough."

He tooled the curricle around the end of the row and into the alley. The stalls behind Dillard's house stood empty. Ryder tied the horses and swung Miracle down onto the cobbles. He led her up to the back door and hammered at it with the butt of his whip.

There was no answer. He tried the latch. The door was locked, but a faint scuffling echoed from the other side.

Ryder knocked again, more softly this time. "Is someone there?"

"I'm not to open the door," a child's voice answered. "Pa says no one's to come in, 'less he says so. Not even the baker, though he hasn't brought us any bread for days and days."

Miracle exchanged one glance with Ryder before she bent close to the keyhole. She kept her voice calm, though stark fear froze her bones.

"Is that Amanda? We've never met, but I'm your aunt Miracle, and you have four little brothers and sisters. I sent you a little muff last Christmas. Do you remember?"

Silence.

"The muff was white fur. It had a little border of silver braid and a pocket for a handkerchief. I sent it to you all the way from London. Now I've come to see you myself. Won't you let me come in?"

"I'm not to," the child whispered. "Papa said so."

Ryder pulled out a coin. Sunlight glanced off the copper.

"Would you like a penny to put into the pocket, as well?" Miracle asked. "I have one here. A bright new penny."

"Can I buy a bun with it?"

"You can buy as many buns as you like."

A chain rattled. Bolts clunked. The door swung open to reveal a little girl. She peered up at the visitors from a tear-streaked face.

Miracle crouched down to the child's level and made herself smile as reassuringly as possible. "Thank you, Amanda. You're my eldest niece and I'm very pleased to make your acquaintance. Here's your penny! You're six years old, aren't you?"

The girl grabbed the coin, then thrust a forefinger into her mouth. She stared up at Ryder with eyes like dinner plates.

"This is my friend," Miracle said. "Where's your mother? We thought we heard a baby crying."

"Mama's upstairs," the child said. "She's crying, too."

"Is there a maid with her?"

"Just Simon and Freddy and George and the baby. Perky's left."

"Your governess, Miss Perkins? She left? Is your mama sick?"

Amanda shook her head.

"Is there a footman, or a scullery maid? Where's your cook?"

"Everybody left. And Papa's locked in his study and he won't come out."

"Your papa is my brother, as Simon and Freddy and George are your brothers. May we come in?"

The child nodded and ran ahead into a long hallway.

Ryder closed the back door behind them. "This kitchen's a shambles," he whispered in Miracle's ear. "I think she's been fending for herself."

They reached the foot of the staircase. Amanda started up.

A door in the hall banged open. "Who the devil are you?" a dark-haired man shouted. "What the hell are you doing sneaking about in my house? And it *is* my house, I tell you! Still my house!"

Ryder spun about. The man's bones were a masculine version of Miracle's. His hair was the same glossy black, though it stood up in wild tufts on the top of his head. His eyes were red-rimmed and bloodshot, as if he had been up all night.

"Mr. Dillard Heather?" He bowed when his offered handshake was ignored. "Ryderbourne. At your service, sir. This is your sister, Miracle. I trust you'll welcome your own flesh and blood?"

Dillard stared in a stupefied silence. His breath reeked of brandy. "Miracle?"

She clung to the banister and tried to smile. "It's really me, Dillard!"

Her brother seemed torn between hope and panic, like a dog that longs for a bone but fears to be beaten. "You heard the news, eh? Came to help the crows pick over my carcass?"

"What's wrong, Dillard? Where are your servants? Why are Mary and the children hiding upstairs?"

His face crumpled. Dillard started to weep into both hands. Terrible, racking sobs.

Ryder looked away. Distress hammered in his blood that this should be Miracle's homecoming. Nevertheless, he stepped back and allowed her to go to her brother. She put her arms about his shoulders.

"It's all right, Dill," she said. "What's happened?"

Dillard hugged her, then set her back to examine her face, as if he thought she might vanish at any moment. "You're an angel, Mirry, really an angel. Been drinking, that's all. Glad you could come. You've grown as pretty as a picture."

He turned to stumble back into his study. Tears spilled down Amanda's white cheeks as she watched her father disappear. Miracle took a deep breath, then turned to the little girl and smiled with stunning equanimity.

"Let me take you upstairs, Amanda. Your papa isn't very well, but I'd like to get acquainted with your mama and the rest of my nephews and nieces. Then we'll see about getting those buns, shall we?"

The child nodded and took Miracle's hand.

"I'll take care of your brother," Ryder whispered as she stepped past him. "But it will be dangerous to stay here very long. Hanley may already be searching Manchester for families named Heather."

She gave him a valiant grin, though he thought that her heart had simply snapped in two. "I'm aware of that. It's just a risk we're going to have to take."

"You're all right?"

"I'm only concerned that the rest of the children are hungry, too. Nothing else matters much compared to that, does it?"

With the child's trusting fingers locked in hers, Miracle disappeared up the stairs.

Ryder looked after her for a moment. Any other young lady of his acquaintance would probably have dissolved into hysterical tears, and demanded he forget everything except her personal misery. Instead, Miracle had instantly seen that the child's distress was more important than her own.

Yet the clock was ticking. Hanley knew that she was fleeing north. Unless they could recover the bag and learn why the earl wanted it, her life was still in danger.

Dillard had already poured himself another brandy. Other than the tray holding the decanter and glasses, every surface in the study—desk, chairs, shelves, most of the carpet—was covered with a confusion of papers.

He looked up as Ryder strode in. "Friend of Mirry's, eh? Have a drink, sir!"

Ryder took the glass from the man's hand and set it back on the tray. "You've had enough, Mr. Heather."

Dillard fell back into a chair, crushing letters and bills as he did so.

"What is it?" Ryder asked. "Bankruptcy?"

"How the devil did you know that?" Dillard stared up as if he saw ghosts. "Did the bailiffs send you?"

"No one sent me. I merely escorted your sister here."

"Then, for God's sake, take her away again, Mr. Ryderbourne."

"Lord Ryderbourne." Ryder pushed aside a jumble of account books and propped his hip on the desk.

The handsome mouth compressed, as if the man choked back dismay. "Mirry's latest protector, eh? No need for pretense, m'lord. I know what my sister does for a living. It's my shame as much as hers."

Ryder refrained from punching the man's jaw. "Stand up, sir!"

Dillard staggered to his feet. "If I'd had the courage to do it, I'd have blown my brains out, so be damned to you and your damned judgmental airs, Your Lordship!"

"You have a wife and five children, sir. And you're not in jail yet."

Miracle's brother clutched the edge of the desk. "Creditors'll turn us out, bag and baggage, and put the whole lot up for sale. My bairns'll be turned out to starve and I'll see the inside of a debtor's cell, whatever you say."

"I'm not in the habit of saying things I don't mean, Mr. Heather. Put your arm about my neck and come with me!"

As if someone else pulled his strings, Miracle's brother did exactly as he was told. Ryder supported his weight and dragged him into the kitchen, then bent the man's head over the sink. Dillard stood helplessly, staring down into the mess of dirty dishes, as Ryder worked the pump. Even when the sudden rush of water poured over his hair, he still stood passively, turning his face slowly from side to side.

"Sober yet?" Ryder asked.

Dillard gasped for breath. "Nay. 'Appen it'll ta'e more than that."

Ryder cranked the handle again. More water cascaded. "Is that enough?"

He shook his head, flinging droplets like a dog fresh out of a pond, then shuddered.

" 'Appen so!"

Ryder grabbed a towel from a hook beside the range. "Sit down in that chair and dry your hair. I'll get a fire going."

Dillard sat down. Water trickled into his collar and cravat. "Y'r Lordship nedna fix th' fire. Ah'll do it."

"Speak in plain English, sir, if you please."

The man shivered and closed his eyes, before pulling himself together with a visible effort. "I'm not much of a man, am I?"

Ryder built a fire, then filled the kettle and hung it over the flames. "That's up to you. Brandy rarely offers a very sound path out of trouble."

"It wasn't exactly a conscious decision," Dillard said with

a little flash of wry humor. "You could say that one thing led to another."

Ryder crossed his arms and stared down at him. "You had some success in your business. You borrowed. Expansion brought more profits. You borrowed some more. As your business grew, you made investments. Some of the ventures seemed a little risky, but you took delight in those unearned returns. After all, you'd had to work so damned hard for everything else, and it was the only way to really make your money grow fast enough."

Dillard rubbed the towel around his neck. "Perceptive, an't you? It worked for a while."

"And it might have kept on working, except that your lifestyle became ever more extravagant. You bought this house and kept a carriage, long before you could afford it. You hired a full staff and a governess for your children. You even took lessons in how to speak as a gentleman—hired a superior valet, probably. Meanwhile, your family was never denied any luxury."

"Had to project the right image. All successful business is built on bluff, Lord Ryderbourne."

Ryder glanced around the untidy kitchen. He was coldly determined that Miracle must never know the worst of this.

"No doubt. Yet too many of those investments turned rotten. Capital started hemorrhaging. When you couldn't pay your servants, they left. In the end everything imploded like a house of cards. Now your creditors are dunning you and threatening to call in your mortgages. So you had a quick drink to calm your nerves—then another. Is that about the size of it?"

Dillard's mouth worked. "I'm not the first man to make a few bad judgments."

"And you won't be the last. There's only one part of this story that really stinks to high heaven, and I could beat you into a damned pulp over it."

The damp head jerked up. Dillard's eyes were still rimmed in scarlet, but he was halfway to being sober. "What the hell do you mean?"

Ryder leaned forward. "Your sister's savings. You embezzled them, didn't you? You lost all of Miracle's money, as well as your own."

The towel crushed beneath clenched fingers. "How the devil did you guess that?"

"Because I'd probably have done it, too—grasped at any straw, however dishonorable—before I saw my children starve."

Miracle's brother stared up in silence for several moments, breathing hard. "I only borrowed it, little by little," he said at last. "I promised myself that when things came right again, I'd pay her back with interest. I never meant—"

"Yet it's gone." Ryder pushed away to stalk about the kitchen, opening jars and boxes.

Dillard stood up and tossed down the towel. "You won't find any tea or coffee, my lord. Cook took it all in lieu of her unpaid wages."

Ryder glanced back at him. "You might have mentioned that before I filled the kettle. Never mind! I need to know about a bag that Miracle sent here for safekeeping. A Mr. George Melman delivered it."

Dillard flushed and bit his lip. "I don't have it."

In one stride Ryder held Miracle's brother by the throat. "Did you steal that from your sister, as well?"

"I'm facing ruin! So, yes, I took a quick look inside, but though I was tempted to sell the jewels, I didn't!"

"Though you no longer have it? What happened?"

"Patrick O'Neill barged in just as Melman arrived. He'd probably been watching the house. He grabbed the bag and tipped the contents onto the hall table."

"This O'Neill is one of your creditors?"

Dillard nodded. "He took the jewelry, though he said it still wasn't enough to settle my debts."

"And the other things?"

"I thought the bailiffs would seize all of Mirry's things along with mine. So I asked Mr. Melman to keep the rest safe until sent for."

"Then you did cling to a modicum of honor. Did Melman leave an address?"

"He's a traveling preacher. He went north toward Lancashire and said he'd get in touch later."

Unable to stop himself, Ryder laughed. "Then I ask only one thing of you now, Mr. Heather: Your sister is not to know any of this."

"If she asks me about the jewelry, I don't see how I can keep it from her."

"Tell her the truth about Melman bringing the bag, but you're to screw your bloody mouth shut about losing the rest of her savings. Let her think that you had a spot of trouble, but now your investments have turned around."

"But I can never pay her back!"

"Yes, you can. I'm going to make you a loan."

Color flooded Dillard's face. He collapsed back into his chair. "A loan, my lord?"

"You heard me."

Miracle's brother laid his head on the kitchen table and began to sob.

RYDER rubbed down his horses and left them in Dillard's stable, then he strode around Manchester like an avenging warrior angel. It took most of the morning.

The first item of business was to send a baker's boy to Dillard's house with a load of bread and buns and meat pies. A dairy maid took fresh milk, butter, and cheese. The grocer's lad brought apples and cabbages and potatoes, followed by packets of tea and coffee and chocolate. The butcher sent beef and sausages.

The children were to have a feast, courtesy of their aunt Miracle.

It took a little longer to visit banks and businessmen, but each of Dillard's creditors was flattered or cajoled or threatened, until he agreed to refinance. The mortgage on the house was transferred into Lord Ryderbourne's name, then paid off. Tradesmen, blacksmiths, leather suppliers, servants—everyone with a claim against Mr. Dillard Heather or his family—saw bills settled in cash. Only O'Neill was impossible to find. He had gone back to Ireland.

No doubt there was fraud buried in some of the transactions. No doubt some better bargains could have been struck, if Ryder had taken more time. Yet he didn't care what it cost. He only cared that Miracle never find out that her brother had betrayed her.

He found the governess through a ladies' employment agency. No, Miss Perkins had not yet found a new post. Yes, her references had always been excellent, but most families preferred a younger governess these days. It did not help, alas, that she had left her last employment in such haste.

Miss Perkins opened her door to reveal a shabby space brightened with brave touches of gentility. Quietly spoken, with soft, dark eyes, she was thrilled to return to the Heather family right away. His Lordship was most kind. She missed the children more than she could say. Though she allowed no hint of distress to pass her lips, it was obvious that Perky had been on the verge of destitution herself.

Ryder strode back into the more prosperous streets and stopped briefly opposite Dillard's place of business. The sign above the window was picked out in gold letters on black: DILLARD HEATHER, BOOT AND SHOE MAKER.

As soon as Hanley came here, he would track Miracle in an instant. Meanwhile, it was impossible for Ryder to keep his own presence and his interest in the Heather family a secret. He was the favored elder son of the Duke of Blackdown. Manchester had probably never before witnessed this much bowing and scraping.

By the time he returned to Dillard's house, it was late afternoon. Ryder knew a moment of real dread as he strode up to the front door. If the earl had already been here—

But his man was still on watch, and Miracle opened the door to smile at him. His heart leaped at the shine in her eyes.

"I'm prepared to wager that the only person who's not eaten yet is you," she said.

He pulled her into his arms for a quick kiss. "How did you guess? No dramatic changes while I've been gone?"

"Nothing, except that a remarkable wave of cheer has been sweeping the household."

"Thank God! The delay was more than a little unnerving."

"Fiddlesticks! Now that she's eaten, Amanda would be more than a match for Lord Hanley."

She led him through to the kitchen and set a hot meal in front of him. Ryder inhaled the savory steam—God, he was starving!—then glanced about. The room was spotless: crockery washed and put away, floor scoured, grate shiny with fresh blacking. Miracle's hands showed how hard she had worked.

"The elves have been busy while I've been gone," he said.

"Always a good idea to have connections among the wee

folk." She sat opposite him and propped her chin on both fists. Dark waves framed her face. He yearned with sudden desperation for her to really give him her heart. "Miss Perkins came back and Dillard says his affairs are taking a turn for the better. Your doing, of course?"

"I'm making him a loan, that's all. His business is sound enough. It just needed a quick infusion of capital."

Her mouth quirked and she looked down. "So he panicked over nothing?"

"If you like. I'll send my Mr. Davis from Wyldshay to advise him how to better manage his cash flow in future."

Miracle turned her head to stare out at the bright summer afternoon beyond the small window. Her profile, as always, took away his breath.

"Dillard's wife, Mary, is expecting another baby in a few weeks. She slipped on the bedroom carpet four days ago and has been confined to her bed. Dillard is with her now, and Miss Perkins is taking care of the children in the nursery."

"He told you about Mr. Melman?"

She nodded. "But everything else seemed so much more important."

A slight noise in the doorway made her look up. Dillard walked in and laid a hand on Miracle's shoulder, then he sat down beside her.

"I'm sorry to entertain you in the kitchen, my lord. By tomorrow I'll be able to offer you both better hospitality."

Ryder laid down his knife and fork. "I regret that pressing business takes us away this afternoon, sir. Miracle would like to recover her bag from Mr. Melman without further delay."

Dillard pinned Ryder with a defiant glare, then he shook his head and bit his lip.

"Then another time, Mirry," he said.

She put her arms about her brother and hugged him. "You won't be able to keep me away, sir."

AMANDA woke up with a start. She choked back a sob, but then she remembered: Everything was going to be all right, after all. Perky sat snoring gently in the nursery armchair. Simon and Freddy and George were still asleep, after being put down for a nap. Aunt Miracle and the nice man who'd sent all that food had left, but a bright copper penny gleamed on the little table next to her bed. She'd eaten as many buns as she wanted and she'd been allowed to keep the penny, as well.

She wriggled into her dress and thrust the penny into her pinafore pocket.

Mama and Baby Charlotte were asleep, too. Papa had flung himself onto the chaise longue in Mama's bedroom. Snores rattled in his throat. He didn't wake up, even when she shook his shoulder. There weren't any servants yet, though Papa had said they'd have new maids and a cook by tomorrow.

So she alone was awake in the whole world. Amanda wandered about the house, looking into all the rooms, just in case.

When a staccato sound echoed from outside, she rushed into the front parlor to look out. A carriage! Perhaps Aunt Miracle and that nice man had come back already! She ran into the hall and tugged open the front door. Her heart thumped like a rocking horse. A carriage had stopped in front of the house.

She almost raced down the steps to meet him, but the man who stepped down wasn't Aunt Miracle's friend. Neither was it any of those nasty men who'd been coming to the house to shout at Papa. This newcomer was an absolute stranger.

He strode up to her and bent down. "This is the Heather household?"

Amanda stuck her finger in her mouth. She was suddenly afraid, so she clutched hard at her penny.

"Don't deny it, little miss! I had the directions from Mr. Miles, apprentice at your father's business." He crouched lower and smiled. He had bright blue eyes and yellow hair, but she did not like his smile. "What do you have in your pocket, sweetheart? Something for good luck?"

"My new penny." Amanda reached into her pocket to show him the protective power of the shiny copper coin. "My aunt Miracle gave it to me and made everything come right again. But she's gone away again now."

"Hah! So she was here?"

Amanda nodded. "And her friend sent me all the buns that I wanted, and Perky came back, and Mama stopped crying."

The stranger's mouth twisted and he straightened up. The dung sweeper boy was trundling his barrow up the street.

"How long ago did they leave?"

"Hours ago!" Amanda backed inside. "But you can't come

in to make Papa ill again. And you won't catch my auntie and that nice man, either. They've gone to Lancashire to find their friend, Mr. Melman. I know, because I heard Papa tell Mama all about it. So you can go home right now and leave us all alone!"

The man laughed.

She slammed the door in his face. Boots rapped as the man walked away. A sudden cry scared her so badly that she sat down on the floor and closed her eyes, but at last hoofbeats echoed as the man's carriage trotted away up the street.

Amanda stared at her penny. It was the best good luck any little girl had ever had, better than a rabbit foot. It had made her so brave that she had chased away that bad man all by herself.

CHAPTER FOURTEEN

"𝓘 ASSUME THAT I'VE NO MONEY LEFT," MIRACLE SAID. "Dillard managed to lose all of my savings along with his own, didn't he?"

Ryder leaned back against the squabs. They had climbed into this larger carriage on the outskirts of Manchester, leaving the curricle behind. The coachman and groom had come down from Wrendale. Now, in the velvet dark of the August night, they were speeding north directly up the turnpike, with the groom discreetly asking after George Melman at every tollhouse.

"Why do you say that?" Ryder asked.

"Because if my brother hadn't already lost all of my money, he'd have asked me for a loan, instead of you. I didn't want to bring it up while we were still in Dillard's house, but that's what happened, isn't it?"

He frowned at her. "Perhaps. But he'll pay you back."

"With money you'll give him?" She laughed. "God, Ryder! Allow me the dignity of embracing my own ruin for at least a few moments, before charging to my rescue with showers of gold."

"You make me sound like Zeus visiting Danaë."

"Except that Danaë could be impregnated and I cannot."

Even in the darkness she saw him flinch. "You cannot stop my lending funds to your brother."

"But I won't take your money, even if it is channeled through Dillard."

"For God's sake!" Dark color burned over his high cheek-bones. "Then how the devil will you survive? You're penniless, Miracle."

"Let's find George Melman first," she said. "If we don't recover my bag before Hanley does, talk of my survival may be moot."

Ryder leaned forward to clasp her fingers. "We'll find it."

His palm felt warm, his pulse vivid with the masculine force that seared into her bones. Lovely! Lovely! Desire pooled, hot and urgent, though her heart faltered. *Coward!*

With her free hand she unsnapped the clasp at her throat and dropped her cloak from her shoulders. He inhaled, one quick snatched breath, as if he were suddenly robbed of air.

"Whether we find him or not, I defy the cold night and the threat of immortal notoriety. I defy death on the gallows, as I defied life in the cotton mill. Make love to me, Ryder?"

"Don't tempt me. I burn for you."

"Then let me quench that fire. It may be the last time."

"I cannot—" He choked and tipped back his head. "You know that I cannot deny you."

"Then let's make love!"

"In the carriage?"

She laughed, giddy with fear and desire. "Yes, of course! You defied dragons in your cradle. Have you never made love in a carriage?"

Ryder spun her between his spread thighs. He flung one foot up onto the seat, so she was cradled against his bent knee. He was already aroused. She rubbed her palm over that magnificent promise, then unbuttoned his waistband to caress naked flesh.

She knew what she risked. She was a courtesan. Each time they made love, she only proved it again. Each time was just one step closer to the day when he would give her a necklace or a bracelet, and say good-bye. However much Lord Ryderbourne declared his love—and however real her love was for him—that would, in the end, be her fate.

But now he was on fire for her.

He moaned as if wounded, but his mouth closed over hers, hot and searching. His hands sought the curve of her flank, his strong fingers kneading her buttocks. Flame scorched over her skin, delivering desperation and anguish and a searing, deep elation. She twisted in his arms to tug her skirts out of the way. His palm rubbed her breast through the fabric of her dress, then he teased her nipple into aching hardness.

The carriage rocked over a bump. Before she could take charge once again, he set her back onto the opposite seat. For a moment, she was bereft.

"You'd still be Sir Galahad, even now?" she whispered.

"No! God! I lost all claim to that title long ago."

"I want to pleasure you," she said, sliding one hand over his thigh. "Let me!"

"What if it's my turn now?" He pinned her with both hands as he slid down to kneel on the carriage floor. Moonlight gleamed on his disordered hair; his mouth, already swollen with kisses; the quizzical, teasing glint in his eyes. "The question is: Will you let me pleasure you?"

"I can't deny you," she said. "How the devil did you think I ever could?"

He pushed up her skirts and stroked her thighs. She lay back on the seat, whimpering with pleasure. With delicate grace, his lips followed his fingertips.

"You'll have to teach me to do it right," he said, between tantalizing little kisses.

"Your own nature will teach you."

"Good," he said. "I've been wanting to do this for a very long time."

She groaned as his tongue followed his lips. Licking and kissing, sweetly fleeting little caresses. Feeling terrifyingly vulnerable, she braced her feet on the opposite seat and gave herself up to his subtle exploration. His tongue flicked. Untutored, but with exquisite sensitivity. Her entire being dissolved into a rush of moisture.

The carriage rocked. The horses clopped on. Ryder slipped both hands beneath her bottom and began to devour her.

When he opened the flap of his trousers, she was already lost.

DAYLIGHT began to filter through the carriage windows. A dull, drizzly daylight, as they skirted the edge of the Yorkshire Dales. Ryder gazed down at Miracle's face. Her lips were slightly ajar, as if she would whisper mysteries, or offer a kiss to a ghost.

He smoothed her hair back from her forehead, and she smiled up at him. His heart, lost long ago, ached for a safe berth in that smile.

"Are you hungry? John Coachman says there's an inn just ahead, and we're already very close to Mr. Melman."

Miracle combed her fingers through her hair. "I believe I'm in a very sorry shape to appear in public."

"You've never looked lovelier. You remind me of springtime maidens and innocence."

She glanced up at him and laughed. "How can you say that? After last night!"

"Even last night."

"Don't, Ryder! Don't forget what I am! A paramour and a gentleman are supposed to enjoy a light friendship dominated only by pleasure, where hearts are not involved."

"It's usually the man who says that, so he can discard his mistress as the fancy takes him."

"Women can also pretend to love, while they're really only mercenary."

"But that's not the only reality, is it? The carefree ladybird who goes merrily on her way when her protector abandons her?"

Her skirts rustled as she moved to sit on the opposite seat. She felt so vulnerable to him, stripped to her soul, as if she could never again tell him anything but the truth.

"I don't know. I've never known any harlot, even the most jaded, who doesn't carry the scars of some man's cruelty buried deep in her heart. She may cover it up with brassy bravado, or take to drink, or opium, or weep in silence when she thinks she's alone. And yes, some become vindictive or try to defend themselves through greed. But most courtesans once, long ago, dreamed of true love, even if they know now through bitter experience that their fate is going to be quite different."

"You dreamed of true love with Guy?"

"Yes, of course. I was young. He seemed to be everything a girl could—" She broke off and twisted her hair into a knot. "Your cousin's been a good friend to me, Ryder. Though there were a few more times after we first parted ways, it's been many years now since we were lovers. I've carved my own path through life. I wouldn't have it any other way, and neither would Guy."

Hens squawked as the coach turned into the inn yard, scattering the birds into raucous complaint.

Ryder wrenched his mind back to the problem at hand. Did he really need to know how she and Guy had loved each other? A new solution was forming in his mind—one so outrageous that he must question his sanity even to entertain it.

"You look as if a ghost had just walked over your grave," Miracle said.

The carriage stopped. The groom from Wrendale opened the door.

Ryder smiled at her as if nothing were wrong. "I was just making up my mind to something. Meanwhile, perhaps we'll find Mr. Melman here, eating his bacon and perusing his Bible. Shall we go in and see?"

An hour later they sat with the preacher in a private parlor. Miracle's bag lay on the table. His face shining with honest good fellowship, George Melman stood up and bowed.

"Glad to be of service, ma'am. Though I apologize that I couldn't prevent the Irish gentleman from taking some of your valuables."

"Can you describe exactly what was taken?" Ryder asked.

The preacher shrugged. "I didn't pay it that much attention, sir. Necklaces? Earrings, perhaps? The lady's brother would remember better, no doubt. Now I must return to my work."

The men shook hands. As soon as Mr. Melman left the room, Miracle seized the bag and tipped the contents onto the table. She sorted through them, then glanced up at Ryder.

"You're going to think I'm insane," she said. "Apart from this bracelet, it's just a lot of rubbish: fans, combs, hairpins, a sewing kit, three nondescript novels. I must have been mad when I packed it."

"No. You were afraid." He picked up a book and turned it over in his hands. "May I destroy this?"

"Why?"

"Whatever Hanley's searching for, it's something he believes could ruin him. Perhaps papers are hidden in the binding. I need to break page from page to make sure."

"Yes! Yes, of course!"

He took a knife and slit the cover, then broke the back and cut stitches. Pages drifted into heaps of disconnected scenes. Words tumbled haphazardly into incoherence. The other two volumes received the same treatment.

"Nothing but dry paste and broken words." He tossed down the last cover. "If the authors could see this, they'd never forgive me."

They searched through everything again. Eventually Ryder sliced into the bag, separating the cover from the lining.

"Nothing!" Miracle bit back despair as she sorted through the items once more. "It's just meaningless detritus. This bracelet should have some value—I'm lucky that the Irishman missed it—but nothing else here could possibly be of importance to Lord Hanley."

Ryder leaned back, his eyes thoughtful, as he nodded his assent.

"So this has been a wild-goose chase, after all. When the earl finds out that I don't have his treasure—whatever it is—he'll bring murder charges."

"No, he won't."

"Yes, he will. Your mad quest has come to an end, Ryder. I should have gone straight to Liverpool."

"Hanley's men will be watching for you at the ports."

"That's just a chance I'll have to take." She tossed the bracelet. Light sparked in the little diamonds. "This is worth enough to pay my passage into a new life, I should think. Unless I was rewarded for my labors with paste?"

"How dare you!" Ryder seized her wrist, cold and determined, though he did not raise his voice. "How dare you throw your past into my face!"

"Because that's exactly who I am, my lord. All the fairy tales in the world won't bring about a happy ending now."

Knuckles rapped at the door. Ryder opened his fingers and released her, brows contracted as he faced the interruption. "Come!"

The groom from Wrendale stepped inside and touched his forelock.

"Yes?" Ryder said. "Out with it, York!"

"Mr. George Melman has left safely, my lord, but another gentleman is asking for Your Lordship in the taproom. Lord Braughton is with him."

Miracle glanced at Ryder's face. "Braughton?"

"The local magistrate. Pray, continue, York."

"The first gentleman described Your Lordship and the lady very minutely to the innkeeper. A burly fellow that I'd guess is from Bow Street is waiting in the yard. Other men are watching the rear exits. The innkeeper said nothing, but plenty of other travelers saw us arrive."

Miracle pressed one hand to her mouth. Icy fingers trailed dread down her spine. "It's Lord Hanley! I must escape, while I still can—"

Ryder smiled, though his smile spoke of headaches and thunder. "You can't escape."

"He'll denounce me, and he's brought the law with him this time."

"Remain here," Ryder said. "York will stay with you. I'll take care of Hanley."

She dropped her head into both hands, fighting the shakes that had seized her limbs. "You mustn't kill for me, Ryder."

"That's my choice, not yours." His fingers briefly touched her shoulder. "But for all his crimes, I don't know yet that the earl deserves to die without trial."

"You still have faith in the courts? Of course, duke's families make the laws, while common folk get hanged. It was easier to be brave when the threat seemed more remote, but I'm genuinely terrified now."

"You don't need to be afraid," he said. "No one's going to die over this. Not even Hanley. And certainly not you."

Miracle stared at the miscellany still scattered on the table: the broken books, the pretty combs, a silk fan with a painted scene of Venus and Adonis. She had struggled so hard for security, sacrificed so much, and she had nothing left to show for it but frippery.

"I saw some thieves face the scaffold once," she said. "Two men had been condemned together, and my carriage was swept along in the crowd. I don't remember any gallantry or fine speeches, but I do remember how one man shouted and struggled—and then the terrible gurgling silence—before the mob began to roar."

"I'll be back for you." He looked back from the door with a bittersweet smile. "You don't need to be brave. It's all going to be fine. Just wait here with York, then be ready for another long, hard journey."

With the thunderclouds still massed in his eyes, Lord Ryderbourne swept from the room.

IT had happened sooner than he had hoped, but it was inevitable that Hanley would catch up with them. Ryder strode out into the taproom with his heart on fire. The earl and Lord Braughton were talking intently to some other travelers. No doubt, as York had reported, the inn was surrounded by Hanley's men. There was no escape for Miracle, but one.

Now that the moment had arrived, his decision filled him with a visceral, wild excitement. After this day—whatever the consequences, and they would no doubt be terrible—there would be no going back.

"Hanley!" he exclaimed. "What a pleasant surprise! We're making a habit of running into each other in obscure hostelries."

The earl spun about as if, flayed, he was raw to the touch. "Good God! Ryderbourne! Still merry as a cricket? Thanks to the ministrations of a certain lady, no doubt?" His eyes narrowed, but tension worked at a muscle in his temple. "We've already ascertained that she's with you. Pray, don't attempt to deny it!"

"Of course, but let's not be indiscreet." Ryder turned to the magistrate. "Delighted to see you again, Braughton! I trust we may welcome you and Lady Braughton to Wyldshay soon? Or to Wrendale, if that's more convenient? The duchess is burning to share all the latest gossip, as soon as she and the duke come north."

Braughton smiled with obvious discomfort. "My wife would be honored, Ryderbourne! Most kind!"

"Not at all! However, Hanley and I have a little private matter to discuss—very much to his interest, as it happens—and I've already led him a merry enough dance across England. You'll forgive us, I'm sure?"

The older man bowed. "Any affair between gentlemen is best settled privately, of course. Yet Lord Hanley implied that I might need to take some action here in my official capacity as magistrate."

"About my chestnut mare, no doubt?" Ryder turned back to Hanley as if having to explain something to a child. "After stealing one of my best saddle horses, some ruffian has been using her for highway robbery. Damn his eyes! He even used her to lift my own watch."

"I remember the mare." Hanley took a pinch of snuff, though loathing flickered in his eyes. "The same damned thug took my watch, as well. If it were in my power to bring it about, I'd see the man hanged."

"Me, too," Ryder said. "The most insolent fellow imaginable! But you have a habit of losing things, Hanley, whereas I have a habit of finding them."

The earl's snuffbox snapped closed. "What the devil do you mean, sir?"

"Simply that your most important recent loss has been found. Happy news, I trust?"

Hanley's lips pulled back as if he faced a ghoul. He fumbled clumsily with the snuffbox.

"Nothing here to concern you, after all, Braughton," he mumbled. "Seems I brought you from home on a wild-goose chase. I apologize."

Lord Braughton glanced back at Ryder. "You've recovered Lord Hanley's missing timepiece, sir?"

"No, alas, I found something quite different. However, Hanley was kind enough to put out a search for my mare. I must thank him."

"Then while you gentlemen exchange news, I'd best return home. Send a description of the stolen horse to me, as well, Ryderbourne. I'll put some of my lads onto it right away."

The magistrate bowed, turned on his heel, and left.

"Are you quite well?" Ryder asked Hanley. "You appear to have swallowed rat poison."

"Damn you to hell, sir!"

"Why? Because a certain lady is in possession of something that you might find embarrassing?"

Hanley swallowed hard. "Then she does have it! The bloody whore! Where is she?"

"Safe."

"Safe?" The earl laughed with leering bravado. "I already know that you've left her holed up in a private parlor with one of your grooms. Careless of you, Ryderbourne, unless you prefer to share your women with all and sundry! There's not a man jack among my servants who'd not sample a whore's wares, if given the chance."

"No doubt. However, there's no whore in the case this time," Ryder said. "As for the other matter at hand, shall we discuss it in more privacy? Over a glass of wine, perhaps? Your agitation is attracting some attention, which you might find unwelcome in the circumstances."

His eyes hollow, the earl glanced about. "If you expose me publicly now, I swear I will kill you."

"Perhaps. But then, you have control over something that I want, as well. We dislike each other, but neither pleasantries nor insults are necessary. I have a very simple proposition to make."

Ryder led the way to a private table in a corner and ordered wine. Hanley had regained control of himself, but a tinge of green still lurked at the turn of his nostrils.

"You intend to negotiate for her life?" he said, leaning forward. "Your silence for mine? Why should I believe you'd keep your half of any such bargain? Can you give me one good reason why I shouldn't bring charges against her right now for Philip Willcott's death?"

"If you do, I will ruin you."

Ryder calmly poured wine and watched Hanley toss it back. Perhaps if he stayed as close to the truth as possible, his ruse might yet work, though the sheer enormity of this bluff almost took his breath away.

"How the devil did you find out?"

"Before you and she boarded your yacht in Exeter, Miracle sent a bag of trinkets to her brother for safekeeping. A preacher carried it north for her. Surely you found out about that?"

The earl glanced away, his eyes haggard. "Eventually. A maid at the inn saw her pass the bag to a stranger under my bloody nose, though it took a while for my fellows to get the story out of the girl."

"But when they did, you guessed immediately what the bag must contain."

Hanley's fingers clenched on the stem of his glass. "It wasn't in her rooms. Willcott hadn't left it on the yacht. Where else could it be? God! If I had learned earlier about that whore's treachery—"

"So unfortunate! Especially once you learned that the preacher had been to her brother's house, but that the man had already left again with most of the bag's contents intact. Who told you that? The street sweeper?"

"I broke his arm for him. Why the hell did the preacher keep it?"

Ryder forced himself not to lean across the table to choke the life out of his enemy. "It's a long story, and not one that concerns either of us. Fortunately, Melman turned out to be an honest man, happy to return another's lost possessions. So I found it first."

Hanley's skin gleamed like damp limestone. "Then you've read it?"

"A little dishonorable for one gentleman to read another's secrets, but necessary in the circumstances, as I'm sure you'll agree."

"And the item is now in safekeeping to be revealed publicly, no doubt, if you were to meet with any sudden misfortune?" Hanley stared down at his hands, heavily laden with rings, and grimaced. "I should have shot you when I had the chance."

"You never did have the chance."

"*Never?* But now you propose that if I swear not to bring charges against her for Willcott's murder, you'll *never* breathe a word about what you've learned?"

Ryder nodded. "She will do the same. Her life is adequate surety for our silence, I would think."

Hanley poured himself more wine. The neck of the bottle rattled against his glass.

"While she's your mistress, perhaps. But once you've left her behind, your hatred for me will override all this gallantry to a harlot." His lips twisted as he glanced up. "Or perhaps you've forgotten what happened at Harrow?"

"No. I've not forgotten."

"And you've never forgiven it, either, have you? Any more than I have!"

"We were boys. It's of minor importance now."

Hanley drained his wineglass. "While you're besotted with her body, perhaps. But you'll get tired of her. You'll abandon her for another harlot. You won't give a damn whether she lives or dies, and your *never* won't mean a damn thing. Then you'll have your revenge and expose me. Why shouldn't I see her hanged first?"

"Because of what I'm about to tell you." Ryder took off his simple gold ring and spun it on the table. "The one event that will make you certain that, as long as I live, you'll be absolutely safe."

Hanley almost knocked over the bottle. He grabbed and steadied it, his knuckles white on the neck. Then a smile slowly creased his cheeks, before he laughed aloud.

"Oh, God! Will wonders never cease? If you're really that much of a fool, Ryderbourne, I think we may have a bargain, after all." He leaned forward, his eyes frosted with ice, and slapped his palm over the ring, then held it up to the light. "But I'll not give you more than twenty-four hours to do it."

MIRACLE sewed up her damaged bag, even though her vision was so blurred that the stitches ran crooked. If she simply sat here and did nothing, she would go mad. Why hadn't she fled to the coast while she still had the chance? Why had she allowed herself to revel in the company of a duke's son, who had—in the end—nothing to lose?

York stood respectfully in the corner and stared off into the distance, but if she tried to leave the room, he would stop her. Ryder's servants had such absolute faith in him. Yet Lord Hanley was likely to burst in at any moment with the local magistrate, and she would be arrested.

Under oath she would tell the truth. She had killed a man. She deserved to die.

Yet there was a terrible irony in the idea of a whore losing her life, because she'd been fool enough to first lose her heart!

Miracle tried to flip open her fan with the elegant gesture she had perfected over the years. Ivory snapped as her fist suddenly clenched. Using both hands she spread the fan on the table. Adonis was ruined. She had just crushed him against the Goddess of Love, and the embrace had destroyed him.

She bit her lip and looked up. York was still gazing steadily at the wall, but she thought she saw fear in his eyes. She and the groom were cut from the same cloth, after all. For all of his fine manners, York had no doubt also been born in a cottage.

Men like Ryder snapped their fingers at sudden death, faced with bravado and dash on the dueling ground or the battlefield. Only people like Miracle and York lived with the threat of a slow strangling from the hangman's rope.

Could she find the courage to face the gallows alone? Would the thought of the cold, distant stars be enough to sustain her?

She was determined to face the inevitable with as much dignity as possible, but she did not want Ryder there. What if she broke down, begging and screaming in the language of a mill child who had once pleaded in vain not to be locked in a dark attic? Though perhaps he would send her a bottle of brandy or a tincture of opium to dull her senses, if she asked for it?

The door burst open. The fan fell to the floor as Miracle leaped to her feet, but it was Ryder, alone. He looked wild, like a falcon bating on its perch.

"See to the horses, York!" he said. "We're leaving right away."

The servant bowed and hurried out.

"What happened?" Her heart hammered, choking. "Where's Lord Hanley?"

"Gone!" Ryder stooped to pick up the fan. His eyes veiled, he gazed at the spoiled painting for a moment.

"What are you concealing from me? You made some kind of a bargain with him? What did it cost you?"

He tossed the fan aside. He seemed feral, dangerous. "Nothing that I care about and far less than I'm gaining."

"Then you threatened him? Oh, God! You told Lord Hanley that we'd found what he's searching for, didn't you?"

"I implied it rather heavily." Ryder looked up and smiled, as if at some secret triumph. "Hanley certainly believes now that I could ruin him. I've no idea what his secret is, but he'll do anything—even let you go—rather than have it revealed to the world."

Knees weak, she dropped back into the chair. "Then, since this is all based on bluff, you've bought us time, but no more."

"Time is all we need." He caught her hand and pulled her

to her feet. "You're not going to die, Miracle. Does anything else matter?"

"You're taking me to a ship?"

"I'm taking you to a new future, but we must leave now, before Hanley changes his mind."

She swallowed hard and pulled away. She was certain that Ryder was concealing some staggering secret. She was equally certain that he was not going to tell her. Yet she would not be arrested, after all? She felt giddy, as if he had poured champagne directly into her veins.

He escorted her out to the waiting carriage, but he did not climb in beside her.

York ran out with a gray saddle gelding. Ryder swung onto the horse and leaned down with a quizzical smile.

"There are some other things I must do right away. I'll meet up with you later."

The coach horses pulled forward. Ryder spun his mount on its haunches and sped away. A shaft of sunlight blazed as blue-white as Rigel in the gelding's mane and tail.

If Miracle never saw him again, it was an image that would haunt her until the day that she died: her knight errant, as determined and powerful and terrible as thunder, riding away toward the hills, his pure heart—because of her—now sullied by duplicity.

Meanwhile, her future security was still built on sand. If Lord Hanley found his missing document and realized how he'd been tricked, nothing could save her. Ryder would grieve for a while and then he would forget her. One of those far more suitable young ladies would marry him and give him sons.

There was real comfort in the certainty of his eventual happiness.

Perhaps that—more than thoughts of the great, impersonal universe—would give her the strength, when it came to it, to face death with some serenity.

Yet Miracle had been mostly awake for several nights. In the end, from pure exhaustion, she slept.

VOICES were giving orders. Miracle woke with a start. Her pulse jolted into a pounding panic, but she was still in Ryder's coach.

The sun hung low in the sky. The bustle betrayed only that the horses were being changed yet again, or perhaps that they had stopped for a meal. For most of the long journey she had barely surfaced from her troubled dreams.

She had no idea where York and John Coachman were taking her, but they had not gone southwest toward Liverpool. Instead they had passed north through Carlisle and over the Esk River. They must be well into Scotland by now. Perhaps Ryder planned to send her all the way to Leith, before she found passage out of Britain?

York flung open the door. "We've arrived, ma'am. This is Mossholm, near Annan."

Miracle brushed both hands over her hair. "Annan? Then we're traveling west along the Solway Firth, not north any longer?"

"Yes, ma'am. Lord Ayre is far from home, but Lord Ryderbourne sent word ahead. We're to stop here for the night."

Miracle climbed down from the carriage. She stood in a courtyard, flanked by stables and outbuildings, but dominated by a towering castle. Light from the setting sun sparkled in a multitude of tiny leaded windows and reflected from dozens of conical turrets. Mossholm seemed encrusted with rubies, as if it had stolen the light from Antares.

Struck by the strange fancy of it, she laughed. "So Lord Ayre lives in a castle from a fairy tale? Is he another enchanter?"

York gave her a puzzled glance. "I believe His Lordship is mortal enough, ma'am. Lord Ayre is an old friend of Lord Ryderbourne's. You'll be safe here."

She was welcomed inside by the housekeeper, who bobbed a respectful curtsy as if the guest really were a lady. After an excellent meal in the wood-paneled dining room, Miracle was shown up to a guest chamber. The house seemed warm and well loved, but she asked no searching questions about her absent host, who had allowed Ryder the use of his home at a moment's notice. Though it was, of course, only another example of the extraordinary reach of a duke's eldest son.

Would nobody, ever, deny a St. George anything?

Fear intruded, like a flickering shadow. Perhaps he was not coming, after all. She would not blame him if he had simply gone back to London. No lover had ever stayed before. Why should Lord Ryderbourne—who could have any woman he wanted—be any different?

A summer squall blew in that night to whip about the turrets and moan down the stairs. Miracle lay awake for a long time, wryly aware that she had slept away half the previous day. She felt oddly suspended. It had been such a strange journey from the apprentice house to this Scottish castle. Did she regret any of it?

Only Hanley.

As for her Sir Galahad, it might almost be worth facing the gallows to have had these last weeks in his company. Miracle turned over and buried her face in the pillow. Drifting on the edge of sleep she almost thought she could feel him, warm and strong, in the bed next to her. Her lips shaped his kisses. Her mouth sighed with longing. Her heart knew deep, lovely tremors as her body remembered him. Perhaps Mossholm really was enchanted, after all?

A shutter banged. Startled fully awake, she stared at the dark windows, while yearning surged, hot and sweet, for a lover she might never see again.

When she next opened her eyes, it was to sunshine and a blue sky morning. After breakfast she climbed up into one of the turrets, where she could look out over Scotland. Water glimmered. The road east, back along the Solway Firth, twisted away toward England like a discarded piece of trimming.

Something was moving.

She watched the black speck as it came closer. A carriage rolled west toward Mossholm: a curricle drawn by two horses. Still several miles away as yet, a lone horseman thundered after it.

A quick stab of fear made her heart freeze for a moment. Miracle leaned both hands on the sill, watching the carriage and the horseman, as if they were portents of death.

As the curricle reached the last stretch, where Mossholm's driveway split from the main road, the rider drew level and leaned down to speak to the driver of the curricle. His saddle horse spun about, its mane and tail streaming in the wind like spume off a wave.

The horseman lifted his hat and turned to ride on. His dark hair whipped in the breeze.

Ryder!

Miracle sped down the stairs. She stopped herself at the last minute, before she raced out into the courtyard like a child. But when the footman opened the door and Ryder strode into the hall, she was standing at the foot of the main stairs, waiting for him, with her pulse pounding its aching desire in her veins.

"I wasn't sure you would really come, after all," she said with a wry smile. "However, I'm now as rested and refreshed as poppies after rain, and ready to travel on to Leith."

Ryder halted in his tracks. His eyes were very dark, as if the gale still tossed there. "You doubted that I would come?" He tossed his hat to a footman. "But I gave you my word!"

Suddenly afraid, she wrapped her fingers around the newel post for support. "Did Lord Ayre arrive with you?"

"Ayre? No. He'll get here later."

She felt awkward, as if the mill child had taken hold of her tongue. "I was watching from one of the turrets. You stopped to speak with someone in a curricle."

"George Melman. I asked him to come. He's driven half the night to get here."

"Why?" she asked. "He's found Lord Hanley's missing papers?"

Ryder walked up to her. The storm clouds still threatened thunder, but he bent his head to kiss her lightly on the mouth. She controlled her surge of longing and returned his kiss just as lightly, as if they were simply friends.

"No. Nothing like that," he said. "He's going to marry us."

CHAPTER FIFTEEN

"ᴅON'T JOKE ABOUT SUCH THINGS," SHE SAID. "WHY DID Mr. Melman really come?"

Ryder choked down the torrent of desire that flooded his bones. He burned to explore her mouth, deeply, thoroughly, but he took her by the elbow, instead, and ushered her into a withdrawing room.

Miracle stood beside the cold fireplace as Ryder strode away across the oak floor. Whatever the confused passion of his feelings, he would not use touch to persuade her.

"Sit down, please, Miracle. I'm not joking."

Ranked around the walls, a row of stags' heads, remote and majestic, gazed down from black glass eyes. Chairs and a chaise longue were arranged around a fine Turkish rug in front of the grate. At the far end of the room, a pianoforte stood near a deeply recessed window. Apart from the piano, Ayre had touched nothing at Mossholm since he had inherited it.

Miracle sat down on a delicate gilt chair and folded her hands. The movement was lovely, pure and simple and grace-ful. Her eyes seemed fathomless, that deep, rich chocolate, but a faint blush of angry pink brushed over her cheekbones.

"Then what the devil did you mean?" she asked.

He swallowed hard. If she tried to defy him, he would beat down her resistance, whatever it took.

"There's only one circumstance that can possibly demonstrate conclusively to Hanley that I care enough about your fate to remain silent forever."

"About a secret that you don't really know."

"Yes, but Hanley thinks that I do. He already hates me, and he has good reason to believe that the antipathy is mutual. He fears that I'd do anything to damage him and damn the consequences. He'd never believe that I'd keep faith for the sake of a mistress." He took a deep breath and spun to face her again. "However, he knows with absolute conviction that I'll keep silent forever for the sake of a wife."

The color deepened in her cheeks. "Are you mad?"

"I've never been more sane in my life."

"You cannot possibly marry me!"

He strode forward, even though it meant that he towered over her. "I can and I will."

She leaped up, her eyes blazing. "Have you gone finally, irrevocably lunatic? You cannot force me to wed you."

Something snapped in his chest, as if a leather belt had been stretched to the limit around his heart and finally given way.

"Devil take it, Miracle! I knew you'd try to defy me in this. But give it one second's consideration! If you don't marry me now, I won't be able to save you. You'll hang!"

She walked away with an oddly icy calm. It infuriated him. "You can help secure my passage out of the country, instead. Surely that's not beyond your powers?"

His fists clenched. Ryder forced himself to sit down.

"If we don't marry right away, Hanley will know I was bluffing. His revenge will be instant. You'd be arrested as soon as you tried to leave this house. Then you'd tell them the truth about Willcott, and be hanged."

Miracle stopped beside the piano, her back rigid. "Lord Hanley knows that I'm here with you right now?"

Ryder buried his forehead in both palms, his fingers clenched in his hair. "Hanley refused to accept that I could possibly be in earnest, until I gave him the exact time and place, and promised that the marriage would take place before impeccable witnesses."

As if her knees had simply folded, she collapsed onto the piano stool. "Lord Ayre?"

"We shall marry in Mossholm's chapel this morning. Ayre and his mother, the dowager countess, will be our witnesses. I

cannot ask either of them to lie about this. Hanley is bound to
have agents watching the place."

"I can be smuggled out past them."

Ryder jerked up his head. "Damn you, Miracle! I won't
take that risk."

"So this is why you had me brought to Scotland?" She
spun about on the stool and flung open the lid. The piano rang
softly, like a muffled bell.

"Scottish law allows us to marry without banns. If you want
to live much past tomorrow, we'd better make that a reality."

Her fingers struck the keys. Three chords echoed, one after
another, with absolute assurance, to be followed by an angry
storm of notes, as if lightning raged from the hammers. He
stared at her, struck to the heart by her passion and power.

"I learned to play when I was eleven." Her voice rang as
the chords crashed and boomed. "Sir Benjamin Trotter hired a
music master for me, so that I might become a proper lady.
I've not let that education go to waste. However, I didn't plan
to be a duchess."

Ryder leaped to his feet and strode to the window. "Even if
Hanley learns later that we have no more idea of his secret
than of the dark side of the moon, as long as you're my wife
he can't touch you."

"And for that faint assurance, you'd transform a temporary
ruse into reality? We'll exchange vows to love and cherish for
all eternity? Even if it means that a whore is to become a St.
George?"

"Why the devil not?" His blood raged in a host of uncomfortable emotions. He knew that she was right. He also knew
that he wanted this very badly and would do almost anything
to get it. "It'll be no harder to play the duchess than it was to
play Ophelia."

She stopped playing in mid-movement. Silence resonated,
then she buried her face in both hands and began to laugh with
a terrible hilarity.

"Aye, but 'appen tha canna ta'e t' mill oot t' lass, can ter?"

"What the hell are you saying?"

Her fingers strayed over the keys, offering a soft lament.
"That I'm a mill girl. That I'm a courtesan. Not even you can
make my past disappear. I cannot become your wife. I'm a bird
of paradise, a bit of muslin, a whore, a strumpet, a moll, a—"

"It doesn't matter!"

She glanced across at him, her eyes blazing. "God, it does matter and for a host of reasons! Let's begin with the most obvious: Your family would never forgive you. Society would never forgive you. You would never forgive yourself."

"That's rather up to me, isn't it?"

"No," she said with appalling calm. "It's not only up to you. It's my life, too."

Cold sweat trickled down his spine. Everything she had said was true. He knew it. He had faced it. He had made his pact with Hanley anyway. If she would not agree, then he must play the trump card.

"Not unless you prefer the gallows," he said. "Because that's the only choice you have left, Miracle: marriage or death. It's too late now for anything else."

"Then what a pretty bargain you made with our enemy!" Her fingers picked out a slow dirge in some haunting minor key. "So Sir Galahad will marry his paramour. He'll defy thunder and headaches for a misalliance that boasts to the world that he's truly besotted. May I have poppies for my bridal wreath?"

"Wreath?"

A merry dance tune rippled through the room. "A slip of the tongue. Obviously I meant my bridal bouquet. So what flowers would be appropriate? Pansies and rosemary?"

Ryder thought he might shatter. How dare she? How dare she negate his love and the enormity of the sacrifice that he was, in reality, making? Did she think that he hadn't already thought through all the ramifications of this? Why couldn't she see that he couldn't bear to live without her?

He crashed one fist against the folded wooden shutter. It boomed like a drum. She stopped playing.

"I've struck enough bargains. This is the last one. You'll never be poor again. You'll never have to be afraid again. You'll live in absolute security for the rest of your life. Are you too proud to accept it? Too fond of all those noble ideals learned in some lecher's library and used whenever it suits you? You would *die* rather than marry me?"

The piano lid crashed down. Miracle snarled at him like an avenging fury, beautiful and terrible, the embodiment of dark desire.

"Too proud? Too *proud*? I've fought too damned hard for

life, ever since the day I was born, to embrace death over any noble principle. Only an aristocrat like you would ever contemplate anything so foolish. People like me fight the darkness until the moment the noose tightens. We'll perjure and plead and struggle like demons, before we'll willingly let anything blot out the sun. But how dare you speak of Sir Benjamin like that?"

"Like what?"

"A lecher, you said. Your voice dripped with so much abhorrence that you couldn't even bring yourself to say his name. But Sir Benjamin Trotter saved me from the mill. He saved me from ignorance and poverty and misery and hunger. He saved me from going deaf. He saved me from losing a hand in the looms. He opened up the world to me in that library you scorn with such distaste—a world of learning and beauty and reverence. He gave me a real home, and I loved him."

He felt stunned, as if he had taken a blow to the head. "You *loved* him?"

"It was what I learned from Sir Benjamin that made me who I am. It was thanks to him that I could pick and choose my lovers in the terrible years after he died. The education he gave me saved me from walking the streets, offering myself to sailors for sixpence." She stalked up to him, lithe and lovely and dangerous. "The only man I've ever taken to my bed that I didn't really choose was you, Lord Ryderbourne."

"Then why didn't he marry you?"

Her eyes were pools of black. "Sir Benjamin thought that I wasn't old enough to take such an irrevocable step. We agreed to wait till I was eighteen. Then he died."

"Yet he took you to his bed."

"We mill girls mature young," she said. "And as I just told you, I loved him."

Ryder reeled away. She had loved Sir Benjamin Trotter? She had loved Guy Devoran? Maybe she had even loved Jack, his own brother? Yet she could not love him, Laurence Duvall Devoran St. George, the man destined to become Duke of Blackdown. Of all the men she had ever known—other than Hanley—only he could not win her heart?

"Sir Benjamin may have saved you from the mill," he said, precisely enunciating each word. "Only I can save your life.

So I assume that—in spite of your misgivings—you will still marry me?"

She marched up to the door. Her fingers gripped the latch, but she pressed the other fist to the panels and leaned her forehead against it. "There's not a whore in London won't cheer when she gets the news that one of her own has snared Lord Ryderbourne. I'll be the toast of the taverns and the anathema of the drawing rooms." She spun about, her chin high and her cheeks burning. "So of course I will marry you, though we will both live to regret it."

"Good," he said, though his triumph yawned like an empty pit in his gut. "Ayre and the dowager countess will have arrived by now. They'll be waiting with Mr. Melman in the chapel."

He walked up to offer her his arm, but she wrenched open the door and whirled away.

"Don't touch me!" she said with a sudden wry laugh. "If you touch me just now, I'll shatter into tiny pieces to be swept up and tossed away like broken glass."

He was lost in an ice storm. "But we're about to be married!"

"Yes, and you break my heart, you mad St. George. Why didn't I insist that you leave me to drown? I'd have saved you from making the biggest mistake of your life."

"Whatever price is exacted, Miracle, I'm prepared to pay it."

"Are you? I can at least promise that you'll always have a way out."

A shaft of sunlight beamed down from a high window, firing her dark hair with mysteries, lighting her cheekbones with the glimmer of transcendence. She was lovely enough to weep over.

"You would deliberately give me grounds to divorce you?" He felt incredulous.

"If I thought it was really forever, do you think I'd agree to this wedding? Whenever you wish to untie this injudicious knot, let me know. Parliament won't hesitate to free you, if your wife is caught in adultery."

Ryder seized her by both arms. "If you ever cheat on me—"

"Oh, stop!" she said. "Those are my terms. You've no choice but to accept them. Now, if we're going to swallow our despair and get married, we mustn't keep Mr. Melman waiting."

* * *

It was not how Ryder had imagined his wedding. As he and Miracle exchanged vows, Lady Ayre sat alone in front of a gathering of servants. Miracle was wearing her plain traveling dress, the only concession to the occasion a bouquet of white roses from Mossholm's garden, bound in blue ribbon and offered at the last minute by the dowager countess.

Lady Ayre was a tall, gaunt woman with silver-red hair. Though she watched the ceremony with shrewd blue eyes, she did not know who Miracle was, of course. She knew only that her son's friend wished her presence for his sudden marriage and that she was their only claim to respectability. Her Ladyship would obviously do anything for her son, who would apparently move heaven and earth for Ryder.

Ayre himself stood to one side, his face grave as he gazed steadily at Miracle. Ryder consciously noticed for the first time how bright his friend's hair was, how stern his features.

Tall and lean, Lady Ayre's only son was a red-gold Scot, but the skin over his cheekbones was a smooth gilt tan, as if he were cast in metal. Like any ship's captain who had sailed exotic oceans, his eyes encompassed the heavens. He caught Ryder's glance and his cheeks creased in a friendly smile, but ardor lurked in those sky-blue depths: an ardor composed of both admiration for a lovely woman and unabashed desire for her.

Ryder knew a sudden urge to wipe his friend from the face of the earth.

But the service was over. Ayre stepped forward to shake his hand and kiss Miracle discreetly on the cheek. Mr. Melman offered his congratulations. Lady Ayre tendered a few wryly correct comments, then walked from the chapel with her son, leaving the preacher with Ryder and Miracle to oversee the signing of papers.

Mr. Melman's carriage was waiting. As Ryder saw him to the door he pressed a purse of gold into the man's hand.

"For your flock," he said. "With the thanks of myself and Lady Ryderbourne."

After a last exchange of good wishes, the preacher was gone.

Miracle lifted the white roses to her face and inhaled.

"What now?" she asked, glancing up at him beneath her heavy lashes. "You'll send news of our wedding to Hanley, I assume?"

"I'll take it to him myself."

"Ah! Then what happens to me?"

"Ayre and his mother will escort you to Blackdown Square. It shouldn't be too uncomfortable a journey. You'll stop every night in the very best posting houses. Lady Ayre will take care of you."

Loose petals drifted to the stone floor of the chapel, releasing more scent. Miracle turned to face him, her eyes searching his. "So now that you've saved my worthless life, I'm to be packed off to London with your fascinating friend? You trust me in his company?"

He grinned, though his heart felt close to devastation. "I trust Ayre. Besides, his mother will be more than adequate chaperon on the journey, and he knows perfectly well that if he breaks faith, I'll kill him."

She bit her lip and began to shred another rose. "Will I ever see you again?"

"God, of course! I'll send for you as soon as I can." He stared at the trail of white petals as she turned away. "It's up to you, of course, whether you come."

Her shoulders tensed, but she laughed. "If you send for me, wild horses wouldn't keep me away. How else can I wreak my revenge on you?"

The door creaked as Lord Ayre stepped into the chapel. His good looks had turned many female heads in the past. It had never bothered Ryder before, but it did now.

"Our carriage is almost ready," the Scot said. His smile seemed only coolly assessing. "Lady Ayre wishes to start out as soon as possible. If that's convenient, Lady Ryderbourne?"

Miracle plucked one rosebud from the remains of the bouquet and tucked it into her hair. The folded petals caressed her cheekbone. Ryder stared at her, fighting visions of Ophelia, and poppies, and the intimation of tragedy. He was not even going to be able to kiss her good-bye?

"Yes," she said. "Thank you, Lord Ayre. If you would allow me one quick visit to my room, so that I may pack a few last minute things?"

Trailing petals and heartbreak, she walked away toward the door.

Ayre shook Ryder once again by the hand. "Delighted to escort your new wife to London, Ryder, but what the devil's so important that you aren't taking her there yourself?"

Before Ryder could reply, Miracle turned from the doorway. She gave Ayre her most dazzling smile, betraying both courage and irony. Possessive jealousy pierced like an arrow.

"My new husband must go alone and immediately to Wyldshay," she said. "He has to break the news of what he has done to his mother."

THE high towers of Wyldshay could be seen from miles away. The dragon banner hung limply beneath blue summer skies. It had been a long and exhausting journey. As soon as he had left Hanley, Ryder had traveled day and night without stopping, more than three hundred and sixty miles in thirty hours.

Shadows flitted as his carriage rolled over the arched bridge and pulled up in the courtyard. In spite of the mad distress of the previous three days, he was home. The tall towers and echoing halls offered balm to his bruised spirit.

Ryder strode first to his own rooms to bathe and change. His valet shaved him and trimmed his hair without comment, as if it were perfectly normal for Lord Ryderbourne to stalk in without notice after an unexplained absence, looking like a Gypsy. A footman brought sandwiches and hot coffee. Ryder ignored the food, but swallowed one bitter cup before he went in search of his mother.

Miracle had seen straight into his heart, as always. He could not dismiss the reality of his identity. Without the unlikely support of the Duke and Duchess of Blackdown, their marriage would be destroyed.

He found his mother, small and precise, walking in her rose garden. The air was heavy with scent. Hot sun beat down on stone walls and a pretty ranking of statuary.

As Ryder strode toward her along the gravel path, she glanced up from her contemplation of an overblown red rose. Beneath the shade of an ivory silk parasol, her eyes seemed both wary and fascinated, as if she watched a very interesting stranger who might offer her either solace or calamity.

He halted and bowed. "Your Grace? I trust I find you well?"

"My roses are infested with greenfly," she replied dryly. "Patterson should spray them with soapy water."

"I'll see to it. I must apologize if the gardeners neglected their duty while I was away."

She arched an elegant brow and moved her hand. The rose exploded in a rain of red petals, leaving only the spiked, naked heart.

"I see you are burning to unburden yourself, sir. Can you offer an account of your adventures fit for a mother's delicate ears?"

"Probably not," Ryder said. "Though I have important news, all the same."

The duchess laughed and tucked her hand into his elbow. "Come, let us walk and you may tell all. Hanley came here. I have no idea what embroils you with such an unpleasant person, but I thought you should know that he expressed both impertinent interest in your affairs, and a cock-and-bull story. Did Guy Devoran find you?"

"Your Grace's perception is, as always, uncanny. Guy made an impeccable messenger, and I owe him more than I can say. So thank you."

An iron gate led into a walled courtyard. The duchess released Ryder's arm as he opened the gate for her. She folded her parasol and sat down on a bench beneath the thick branches of an ancient cherry tree.

Leaves shaded her shrewd gaze. "I feared that you were about to make a bargain with the devil."

Ryder began to pace the flagstones. "I was and I did."

"I fear that this accommodation with Hanley involves something rather more than gaming debts, or a quarrel over horses?"

He spun to face her. "Yes," he said. "I have married his mistress."

Silence fell like a cudgel. Ryder stared at his mother, appalled that he had broken it so clumsily. For the first time in his life he had robbed the duchess not only of words, but of all semblance of life. She sat encased in absolute stillness, her face dead white, her lids closed.

Sound rushed back—the rustle of leaves, a gull shrieking far overhead—and she opened her eyes: the same deep green fringed in dark lashes that looked back at him every morning from the mirror.

"Is this marriage legal?" she asked with appalling calm.

"We were married at Mossholm. It's not only legal, but I have no intention of ever breaking it."

Color burned over her exquisite cheekbones. The duchess clutched hard at her parasol.

"Hanley's mistress is a well-known flower of the demi-monde. I have never, of course, met her, but I make it my business to know the society gossip. I believe she enjoys the unlikely name of Miracle Heather. A steady stream of trinkets would have secured her professional favors, along with all the protestations of love you could have wished. Yet you have *married* her?"

"Yes."

"Does Lady Ayre have any idea what kind of creature she sponsored?"

"Ayre's probably told her by now. He's bringing them both to town."

"The beautiful Lord Ayre? You'll be cuckolded before they reach London."

"I will not." His boots rang on the flagstones, echoing the pounding in his heart. "Though Miracle offered to do it—to give me grounds to divorce her, if I wished."

His mother's lips curled. "The future Duke of Blackdown is a great catch for any lady, even a royal princess, were one available. Should her husband choose to keep a paramour in town, a wife with the proper breeding would accept it. Did that option not occur to you?"

"That's not the kind of marriage I want."

"This creature is a great beauty, I assume?"

"Yes," Ryder said. "Exquisite. But she's far more than that: honest, clever, wise—"

"And her skills as a lover are unmatched." The duchess tossed aside the crushed silk and stood up. "No one cares whom you bed, sir. Everyone will care whom you have wed. I can only assume that you have lost your mind."

"On the contrary, this is the sanest thing I've ever done."

Small and perfect, the duchess stepped forward into the sunlight, where she blazed like a flame. "No court in England would agree."

He stepped closer. "You would try to have me declared mentally incompetent in order to challenge this marriage?"

The duchess stood rigidly upright. The green eyes flashed. "If that is what it takes!"

"Before you say anything else that you'll live to regret, Your Grace, I would ask only that you meet her. As soon as Miracle arrives in London, I'll bring her here."

"I will not have your harlot brought to Wyldshay."

Ryder strode to the gate and set his hand on the latch. A fist seemed to have closed in his chest.

"Miracle is my wife. If Your Grace does not welcome her here with the respect due the future duchess— If you so much as look at her askance, or make her uncomfortable in any way— If by the slightest action or omission you let her know that you despise her, or her humble origins— I will turn my back on Wyldshay. You won't see me again, until I return to claim the title. If you're still living when I become duke, you will—with all due respect—be shown the door. The choice is yours, Mother."

Silk rustled. The duchess sat down. "She is already carrying your child?"

"No." Ryder leaned his fist against the stone wall as rage and pain surged through his blood. "Miracle can never have children. She miscarried when she was very young. She's barren."

"Then you break my heart and will shatter your own."

"Why? It will only bring about your greatest wish: Jack will become Duke of Blackdown when I die. He won't welcome it, but it won't do him any harm."

The duchess took a deep breath. She seemed truly stricken, but she would never allow herself to lose control. Jewels burned in the depths of her eyes. "Only a few months ago you offered your brother nothing but chastisement for his sins with Anne. It was intolerable to you that he would break with the moral norms of English society. Now you would marry your mistress and charge his life with entirely different expectations?"

"I was wrong to judge him. I didn't understand—I knew nothing of passion."

"A passion that binds you so deeply now that you will even forgo having sons?"

Ryder pushed away from the gate and walked up to her. "Yes," he said. "Though I always wanted children."

She returned his scrutiny calmly, but a terrible vulnerability lurked in the tiny wrinkles at the corners of her mouth. "How can you think for one moment that I will support you in this calamity?"

"Because I'm asking you to do so. Because I'm your son. Because if you don't, you may never see me again. And, perhaps, because it's the only way you have left now to demonstrate that you care for me at all."

She glanced away as if grief welled up from some deep, forgotten place. "You would blackmail me with my own love for you?"

"Why not?" Ryder sat down on the bench next to her. "After all, it's what you've done to all of your children, since the day we were born."

"*Touché!*" The duchess clasped his fingers, then looked up with another small laugh. "We are an overly complex family, my dear. But you are my firstborn son. Can you really doubt that I love you?"

"I've always doubted it, but it would seem that love is capable of infinite diversity. I beg that you won't force us to be parted over this, Your Grace. Miracle holds my heart in the palm of her hand. I refuse to live without her. If you force me to choose between my wife and my family, though it break my heart, I won't hesitate to choose my wife."

She closed her eyes, as if she hid sudden tears. "They say we should be careful what we wish for. I have wished for your marriage. I have wished—believe it or not, as you will—for your happiness. I hoped you would find a wife you could love. Now you tell me that you have. Does she love you?"

"I don't know," Ryder said.

"She has enjoyed many other lovers, of course."

"More than you, no doubt, but probably fewer than Lady Oxford."

The duchess laughed. "Yes, perhaps a former courtesan will prove more faithful to her marriage vows than many ladies of our own class. Yet you will always meet men who have known her, Ryder. For the rest of your life, every man who looks at your wife might be remembering her in his bed. You can tolerate that?"

"It's a risk I'm prepared to take—even if my own brother was among them."

"Your brother?"

"It's possible. I don't know."

"You haven't asked her?"

Ryder buried his head in both hands. "No, and I never shall. It doesn't matter. Anne has Jack's heart now. But if you give this marriage your backing, no man in England—not even my own brother—will ever dare to drop a hint that he even met Miracle before, let alone that he ever knew her."

A little breeze sighed through the cherry leaves and agitated the trimmings on the duchess's dress. Once again she sat in silence, her hands folded in her lap. She appeared to be studying the flagstones.

"I need your support very desperately, Mother. Without it, I'd have no choice but to take Miracle abroad. Otherwise—whatever I tried to do to protect her—the jackals would tear her apart."

She glanced up. "Am I not to be allowed at least a modicum of outrage first?"

"I was expecting it. Just as long as any wrath that's going to be experienced because of this impolitic gesture breaks on my head and not hers."

"You are, of course, very deeply in love. No other lady will ever live up to the charms of this courtesan. Perhaps you are right. Yet I don't know whether even I can force society to accept her. Gossip will drag us down like an undertow."

He took her fingers and briefly kissed the knuckles. "So a few old biddies will turn their backs, and the highest sticklers will refuse to receive her. Everyone else will follow your lead, especially if it's done with enough panache. You'll no doubt find it vastly amusing."

She lifted her hand to gaze at her rings. Emeralds scattered the sunlight. "Blackdown would have to agree."

"The duke will go along with your decision in this, as he has in almost everything else concerning your children, since the day you first presented him with me. No one else has your influence in society."

"Very well," she said, dropping her hand. "Bring your bride to Wyldshay! If she is everything that you say, I will indeed defy the world to save her. However, if she is what I fear, then I will use everything in my power to secure your divorce."

"She won't fight you in that," Ryder said. "The marriage was my idea, not hers. She's already offered to do anything necessary to free me. I have only to ask her."

"Then she is a clever woman," the duchess said. "But I have already guessed that. Now, if you are quite through with your revelations, sir, I suggest that you go back to your rooms and get some rest. It is obvious that you have not slept in days."

Ryder stood and bowed. "Your Grace!"

"Oh, go!" the duchess snapped. "You are dead on your feet, and before I start planning what to do, pray allow me the courtesy of weeping about this in private."

MIRACLE offered quiet thanks to Lady Ayre and her son. The countess waved good-bye as their carriage bowled away. Lord Ayre had been polite but distant for the entire journey. His mother had been generous, without being familiar. Yet all three of them had understood the potential that lay in the situation.

Whether Miracle was married or not, no man, ever, would not believe that of her.

Nothing seemed to be changed in Blackdown Square, except the locks. Hanley had once possessed a key, of course. Ryder must have seen to it that the earl no longer had access to the house, before he had first left London to come after her.

Miracle was forced to knock to gain entry to her own house—no, Ryder's house.

She owed him everything. If he asked for it—even if it destroyed her—she would free him. Even if that meant the heartbreak of being found naked with another man. Even if that man was as casual about his admiration as Lord Ayre.

Izzy threw open the door and curtsied deeply, her face red with delight. "Oh, welcome home, Lady Ryderbourne!"

Miracle stared at the maid in amazement.

"Lord Ryderbourne's waiting for you, m'lady," Izzy said. "His Lordship's already been here for two days, and he's had me clean the place from top to bottom, but he said I could take myself off as soon as Your Ladyship arrived. Is that all right?"

"Yes," Miracle said, her pulse pounding. "Yes, of course."

The girl bobbed another curtsy and disappeared.

Ryder was here!

An extraordinarily mundane conversation ran through her head—*You had a pleasant journey? Lady Ayre took good care of you? My friend, Lord Ayre, he saw to your needs?*—before it pitched into painful lunacy: *Am I free of my imprudent marriage? Did you learn all the splendors of yet another man's body? Am I already cuckolded?*

Miracle took a deep breath and pulled off her hat before she walked into her sitting room. Ryder was standing by the window. Sunlight haloed his dark head. He turned to face her as she entered.

Her heart lurched like a spring hare. Desire for him shook her from head to foot, passing in hot waves through her blood, flooding her—mind, body, and soul—with longing. Stunned into a desperate silence, she dropped her reticule.

Ryder merely stood as if turned to stone, gazing at her with fire burning in the depths of his eyes.

Heat burned in her own heart as Miracle wrenched her gloves from shaking fingers. The soft kidskin fell to the carpet.

Passion flared in the sharp angle of his nostrils and the tension around his mouth. Never releasing her gaze, he wrenched away his cravat, then wrung his collar back from his neck with one hand.

Hectic flames licked over her belly and legs. A sweet heaviness scorched between her thighs. Shaking from head to foot, she unbuttoned her pelisse and dropped it from her shoulders.

Fighting for breath, he tore open buttons and shrugged out of his jacket.

Head high, pulse frenzied, her heart possessed, Miracle stepped out of her shoes.

Fire roared about him, as if he burned in his own light, like an angel. He ripped off his waistcoat, buttons rolling behind him as he strode across the carpet.

Consumed by frantic desire, she stepped forward to meet him.

He lifted her in his arms, bent his head, and kissed her.

Tears burned as she kissed back, meeting the hot velvet of his tongue, the sweet potency of his lips. His lean, hard strength pressed against her breasts and belly and thighs. Without a word, still kissing, he spun her across the room.

As they traveled he unfastened her dress, one button at a time, until it sagged from her shoulders. She clung to his lean waist, laughing and weeping. His lips burned over hers, ardent and open, yet dulcet as warmed honey.

A trail of garments followed them from the sitting room to the bedroom. He kicked off his shoes. Her dress fell away. Still kissing, Ryder unbuttoned his waistband and wrenched at the hem of his shirt with one hand.

Wrestling tongue to tongue, Miracle slid her hands beneath the fine linen. Her palms feasted on firm, naked flesh, the delectable muscling of his back and belly and chest.

She was as liquid and hot as the sun, burning with infinite fires, casting great streams of light into the cold universe. Ryder circled her, until they spun together in a dance of cosmic flame. Like twin stars. Like Lesath or Acrab in Scorpius, the slayer of Orion.

Ryder kicked the bedroom door closed behind them, then swept her to the bed. He lifted her onto the white sheets and buried his face against her neck. Scorching tremors rippled as he suckled the sweet spot at the base of her throat, then nipped at the lobe of her ear. His breath caressed like a dragon's.

Dressed in nothing but shift, stockings, and corset, she fell back against the pillows, her soul shattered with delight.

He drew back only to tug his shirt off over his head. Grinning like a fool, he wrenched away his trousers and underwear, then stripped off his stockings. Gloriously naked he fell onto the bed beside her.

Her mouth, her thighs, her entire being welcomed him as he rolled over her and started kissing her again. Long, trailing kisses along her jaw and down her neck. Exquisite little nibbles in the sensitive hollows of her throat.

Longing consumed her. She wanted to touch him back, drive him even wilder with her own caresses. Yet he held her hands pinned to the bed with both of his, and used only his mouth to pleasure her.

She was fired with helpless ardor. Her skin glowed beneath

his lips. Her nipples swelled erect beneath his tongue. The fire raged, all consuming, when he laid her as open as if his mouth plundered the heart of an iris. She cried out, writhing as the scorching intensity almost consumed consciousness.

When he slid inside her at last, she was lost, already burned away to pure gold. Her body convulsed in exquisite pleasure, lost, lost. Yet at each thrust he demanded still more. More openness. More vulnerability. As if at each long, lovely stroke, he delved ever more intimately into the depths of her soul.

She quivered like a violin string, the wrenching tremors thrilling as if she had become nothing but responsiveness.

As light flooded her mind, she found the beauty of his back and the strong thrust of his buttocks, so he must have released her hands. She didn't know when.

Her mouth found his, tongues touching and caressing in blissful rapture, so he must be kissing her again. She didn't know.

Miracle knew only this white-hot, passionate surrender to the only man she had ever let herself love totally and completely, though it broke her heart.

SHE woke wrapped in his arms. A candle flickered beside the bed. The rest of the room lay in darkness. She sat up. Ryder propped his dark head on one bent elbow and smiled up at her.

"I slept?" she asked.

"About eight hours. It's well past midnight. Are you hungry?"

"You've asked me that before—"

"And I trust I've satisfactorily fulfilled your appetites, Lady Ryderbourne?"

"Only you will ever do so," she said. "Yet the world will destroy us."

"Not if my mother decides otherwise."

Miracle bent her head and kissed him quickly, before she slipped from the bed and grabbed a dressing gown.

He had taken possession of her as soon as she had arrived, as if to obliterate the memory of the other men who had shared her bed. It wasn't necessary. She loved him. Only him. Only he had ever moved her so deeply. Only he stripped her of all artifice and left her nothing but blissful absolution.

But women like her did not marry duke's sons. Society was not made that way.

"Not even a duchess can remake what I am," she said. "You should have hidden me in a bower, as Henry the Second kept his Fair Rosamund—until his secret mistress was poisoned by Queen Eleanor, of course."

He smiled back, though not with real joy. "For God's sake, I'm not a king. I'm not even the duke yet. The Earl of Berkeley married a butcher's daughter, and the world survived. As soon as it's light, we'll go down to Wyldshay. My mother wants to meet you."

"Does she? I very much doubt it. Did you threaten her with fire and brimstone, and make her afraid that she'll lose you? As soon as the chance presents itself, she'll see me to the devil."

"Perhaps," he said.

"I've had a long coach journey in which to think about this," she said. "I must ask this, Ryder: Is there anything really between us but passion? We've known each other for such a short time."

"Long enough to know the truth."

"The truth is that I made love to Hanley in that bed. You cannot negate that, however much you think that you love me. The knowledge will eat away at your heart. You'll get tired of me—"

Ardor burned in his eyes, as if she were a single fascinating flame. "No."

"But when—"

A loud banging echoed. Ryder spun naked from the bed, lithe and lean in the candlelight. He was so beautifully made: all muscle, his belly taut, his buttocks lovely. The racket clanged again. Ryder pulled on his trousers and strode from the bedroom, barefoot and naked from the waist up.

Miracle followed him out through the drawing room and into the front hall.

Her hair tied in curling rags, Izzy had crept up from her bed off the kitchen, but now she stood staring at the door with enormous eyes, doing nothing.

The knocker hammered again. Ryder flung open the door.

Rain sheeted along the pavement and across the cobbled street, beating over the roofs of the houses.

A gentleman in a long cloak swayed on the step. Water dripped from his chin and ran in dark rivulets over his shoulders.

"Good God!" Ryder said. "Dartford? You're foxed, sir!"

"Very," Dartford said. "Drunk as a lord! Mush see you!"

Ryder stepped back. "You'd better come in and have some coffee."

"Only sober when I'm gambling. Can't afford to drink then. Have a message for you, Ryderbourne. Owe it to Miracle."

Miracle clutched her robe to her throat with both hands as Lord Dartford stepped inside. Ryder glanced at her as she met Dartford's wild, wet smile with one of her own.

"Please get dressed, Izzy. Bring hot coffee to the drawing room."

Izzy curtsied, then ducked away back to the kitchen.

Dartford tore off his hat and shook out the water. He stepped up to Miracle and bowed unsteadily.

"Don't want coffee," he said. "Came to warn you. Hanley says you're guilty of murder. Going to see you arrested before dawn."

CHAPTER SIXTEEN

"*I*T CAN MEAN ONLY ONE THING." SHADOWS LEAPED ON THE bedroom walls as Ryder shrugged into his clothes. His voice was intense, filled with determination. "Hanley's found the bloody papers, so he knows I was bluffing. And since he's confident enough to threaten you, he must be certain that I cannot have seen them and have no idea of their contents."

Dread turned in her stomach, but Miracle was determined not to let him see it. She sat down on the edge of the bed to pull on her half boots.

"Ah, well! Marry in haste and repent at leisure. I just hadn't planned to repent on the scaffold."

"You won't have to, Miracle." He wrung one hand over his hair. "For God's sake! You're my wife. You don't need to be brave any longer."

She smiled at him, though her unsteady heartbeat threatened to engulf her.

Fingers scratched at the door. At Ryder's command, Izzy stepped in. Her hands plucked nervously at a hastily donned apron.

"Yes, Izzy?" Miracle asked.

"Lord Dartford fell asleep, m' lady, in the chair. Shall I bring the coffee in here?"

"If you please," Miracle said. "And fetch us some hot toast with butter, as well."

"Very good, m' lady!" The maid turned to leave.

"Wait!" Ryder said.

Izzy flushed and bobbed a curtsy. "Yes, m' lord?"

"Did someone visit this house, perhaps just before I arrived a few days ago?"

Miracle felt the blood drain from her face. With sudden insight, she followed Ryder's reasoning. Lord Hanley must have had very good reason to think that she'd had his papers to start with, or none of his behavior made sense.

"Sit down, Izzy, and answer Lord Ryderbourne. Did Lord Hanley come here again recently? Was he looking for something?"

Izzy plumped onto a chair, her eyes filled with doubt. "I never meant no harm, m' lady. But His Lordship said as how he'd have me taken for a thief if I didn't give him what he wanted. Though it was mine!"

"What was yours, Izzy?" Ryder asked.

The maid's mouth crumpled. "My Bible, m' lord. The one my mother gave me, though I never could read it too much. Too many long words and the print was too little."

"You gave Lord Hanley your mother's Bible?"

Tears spilled as Izzy glanced up. "He came here the day before Your Lordship arrived. He said I must have something that was really his—a book or something like that. I told him I didn't have nothing, but he said that I must have and if I didn't let him have it, I would hang. He gave me three days to think about it, but I wasn't to tell nobody." Her voice broke. "Though I only had the one book."

"But you were afraid. So you gave him your Bible, hoping that would satisfy him? When was that?"

"Yesterday evening, m' lord. I was so glad to have thought of it. Lord Hanley had a man waiting at the corner. He said I was a good girl and he gave me a shilling." She wiped her eyes on a corner of her apron. "Was that wrong? I never meant no harm!"

"It's all right, Izzy," Miracle said. "Lord Hanley's angry with me, so he thought to annoy me by upsetting you. Now, go and dry your eyes, then fetch us the coffee and toast. You only did what you thought was right."

The maid nodded and stumbled from the room.

Ryder's eyes shone with intelligence and ironic self-mockery. He ran his fingers through his already disordered hair and laughed.

"It's not funny!" Miracle snapped.

"Yes, it is! Though I'll get Izzy's Bible back for her, if I have to wring Hanley's damned neck."

"I thought it was the wringing of my neck that was at issue. So Izzy had his papers here all along. Alas, it would appear that you married me for nothing."

He spun about to face her, all laughter gone. "I married you because I want you for my wife. The only element of this farce for which I'll have a hard time forgiving myself is that I didn't guess about Izzy. After all, Hanley was so certain that Willcott had hidden something here that he ransacked the place. He only assumed you'd inadvertently taken the papers with you, when that failed."

"Which allowed him to believe, for a moment at least, that we'd found them."

"Alas, I must be a damned poor actor. He obviously suspected that I might be bluffing. Then he remembered Izzy."

"Thus he came straight back to London, while you were at Wyldshay and I was still traveling with Lady Ayre, and the papers slipped out of this house under our very noses."

Ryder tossed a few personal items into a bag. "But how the devil did Willcott get access to your maid's family Bible for long enough to hide something in it?"

"Does it matter?" Miracle asked. "Unless this is a double bluff, Hanley now has the papers and he's no longer afraid of you."

"Then he should be."

"Not enough! He intends to drag me from my bed—in spite of our Scottish wedding—and have me thrown into jail."

He smiled as he pulled her to her feet. "Hanley can only risk that here in London, in the hopes that an accusation this soon would force me to repudiate our marriage and wash my hands of you."

"That's an option," she said.

He lifted her hand to kiss her wedding ring, his eyes ocean-green as he glanced up at her beneath his lashes. "Never!"

She closed her fingers around his. "Or perhaps his excess of elation will bring on an attack of apoplexy and solve the problem?"

"There is no problem. Everything will change once we reach Wyldshay. Hanley might think he can create a scandal right now for me personally. He'll never risk alienating the Duke and Duchess of Blackdown, once they've thrown their public support behind you. After all, he has no more proof of his accusations than we have of his secret."

"And he's no fool, of course. But now my future depends on your mother?"

"Don't worry! She'll like you."

She pulled his head down to hers with both hands, then pressed a brief smile against his lips. "Ah, you foolish man! Her Grace may like me. I may like her. But she'll no more accept this marriage than dye her hair pink. Fortunately, Wyldshay lies near the coast, doesn't it?"

"It won't come to that, Miracle. But if it did, I'd go with you."

It was not true, of course. He might think it was true, but future dukes did not abandon their titles and lands for their mistresses. Not even when they had married them. If Ryder were forced to choose between his wife and his inheritance, Wyldshay would win.

"We should go," she said. "It's already closer to dawn than is comfortable. I'd prefer to be gone by the time Lord Hanley gets here."

"Thanks to Dartford, you will be." Ryder picked up the bag and strode to the door. "He was one of them, wasn't he?"

"One of whom?"

"One of your lovers."

A sharp pulse of fear plummeted into her belly, one even more profound than when Lord Dartford had first delivered his news. "Yes. How did you guess?"

"That smile that you exchanged at the front door." His expression was guarded. "The one full of regret and dashed dreams. I trust it's not a smile that you'll ever bestow on me."

"I've married you," she said. "We've exchanged vows. I'll never give you that smile, unless you ask for it."

"Did Dartford ask for it?"

"Don't do this, Ryder!"

"I'm only grateful that your past lover still holds enough affection for you that he came here to warn us."

"It's also fortunate that you decided not to run him through as soon as you guessed."

"I'm not a particularly brilliant swordsman." His laugh barely concealed his distress. "Though I'm pretty damn good with pistols."

"I will tell you only this: I don't love him. He doesn't love me. We parted amicably."

Ryder stared at the door. "And my right arm would get pretty damned tired, if I were to call out every man you've ever known?"

"More than tired. You'd be wrong. Lord Dartford's a good man."

The trace of bitterness dissolved as he smiled at her with genuine amusement. "When he's gambling like a fiend, but sober, or when he's more honorably employed, but foxed? Don't worry! I like him."

"Though right now you'd like that coffee and toast a great deal better."

"And I'd like it best," he said, "if we were already at Wyldshay."

"Ah, yes," the duchess said as Miracle curtsied. "Exquisite, indeed!" Her velvet voice cloaked a core of pure steel. "Of course, I am not surprised. Pray, come in and sit down."

"Your Grace is most kind."

Miracle walked across the thick carpet and took the indicated chair. She was alone with the Duchess of Blackdown in an elegant withdrawing room, high in an ancient round tower at Wyldshay. An arrow-slit opening had been enlarged long ago to create a more modern window, but the stone heart of the medieval keep still beat steadily in the ancient beams and in the worn carvings over the fireplace.

"We are presently in the oldest part of the castle," the duchess said. "The Fortune Tower was built by Ambrose de Verrant in 1104 to replace the wooden keep that his grandfather erected after the Conquest. This island has been a fortress for over seven hundred and fifty years."

"I understand that it still is," Miracle said dryly.

The duchess smiled, with a certain appreciation, but without real humor. Precise and dangerous, she glanced up at a portrait over the mantel: a young man wearing the fur-trimmed robe and jeweled cap of the Tudors. He held a rose in one hand and a sword hilt in the other.

"Do you, indeed? Should I also point out that Ambrose and his grandfather were little more than bandits? Or that the handsome young earl in this portrait made his fortune by supporting Henry the Eighth in the dissolution of the monasteries? The St. Georges have been ruthless for many centuries."

Miracle took a deep breath. She had expected a duel of sorts, but this was an already unsheathed blade.

"Your Grace doesn't need to remind me," she replied. "The power of the Blackdowns stands in stunning contrast to my own birth and background, and I couldn't be more aware of it."

"I do not assume that you are stupid." Ryder's mother glanced at her with the considered green gaze of a pagan goddess. "Far from it! It took a very clever woman to ensnare my son. Yet this imprudent marriage cannot be allowed to stand. You must realize that it is within my power to have it dissolved?"

A knot tightened in Miracle's stomach. "I've assumed all along that would be Your Grace's intention. I shan't stand in your way."

"Then you do *not* intend to fight me in this?" The duchess raised one elegant brow. "How much money do you want?"

Miracle swallowed a sudden passionate rage, before she lifted her chin and replied with deliberate coolness. "I have very little in this life, Your Grace, but I assure you that I will not take your money, nor your son's. I shall free Ryder for his sake, not yours. And since I am neither your servant nor your dependant—"

"Your temerity astounds me, madam!"

It was a tone designed to strike to the heart. Miracle felt its impact, but she stood up and faced the duchess with rigid dignity.

"I may have been born in a cottage, but I learned long ago that it's up to me to maintain my own integrity, since no one else will do it for me. I've done my very best to convince your son of the foolishness of our marriage, and—if it can be done without further damage to him—I would welcome Your Grace's help to free him."

The duchess stalked to the window. Trembling ribbons from her tiny lace cap trailed over her back. "Why should I believe that?"

"I know the world that we live in."

"No doubt! So why did you agree to the marriage?"

"Your son can be very stubborn."

"A family trait," the duchess said with a hint of wry humor. "Unfortunately, Ryder thinks that he loves you. He doesn't want to believe that his love cannot possibly survive the reality of your past."

Miracle closed her eyes for a moment to blot out the pain. "Did he also tell you that I'm barren? I cannot give him sons. He claims not to mind, but he would only care more passionately with each passing year—"

"Yes, I am afraid of that, too." The duchess turned. Her wheat-and-gold hair glimmered as if the sun flamed behind a cloud. "Yet even if his love were able to withstand all of this, would yours?"

Grief burned like a hot iron, but Miracle masked it and stood her ground.

"The state of my heart is irrelevant, Your Grace. Isn't that what this discussion is all about? It's obviously to everyone's benefit to maintain the social order. My father was a laborer who sold me into servitude. I've worked on the stage. I've traded my favors for protection. This marriage is best set aside, before it does Ryder real harm."

"I am so glad that you understand."

"I've always understood," Miracle said. "Only one class of men is born, raised, and educated to govern. The stability of England depends on the wise choices of men like your son."

"Wise choices that include marrying a lady of his own rank." The duchess walked forward. Light from the window glimmered behind her. "So you are not a revolutionary, Lady Ryderbourne?"

The Tudor earl gazed down with disdain, his lips curved in a slight sneer. Miracle's pain began to dissolve. The duchess was only stating the truth, after all. Perhaps if they joined forces, Ryder could also be brought to agree?

"I'm more of a pragmatist, I think. Society weddings help preserve the great estates, which support half the population. Who else but a hereditary aristocracy would cherish their fields with such care, or plant trees that won't mature until generations later? It's a patronizing system, but that's the reality we face. Whether it's right or not, it's not within my power to change."

The duchess's green gaze seemed to encompass the world. "Even though a certain number of puffed-up fools sit in the House of Lords and the Commons?"

"Yes, I know," Miracle said with a wry smile. "I've slept with one or two of them."

Ryder's mother laughed. "So what would you change, if you could?"

Miracle had begun to feel a little surreal. Whatever she had expected from the duchess, it was not a discussion of politics. Though class differences lay at the heart of their impasse, didn't they? Duke's sons did not marry the daughters of laborers, and they never married courtesans. Yet there was nothing to lose by answering honestly.

"I'd like to see a world with more justice and less indifference to human suffering. On the other hand, I've no desire to see England at the mercy of the mob, which I also know, since I was born amongst them."

Ryder's mother gazed thoughtfully up at the portrait. "Even though at present many intelligent, resourceful men born to the wrong class see their leadership talents go to waste?"

"Half of the population of every class goes to waste, Your Grace," Miracle said. "I've read Mary Wollstonecraft, but I don't expect to see women gain their rights in my lifetime. Only men have real power in England. All of the rest is just talk."

The duchess glanced at her with something of real interest, even compassion. "Now, that is arrant nonsense, and you—of all females—must know it. We claim that men are strong, but ladies are the strong sex. No man ever achieved his full potential without the right woman at his side."

"And in Ryder's case, the right woman must be a lady and a virgin. I understand."

"Yes, indeed! After all, what would happen to England if

the social rules were broken with impunity and peers chose their life partners for love?"

"I don't know," Miracle said. "But perhaps there'd be more tenderness toward children and more kindness toward the less fortunate."

The duchess stalked back to the window. "You think that I do not love my children? Sit down and answer me honestly, please."

Miracle dropped back to her chair. "It doesn't matter what I think, but Ryder's convinced that you've always loved his brother better."

"All parents label their children," the duchess said. "Ryderbourne was the strong one. He is pure gold at the core. His future was not only secure, but predestined. I knew from the day he was born that he would make a splendid duke. Yet nothing was certain for Lord Jonathan, five years younger. He had the fragility of genius and a dark shadow lurked in his soul. I was terrified for him. Perhaps in my anxiety for my younger son, I sometimes neglected my elder. Do you think so?"

Miracle clenched her hands as if she had been cast adrift in dangerous waters. "You must ask him."

"Was Lord Jonathan once your lover, also?"

Shock stabbed like a knife. Miracle felt almost faint, before a renewed surge of anger forced her back to her feet. She did her best to keep her voice level, though the hurt burned.

"I've tried to be honest with you, Your Grace. You've responded by setting me a trap. The gentlemen I've entertained in the past are none of Your Grace's business and you know it. Yet I cannot refuse to answer, because then you'll assume that it's true—and if you tell Ryder that his brother once loved and left me, you'll sign the death warrant for his soul."

"That will be my decision, not yours," Ryder's mother said in a voice like steel. "But I will know the answer."

"Then the answer is no, Your Grace." Miracle stalked to the door, her heart filled with scorn. "Though I met him many years ago, Lord Jonathan never shared my bed. What do you really think I am? I've been a courtesan since I was sixteen, but in my entire professional career I've known only six men. *Six!* There are many society ladies who've been far more promiscuous than that."

"No doubt." The duchess was a sword blade, the embodiment of power.

"Yet because I was born to life in a mill, because my contracts with those gentlemen were not blessed by the church, because money changed hands directly, instead of through dowries and settlements, I am forever proscribed. I accept it. I've done my best not to hurt Ryder, nor break his heart. I did not want—nor scheme for—this marriage. But I neither will, nor can, control him. Because he is, as you say, pure gold at the core, he wished to save my wretched life. Or perhaps he didn't tell you that I'm not only a harlot but a murderer?"

The duchess turned from the window and smiled, with a strangely sardonic glint in her pagan green eyes.

"Good Heavens! Murder is not hard for society to forgive. Nor is promiscuity, as long as it is cloaked by marriage vows. No, it is the very honesty of your past relationships that is the problem."

"There will be no problem," Miracle said. Prickles of outrage still danced along her spine. "To save Ryder from any more pain, I'm prepared to leave England tomorrow."

"Leave England? Why?" The duchess stepped forward. "You do not believe that it is also within my power to save this marriage, now that I have decided to do so?"

The latch burned beneath her suddenly cold fingers. "Save it?"

"My dear child, I am not your enemy," the duchess said gently. "After all, we love the same man."

The room began to spin in lazy arcs, as if the planet had lost its bearings and swung off into space. Miracle fought for balance as she turned from the door.

"You're trying to tell me that you will give this mad marriage your blessing?"

"That is exactly what I am telling you." The duchess walked steadily across the carpet. Her eyes seemed only wise and tolerant. "You will forgive me, I trust, if I felt that I had to test you a little first?"

"But I thought the nation would fall apart if future dukes married their mistresses?"

"Nonsense! I will not break my son's heart for the last century's values, when his life may last almost to the end of this one. Winds of change are already blowing through England.

We shall see franchise reform within five years, and eventually the power of families like mine will wane. However, if this marriage is to stand in the meantime, we have a great deal of work to do."

"But I'll never be accepted in society!"

Ryder's mother laughed with genuine mirth. "My dear child, I saw you play Portia once. You are a brilliant actress, which is really all that it takes to be a duchess."

"Our conversation just now wasn't acting, Your Grace." Miracle trembled as if she had just withstood a storm. "You did your very best to tear the truth out of my heart, and succeeded."

"It was absolutely necessary for me to discover who you really are, Lady Ryderbourne, before I commit the resources of the duchy to saving you."

Miracle stumbled to a chair and sat down. "I don't understand."

The duchess waved one hand. Her rings, brilliant, priceless, sparkled in the sunshine. "I once told Lord Jonathan that one of only two reasons justifies the choice of a bride for any son of mine: brilliant social consequence, or—failing that—true love. You love my son with all your heart, and he loves you."

"Yes," Miracle said. She felt flayed to the soul.

"However, if Ryder is to make a well-known courtesan into the future Duchess of Blackdown, we must make sure that he doesn't have to sacrifice more than he can bear. We shall begin with another wedding."

"I'm entirely outclassed in this game, Your Grace. Another wedding?"

"My son cannot be seen to have wed in haste, as if he were ashamed of his bride. You must become impregnable to gossip. The first step is to hold a new ceremony here at Wyldshay, with the entire peerage fighting for an invitation."

"You can do that?"

"My dear child, the Duchess of Blackdown can command the King, if she so chooses."

RYDER paced restlessly along the wall walk behind the battlements. Why the devil had he allowed Miracle to see his mother alone? His first reaction had been to insist on accompanying her. Yet Miracle had been quietly adamant about answering the duchess's summons without him.

Would his mother simply try to demolish the woman he loved? How would Miracle react, if she did?

And what future, really, could their marriage have? He already held a seat in the Commons, and he would become a powerful peer in the Lords one day. His wife had an important role to play in society. It had all been too easy to ignore while adventuring with Miracle on England's byways, but here at Wyldshay that cruel reality could no longer be denied.

If he walked into any social gathering in London with his new wife on his arm, every lady in the room would turn her back.

Ryder stopped and gripped the parapet with both hands. A neat patchwork of well-tended woods and fields stretched down to the distant sea. Closer at hand, the castle cast its dark silhouette on the broad surface of the River Wyld. He could even make out his own shadow, rippling on the moving water where it spread about the roots of the castle.

He loved his home with a profound passion. Wyldshay defined his identity and gave him his bearings.

Yet for Miracle's sake, he would give it up and never see it again. Lord Jonathan, his younger brother, had taken his bride and disappeared into the wide world. If necessary, Lord Ryderbourne would abandon his inheritance and do the same.

Though he knew without question that he would do it, the pain of the thought drove him to grip the cold stone until his hands became numb.

A small shush of silk sounded behind him. Ryder spun about.

"Mother!"

The duchess gazed at him without speaking for a moment, then she walked up to stand next to him. Ribbons fluttered. The breeze tore loose a few strands of blond hair to whip about her cheeks. He recognized with vague surprise that he had never seen his mother even slightly disheveled before.

"I have fought all my life for the power of Wyldshay and the continuity of the Blackdown name," she said. "It is my life's work. I will not see it destroyed."

Ryder turned his back on the view and leaned his hips against the merlon. "Where's Miracle?"

"I have sent her to the duke. Blackdown, being male, will be charmed by her wit and her beauty, though he is most annoyed about your hasty marriage, of course."

"So he told me. It doesn't matter. I'll take Miracle away from here tomorrow."

"Will you? What a shame!" The duchess gave a small, elegant shrug. "I have just put your wife through a painful little trial, and would hate to see that wasted."

"What the devil did you demand of her?"

Her green eyes searched the sky, as if she might find answers to some problem in the clouds.

"I demanded simply that she show me her mettle. Tearing into the souls of others is an indispensable skill for duchesses, and it was absolutely necessary. If your wife is to take my place one day, she must be able to carry off the part. Fortunately, she has the necessary pride and the necessary backbone."

"God! I could have told you that."

The duchess turned to face him. "Pray, do not frown at me like a dragon, sir! You are hardly objective. However, Miracle is intelligent, well-educated, thinks for herself, and has a splendid natural dignity. And she is indeed quite stunning to look at, which always helps, especially with the men."

"And did she forget to mention," Ryder asked, "that she can also sing and dance and play the piano?"

The duchess laughed. "Don't be obtuse, Ryder! I am trying to tell you that I shall move heaven and earth to save your marriage."

He stared at her in silence for a moment, while his heart raced.

His mother linked her arm through his. "I was far more afraid for you when I thought you might marry Lady Belinda Carhart. We claim that the ideal is for virgins to marry. It is utter nonsense, of course."

"You astound me," Ryder said. "I seem to recall that Jack was hauled very thoroughly over the coals, after what happened with Anne."

"The two situations are entirely different." They turned to walk along the battlements together. "I feared that your brother was about to disclaim moral responsibility after he had stolen a young woman's innocence. In your case, I think, it is rather the other way around."

He was forced to laugh, though a small pain still fired at the thought. "Yes, my wife is undoubtedly more experienced than I am."

"And does that disturb you? Do you think her past means anything more than yours? Or are you still tempted by every pretty new face?"

"For God's sake! I'll never look at any other woman as long as I live."

"Oh, yes, you will! No one can remain married for a life-time without meeting some other man or some other woman, with whom—had things been different—she or he might have fallen in love, instead. But you may look without harm and not act on it. Miracle understands that. She knows in her bones that no other man, however charming, could ever match up to what you and she will create together. Thus she will never be disturbed by your casual admiration of another lady, and she will never risk losing your love for any passing fancy of hers. A virgin bride, on the other hand, will always wonder what she might have missed. Sooner or later, she may decide to find out."

"Your Grace, I am stunned. You would say the same for my sisters?"

"No, of course not." The duchess glanced up at him. "Their suitors would not agree with such a practical philosophy. The price my daughters would have to bear for rebellion is too great. But if a reformed rake makes a good spouse, then so may a courtesan who has genuinely lost her heart. The men in her past can only help to keep a woman honest, if every one of them was a mistake."

"Why the devil are you telling me this, Mother?" Ryder asked.

"Because other men will always pay attention to your wife." They reached the small door to the spiral stair. The duchess released his arm. "I shall support this imprudent mar-riage, Ryder, but only because Miracle can carry it off. I shall face down the world to see your new wife accepted, even feted, in society. But if you cannot control your own misgiv-ings about her past, you will destroy her yourself."

"But I love her," he said.

"Enough to empty your heart of doubt? Meanwhile, if I am to save this marriage, the duke and I must leave immediately for London. A new myth must be created, in which Miracle becomes an object of admiration and sympathy, instead of outrage. Everyone who ever saw her onstage, or heard her name mentioned with contempt, must wipe that memory clean."

"And Hanley needs to be reminded that he cannot persecute a St. George without repercussions."

"You are my son," the duchess replied. "I would tear Hanley apart and use his guts for fertilizer before I allowed him to damage you or your wife any further."

"He was her lover," Ryder said. "He betrayed her."

"And you still cannot forgive that, can you? Even though possessive jealousy is death to love."

He opened the door for her. "For God's sake, I'm not jealous of Hanley."

"Nevertheless, men will always flock to her. So I think you should at least know," the duchess said as she turned to leave, "that your fears about your brother are unfounded."

THE duke and duchess had been gone for five days. Five days of idyllic privacy for Miracle and Ryder.

They had walked and ridden and explored and talked, as if at every moment they might meld into one mind, one purpose.

When it rained, Ryder led her through the strange labyrinth of towers and rooms and courtyards and gardens that formed Wyldshay Castle.

When the sun shone, they rode out together over fields and through woods, or sometimes tied the horses to stroll on the shingle beneath the tall cliffs.

They made love.

Achingly, passionately beautiful love. As they exchanged lingering caresses, Ryder slowly peeled away the last of her defenses. A knot of pain seemed to be unraveling in her soul, one she had lived with so long that she had not known that life was possible without it.

He is gold at the core.

Her heart opened in wonder at each perfect moment. Miracle almost forgot her last few fears about Hanley.

The sixth morning bloomed into a stunningly sunny day that had wound down into a hazy sunset, before fading into this clear, warm twilight. The horses picked their way along a rocky path that led out onto the top of a promontory.

Miracle filled her lungs with salt air as she pulled up her mount at the base of a shadowed round tower, built centuries before on the top of the cliff.

Ryder swung down and tied his black gelding to a ring in the stone wall.

She gazed at his long legs and strong back. She was so very desperately in love. The summer was beautiful. She was safe. And now her husband had brought her to this strange round tower for a surprise.

"We call this place Ambrose's Folly," he said. "Let me help you dismount."

Her new riding habit reflected her status as a future duchess. As if by magic, dressmakers had appeared to produce her new wardrobe. Every garment was restrained, yet stunningly elegant.

Ryder lifted Miracle easily from the saddle to kiss her with unnecessary thoroughness. As if the surf far below had entered her veins, her heart began to pound.

She took his hand and let him lead her. A cracked stairway wound around inside the tower, then brought them out onto a flat roof surrounded by battlements. Miracle stepped straight into the heady scent of roses. She glanced down. A scattering of white petals lay beneath her feet. Each step released spiced perfume into the night air.

Ryder kissed the back of her neck.

"It's the second week of August," he said. "Time for the Perseid meteor showers. I thought we might sleep out here under the stars to watch them."

A bed of silk cushions and coverlets beckoned from the center of a rich carpet. A small table held a light supper and several bottles of wine.

"We'll feast like Roman senators," she said, "sprawled on cushions."

Ryder laughed and tugged her down onto the bed beside him. He opened wine and lifted the covers off dishes. As they ate, twilight deepened into true darkness. The planets eased into being. One by one the stars winked into existence, and the summer constellations began to take shape.

Replete, Miracle rested her head on his shoulder to stare at the sky. His fingers stroked her neck. Beneath the peace of a brilliant heaven, they slowly disrobed each other, one garment at a time, while a gentle surf surged at the base of the cliff far below.

Desire flowed in rose-scented streams through Miracle's blood. The profound, thrumming silence of the night was broken only by their whispered sighs and small groans as Ryder pleasured her and she pleasured him back. It was so effortless, this loving: the simple, open exchange of delight. Her hands strayed over his lean muscles. Her mouth fired with sensitivity as he kissed her, then throbbed with rapture as he deepened the kiss.

A slow, dreamlike lovemaking, filled with profound sensuality, as the heavens filled with stars like daisies on a lawn.

The first star fell: shooting across the night sky, as if a diamond broke loose from black velvet to plunge into the sea.

Ryder stroked his hand up her thigh. "You saw that?"

She slipped her fingers along his spine and pulled him closer. "Yes," she said. "Ah! And there's another!"

His arousal nudged her hip. His hands moved to capture her jaw. His tongue teased hers in deep, star-drugged kisses, while larger gems began to flash across the sky, burning colored streaks across the heavens.

His eyes were black pools of intensity, his breath as shattered as hers, as he entered her. She responded with quivers of sensitivity so acute that her vision almost slipped away. Yet her mind filled with the explosion of shooting stars, as Perseus flung his meteors across the sky and into the ocean. Perseus who slew the Medusa and married Andromeda, so that he and his wife might take their place forever in the heavens.

Her ears filled with her own quick breath. Her nostrils filled with the scent of roses and man. Her fingers dug into Ryder's shoulders. Miracle opened her eyes again on that immense sphere of stars and the smiling face of her lover, his dark hair tumbled over the sheened skin of his forehead.

She smiled back at him as a single white star, full of brilliance, scorched across the sky, leaving a long trail of splendor.

Ryder threw his head back in rapturous concentration. She pulled up her legs, drawing him deeper, ever deeper, inside. Her voice mingled with his as every atom in her body thrilled in response—until, as she felt the spill of his seed, she thought she also heard the faraway sizzle of that one last great shooting star plunging headlong into the ocean.

"MY lord," the footman said, holding out a silver tray. "Lord Braughton's man awaits a reply."

Ryder tore open the letter and scanned it. Miracle glanced up from her breakfast. She had returned from Ambrose's Folly ravenous, and had been as hungry as a tiger for the three days since then.

He read the missive in silence, then looked up with a slight frown, before he smiled at her.

She smiled back. She had been filled with deep content ever since the meteor shower, as if her entire body was aware of some profound change that her mind could not yet quite grasp. She knew only that her heart felt open and free, completely secure in his love—though she was hungry.

"Alas, our idyll is interrupted," he said in answer to her unspoken question. "Beauty's been found. The ruffians who stole her will stand trial next week. Lord Braughton wants to see them hanged. He would like me to give evidence."

"Hanged?" She shivered. "You must go back to Derbyshire?"

"There are other witnesses. A letter from me would probably suffice."

"To take away three men's lives? You don't even have to be there?"

He stood up, walked around the table, and kissed her. "No, but I'm going, all the same. If I want to make certain that their sentence is commuted, I'd better go myself. They didn't take our lives when they had the chance. Why should we take theirs? I'll be gone for only a few days. Will you be all right?"

"Within the strong walls of Wyldshay? Of course!"

"I hate to leave you, but I don't think it wise to take you away from here just yet. Not until the duke and duchess get back."

"Then go! Your mother has no doubt already cowed Lord Hanley. Since he knows now that we have no idea of his secret, I'm no threat to him. Of course I'll be safe. And you owe it to Beauty to bring her back yourself."

"I knew you'd understand," he said. "Can you also understand how very much I love you?"

She gazed up into his eyes and grinned. "Oh, I think so! After all, it's almost as much as I love you."

RYDER sent Beauty home with a groom. He made a quick visit to Dillard to make sure that Mr. Davis had his brother-in-law's business well in hand. Then he was forced to stay on at Wrendale, pacing with impatience, when the trial took far longer than he had hoped. But in the end he saved Bruiser and his friends from the hangman, though he doubted that they were grateful to get seven years' transportation, instead.

Though he burned with impatience to get home, when his carriage rolled back south at last—carrying him back to Miracle—Ryder leaned back against the squabs and smiled wryly to himself.

Messengers had brought word from Wyldshay every day. Back in London from her rounds of various country houses, the duchess was launching a whirlwind of preparation for their new wedding. His mother's influence in society was immense. It might just be enough. Perhaps fortune favored the brave, after all!

In which case, perhaps Miracle's mother had known exactly what she had done, when she had named her new baby.

The carriage rocked as it turned into an inn yard. Ryder climbed down and glanced about. The White Swan, where he had once suffered through a bitter breakfast with Hanley. Ostlers swarmed once again about his carriage.

He laughed and strode inside to order a late dinner. As he entered the parlor, a brown-eyed man in a caped riding coat grabbed him by the elbow. It was Guy. Dread coursed through Ryder's heart at the look on his cousin's face.

"Ryder? Thank God I ran into you!" Guy said. "No, nothing's happened to Miracle. Not as far as I know."

"Yet you look like a man with too many days' hard riding behind you. What the devil is it?"

Guy released Ryder's arm and ran his fingers through his hair. "I've found Philip Willcott."

CHAPTER SEVENTEEN

THE BUSTLE OF THE INN FADED TO A BLURRED HUM AS RYder stared blankly at his cousin. *"Willcott?"*

"He's alive."

Sounds sprang back into focus. Miracle had never admitted to grief or guilt—and for God's sake, she'd been justified in defending herself—but Ryder suspected that she still saw the incident with Willcott as a stain on her soul. But how the hell could the man be alive? Elation warred with a whirlpool of misgivings.

He guided Guy inside, commandeered a private parlor, and ordered wine and a tray of bread and meat. Real exhaustion lurked in the brown eyes. Without food and drink, Guy might simply drop, and it would anyway take several minutes to change the horses.

Ryder filled two glasses and gave one to his cousin. "You didn't kill him when you found him?"

"For what he did on the yacht? It's a little more complicated than that!" Guy flung himself into a chair as Ryder paced the small room. "He outwitted me. I lost him again."

"Yet Miracle isn't a murderer. Thank God for that! Though she did stab him?"

"Yes!" Guy gulped down wine. A little color came back to his face. "Everything up to that point happened just as she described. I got that much out of him, at least. Hanley must have found him after Miracle had already fled in the boat. I don't know if Hanley thought he was dead or not, but he flung him overboard. If Willcott *had* died then, Hanley—not Miracle—would have killed him. However, Willcott regained consciousness when he hit the water. He began sinking like an anchor, but he didn't dare shout for help, in case Hanley simply shot him like a dog."

"He must have thought he was about to meet his Maker," Ryder said dryly.

"He did."

Ryder tore a chunk of fresh bread from a loaf. It was as important to maintain his own strength as Guy's, though his dread was rapidly coalescing into real fear.

"He did what?"

"He did meet his Maker, or thought that he had. Willcott swam until he was exhausted. Then as he sank beneath the waves again God appeared to him in a blaze of white light. He was swept down a bright tunnel, cradled in the lap of Christ. When he was eventually cast—like Jonah—back onto the bosom of the waters, he found himself in a small boat in the company of some freebooters. Assuming from his sorry state that he was a fellow renegade who'd fallen foul of the revenuers, they carried Willcott with them to France."

"So where the devil did you find him?"

"North of here. God told him to track Hanley down and destroy him. Willcott chased down some more evidence about Hanley in France, then came back to England. When he learned that the earl had gone to Derbyshire, he followed him."

Ryder choked down his burning urgency. He must know all the facts before he acted on his growing terror.

"Did he tell you what secret he'd been holding over Hanley?"

"He not only told me, he gave me proof. There were several copies, apparently."

"Proof of what?"

Guy tugged out a folded document and threw it on the table. "A French marriage. The fourth Earl of Hanley took a wife in France before he committed bigamy by marrying again in England. Evesham Forbes Frobisher was thus born out of legal wedlock. He's no more the fifth Earl of Hanley than I am."

Red liquid spilled as Ryder spun about. "Willcott's gone to find Hanley now?"

Guy gulped wine and nodded. "He discovered that Hanley—Mr. Frobisher, I should say—had already returned to London. I was hot on his heels when I saw your carriage pull in."

Heart racing, Ryder set down his glass. "I know you need food and rest, Guy, but you can eat and sleep in my carriage. We must get to Wyldshay."

"Wyldshay?"

He seized his cousin by the lapels and dragged him to his feet. "For God's sake, Guy! Even if Hanley kills Willcott the second the man arrives in town, multiple witnesses—including you—can testify that they recently saw him alive. Miracle's not a murderer and never was. So Hanley holds nothing over me, after all. Yet if Willcott admits that he gave you these papers, Hanley will know that you'll share them with me."

Guy swayed on his feet, but he began to wrap bread and meat into a napkin. "He won't trust you to keep quiet?"

"Never! Our antipathy runs too deep."

"In which case," Guy said, "Willcott's existence just rather tipped the balance of power, didn't it?"

"Exactly! As soon as Willcott reaches him, Hanley will know that his worst enemy has evidence that can destroy him. With Miracle proved innocent, he no longer has anything he can use to make me keep quiet about it. So what the hell does he have left now, except revenge?"

MIRACLE gazed at the darkening sky beyond the window in Ryder's bedroom. It was almost time to go down for her light supper, but she often seemed to feel suddenly tired like this. She may have impressed the duchess with her cool manner, but now that Ryder had left, her appetite had disappeared.

Sheer nerves made it hard even to face breakfast in the mornings. Sometimes she could eat a little dry toast and drink tea. Other days she ate nothing and still felt like retching.

Her one comfort was to retreat to her husband's rooms off the Whitchurch Gallery. The Whitchurch Wing was separated from the rest of the castle by a series of courtyards. Though a medieval tower rose majestically above it, Ryder's private domain was elegant, simple, and peaceful, and she loved it.

She lay fully clothed on the bed that they had shared every night since he had first brought her to his home, except for that one magical night on the roof of Ambrose's Folly, when she had thought that the falling stars had entered her soul.

Gathering darkness played across the room. Miracle wrapped her arms about Ryder's pillow and buried her face in the clean linen. Every day a messenger brought a little note, filled with humor and wry observations. She missed him with an anguish like a wound. Though the maids had brought fresh sheets the day he had left, her breasts ached at the faint shadow of his scent.

Something touched her shoulder. Miracle opened her eyes. One of the maids stood over her, nervously twisting her fingers in her apron.

"Yes, Jane? What is it?"

"Your supper is ready, m' lady, and there's a gentleman to see you. He's waiting in the Great Hall. The footman told him you were not receiving, but he was most insistent. He said you'd want to see him, that he had news about Lord Ryderbourne."

She was instantly awake. "Did this gentleman give his name?"

"He said you'd know him, m' lady. He arrived in a fancy carriage with a crest. He said he's been here before as a guest of the duchess. He acted like he expected to be invited to stay to supper."

Miracle crossed to her washstand and splashed water on her face. Since her husband controlled fleets of paid envoys, she doubted that any gentleman was bringing her a message from Ryder, but had her past decided to pay one last visit, after all?

She stared at her face in the mirror for a moment. The face that had been both a blessing and a curse. The face that had saved her from starvation. The face that had given her to Sir Benjamin Trotter, who had loved her.

And to six men who had not.

Guy had been one of them—though he had never quite believed that—and there was Hanley, of course. The names of the others ran through her mind: Richard Avedon, Lord Dartford, Sir Robin Hatchley, Lord Burnham. She had nothing to fear from any of them. Perhaps her mystery visitor was Dartford, sadly foxed, who still thought it more discreet not to tell the servants his name, since her husband was away and he had once been her lover.

She was hardly in the mood for company, yet she allowed Jane to comb out and rearrange her hair, before helping her into a fresh dress.

Miracle took one last look at herself before she left the room. The lady of the night was gone. In her place, Lady Ryderbourne, a future duchess, stalked down through the castle in a stunningly elegant gown of white satin, while every maid and footman stood to attention as she passed.

The Great Hall was empty.

The carriage rocked dangerously as John Coachman drove the horses south through the night. Wishing only for yet more speed, Ryder told Guy everything that had happened since they had parted at Wrendale.

"So you really think Hanley will try to harm her?" Guy asked. "Yet surely she'll refuse to see him? Wyldshay is full of servants who'll sacrifice themselves before letting any harm come to a St. George."

"Servants? God! However loyal, how the devil can servants be expected to stand up against an earl?"

"Hanley isn't an earl."

"No one else knows that as yet, I imagine, except you and me and Willcott."

Guy turned his head to gaze from the window. His skin still looked pale. "Why the hell do you hate each other?"

Ryder tipped his head back against the squabs. Revulsion and rage mingled hotly in his blood, driving his pulse into thunderous new rhythms as he recalled what had happened at Harrow. He had been barely more than a child in the hands of an older boy. Yet that boy had come into his title, and Lord Hanley had become, to all appearances, a perfect English gentleman.

He had buried all of those memories so deeply he had genuinely almost forgotten them. Until he had rescued a woman with bruises like accusations on her skin, and learned that she'd been Hanley's mistress.

"It doesn't matter," he said. "It's all in the past."

His face ghostly, Guy glanced back at his cousin. "I wish I could believe that."

"Forget it! Did Willcott explain why he hid a copy of the papers in Izzy's Bible?"

"He'd come across evidence of the French marriage and he was blackmailing Hanley, as we surmised. Willcott knew that Hanley would ransack his rooms as soon as he had the chance, so he took his proof to Miracle's house. It wasn't hard, I imagine, to secrete it in the maid's room."

"And as it turned out, that was a perfect hiding place—until Hanley thought it all through and guessed what Willcott had done."

Guy rubbed a thumb and forefinger over his eyes. "But why the hell create the scene on the yacht?"

"That was probably genuine. Miracle can drive almost any man wild with desire, even when she'd rather not. So when Willcott offered to trade all the damning evidence for Miracle's favors and—no doubt—a very large sum of money, Hanley must have believed him."

His cousin looked up. "But you think Hanley intended a double cross?"

Ryder nodded. "How could he trust Willcott to keep quiet forever, however much he paid him? So he'd promise the money, sacrifice Miracle, learn the location of the papers, then turn Willcott adrift in a boat without oars in a spot where the currents would carry it straight onto the rocks of the next headland."

"Though Willcott must have already told Hanley that he'd hidden the papers amongst Miracle's possessions?"

"I imagine he told him on the yacht that night. It was the truth, after a fashion. He probably refused to explain exactly, till after he'd secured the money, but a half truth was necessary to win Hanley's confidence. However, Miracle put a little damper on everyone's plans when she put a knife into Willcott's shoulder. Now, get some sleep, Guy! There's nothing more we can do now, except pray."

Guy pulled a rug up over his shoulders and slumped into a corner of the carriage. In a few moments, he was asleep.

Ryder sank his head into both hands and tried to bury his fear. He even tried to pray, for Miracle's safety, for her love. Yet another thought intruded, as he looked up to see Guy settle into the deep slumber of exhaustion: a generous man, his cousin, to knock himself out for a woman who had already pledged herself to another.

MIRACLE shrugged and gazed about the Great Hall. The room was dominated by images of St. George and the dragon. Perhaps the gentleman had lost his nerve, after all? Which meant that her visitor was almost certainly not Lord Dartford.

She turned to speak to the footman. "A gentleman came here asking for me, Duncan, but he didn't give his name?"

"That's right, my lady, but he's gone now."

"Gone? You mean his coach already left?"

"Yes, my lady. A few minutes ago."

"Can you describe the crest on the door?"

The footman shook his head, but he went to question someone from the stables. Miracle waited with a vague sense of unease.

Duncan's shoes resounded heavily on the floorboards as he came back. "The coach was damaged, my lady, but recently repaired. The head groom says it looked like a bullet had gone through the door panel. He made this little sketch of the crest."

He held out a slip of paper.

There was no need, of course, to look at it.

THE carriage rolled on, its lamps carving a faint path through the darkness. Guy still slept. Ryder stared from the window at the shrouded countryside. Thick clouds hid the stars. Lightning crackled from one ominous mass of blackness to another, followed by long, low peals of thunder.

God! If only he could tear open the night to fly like a raven straight to Miracle's side!

There was no way to travel any faster than this. He forced himself to lean back and close his eyes.

"Aren't we almost there?" His cousin pushed down the rug and stretched. "Must be close to dawn?"

Ryder glanced at his watch. "Not according to this. Bloody timepiece must have stopped."

He leaned forward to glance from the window, then he wrenched down the glass. Shock ripped into his gut.

"What the hell?"

An angry red bruise colored the sky to the south, as if the devil were smelting iron in the clouds. For several long minutes as the carriage rolled closer, Ryder stared in silence. At last he was able to distinguish the sharp agony of battlements silhouetted against the red glow. The spiked outline of roof turrets and flagpole. The dread bulk of the Fortune Tower.

Shock coalesced into terror, while incoherent prayers tumbled through his mind.

The base of the clouds above Wyldshay flamed like a furnace.

He slammed his fist into the side of the carriage, then tore both hands through his hair, as if he could wrench the torment out of his heart.

Guy grabbed him by the wrist. "It's no use, Ryder. There's nothing we can do till we get there. The horses can't possibly run any faster."

Ryder forced himself to take several deep breaths, before his anguish completely blocked his throat.

"I know that," he said. "But I left Miracle there alone. And the bloody bastard has set fire to Wyldshay!"

MIRACLE dreamed of him: warm, passionate, thoughtful, lovely. Lord Ryderbourne!

Yet buried doubts also stirred—as if she were being prodded by hobgoblins—making her toss restlessly in his bed. Thunder boomed through her dreams, threatening heartache.

Or is it just that poppies are known to bring headaches and thunderstorms?

Surely love would be enough?

Yet she woke to sudden fear, as if a goblin jeered at her: *How do you like your fool's paradise?*

Thunder still rolled, but the sound had become a dull roar, like a waterfall. A faint crackling underlay the sound, as if the water fell onto dry sticks.

"I asked you," the voice said again. "How do you like your fool's paradise?"

Miracle gulped down plain terror, then pushed her hair from her forehead with both hands and sat up. The clock marked only a few minutes past midnight, but a faint red glow was shining in at the window, and a man with an oil lamp was standing at the foot of her bed.

For one long moment she stared at him, while her heart rattled madly in her chest.

"He loves this place, doesn't he?" Lord Hanley asked. "He even thinks that he loves you. Too bad he's about to lose all of it."

She swallowed hard. Smoke wafted in the open window. "There's a fire," she said. "We may not have very much time to get out."

Footsteps pounded in the corridor. Someone shouted, then rattled at the door.

"It's locked," Hanley said, lifting the lamp higher. "And in case you hadn't noticed, I'm holding a pistol in my right hand. Both loaded barrels point at your heart. Get up!"

Miracle swallowed hard. Life beat fast in her veins. She did not want to die.

"In nothing but my nightgown? In front of a gentleman? Sir, you shock me!"

Lord Hanley stepped forward. Red glinted on his weapon. "Don't try to be clever, Miracle! Do as I say!"

"Well, of course! I would never argue with loaded pistols." She clambered from the bed. *Buy time! Buy time!* "Yet I had planned to die on the scaffold. Ah well! It's been a short life, but a sweet one. I regret none of it, except you."

He thrust the gun into her ribs. "Be quiet!"

Voices shouted her name from the hallway. She heard Jane and Duncan: Ryder's people, trying to save her. Something heavy thudded into the door. They were trying to break it down.

Lord Hanley threw the lamp. Glass exploded into flame, devouring oil as it spilled across the floor.

He clapped one hand over Miracle's mouth and marched her to another door hidden in the paneling. He slammed it open with a blow from his pistol butt and pushed her through ahead of him. A spiral stair coiled up inside the walls of the Whitchurch Tower.

Miracle stumbled up, the steps rough on her bare feet. At

every third or fourth turn, an arrow-slit window looked out. She saw nothing but red.

Hanley thrust her out onto the roof walk behind the battlements and slammed another door closed behind them.

"I want you to watch as his home burns to the ground," he said. "I'm only sorry that he's not here to see it, as well."

A furious red glow was eating its way steadily up the walls of the Docent Tower. The stables were already ablaze. The Fortune Tower stood out like an angry black fist in stark contrast.

"How did you know that a stair led up here from Ryder's bedroom?" she asked.

"He told me. Many years ago. At Harrow."

"When you first fell into disagreement? What on earth did he do to you?"

Hanley thrust her up against the battlements, cruelly twisting her arm. Stitches tore at the shoulder of her nightgown.

"It's more a matter of what I did to him. Shall I tell you?"

She forced herself to laugh, though fear beat at her. "If you like! It makes no difference to me. I really don't care to know any more about him."

He released her and stepped back. His eyes were cold, his handsome face rigid.

Lord Hanley did not look mad. He looked like a man with a broken heart.

"You don't even love him, do you?" he asked.

Forgive me, my love! But I want to live for you, if I can. If he knows how much we care for each other, I fear he will kill me out of hand.

"Love? Are you serious? He just fancies me in his bed, that's all!"

"You little bitch!" The pistol wavered as if he gripped it too hard. "Did you truly think you could get away with this? That a strumpet could marry into one of the first families of England? That a harlot could ever become a duchess? That after sharing all those nasty whore's tricks in my bed, you could really invite the rest of the peerage to a grand wedding here at Wyldshay?"

"Well, no," she said. "I suppose not. But it was worth a try. After all, he has more money than you ever dreamed of."

"Used to have."

Hanley leaned his hips against the high wall behind him. Red reflections glowed on his face and in his silver-blond hair, but his eyes glittered like ice.

"Yes," Miracle said, turning to gaze down at the flames. "I suppose Wyldshay will cost a little more to rebuild than the door panel on your coach."

He stepped forward again to grasp her by the chin, then twisted her, so that her stomach pressed hard against the merlon.

"Yet perhaps he won't wish to, when he finds his wife's body. Not quite so pretty, after she was burned alive."

"How very unoriginal!" she said. "If my corpse is to burn, how on earth will he know whether or not I was raped—or do you intend to do that afterward?"

He stood for a moment as if frozen, then—still holding her by the chin with her head pulled back—he thrust his other hand beneath the hem of her nightgown.

Far below, in the courtyards and gardens, a scurry of figures had organized itself into bucket chains, bringing water and flinging it at the tortured stone walls. Horses surged blindfolded from the stables. A procession of maids carried paintings and armloads of valuables across the arched bridge.

On the edge of the river men were working feverishly at some kind of pump. Another group dragged hoses. The roof of the stables fell in with a roar, but a spray was starting to play across the base of the Fortune Tower.

Even without its master, Wyldshay fought for survival.

As did Miracle Heather.

Hanley's hand, still holding the pistol, stroked unsteadily up her thighs, until her gown was rucked up over her bottom. His breath roared hot in her ear.

"One last time, then, Miracle, before we both die!"

"Did you forget," she said through gritted teeth, "that I'm not a fine lady who'll lie back and squeal while you take your rotten pleasure?"

She locked her fists together and hammered her elbow into his groin. Hanley doubled over. The pistol skidded away across the stone pavement. Miracle dived after it, but he caught her by the ankle.

Writhing like an eel, she rammed her bare heel into his face. He grunted, but hung on, his fingers biting into bone.

It was a blind, bitter rage. All the hurt. All the pain. Childhood years of hard labor and fear. The dread of hunger and desperation and poverty that had led her to accept carte blanche from him, even when her instincts screamed a warning.

With the same grim determination that she had once shown Willcott, she kicked out again. Hanley swore and released her.

Wriggling back across the cold stone, she tried again to grab the pistol. Hanley lurched to his feet. Her fingers closed on the gun. As he started toward her again, she took aim and fired.

He cried out, then fell like a tree.

Miracle dropped the pistol and stumbled back to the door that led to the spiral stair. The oak was at least two inches thick and heavily banded with iron. She set her hand on the latch to wrench it open, then let go with a gasp. The handle was hot.

She glanced back at Hanley. Handsome, broken, his fair hair glimmering, he lay like a corpse.

Now that she was free of his direct attack, she was afraid enough to weep. Smoke leaked from the keyhole. The rooms below must be roaringly alight by now. The staircase was probably on fire. As far as she knew, there was no other way down.

Yet life still blazed its demands. Whether in the end she lived or died, she would strive for life with every ounce of her being. Miracle glanced up and whispered a quick prayer—blasphemously offered not to God, but to her husband's love. She would tear the clouds from the heavens, if that would prevent Ryder having to find her dead body.

Thunder boomed directly overhead. A bolt of lightning sizzled into a field on the other side of the River Wyld. Every stone leaped into sharp relief. A gutter ran down the wall of the turret. She reached up to dip her fingers into a bend in the lead. Water still lay there from the last rain.

With frantic fingers she tore the ripped sleeve from her nightgown and sopped it into the fluid. She splashed more water over her nightgown until she was soaked. With the wet sleeve wrapped over her nose and mouth, she set her hand on the door latch.

The oak planks roared as if they held back lions.

She began to turn the handle, her face damp with rainwater and tears. *My dear Ryder, give me the strength to live for you!*

"Miracle! For God's sake! Don't!"

She whirled about. His hair wild about his face, Ryder hauled himself up over the battlements. He had stripped down to shirt and trousers, and he carried a coil of rope slung over one shoulder.

"Unless you want to die, don't open that door!" he said. "The whole bloody tower beneath us is on fire."

Miracle smiled at him with the smile that she might reserve for angels, and fainted.

AN ocean lashed into her face. She was adrift in a dinghy with no oars. She had just killed a man. She deserved to die.

"Miracle!"

She looked up into the pure green gaze of Sir Galahad. Lightning blazed from cloud to cloud. A downpour beat from the darkness, soaking his shirt and face and hair. He was holding her tight to his chest and striding with her toward the battlements.

"I love you," she said. "Is it raining?"

Ryder nodded, his hair plastered to his forehead. "You fainted. The rain will help save the rest of Wyldshay, but this roof is threatening collapse."

"You climbed all the way up the wall from the river?"

"Yes, but we must get down right away. Can you stand?"

She glanced at Hanley, still lying where she had shot him. She shivered.

"So I've killed another man?"

"No." Ryder set her on her feet and busied himself tying knots in the rope. "No. Anyway, you never killed the first one."

Lightning cracked again. Miracle leaned both hands on the wet stone and looked out. Rain swept in sheets across the fields to thrash into the castle, dumping torrents onto their heads. The stables still burned, but the frenzied flare had softened to a dull, bruised glow, hissing beneath the storm.

"I don't understand." She still felt a little giddy. "Willcott?"

"I can't explain now, but Willcott's alive. As for Hanley, he's not dead. You shot him in the leg. He fainted from pain and pure bile, probably. You didn't kill anyone, Miracle."

"No," another voice said. "But I did."

Ryder thrust Miracle behind him and spun about. He seemed carved from wet stone.

With one hand pressed to his thigh, Hanley had pushed himself up to sit propped against the wall. "Willcott's body will be found in an alley in London. No one will associate it with me."

"So you killed him?" Ryder tied loops of knotted rope about Miracle's body. "Once you knew that Guy and I had seen the papers, what difference did Willcott make any longer?"

The downpour streamed. Hanley's head seemed to be plated in silver, as if he wore armor.

"It's what I should have done to start with, when Willcott first hinted that he knew secrets that could ruin me. Yet he said there were more copies, that if anything happened to him, they'd be made public."

"Though you still took the gamble on the yacht?"

"Once he admitted that he'd hidden the only copies in England amongst Miracle's things, the risk seemed worth it. Who'd go to France to look for the rest?"

Hanley grimaced and lifted his palm from his leg. His fingers were sticky with blood.

Ryder picked up Miracle's torn sleeve and tossed it to the other man. "If you want to get off this roof alive, you'd better bind that."

"No!" Hanley said, striking out with his free hand. "Leave me be! I'm damned if I'll let you see me ruined."

"For God's sake! I can't leave you up here to die."

"Why the hell not?" Hanley laughed. "I've rather burned my bridges, as well as your home."

"Bind the wound!" Ryder tied the other end of the rope about a merlon. "As soon as I've seen my wife safely down off this roof, I'll lower you next."

"So you really intend to remain married to that whore? You'll besmirch your entire family and contaminate the purity of your blood by attempting to ennoble a creature from the gutter? Then you'll hold *me* up to ridicule?"

"Manners, not birth, maketh man," Ryder said. "Why do you assume that I'll blackmail you as Willcott did? The sin, if there was one, was your father's, not yours."

Hanley stared at him. "You really think I'll let you give me my life?"

"If you want it. As for Willcott's death, I've no proof against you, and you know it. That's entirely up to your conscience. The man's no bloody loss to the world."

"But everything I have was entailed with the title. If the truth comes out that I'm a bastard, I'll be a laughingstock."

Ryder looped rope around another merlon, where he could brace it. "For all I know, Willcott made up the whole sorry tale and had forgeries made in France. There was enough chaos after the Revolution to make that possible."

Hanley tied the sleeve about his leg. "But you've always hated me."

"No," Ryder said. "I did once, but I forgave it all a long time ago. The only thing I can't forgive is how you tried to use Miracle. For that, once your leg is healed, you'll be pleased to give me satisfaction."

"And why not first see me drummed from the Lords?"

"You have a wife and children, sir. If anybody's innocent in this whole bloody mess, it's your little son."

"When you spread the word, they'll all be beggared."

Ryder lifted Miracle onto the battlements, kissed her quickly, and made ready to lower her from the tower.

"Devil take it! Haven't you grasped yet that I'll keep silent for their sake? So will Miracle and Guy Devoran. You've no cousin who's being cheated of his inheritance. Nothing's to be gained by ruining you, sir!"

Hanley staggered to his feet. "Do you think that I wish to live beholden to you, waiting every day to be denounced? What the hell do I have left to live for?"

"Not much, I admit," Ryder said. "Because once you're healed enough, I still intend to kill you."

"So you would offer me a gentleman's death on the dueling field? Then let me take a gentleman's death here and now." Hanley nodded at the gun left lying where Miracle had dropped it. "There's still one ball left in that pistol."

Miracle gasped as her husband kicked the pistol within Hanley's reach. The blood-soaked fingers reached out and grasped it. As Hanley raised the pistol, Ryder lowered her over the wall.

She spun out into space, lost in the lashing darkness, but a shot rang out, the sound oddly muffled by the rain as she spiraled down toward the black river.

Hands reached up to catch her. Guy was waiting in a small boat at the foot of the tower. He untied the rope from her body and flung his cloak around her shoulders, before pulling her down onto the seat beside him.

"Ryder!" she said, clutching Guy's arm. "He's up there with Hanley. He gave Hanley the pistol. I heard a shot."

Guy hugged her to his side and stared up into the roaring darkness. "Ryder's the best man I've ever known," he said. "Have faith, Miracle!"

The end of the rope snaked back up the wall. Miracle sat wrapped in Guy's embrace with her blood frozen in her veins.

"I can't bear it," she whispered. "I could never go on without him. I don't deserve him, but surely God can't take him away from me this soon?"

"It's all right," Guy said. "Ryder loves you. He won't die for nothing."

Lightning flashed again. A man was dropping hand over hand down the wall with the aid of the rope.

Flames burst from the top of the Whitchurch Tower with a sudden roar. The upper half of the rope whipped away into space. The man hanging from the lower end plummeted like a falling stone into the river.

Spray splashed. The boat rocked. Guy thrust off with the oars. Frantic with fear, Miracle scanned the black water for several long moments, before a dark head surfaced and shook spray like flung diamonds.

Wet sleeves flashed white as the man's arms cleaved the water. In a couple of strokes he swam up to the boat. His strong hands grabbed the gunnel.

"Hanley said he'd rather die," Ryder said. His face looked ravaged. "So I gave him the pistol and he shot himself."

CHAPTER EIGHTEEN

"I DO HOPE," THE DUCHESS SAID AS SHE EXAMINED THE ruins of the Whitchurch Tower, "that all this was worth it?"

Ryder glanced up at the blackened stone walls, the soaked remains of burned beams and plaster, and hugged Miracle to his side.

"To keep Miracle alive? What the devil do you think, Your Grace?"

"I think Hanley made some most injudicious choices. The duke is furious. I have, however, put it about that the earl perished heroically trying to assist with the fire."

"Instead of starting it?" Guy asked. "He set the blaze in the stables first, knowing that the hay and all those dry wooden partitions would go up like fireworks. Thank God the grooms knew how to get the horses out."

"Yes," the duchess said. She turned and led them back into what had been Ryder's bedroom. Parts of the floor were missing. All the contents had been destroyed by either smoke or water, or both. "I understand the staff also made heroic efforts with those newfangled pumps of yours, Ryderbourne?"

Ryder nodded. "Yes, the servants were splendid."

"Exactly as you had trained them to be. If they had not kept their wits about them, the fire would have spread to the rest of the castle." The duchess stared up at the peeling wall near what had been her son's bed. "However, I regret the loss of that painting. I was fond of it."

"But why make Hanley into a hero?" Guy persisted.

"He leaves a widow and several young children," the duchess said. "No one—not even Blackdown—need know anything more, except those of us in this room. I want no further scandal attached to Miracle's name. It is difficult enough to continue with the wedding arrangements as it is."

"How many high sticklers have threatened to turn up their noses?" Ryder asked.

The duchess stalked out into the fresh air of a courtyard. "I can only say that I have done my best. Only time will tell whether curiosity will win out over prejudice. However, we must make plans to go forward. Fortunately, other than your rooms and the stables, the rest of Wyldshay is relatively untouched. Though I am most annoyed about the St. George tapestry that Duncan hauled out of the Great Hall. Along with several undistinguished portraits of your ancestors, for which I can hardly pretend grief, the tapestry escaped the fire, only to be half-ruined by the rain."

"Then you think the wedding can go forward as planned?"

"It must."

"Even at the risk that no one will come?" Ryder asked.

"My dear son, the Duchess of Blackdown does not gamble her influence and reputation for nothing. Should we decide that Wyldshay is too greatly damaged, Arthur has offered us Stratfield Saye for the wedding."

"Arthur?" Miracle asked. For no apparent reason, she felt a little faint.

The duchess glanced at her. "My dear child, surely the Duke of Wellington was not yet another of your lovers?"

"No," Miracle said. The walls of the courtyard had begun to spin in long, lazy arcs. "I wasn't thinking of the living man. I never met the Iron Duke to speak to. I was thinking of his face on an inn sign."

The duchess stared at her for a moment, then she turned to snap at her son.

"Ryderbourne! Help your wife to sit down!"

"It's all right," Miracle said. "I'm quite well!"

"I hope so," the duchess said, "since you are quite obviously with child."

"You really didn't know?" Ryder asked.

Miracle gazed up at him. He had carried her into the set of guest rooms where they had been living since the fire, laid her on a chaise longue, and was cradling her head in his lap.

"I thought I was just worried about the future," she said. "Sometimes I felt sick in the mornings. I even missed my courses, but I assumed it was anxiety about the wedding. How could I guess it was a baby?"

He seemed lit from within. "I cannot begin to express how I feel."

She reached up to stroke his face. "Do you think our son may have been conceived in a bolt of heavenly fire, the night of the meteor shower on Ambrose's Folly?"

"Very possibly. If it's a boy, should we call him Ambrose?"

"I don't know," she said. "Part of me hopes that we have a girl, because no baby of mine is ever going to ride in that dreadful dragon carriage you keep at Wrendale."

"But our first son will be a future duke," Ryder said with a grin. "You'd deny him his heritage?"

"Only those parts of it that might have been damaging to you." Miracle sat up and dropped her feet to the floor. "What really happened at Harrow, Ryder? Will our sons have to suffer the same way?"

He pushed to his feet and strode away across the room.

"I suppose we shouldn't have any secrets." He spun about to look back at her. "Should we?"

She stood and walked up to him. "No, we shouldn't, though it might take a lifetime to share all of them."

"We have a lifetime," he said.

Miracle studied his face. "Yet I will tell you now about those other men who came between Guy and Lord Hanley, if you wish. I used to think it would be disloyal for me to do so. Now that I know that you are part of my heart, you deserve to know that it wasn't as bad as you might have feared."

"I don't really care," he said, "except insofar as it was painful for you."

"No. I think you have cared very much, Ryder."

"I cannot bear to think that you were used casually or cruelly." A shadow flitted over his face. "Why else would you have chosen to favor Hanley?"

"My only real mistake! But after Guy there were only four others: Richard Avedon, Lord Dartford, Sir Robin Hatchley, and Lord Burnham."

The shadow lifted a little as he smiled down at her. "All good men, though Avedon's a bit of a fool."

She gave him a wry grin. "I did not keep company with him for his brains."

He laughed. "And then he married—and Hatchley, as well?"

"Exactly. Being young men of a certain integrity, they each decided not to keep a ladybird after that."

"But Dartford's a bachelor."

"Alas, Lord Dartford's a little too fond of his wine and the tables. After one run of bad luck, he was on the brink of leaving the country, so he introduced me to Sir Robin."

"And Burnham died in a hunting accident, didn't he? I'm so sorry, Miracle."

"Yes," she said. "He was dashing and amusing and very kind to me. I think I could almost have loved him. When they brought his body back on a gate, I was a little . . . distraught, as you can imagine."

Ryder put his arm around her shoulders and led her back to the chaise longue. "And Hanley was there?"

"Yes. He seemed kind enough and I was numb to anything else. Three weeks later I accepted his offer."

"Yet he intimated some rather dreadful things about you."

"Did he?" She looked up at him, her heart open and entirely at peace. "Perhaps that was simply a reflection of the way he felt about you. I was with him once when you entered a ballroom. He insisted that we leave right away, then that night he demanded that I tie him down and beat him with a riding crop. We argued very terribly when I refused. I don't think he ever quite forgave me: not for my refusal, but because he had broken down in front of me, and revealed something he wanted to keep hidden forever. What horrors lay between you, Ryder?"

"Nothing that matters now." He took her hand and stared at her fingers.

Miracle closed her palm over his. "You don't need to tell me, not if it's too painful to you."

"Painful? No. Not anymore. I had simply buried it. I was not even his primary victim. Yet I will tell you, because I would leave nothing hidden in my soul."

She leaned her head against his shoulder and waited quietly.

"I suppose it's just what boys do," Ryder said at last, "when they're torn from their homes and left without much adult supervision. I wasn't quite prepared for it, because I was the first St. George to go to a public school. My father was taught here at Wyldshay. It was the duchess's idea that her sons learn to get along with other boys. Of course, she had no idea what form that might take."

"You'd never met Hanley before?"

"Not to speak to. He was three years older. Yet he took an instant dislike to me. I'd not been there long, when he led a gang of older boys who subjected newcomers like myself to what they liked to call an initiation. I resisted. They held me down and did it anyway."

"And it was something pretty barbaric, I assume?"

He leaned back and pulled her head down onto his shoulder. His fingers stroked softly over her hair, as if he took deep comfort in her presence.

"Hanley held our faces under water until we thought we were drowning, while his friends tore away our trousers. It was meant to be both terrifying and sexually degrading, but I was lucky. I was able to hold my breath far longer than most. All those years of swimming in the Wyld, no doubt. When they let me up for air, I fought back like a demon and was knocked out. Probably a blessing. I have no memory of what happened next."

"Only the knowledge."

"My primary emotion was a deeply outraged pride. There's very little fun, after all, in assaulting an unconscious carcass. Yet little boys in those circumstances form very deep friendships, and a boy that I loved like a brother wasn't so fortunate."

She shuddered. "He was raped?"

His fingers stopped for a moment, then he kissed her forehead. "Though he had the courage of a tiger, my friend was fine-boned and small for his age. He didn't stand a chance. If we hadn't shown Hanley that we couldn't be intimidated, we might have been attacked over and over again. So my friend and I swore a pact."

"Lord Ayre must have looked like an angel when he was little," she said.

"How the devil—?"

"Never mind! That's his secret, not ours. It was just something that he said when we were traveling down from Scotland, to the effect that the ties between you were unbreakable. And his mother must have had some reason to be so very forbearing. So you organized yourselves to take revenge?"

Ryder kissed her again. "With all the fiendish ingenuity of little boys. Hanley didn't get a moment's rest. He never knew what humiliating surprises lay in wait, until he went up to Oxford."

"Then he didn't retaliate further against you?"

"He tried to, but I think our outraged defiance simply defeated him. That's what he could never forgive: We refused to be cowed."

"Perhaps he was ashamed, as well," Miracle said. "I don't think he really wanted to be cruel."

"No. He wanted to win acceptance. A display of ruthless savagery always impresses other boys."

"It was the same in the apprentice house. I was glad to be a girl and separated from the boys' dormitories. The girls' nastiness was mostly confined to words and petty meanness. But the boys always fought a ruthless struggle for leadership."

"Yes, I suppose that's how it was at Harrow," Ryder said.

"And Lord Hanley was always so desperate to assert power," Miracle said. "He knew you'd grow up to outrank him, and that's probably why he singled you out. Do you think he suspected even then that he might be illegitimate?"

"God knows!"

"It would explain a great deal. Yet you forgave him in the end, didn't you?"

"If it hadn't been for Hanley, you and I might never have met. Though I'm glad that our child wasn't conceived until after I'd emptied my heart of my loathing for him."

"That night on the roof of the Folly, I think the heavens conspired to erase all the pain of the past," she said. "Until I met you, I had never known that sex could be made radiant with love, that life could be made radiant with love. A heart filled with love leaves no room for hatred."

"Then we'll marry this time like two virgins, after all," Ryder said with a grin.

"With one of them carrying a child? That sounds a little blasphemous! Let's just say that we shall marry again with our hearts filled with brilliance."

THE day of the wedding dawned under promising blue skies. Carriages had been rolling into Wyldshay all that morning and most of the previous day. The castle was bursting at the seams. The Whitchurch Wing had been cleaned up and repairs begun, but Ryder and Miracle planned to leave for Wrendale immediately after the ceremony.

Dillard seemed stiff and nervous as he moved about among so many aristocrats, but no one seemed to notice. Mary had stayed behind in Derbyshire with her new baby and the children.

"I've turned over a new leaf, Mirry," Dillard said. "Since my latest little daughter was born."

"Mr. Davis has helped set your business to rights?" Miracle asked.

"Aye, and more than that. I've sworn off the drink. It was the ruin of our father. I think it was fair on the way to becoming the ruin of me. I'll never touch another drop."

"Not even my wedding champagne?"

"Not even that," he said with a fond smile. "Especially if I'm to give you away in front of all these damned Tories."

She kissed him. "They may all be aristocrats, Dillard, but they're not all Tories."

"And there's more, Mirry," he said. "You're not completely ruined, after all. Mr. Davis just told me. Some of my creditors were cheats. He's recovered most of your investments, including the jewelry that damned rascal O'Neill took in Manchester. You don't need to marry this rich lord, not if you don't really want to."

"My dear, foolish brother," Miracle said. "I'd wed Ryder even if he were as poor as our father. Like you and Mary, we're marrying for love."

"Then may God bless you with just as fine a family, Mirry," he said. "Now, if you're ready, it's time, I think."

The ancient chapel was filled with the flower of society. Guy was there, of course, sitting stoically beside Ryder's sisters and their aunt, Lady Crowse. Perhaps a few high sticklers were prominent by their absence, but Miracle knew only the confident bliss of a woman in love.

Heads craned, in curiosity, in admiration, as Ryder, tall and elegant in his wedding clothes, welcomed her to his side.

"Dearly beloved," the minister began. "We are—"

A ripple ran through the crowd as if it had been stirred with a stick. Heads began to swivel. The minister lowered his prayer book.

The door at the back of the chapel had swung open. A tall, hook-nosed man strode inside. He gazed about with an air of absolute command, then he nodded his head at Ryder's mother.

The duchess returned the man's greeting with impeccable dignity.

A quartet of footmen in glittering livery entered behind the newcomer and set down a litter. The occupant climbed out. He was enormously fat, his face shining with rouge beneath an old-fashioned wig.

The tall man offered his arm. The two men began a slow progress up the aisle, until they reached the very front.

Every man in the church bowed, and every lady dropped into a deep obeisance. Ryder grasped Miracle's hand.

"Yes, I know," she whispered as she sank into her curtsy. "It's the Duke of Wellington."

He winked at her as he bowed deeply from the waist. "Bringing Mother's ultimate conquest, it would seem."

Miracle stared at the decorations splayed across the other man's capacious chest.

"Oh, God," she said. "It's the King!"

The Duchess of Blackdown glanced up at Miracle and smiled.

EPILOGUE

AMBROSE KICKED AT HIS QUILT AND SQUALLED LIKE A
seagull. Ryder picked him up, then carried him to the
window, where his son could gaze out on his future inheritance. The baby gurgled and reached out his hands toward the
distant ocean, as if he had already fallen in love with the far
reaches of Wyldshay.

After the triumph of the wedding, autumn had drifted by in
the mellow beauty of Wrendale, where Dillard and his family always found a ready welcome. Amanda and her brothers had discovered the glories of a rocking horse with a real leather saddle,
even though their father—soberly rebuilding his business—was
too busy to visit very often.

When winter threatened to close in about the Peaks, Lord
and Lady Ryderbourne had returned south. The Whitchurch
Wing had been completely refurbished. No trace of the fire remained, and Wyldshay was always splendid at Christmas.

The duchess threw parties. Richard Avedon and Sir Robin
Hatchley were among the guests, yet they each seemed
strangely forgetful, as if they had never met Miracle before.
Certainly, they had never seen her like this: carrying a child in
her womb, and in love with a husband of her own.

Ryder had felt no qualms at all as he welcomed them with
their wives to his home.

Spring had called all the St. Georges back to London. The

duke must attend to his duties in the Lords. Ryder had been re-elected to his seat in the Commons. He had tried and failed to buy the mill where Miracle had once been apprenticed, but he was dedicating himself to reforming the law regarding conditions in all the new factories. It was a cause that would probably take him the rest of his life.

Meanwhile, society awaited the duchess and her lovely, mysterious new daughter-in-law, whose life had been so tragic and so romantic. Yet, alas, Lady Ryderbourne was in an interesting condition and expecting her first child, so she couldn't be expected to appear much in society.

No one was surprised when her husband took her home to Wyldshay before the Season was over, yet the last vestiges of Ryder's concern for Miracle had anyway faded away into nothing.

When packets of letters arrived from India, they perused them together. Jack's wife, Anne, was also expecting a baby. They were coming home.

Lord Dartford, after once again losing heavily at the tables, had decided to take a tour of the Continent.

"Your mama suspects," Ryder said to Ambrose. "Though she'd never breathe a word, I know she approves. You owe him more than you know."

The baby laughed at his father and kicked with renewed vigor.

"That's right," Ryder said. "I paid off his gaming debts. Yet Dartford said he'd only acquire new ones, and he'd rather do so in Rome. Your mama would seem to have left a trail of broken hearts. I am a very lucky man, sir, for she has only healed mine."

Something rustled behind him. Ambrose flailed his arms and legs, and smiled like a sunbeam. Ryder turned to see Miracle standing in the doorway.

"The carriage is ready," she said, walking forward to take the baby. "And I'm nervous! I know I shouldn't be, but I am."

He leaned down to kiss her. "Don't be!"

"Yes, I know you bring order from any chaos," she said. "It's your greatest gift, Ryder."

"As yours is to add depth and richness to every day. Anne will love you, and Jack probably already does."

* * *

THE ship from India stood out to sea, her sails furled, as her rowing boat scraped on the shingle. The sailors grinned and doffed their hats as their passengers disembarked: a tall, dark-haired man who lifted his heavily pregnant wife in both arms, then carried her through the surf to the beach.

She laughed up at him, both arms wrapped about his neck. He set her down, kissed her, then strode forward to clasp Ryder by the hand.

"The prodigal returns yet again," Jack said. "But Anne and I will stay around for a while this time."

"God, Jack!" Ryder said. "All I care about is to see you both safe and happy!"

Laughing and hugging, the brothers pounded each other on the back.

Knowing her flutter of nerves was silly, Miracle walked forward, smiling. Ambrose squealed and laughed at the small splash of waves.

"You must be Anne," she said. "I'm so glad to meet you at last. You write such wonderful letters!"

Gray-blue eyes smiled back into hers as Anne held out both hands. "So do you! You already feel like a sister, Miracle. And this must be Ambrose?" She caught the baby's flailing fingers. He locked dark blue eyes on her face and gurgled. "I'm so glad that my baby will have a cousin almost the same age. May I hold him?"

Miracle laughed. "Of course! I'm all in favor of cousins."

"So am I." Anne hefted the baby in her arms, then glanced about. "But where's Guy? I thought he'd be here, too?"

"He promises to visit you very soon, but he thought Ryder and Jack should have this first meeting to themselves. Even the duchess agreed, though the whole family is longing to see you both."

"Ah, the duchess!" Anne met Miracle's gaze, and both women laughed. Ambrose clutched at a wisp of her brown hair. "But Guy's a generous soul. He isn't married yet?"

"No." Miracle swallowed a small grief at what she suspected might be part of the reason. "Though I'm sure that he'll meet someone who can win his heart soon enough."

"I hope so." The baby chortled and flailed his arms, smiling up at his aunt. Anne smiled back. "And when he does, she'll be almost as fortunate as we are."

* * *

RYDER caught his breath, then stepped back to grin at his brother like a fool.

"Come," he said. "We can't keep Anne and Miracle standing out here on the beach." He gestured. "My carriage awaits."

Jack glanced at the two women. Miracle was radiant as she took Ambrose back from Anne.

"Still stunning," he said with a wicked smile, though his eyes were filled with nothing but love for his own wife.

Ryder laughed. "More so than when you knew her years ago?"

"Absolutely! You must be good for her." Jack winked. "And I'm beyond delighted that Miracle is already the mother of a lusty son and heir. It was always my fear that you'd neglect your plain duty, and saddle me with the bloody dukedom in the end."

"I'd have had no compunction in doing so," Ryder said. "But if you and Anne insist on adventuring about the world, I may yet outlive you."

"No," Jack said. "With our own baby due any minute, the adventuring is over. I can't tell you how glad I am that it is."

"Once you've paid your due respects to the family at Wyldshay, you'll be going back to Withycombe?"

"Yes, of course. I'd like our baby to be born there. We'll be only a few hours away." His dark eyes searched Ryder's face. "I trust you and I will always remain close?"

"For God's sake, you're my brother," Ryder replied. "And I owe you more than you know."

"The same goes for me." Jack reached into a pocket. "By the way, I have something for you."

"Brought back from the ends of the earth?"

Jack laughed and nodded.

Ryder unwrapped a small package. A perfect little horse, carved from jade, lay in his palm. He swallowed hard, studying the fine hooves, the ripple of green mane: an almost exact replica of the gift he had destroyed in a heartbroken rage the year before.

Though he had asked Jack to bring him another, Ryder had not really thought it possible.

"You know that I'll always treasure this," he said. "Yet I

treasure you, my own flesh-and-blood brother, even more. I owe you all my happiness, Jack."

"Your happiness? That's not in Miracle's lovely hands?"

"Yes, of course! But if it hadn't been for you, I'd never have had the chance to fall in love with her. So I owe you Miracle, and Ambrose, and my sanity."

Jack gave him a puzzled glance. "But I wasn't even in the country!"

"No, my dear brother." Ryder held out his hands to take his son as Miracle and Anne walked up to join their husbands. "But you've always been in my heart."

AUTHOR'S NOTE

Miracle's detailed knowledge of astronomical facts and figures dates from 1816, when Sir Benjamin first gave her a book that had just been published that year. Having read the same book, I can vouch for the accuracy of her memory, though obviously astronomy has learned a great deal more about the universe since then.

Anne met and married Ryder's brother, Jack, in *Night of Sin*, my first book about Wyldshay, initially published by Berkley in trade paperback in January 2005.

Details may be found on my website at www.juliaross.net.

About the Author

Julia Ross was born and grew up in Britain. A graduate of the University of Edinburgh in Scotland, she has won numerous awards for her novels. Julia now lives in the Rocky Mountains. Visit her website at www.juliaross.net.

Enter the rich world of *historical romance* with Berkley Books.

Lynn Kurland

Patricia Potter

Betina Krahn

Jodi Thomas

Anne Gracie

Love is timeless.

penguin.com

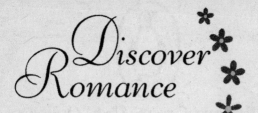